# CRACKERJACK

*A novel by Peter Church*

**Catalyst Press**

Livermore. California

For further information,
write Catalyst Press,
2941 Kelly Street, Livermore CA 94551
or email info@catalystpress.org

In North America, this book is distributed by
Consortium Book Sales & Distribution, a division of Ingram.
Phone: 612/746-2600
cbsdinfo@ingramcontent.com
www.cbsd.com

In South Africa, Namibia, and Botswana,
this book is distributed by LAPA Publishers.
Phone: 012 401 0700
lapa@lapa.co.za
www.lapa.co.za

FIRST EDITION
10 9 8 7 6 5 4 3 2 1
Library of Congress Control Number: 2018946328

Cover design by Karen Vermeulen, Cape Town, South Africa

Printed in Canada

# 1

**At the Sea Point gymnasium in Cape Town, Daniel Le Fleur's trainers** struck the treadmill mat in an even rhythm. His left arm was enclosed in a cast. Perspiration dripped off his chin and trickled down his vest. The diagnostics on the treadmill showed he was halfway through a twenty-minute session. He would much rather be riding his Rush 29 on the mountain.

If he still had it . . .

Seven weeks ago as he descended the dirt track from the King's Blockhouse, three muggers jumped him, pushed him off his bike and over the edge, a two-meter fall. When they came for his cell and Go-Pro, he hooked one bandit with a piece of broken tree stump, could not argue with the other guy's handgun.

He tapped the acceleration lever with his right hand and increased the speed by half a point. In the background, a vacuum cleaner whirred, weights clanged and music barely distinguishable as Rihanna thumped from club speakers. A shiny railing separated the gym floor from a drop into a shallow swim pool. A woman dived in, a blue cap with *Dolphins* written on it, cut through the water like she was propelled by a motor.

The muggers took his bike, his cell, his gear, his helmet with the Go-Pro, left him to walk barefoot down the contour path in his underpants. There was a moment when one bandit seemed likely to stab him, so walking away had some upside.

He closed his eyes. He did not have to imagine the bikejackers stashing his Rush in a ravine, or the trio making their way down the mountain, smoking weed and laughing. A 3G SIM card in the adapted Go-Pro on his helmet automatically streamed its output to the server at his home.

His left calf muscle tightened and he opened his eyes. Down below, the swimmer reached the wall, folded forward, and tumbled over.

Within 24 hours of the attack, all three muggers were in custody. But the bike was gone. Somehow there is always a fourth.

Salt from sweat running down his legs stung the red, blue, and violet cuts and bruises. He checked the display: three quarters done. Tucked in the well alongside the screen of the treadmill, his cell phone beeped. He leaned forward and tapped the phone's screen—two missed calls from the same unidentified number.

He ignored the calls and placed the cell back on top of his car keys and RSA identity card.

Daniel Le Fleur was thirty-two years old, a quarter inch short of six feet, and a little too lean. He had the slim artistic hands of a piano player or a surgeon. His ID photograph identified him as having a light brown complexion with kind blue eyes, relaxed mouth, a sprinkling of freckles on his nose, and medium-length brown hair. He appeared friendly, approachable, though the eyes seemed focused on a faraway object and suggested thoughtfulness, possibly remoteness—at odds with his outward appeal.

By nine-thirty, the traffic in the gym had thinned. The swimmer in the pool was still going up and down, swallowing chlorine and frazzling her mind with repetition. A woman stepped off the treadmill to his left. He sensed her attention, but did not look about.

Gym was a space he resented, from the swipe of the card and the phony welcome, to the stale bodies, mirrors, and mechanical clanking, damp people hoping to improve their physical appearance. Members toiled in claustrophobic sweat halls when they lived in a city of sunshine and fresh air, a mountain to climb five minutes from the city center. But gym was a safe place. That made sense to him. It provided a sense of belonging, of being in the company of others without having to maintain friendships. He had read that on someone's blog.

Maintaining his stride and balance, he toweled his face again and allowed his eyes to navigate the outer perimeter of the space, noting with satisfaction that the cameras he had installed before the gym opened were invisible.

An elderly man mounted the treadmill alongside. His personal trainer, in a black tracksuit, sauntered around the front of the machine and slouched against the railing. The trainer was built like a railway sleeper, short blonde hair, a ruddy complexion and arrogant jaw. His name tag said Kevin. He pulled on the zipper of his tracksuit top. Up and down. Zzzp. Zzzp.

"It's not the same here as Claremont, do you agree?" the client said.

"Yeah," said Kevin. Zzzp. "It's a different vibe here, for sure." He wore a flash watch, sleeves pushed to the elbow.

"How long do you think before the new gym opens, Kevin?"

"Who knows?" He pulled the zipper to his neck, wiggled it up and down in short jerky motions. Zzzp.

"Oh, before I forget, here's your money." The client handed over a wad of folded notes, a fifty rand note on the outside.

"Thanks. Hey, that reminds me, Mr. P. Last week, I didn't check the cash you gave me, but it was only a hundred bucks."

"What's that, Kevin?"

Kevin laughed. "It's not a problem, Mr. P. You only gave me a hundred bucks last week. I didn't count it until I got home." He held out the cash

Mr. P had given him a few moments earlier. "You see it had a fifty on the outside like this, but inside there were only two twenties and a ten. The fifty rand note around them and two twenties and a ten."

Kevin laughed again and pocketed the cash. Zzzp. He glanced over his shoulder then back at his client. "Don't worry. I wanted to let you know. It probably dropped out somewhere. It was a hundred bucks instead of the usual three hundred. But it doesn't matter, don't worry about it."

Le Fleur listened to their conversation, his right hand hovering over the speed lever.

"Oh no, I'm so sorry. We can't have that. I'll put it right, Kevin. For sure, I'll straighten it up."

"Not to worry, Mr. P. I wanted you to know, that's all."

"No. I'll sort you out for sure."

Le Fleur rammed the stop button and wiped his perspiration from the treadmill. Kevin looked across at him. Zzzp. Le Fleur hopped off the treadmill and reached into his tog bag, opened his wallet, removed two hundred rand notes. "Here . . . take this."

Mr. P lost his rhythm on the treadmill, one foot sliding onto the edge. Le Fleur grabbed his elbow and steadied him.

Kevin frowned, his eyes narrowed, hands off the zipper at his sides.

"Here's your money. You played the same trick on your last client. A Mr. C, I think—"

Kevin reddened.

"I'm sorry, what did you say?" said the old man.

"Don't worry about him, Mr. P, this guy is cooked." Kevin twirled his finger around his ear.

Le Fleur dropped the cash at Kevin's feet, picked up his bag and walked away, reached the door of the change room.

A hand gripped his shoulder.

The trainer came from behind and spun him around, gripped his right wrist. "What's your fucking problem?"

Le Fleur blinked. He did not like being involved. Not in anything. Then sometimes he suffered an inexplicable urge to bypass reason and plunge headlong into trouble. "You should steer clear of the petty stuff, Kevin. These old guys are on a fixed income. They can't afford your bullshit."

"What?"

"Let me go."

The trainer backed him into the change room. The swing door closed behind them.

"Or what?" Kevin's face contorted, veins throbbed in his neck.

"What about the cameras?"

The cameras he had installed backed up to a server farm in Gardens. Le Fleur could even tell him the IP address, an unwanted hangover from the days when he collected those unique strings of numbers like medallions.

"There're no fucking cameras here, pal. It's just you and me. Do you want me to break your other arm?" Kevin ran his eyes across three pale blue crosses tattooed on the underside of Le Fleur's right wrist. He released him and smiled. "You've picked on the wrong guy, buddy. If I see you again, I'm going to tattoo my name on your forehead with a screwdriver."

Kevin turned and stalked off. Le Fleur watched him. He doubted there would be a next time. He was going to make damn sure of that.

# 2

**The sea was flat and the sun bounced off its surface.** Le Fleur leaned on the balustrade of his seaside apartment and shielded his eyes from the white light. In his view, a rocky bay stretched to the horizon under an open, blue sky. Compared to his previous residence, a flat with a bedroom the size of a cupboard, his current address was a colossal improvement. But he took no pleasure in his surroundings. He was contemplating the chasm between man and environment and concluded mortality was an instant and his ownership of this space temporary.

He stepped inside, away from the warmth of the day. Van Gogh's *Woman Sewing* appeared on a liquid crystal display above his head. He had been considering the coarse image of a peasant woman for some time. The painting represented doing things as they were always done, and the thought added to his melancholic mood.

The doorbell rang.

Other than the Mr. Delivery guy whose arrival was a regular two to three times per week, the last person who rang the bell was a religious crazy who wanted to save him from being brainwashed by aliens. Before he left, the fanatic offered to sell him a handful of miracle tablets that Le Fleur assumed were Mandrax, a popular local drug initially marketed as a sedative.

He checked a 17" security monitor at the door of his apartment. A woman stepped back from the entrance camera and looked upwards. She had pressed the buzzer of No.4 Crystal Place on Victoria Road. His name did not appear next to the buzzer or on the post box. She must have guessed this was the penthouse perched on top of three other apartments, each looking like white ice-blocks in the sharp sunshine. *More likely she was mistaken*, he thought.

He captured her on the security screen, noticing in order the slim tanned legs, a white skirt flapping like it could blow off, and sunglasses perched on top of her fair head.

Not a crazy or a drug addict.

He had never seen her before.

Toggling the joystick controlling the outside cam, he swept the video's eye along Victoria Road in both directions. This was Cape Town's Riviera, a boulevard posted with palatial guest villas and boutique hotels, a place of perpetual construction where every inch counted, cranes overhead, knocking down the old to put up better.

Besides his caller, there was nobody nearby except a vagrant sitting on bench no.57 on the other side of the road. The bench faced away from the sea, looking towards Crystal Place.

The woman glanced over her shoulder then back at the entrance. She appeared to have arrived in the racing-green Mini which was parked awkwardly, two wheels on, two wheels off the pavement.

"Hellooo there." She eyed the vagrant and pressed the buzzer again.

The vagrant was standing now, long gray hair, tangled beard and chocolate brown suit adding to the disturbing nature of his appearance.

"No, no, no." She pressed No.4's intercom bell twice.

He pressed the intercom receiver. "Yes?"

"Is that Daniel Le Fleur?"

"Who wants to know?"

"My name's Carla, Carla Vitale. You don't know me, but I work for a company called Supertech." She paused. "I need to speak to you urgently. I couldn't get through on your cell."

He thought about the missed calls at the gym. There had been no messages. Hardly anyone knew his number.

"Speak to me about what?"

A breeze flicked at the hem of her skirt. She bent forward, looked directly into the camera. He thought she looked like a model at the wrong shoot venue.

"Oh shit," she said.

He shifted the joystick. The vagrant tottered on the edge of the curb, waiting for a gap in the traffic to cross.

"I think you've got the wrong guy," he said.

"Please. I can explain. Oh my God, there's the scariest looking thing coming towards me."

He scanned back and forth. Few people *he* wanted to see rang the bell of No.4 Crystal Place.

"Please let me in, please, I'll explain. It's about your IT skills. Shit, he's coming towards me."

She pushed on the glass door. Nothing happened. The vagrant was in the street, mounting the pavement, ten steps away.

"Please."

He clicked the door opener, split the screen, watched her slip into the foyer and shut the door. Seconds later, the vagrant slapped his palms against the glass door. The foyer lift opened. The vagrant's face pressed against the glass, arms outstretched as if he were an anguished lover. Then he made like he was jerking off.

Le Fleur was waiting when the lift opened on the fourth floor. In his right hand, he held a remote controller which operated every electronic device in his apartment. It also had a panic button.

"I'm so sorry," she said, breathing ragged, hand held to her left breast. "There's a, like, bergie downstairs who looks like he came out of the storm water drain."

He thought the monitor had short changed her—no makeup, she was radiant. She offered to shake his hand. He changed the remote to his left hand and shook it.

"I've been trying to contact you for weeks."

"I think there's been some mistake."

"You are Daniel Le Fleur?"

"Yes," he confirmed.

She looked past him, along the corridor.

"I'm kind of in the middle of something. I'll walk you to your car if you're scared," he said.

"Please give me a minute, I'll explain."

He looked away. Carla Vitale was obviously used to getting her way. He sighed. What harm could it do? *OK.* She followed him along a carpeted passage through the open door of his apartment. The entrance expanded into a large open-plan living room. The view of the Atlantic Ocean presented through an expanse of glass and open doors, American shutters folded back against the walls. She lowered her sunglasses to counter the white glare, paused, hands on hips, and stared out at the narrow bay with its rocky outcrops.

"Oh my God, breathtaking . . . What's this bay called?"

"Bali."

It was sometimes Bali, sometimes Barley, depending whether you were selling real estate or naming the bus terminals.

She stepped out onto the patio and looked at the sparkling dip pool, Mediterranean sun loungers with sail shades, a barrel of fluffy white towels and folded gowns.

"Your place is so tidy. You live here alone?"

"When I last checked," he replied, surprised by the personal question. He stood behind her, arms folded, his body language conveying she had asked for a minute, was she going to waste it on small talk?

She was two to three inches shorter than him, arms toned, shoulders and waist narrow. Her hair spilled onto the collar of a cream blouse. He guessed her age as late twenties.

"I drive along this road all the time and I've always wondered what these places are like inside."

For an ugly moment, he thought she might be an estate agent.

She leaned against the rail. Below them, Victoria Road snaked along the coast. A burst of speeding cars ripped along the winding road as if they were being pulled on a string. Across the road, a pedestrian tarmac led to a winding descent to the sea.

She wore open sandals with silver loops around her feet. When she smiled, her mouth opened slightly. The fine lines at the corner of her eyes signaled she preferred optimism.

"What happened to your arm?"

"I fell off my bike . . . I don't want to be rude, but you said a minute. What's up?"

"Of course," she answered, smile unchanged.

The central area of the apartment was the size of a beach volleyball court, looked like a working studio, lounge units, big TV, kitchen unit at the far end, two empty easels in the corner. Ibiza style music filtered through speakers mounted in the ceiling. The walls of the apartment were covered with canvas artworks, original oils splashed with reds and yellows and enflaming the classic blue-white beach decor. Huge mirrors on either side of the entrance reflected the blue sky into the room.

"You're a painter?" she asked.

"I paint as a hobby."

If she recognized any of the paintings he had copied, she did not say. Her gaze halted at a large painting on the far wall, showing a haggard character with wild hair, slightly bent, one hand tucked into a sepia overcoat.

"Oh my God, that's the creep outside. Do you know him?"

He nodded.

"I feel dirty looking at him." She shuddered and stepped back from the painting. "The likeness is incredible. Did you do it?"

He nodded again.

*There.* He spotted a glimmer of satisfaction cross her face. *She's a clever operator,* he thought. She had infiltrated his barrier. Worse, it did not concern him.

"What's his name?"

"I call him Aqualung."

"Aqualung. Why?"

"He looks like a character on the cover of a Jethro Tull album."

She did not react; he assumed she had never heard of the band. She turned her back to the painting. "Well, you've got a fabulous place here."

"It's not mine, I rent it. The owners live overseas."

"Oh?"

She circled the room, noticing, on the far side of the room, the solid metal gate which stretched from door height to the floor.

"And the security gate?"

"Paranoid Swiss think the dark people can climb over the fourth floor balcony."

She smoothed her skirt, sat on one of two leather ottomans in the center of the room, and crossed her legs.

*Make yourself at home.*

"So you didn't receive any of my messages?"

"Nope."

"You have no idea what's this about?"

"Tell me."

"You've obviously heard about Nial Townley?"

Indeed, he had. Three months ago, Nial Townley's crumpled Land Cruiser had been found at the bottom of a cliff on the Noordhoek side of Chapman's Peak Drive.

## 3

**Le Fleur resigned himself to lost time.** He fetched a bottle of spring water from a retro fridge positioned against the wall.

"Thank you." Carla bit her lower lip and tears welled in her eyes. She gulped a mouthful.

He sat on the opposite ottoman. An unfinished game of backgammon rested on the coffee table. "Nial Townley, he was CEO of an engineering company?" he asked.

"Supertech."

"I remember. Didn't a fishing vessel spot his car lodged in a gulley at the bottom of Chapman's?" He also recalled that an extensive search failed to turn up a body at the accident scene.

She nodded, tried to speak but could not. He wondered whether she was Townley's daughter or a close relative. He was not sure how to handle her sadness. Should he touch her or pat her arm, or more, put an arm around her?

"I've been over it so many times in my head. Sometimes it feels like I've run out of space in my head for rational thought." Her voice faltered. She took a sip of water.

The pain in her voice was palpable. Why had she come here? He had an uneasy feeling she was not in the wrong place after all.

She turned and looked towards the sea. "There was trouble with a project in Venezuela."

It occurred to him that she was Townley's work colleague.

Carla hugged her shoulders as if suddenly cold in the air-conditioned room.

There was something else, he recalled: twenty million dollars, the amount of money missing from Supertech's bank accounts.

"Nial was my mentor." Her voice was thin and shaky. "He taught me everything. I never guessed anything was wrong."

She lifted her hands to her face and sobbed.

He shifted, uncomfortable.

After a few moments, she rummaged in her bag for a tissue, took a deep breath, and ran her hand through her hair. "Shit, I'm sorry. I promise I didn't mean to do this." She breathed deeply and composed herself. "So they found Nial's car a week after he disappeared. Then the drama *really* began. You know about the missing money?"

He nodded, recalling the rumor: Townley stole the money, staged his

---

suicide, and was cruising exotic destinations with his Brazilian girlfriend. Or was she Columbian?

She flicked a wisp of hair, repositioned the sunglasses on her head. "When word leaked about the money, the shit hit the fan. The banks foreclosed on us. We had nowhere to turn. GALI descended on us like vultures. Do you know who they are?"

He nodded again. GALI was a multinational engineering conglomerate, a new entry into Africa, another European company aiming to take advantage of weak currency and weaker government.

"Whatever happened to Nial that Friday afternoon changed everything," she said. "GALI is taking control of Nial's company and there's nothing I can do about it."

Her eyes were dewy, no mascara to leave streaks. She steadied the quaver in her voice and took another sip of water.

"Sorry, I should explain who I am. You must think I'm some noob in a dress. I am supposed to be the next Managing Director of Supertech."

She did not look like a future MD. He speculated whether she was romantically tied to Townley. *Tears, mentor, he taught me everything.*

"Can you believe GALI Africa offered me a *job* in the new company as a site engineer on the East Rand?"

Her expression tightened, eyes narrowed.

She did not look like an engineer either. He tried to picture her with a hard hat, prowling a construction site—did not come close. She looked like she would be more at home in a tight bikini on a sandy beach.

"Screw them. They can have their fucking job. I'd rather be poor."

He wondered whether her attractiveness was a help or a hindrance to her profession.

He said nothing. He should never have let her in. No one came to No.4. He had no connection to what she was telling him. He was listening to a stranger's problems.

"Nial Townley did not do this. I know with every fiber of my soul. I'll never give up searching for the truth about his disappearance. I'll exhaust every resource I have to find the truth."

*Every resource I have.* He did not want to be one.

He had seen pictures of Nial Townley, a powerful, handsome man. Was he the kind of man to hire an attractive young woman to take over the reins of his company?

"So where do *you* think he is?"

She sucked in her breath like she had contemplated the question a million times. "He's dead."

She forced out the words and they hung in the air like a terrible accusation. He clasped his hands and blew through a gap between his thumbs. He regretted his question. He did not want to share her fears.

"Do the police agree?"

She sniffed and wiped her nose, took a deep breath. "SAPS did a reasonable job. But you know how justice works in this country. Once the detectives have their preferred theory, that's what they investigate. They listened, followed leads, they tried, they really tried. But they've got new cases to investigate. We had the Directorate of Priority Crimes involved. They assigned a senior officer from the Hawks. He's a decent guy. Captain Roly Phakatini. They call him Parks. But they're all so overworked."

She looked at her sandals and wiggled her toes.

"So when nothing happened I got a little desperate. I hired a psychic detective, an expert in parapsychology. She had some success on a pedophile case in the 90's. She had a premonition that Nial's body was dumped in a dam, you know the dam at the intersection between Wynberg and Constantia?"

He did not.

She wiped her fringe from her face, broke a thin smile. "I convinced Parks to drain it. He picked up a massive bill and got shat out by his boss. He hasn't forgiven me."

"Ouch."

Her jaw tightened. "Nial Townley would not steal and he would not kill himself. No chance. Forget about the financial trouble, he had a son he loved dearly. It's impossible. Believe me."

"What happened to the money?"

She blew into her hand. "There's speculation Nial took it to avoid paying creditors in Venezuela. It was actually collateral for the tender we did in that hellhole. The creditor story is fraud. The Venezuelan Government had no right to attach our assets. They have the most crooked government on the planet. Nial would never pay their penalties."

She gently squeezed the plastic water bottle. Le Fleur puzzled over what she had told him.

"What penalties?" he asked.

"They claimed we didn't having the correct licenses. There's a new world order of crime—despot governments ripping off foreign corporations with trumped up claims or fines. We've seen it in Nigeria with MTN, in Brazil with Billiton. But I'd have known if he was thinking about settling with the Venezuelans. We had no secrets." Her white blouse was mildly transparent, the outline of her brassiere visible beneath.

"Everyone has secrets," he said.

She placed her palms on the glass table between them as if offering her nails for inspection. Her hands were small and tanned, short practical nails without polish, a thin silver ID bracelet on her left wrist, gold band on the fourth finger of her right hand. When he looked up, she was staring at him. He imagined she was looking straight through him, that his face was a window and everything inside was visible.

"I knew his secrets! He told me everything. Even the bloody stuff I didn't want to know. We were too close for me not to know if he was planning—" She halted mid-sentence.

He looked away. Her stare was too intimate. It was as if she had perceived what he was thinking.

"We weren't lovers."

He raised his hands defensively, feeling a pang of guilt. He could not deny he had jumped to that conclusion.

"You aren't the first to think it, don't worry. His girlfriend does. The ex-wife, for sure. The Supertech executives. The police. They see tits and ass and wonder how some bimbo *chick* can become the next MD of Supertech. They don't care that I'm a fucking good structural engineer. I know this business better than anyone, sometimes better than Nial."

He frowned. He would not have labeled her a bimbo. Two fragments of her last outburst interested him. *Tits and ass.* He was not used to a woman who spoke so directly. Then again, he was not used to women. The other sentence of intrigue—*sometimes better than Nial*—sounded like she was speaking about him in the present tense.

She took a slow breath as if filling up on courage. "I wasn't fucking him. But..." Her eyes filled with tears again.

He shifted awkwardly and moved his left hand up and down inside the cast.

"God, they say the truth hurts. I don't know why I feel I can tell you this, but if Nial asked me, even hinted, I would've in a heartbeat."

She buried her face in her hands then looked up immediately.

"I've never admitted that to anyone. But it's the truth. I admired him, worshiped him. I know he's dead. I always thought there'd be a time for us one day. Now he's gone."

She sobbed.

*I know he's dead.* He noticed she was back to the past tense.

He reached across the space and placed his hand lightly on hers. It felt cold. Before he could say anything, she looked up fiercely.

"I want you to help me find who did this to Nial," she said.

## 4

**Le Fleur stared at her smooth golden skin, the outline of her breasts, her slender legs.**

It did not seem real. He rubbed his face, feeling suddenly shallow. She was spilling her guts; he was having distracting thoughts. *Maybe that's her strategy,* he thought. She was not dressed for an engineering convention, although perhaps she was and he was misinformed about current trends in executive wear. He withdrew his hand and expelled a mouthful of air. If she knew the demons he wrestled, she would not be soliciting his help.

"This place, and you, it's so not like what I expected," she said.

He did not want her to elaborate. She glanced at him then swept her eyes around the room.

"It's, you know what, the whole *Mr. Robot* scene. Have you watched that series?"

So she was expecting a black-eyed morphine addict in a hoodie with a rucksack? He did not watch the series, did not care to follow another stereotyped hacker suffering social anxiety and depression.

"Who told you I could help?"

"You're the top cyber professional in the country."

He smiled. *Send in the pretty girl and flatter the shit out of him.* He wondered how she got his number. Not from someone he knew.

"You can tap into online systems, access CCTV video networks, cell phone records, and internet—"

"I don't do that anymore. This is a police matter. I'm not a detective."

"You work for the Cybercrime organization?"

"I don't work for them. I *do* some work for them."

A clunk from the fridge signaled fresh ice.

"You have the skills. The police don't have them. They are searching for Nial and the money out there on the street and they can't find either. We need a digital specialist."

"Why do you think they never found his body?"

A month ago, one newspaper ran a story that Townley had been spotted in Mexico. Not that he believed one newspaper story but there was always the outside chance it was true.

"I don't think it's so difficult for a body to go missing on Chapman's Peak," she said.

"What about his phone?"

"It wasn't found. Nor his laptop."

"The police obviously must have accessed and analyzed his phone records?"

"Yes, the state's digital forensic laboratory did it. But we haven't accessed records of other parties."

"What others?"

"There are a number of possibilities, people who may be involved. Sophie Townley, his ex-wife. I would like to see her phone records on the day."

Le Fleur pursed his lips. Was she suggesting the wife did it?

"She's gone to London with Nial's son. That's what she always intended. Nial was opposed to it. Last year, there was a huge custody battle when she pulled a similar stunt."

She paused to take a breath.

"And how about the GALI corporation? Bunch of fucking crooks. One minute they're looking for a partner in Africa, next thing they're boosting their balance sheet with our assets."

Corporate mischief? That was not how he remembered the press coverage. The view was GALI had rescued Supertech from their Venezuelan woes. He looked closely at Carla, wondered whether engineers were clear on the difference between asset and debt.

"You mentioned a girlfriend?"

He remembered a picture gratuitously splashed in the media, tall and dark, a former stripper. The story ran an extra week due to the interest.

"Exactly. Her name is Ynez."

"Is she from Venezuela?"

"Close enough . . . Colombia. Who says she wasn't sent here to seduce him?"

He narrowed his eyes and studied the animation in Carla's. Custody battles, corporate intrigue, government corruption, and lap dancers.

"So I gather you want to obtain their cell phone data and internet activity?"

"Yes, of course. There's motive. And what about the agitators that stirred things up in Caracas? Jorge Ramos is our agent in South America. What does he know?"

He nodded patiently. She had thrown in a token tequila slugging Hispanic. He glanced at his watch.

"We need access to all these phone records."

"Who was the last person to speak to him?" he asked, regretting his curiosity. It would only make it harder later.

She took a sip from the water bottle. "I spoke to Nial at midday on the

Friday he disappeared. After that, there was one other incoming call on his cell and a missed call he made to his wife Sophie. Then there's a call he made to Goldman's in the UK to transfer the money."

He raised an eyebrow.

"We hired a detective to investigate the call he received after I had spoken to him. The number belonged to a woman who swore she had no such number. So you know all sim cards are registered?"

Le Fleur suppressed a smile.

"We subpoenaed the registration details. It is this lady—her electricity bill and bank statement. Turns out she never had such a number and had never heard of Nial Townley."

Le Fleur was silent. A false sim registration. The country was awash with such devices.

"But Daniel, that call was the catalyst. Everything changed after Nial received it. I spoke to him. Everything was fine. He was fetching his kid at school, for Christ's sake."

He nodded. Carla continued.

"Our detective says he can get cell phone transcripts. Incoming calls, GPS locations, SMS, transcripts of conversations. But this was months ago and we haven't seen anything."

Le Fleur shook his head.

"You don't think he can get them?"

"These people aren't suspects. Cell phone service providers require a subpoena from a magistrate's court, at least, before releasing data. The police usually reserve the favor for violent crimes. Even the President's information is hard to come by."

"But do the cell phone providers have that information?"

"The provider has records—call activity, duration, approximate locations. Where calls were made or received based on the distances from connecting towers. I'm assuming *your* detective isn't going the legal route."

She looked glum.

"And actual conversations won't be available from three months ago." He checked the time on his watch. "Look, you seem like a decent person. I'm not going to lie to you. I was involved in computer surveillance work. That's in the past. I'm no detective, I—"

"If we can access cell phone network records—who was calling who, which internet sites were accessed—and security video footage."

He smiled. *OK, so if that's all.* "Like bypass the courts. And the cops. Bribe a technician at the cell phone company."

She looked away.

"I don't do that anymore, I'm sorry."

She remained silent for a moment. When she looked back at him, she was fierce. "So what *do* you do when you're not painting?"

"I'm a day trader."

"You're a gambler? You place your bets on corporate news then wait around to see if they come in?"

He did not react to her scorn. "It's meant to be exciting. So I'm told."

She reached forward and grasped his wrist. "I really need your help. We'll pay you whatever you want."

"It's not about money."

"There's a reward. GALI is offering five million rand for information leading to the discovery of Nial's whereabouts."

"I'm sorry."

Her downturned mouth, flickering eyes, did not diminish her physical appeal. She looked as if she was about to say something then did not.

"Look Carla," he said, determined not to be swayed by emotion or her attractiveness. "I can't help you. I can't afford to be involved in anything illegal again."

## 5

**On a liquid crystal screen, another Van Gogh masterpiece flickered.** His hobby was copying a master. He had settled on Van Gogh as his new subject and spent a week deliberating his next target. *The Potato Eaters* was under contemplation. He felt no attachment to the peasants and their supper under the lamplight. He stepped away and wandered into the kitchen, shifted the rubbish bin behind the door. The kitchen counters were clean, no stacked dishes, no notes attached to magnets on the fridge door.

He sighed, opened the fridge, and stared inside, unsure if he were hungry or not. He removed a brown packet and inspected the contents: Nando's peri-peri chicken, mild, two days old. He replaced the packet and closed the fridge.

He left the kitchen and strolled across the open plan living room. He could still smell her perfume, her disappointment.

He unclipped his cast and massaged his fractured wrist, stared out the window towards the horizon.

What an unusual day.

First the altercation with the trainer . . .

Then a stranger breezes into his apartment asking him to break laws so she can find her missing boss.

Who was the last woman who sat on his couch? Or came through the door of No.4? He could not recall.

He was sure she had come dressed for the occasion, assumed he would fall all over himself to help an attractive woman. He could not tell if the tears and the emotion were part of the act.

There were four internal cameras in his apartment disguised as LED lights. If he wished, he could replay Carla's visit, including their conversation. He also had external cameras covering Victoria Road and linked to software using license plate recognition (LPR). He had customized the system using open source stubs downloaded from a public directory of software, and linked it to the national car registration for tracking purposes.

He looked at the unfinished game of backgammon on the coffee table. He wondered if she had guessed he played games against himself. Perhaps she had wondered about the plunge pool on the patio and the white gowns and carefully folded towels.

He pumped his fist lightly into his other hand then looked at his image in a mirror on the wall. Black long-sleeve T-shirt with "Keep your coins, I want change" logo and straight blue jeans, bare feet. Maybe the *Mr. Robot* thing was not so far off. His hair needed a cut.

She must think he lived a sad and empty life.

He picked up the remote and activated the metal gate on the far side of his apartment. The gate rose automatically, revealing a room of chrome furniture, multiple screens on counters, mounted on the walls and suspended from the ceiling. He named it "The Chrome Room." There were no windows. An array of computer gear twinkled in a large rack. When not in use, his processors mined Bitcoin transactions for a small share of the crypto currency booty. A cooling tower fanned cold air onto the system.

On the far side of the room behind a wooden panel was a spotless work bench with an attached vice. A soldering iron and pair of miniature pliers were the only tools on the bench. Various tools were suspended from hooks on the wall. A glass cabinet consisting of plastic jars containing screws and plugs and connectors was in reach of the bench. A large cupboard on the other side of the bench was closed.

He entered and illuminated the room, examined a scrolling screen of flashing digital numbers and graphs. He paused on a display of the London stock exchange, noticed the Footsie indices were up, all except the tech stocks.

*You're a gambler?*

Day trading had been logical. The thousands of hours playing *Grand Theft Auto* and *Dwarf Fortress* had honed his single-minded assiduousness. Other than concentration, all it needed was good news or bad news. He bought and sold shares online, holding the position for the rest of the day, and sometimes into the next day, before liquidating. Initially he incurred losses, but as his understanding of peaks and troughs grew, his profits increased. The business required volatility not normality or moderation. The enemy was no news. He spent many hours of each day trolling the web for information and opportunities.

But now he had something else on his mind.

He stepped away from the financial screens, pulled on his headphones, and booted his Omega workstation.

He used TrueCrypt to mount a drive then a utility called Tor to tunnel into a virtual connection and hop between proxy servers. Rule #4 of the internet: *Anonymous is legion.* He did not want anybody—Internet Service provider or dodgy marketing company—tracking his browsing history. His screen emulated a DEC VT220 terminal, the characters glowing green pixels on a black background.

In between the day trading, he did special jobs for an organization called Cybercrime.

Two years ago, he had been given a choice of twelve months scrubbing graffiti off Cape Town's infrastructure or putting his knowledge to good use. Cybercrime was a quasi-government organization that operated on corporate funding. They dealt with cyber fraud, phishing, and identity theft. His obligation to repay society for his impetuousness had long since lapsed, but he had stayed connected out of loyalty to the organization's head, Ian Coulson, who had looked after him and never treated him like a criminal.

A week ago, Coulson had given him a new assignment. A gang of ex-bouncers had installed themselves as gym trainers, were extorting cash from the clients.

Le Fleur paused and took a deep breath. What he was about to do went beyond his obligation of installing hidden cameras at the gym. He pictured the old man on the treadmill. *Don't worry about him, Mr. P.* One good turn deserved another.

Using a process of injection, first by locating a staff login screen on their public internet then invoking an SQL string to attack the table where the user's names and passwords were stored, he hacked into the gym's staff record database.

*You've picked on the wrong guy.*

Kevin's surname was Halstead. His membership record listed a pending disciplinary hearing at the gym. Le Fleur typed a short memo to the manager and another to the email address listed under Kevin's personal details:

CHECK LOST PROPERTY FOR YOUR FINAL WARNING.

He then went backdoor into the national car registration database. Many years ago, he had worked on its design and inserted guest logins into every government system he could access.

*I'm going to tattoo my name on your forehead with a screwdriver.*

Using Kevin's ID, he located traffic fines linked to a white Toyota Cressida. He changed the status from "issue summons" to "warrant for arrest."

He logged off the registration system and started a remote program called SearchMe to check whether anyone had recently searched for him on the Internet. In the online world, paranoia was not an affliction, it was a necessity.

His cell rang, unknown caller.

"You were looking good at the Sea Point gym. Any pussy?"

He recognized Ian Coulson's rasping voice.

"You're the one watching their new CCTV all day," he replied.

Coulson laughed. "I saw you shaping up to some muscle head. Good work, Daniel, the owner is delighted with the new surveillance."

Coulson owed the owner of the gym a favor.

"So you decided to lay down some law, Daniel." Coulson chuckled.

Le Fleur paused. *An inexplicable urge to bypass reason...*

"I like to see what I'm dealing with. It makes it feel real."

"It's real all right. We're going to bust those scumbags."

Coulson controlled the single biggest source of tech expertise in the land, and was well connected in business and government circles. Le Fleur had met him once in the flesh, a year ago, outside the Labia theatre after watching the movie *Algorithm*. He had recognized him from a solitary picture on the Internet, Coulson uncomfortable in an oversized jacket, long straight hair flecked with gray, dominating mustache. Le Fleur respected him. Coulson had come through at a low point in his life. They communicated mostly by secure message, and occasionally, Coulson called him on his cell.

"Is everything OK with you, Daniel? How's the wrist?'

Le Fleur touched his cast. "It's on the mend."

"You look after yourself." Coulson ended the conversation.

Le Fleur powered down Omega and checked the time. He had been online for fourteen minutes. He pushed back his chair and stretched. He still could not work out if he was hungry or not.

He exited the Chrome Room and strolled onto the outside balcony.

*I really need your help.*

Carla Vitale. She had wild theories about her boss being kidnapped, a whole cast of suspects. All he could smell was trouble.

Pulling cell phone records of random people was illegal, an invasion of privacy, and a serious violation of his probation. Ditto finding out about porno sites surfed during private and not so private hours.

He did not need that trouble.

He sat on an ottoman and aimed the remote at the LCD screen. The last station he watched was Disney Channel.

Surfing channels without method or concentration, he paused on Bloomberg. The JSE was up half a percent. He had not made a single trade today.

He toggled to Summit, on Business Report: GALI were acquiring Supertech.

Le Fleur leaned forward.

On screen, a man identified as Bruno Pittman, MD of GALI Africa, expounded the potential in Africa. GALI would bring their expertise, he said, create jobs, investment opportunities. Pittman was a squat man in a gray suit and loose tie. His ruddy face glistened with practiced integrity.

---

*Fat chance*, Le Fleur reflected. They would haul the proceeds offshore. Like the arms deal. Africa was a dumping ground for obsolete European shit at inflated prices. Corrupt officials and gullible consumers: Africa was a price.

The interviewer asked what synergies GALI brought to Supertech.

Pittman stated Supertech's local knowledge combined with GALI's international expertise would be a powerful force. He explained that demand in Africa and South America had overextended Supertech's resources and finances and they required a big player to address the opportunities.

Le Fleur concentrated as Pittman spoke. There was something unusual about his face. It was not immediately obvious. It was his eyebrows.

The camera shifted onto someone called Gavin Marx. He was tall and tanned, with a full head of graying hair. His suit was tailored to fit his slim shoulders.

"Gavin Marx represents Supertech management. Gavin, what has been the effect of Nial Townley's disappearance on the staff?"

Marx seemed irritated by the question. His deep set eyes had a haunted look.

"Everyone is devastated."

"Is he out there? Do you think he is out there somewhere?"

"Are you seriously asking me that question?"

Marx put his hand in front of the camera.

The camera panned to an office façade, glass doors with large gold letters: GALI AFRICA, some administrative staff standing outside.

The camera was back on Pittman.

"It's a difficult time," said Pittman. "Nial Townley was Supertech. Supertech was Nial Townley. But we have to go forward."

The camera shifted to interviewer.

"We've been talking to Bruno Pittman, the new MD of GALI Africa, about prospects for the amalgamated engineering concern. Supertech staff members are still visibly traumatized by the disappearance of their founder Nial Townley who has not been seen since twenty million dollars was transferred out of Supertech's company account three months ago."

Le Fleur switched off the TV and wandered onto the balcony, gazed out at the Atlantic in the late afternoon sun, water sparkling with false promise, the cold Benguela current lurking beneath the surface's blue invitation.

Trouble.

For a moment, he felt frozen. The cars below became soundless and his heart quickened.

# 6

**The next day Le Fleur drove south in his white Saab along the M3 highway.**
He connected his cell to the car's speakers and streamed a podcast on
Van Gogh.

At Alison's flower shop in the suburb of Wynberg, he stopped to purchase twelve ivory roses.

Back in his car, the narrator explained why Van Gogh had cut off his ear,
wrapped it in tissue, and given it to a prostitute. It wasn't madness after
all, it was jealousy: his brother, who was also his financial supporter, had
got engaged.

At an old cemetery in adjoining Plumstead, Le Fleur parked and tracked
slowly between rows of headstones. It was six months since his last visit
and he always experienced an initial sense of dread.

He visited his father's tombstone first. *Jake Le Fleur: aged 45.* That's
all it said. He thought he should have added, *"He did everything for
women,"* because that was the truth. Maybe it was some type of addiction,
but it was a painful memory. He imagined his father would have plenty to
say about the visit from Carla Vitale. *What you waiting for? Don't be a wet
dream. Fussy doesn't fuck.*

He removed an ivory rose and placed it on the adjacent grave of some
arbitrary person, a Mary van Breda. She died at 40 years old.

"I'm sure Jake would've liked you too," he said.

A dry wind blew sand along the pathway. He followed the path to the
far end of the cemetery. When his head was bashed in at rugby, his nose
bloodied by a bully, when his father let him down, there was always his
mother's soft voice, her warm nurturing embrace. Maria Le Fleur died at
age thirty-two, when he was eleven. The epitaph read: *Our beloved Maria,
sadly missed by Jake and son Daniel.*

There were fresh flowers at her gravesite, white carnations. He opened
an attached card. The message read: "For a love that cannot be shared."
The card contained a stamp from The Christina Home for Abused Women.

Empty sites flanked both sides of his mother's grave. He could have put
his father alongside his mother, but he had been young and angry. His
father was fucking other women when his mother was still alive. After she
died, his father became worse, his vain and pathetic character bolstered
by the attention of a new woman.

He placed the bouquet of ivory roses on his mother's site, stepped back
and mouthed a silent thank you. He imagined the extent of her sadness:

---

leaving behind an eleven-year-old boy in the care of her relentless husband. He remembered her on her deathbed, trying to mask the fright, the fear, trying to be brave, believing maybe, perhaps there would be a reprieve.

*"Don't worry, everything's OK."*

Whose words were those? His mother to him or him to her? He felt a dry ache in his throat. It could never be OK. His mother would never come back and he would never see her again. The utter desolation of that reality had never left him. At his mother's funeral, his father's attention was already on another woman.

He walked slowly back to his car and left the cemetery, turning onto the main road where the traffic was business vehicles, cars with logos advertising services such as carpet cleaning and plumbing. The hardware stores and video shops gave way to car showrooms. He routed up towards the homebound freeway.

At Hospital Bend, a tight corner intersecting the bequeathed estate of Cecil John Rhodes and the city's public hospital, he noticed another tranche of flat-topped pine trees had been felled. He thought maybe he should paint them before they were completely gone.

On the Camps Bay strip, he bought a platter of fashion sandwiches and ate them alone in an empty restaurant.

Afterwards he stopped at the post office and handed in a parcel slip. The parcel was the size of a shoebox and contained numerous smaller parcels, some no larger than a matchbox. The customs documentation stated: Electronic Equipment. The source country was Israel. Possibly because of that country's political isolation, they produced cutting edge gadgets. Gadgets that he liked to tinker with on his work bench in the Chrome Room.

Back at Crystal Place, he removed his shoes and socks and projected a full size image of Van Gogh's *Wheatfield with Crows* onto the big screen.

He opened and closed his eyes. Like a pinhole camera.

Repeating the process in short intervals, he focused on the Van Gogh painting until his vision blurred. Gradually he shortened the intervals of capture and increased the duration of contemplation. The visual image in his head formed and set—the colors, clouds, movement, road, shapes, proportions, number of crows. When he turned off the projector, he sketched a pencil outline on the canvas without looking at the original.

He pulled a paint-flecked apron over his shirt. His apartment was bathed in sunlight, the glass windows open and curtains flapping gently with a light onshore breeze. Music piped through the speakers. He had chosen Counting Crows' album *August and Everything After,* an old favorite, for inspiration. Rolling his sleeves, he squeezed tubes of oil paint onto his palette, avoiding looking at the intimidating white canvas with its crib lines demarcating the outline of his work. A reasonable copy sold for $50 at a Chinese sweatshop, but financial gain was not his motivation. On a narrow trestle table beside the blank canvas were his tools: jars of brushes, palette knives, soft tubes of oils, bottles of linseed oil and mineral turpentine.

He tried to purge his mind of all thought beside Van Gogh. He needed to be like him to paint like him. Aqualung, sleeping on bench no.57 below, would approve.

He pressed a tube of burnt sienna onto his palette and mixed in the Liquin, scraped the paint back and forth, then applied it directly to the canvas as if smoothing butter on a slice of bread. The smell of the oils lifted his spirit, connected his creativity, and transported him to a wooden-floored school room, the portly art teacher pressing too close and through garlic breath reminding him to paint with his eyes and heart and not with his brain.

Waiting for the first wash to settle, he checked the mountain webcams for weather conditions at the upper cable station. Art soothed his soul, exercise pumped fresh blood into his veins. Combined, they would erase the sadness of his morning visit.

He checked his cell phone for messages or missed calls. There were none.

He could feel an energy rising. At his next birthday, he would be older than his mother when she died.

Returning to his easel, he mixed cadmium yellow, orange, and white with linseed oil and Liquin until he was satisfied with the texture. He repeated the process with cobalt blue and French ultramarine in preparation for a moody sky.

With paints mixed, he assessed the moist canvas and got to work. He began with the sky, crudely slashing paint onto canvas with a palette knife. Moving the brush into the blue paint, he created texture, a primitive effect, the brush strokes giving an appearance of basket weave to create a looming sky.

The bending yellow corn created the contrast between the two primary colors in juxtaposition against one another, highlighting each other's magnificence, the glossy sun kissed corn fields against the brooding and tempestuous sky.

His head was now clear of thought, every stroke a release. He was the

---

madman Van Gogh, his only world the restless vision of the cornfields.

He dipped a clean brush into black paint and added a number of squiggles. In his mental image, there were thirty seven crows, Van Gogh's age when he died.

He made sure he painted them all.

## 7

**The hobo Le Fleur called Aqualung was now seated on bench no.56 on the seaside of Victoria Road.** Unlike no.57, it faced the sea. The onshore wind had died and the bay was a smooth glass surface with white patterns of foam shaped by tide and current. Kelp floated in the placid water like a lazy swimmer.

Though it was deep into autumn, the winter rain was not coming.

Le Fleur handed over a packet of takeaway chicken and sat alongside his homeless friend. A low mesh fence in need of repair separated the pavement from the coast. Further along the road, a neglected narrow path led through a tangle of matted bushes onto the shoreline of exposed boulders and white sand. Not quite the popular Fourth Beach in Clifton but less crowded.

Aqualung's real name was Frederik Patrice De Villiers, a direct ancestor—unsubstantiated—of a long deceased French Commander and local woman by the name of Clara van de Kaap. According to Aqualung, he could have been rich and owned a boat. First the booze got him then he lost a good woman and then a pack of loose harlots took all his money.

"Merci. Très bon."

Aqualung opened the packet and pressed his face into it. Satisfied, he removed the splayed chicken and began stuffing it into his mouth.

Le Fleur scraped his brogues on the cracked cement and stared out to sea.

"What is it, Le Fleur?"

A container vessel inched across the horizon.

"What is what?" Le Fleur asked.

"You look troubled."

He stretched his arms above his head, his cotton shirt clinging to his body. "I'm fine, Freddy."

Aqualung withdrew the chicken and inspected it carefully. Then he bit down, tearing the flesh with his remaining front teeth.

"Trouble is good," he said. "Have you seen the bus stop?"

He reached below the bench and retrieved a brown packet. The cracked concrete and scraggly grass was littered with remnants of other meals.

"What bus stop?" Le Fleur asked.

Aqualung gestured towards the yellow bus stop with a plastic blue roof. An insurance company's advert advocated "Protect what's important." Le Fleur was unsure whether transport actually serviced the bus stop.

---

"Someone sprayed *Fuck da Police* on it."

Aqualung removed a bottle of scotch from the brown packet and offered it. Le Fleur stared at the black liquid in the bottle. "No, thank you."

Aqualung tilted his head and drained the bottle. "Sugar," he said, examining the empty bottle with tenderness. "It's bad for you." He opened his lips and ran his tongue between the gaps in his teeth, savoring the taste.

"You mix Johnny Black and Coke? Jesus, Freddy—" He tapped Aqualung on his dusty coat then examined his hand. Aqualung hurled the bottle into the gnarled shrubbery. It smashed on contact with other discarded bottles.

"Sugar is trouble, makes me feel good." Aqualung belched and inspected the remnants of his meal as if considering whether to eat the soft bones. Then he threw away the box and bones and shaped an imaginary hourglass with his hand movements. "Le coupé cabriolet, this girl in the Mini . . ."

Le Fleur had a vision of Carla Vitale, her slim legs crisscrossed on his couch.

"Le Sucre. What does she smell like?"

"What?"

"I tried to smell her, but she ran away."

"I don't think she wants to be smelled."

Aqualung blew his nose into his hand. He shook off the mucus, closed his eyes, and reached out in a biblical gesture. "I cannot deny my humanness." His mouth tightened and eyes became dark. "I am a prisoner in this grotesque skin, a prince of hearts disguised as a white haired monster fermenting in this withered body."

Le Fleur clapped his hands lightly. Aqualung's eyes fixed on some faraway place. Then he scratched his nose and pointed to the sky.

"She's your sweet thing?"

"I only met her yesterday."

Aqualung laughed, an open-mouthed cackle, chicken smeared on his gray beard. Then he leaned forward and jabbed a dirty finger into the back of his mouth. "She'll make you ache like these teeth."

Le Fleur placed his palm flat on Aqualung's chest, prevented him getting any closer with the oral demonstration.

"Who's the sweet thing's friend?"

"What do you mean?"

Aqualung waved his hand over his shoulder then shaped them in a diamond logo. "A yellow teapot arrived after your sugar arrived, parked, looked up at your apartment then departed."

Le Fleur narrowed his eyes. He had all the technology in the world, but the important stuff was sourced from a hobo. And, Aqualung called a Renault motorcar a teapot. He sucked in the sea air and gazed into the dwindling light across the bay.

"You see, you have that look again." Aqualung checked his watch, a fake TAG Heuer—a gift from Le Fleur—and stood, pressing a hand on Le Fleur's shoulder. "You have this place, money, this life, but what is it you looking for?"

"You should tell me. You are the self-professed white-haired fount of wisdom."

Aqualung swayed back and forth, grabbed onto Le Fleur for balance. When he stabilized, he picked up an old rucksack and threw it over his shoulder. "Do you still wake up and think about dying?"

"Sometimes."

It was not like it sounded—that he thought about offing himself. It was a strange paranoia in which he imagined his last day on earth, a premonition of some unexpected force waiting for him.

"You are troubled by your purpose?"

"Come on now, I have *purpose*. I fight bad and evil guys on the internet."

"You laugh, but this is not funny. Not all who are bad are evil."

Aqualung checked his cell—a R99 text-only special—then stumbled to the pavement. "You must do as you want. You'll wake up thinking of dying instead of living. You'll never change. You'll be like this bench."

He waved his arms in the air and walked slowly away, heading for the Somerset Road homeless shelter.

Le Fleur remained for fifteen minutes, watching the darkness blur the horizon, thinking about Aqualung's words. Why did he have to do anything?

Half an hour later, back in his apartment, he identified the yellow Renault on video surveillance captured by his roadside LPR camera. Using the national registry, the software linked its plates to the registered owner, Apollo Financial Services, which, according to the public CIPRO database, was an insurance brokerage in Cape Town. He thought it was probably some guy stopping to admire the scenery. Even so, he placed the registration on a watch list to see if it returned.

That night he watched *Paranormal Activity 2* on Netflix and fell asleep in his clothes. An hour after midnight, his cell beeped and woke him. There was a message from Cybercrime's Ian Coulson.

```
Heads up. Some chick's been asking
around for tech help to find Nial Townley.
It's not our monkey.
```

He blinked, sent back a terse response.

    Don't worry.

After a moment, his cell beeped again.

    You hear Fallon Trafford's out?

He stared at the message. Deep in the recess of his brain, something flickered and flashed—an image of Fallon, her green eyes and raven hair. For a moment, he wondered whether he was still asleep, dreaming. Then he remembered the strange last two days, the portent for change.

He put down his cell and walked to the window. Outside, the night glittered, the street was quiet.

*You hear Fallon Trafford's out?*

He stripped to his boxers and left his apartment, taking a set of keys. He crossed Victoria Road and descended a dark path through bamboo forest to the Atlantic.

He had not thought of Fallon Trafford for years. What did it matter? So she was getting out of prison.

Carefully avoiding broken glass, he crossed the narrow band of sand and tested the icy water. He removed his boxers and stretched his arms above his head. No clothes, no buildings, no internet, no human creation to distract. Only his body; the cold Atlantic stretching out in a black mass to a distinct horizon; a clear, starry sky, the moon dangling above like a slice of lemon.

Naked in the water, he felt truly free. He could never imagine a life without this freedom.

# 8

**The concrete room was thick with steam.** Fallon Trafford removed her orange sweats and laid them over a matching tunic. She reached behind her back and unhooked her bra then pulled down her cotton underpants. She folded her underwear into her sweats and crossed the floor to the shower area.

A dim light filtered through the barred roof windows. One fluorescent light flickered continually, the other buzzed, as if deliberately intended to irritate.

Three years in Worcester Women's Prison. She had arrived with expectations of being out in a year.

Stepping under the shower nozzle, Fallon twisted the tap and a jet of tepid water washed through her raven hair and ran down her body.

Today, in the cell she had shared with fifteen inmates, her bed was unmade for the first time. On her final day, it was a special privilege to use the ablution block in private after the other prisoners had showered and been herded into the recreational quad.

She cupped her hands and filled them with water.

As a first offender, she could have got off with a suspended sentence. She blamed a fat policewoman from the Peninsula Narcotics and Sexual Offences Squad who wanted to ruin her life. A month before her first automatic parole review, the policewoman had pitched up in Wellington with the Case Management Committee's report.

"An offender must accept that the committing of the crime was wrong. There are poepalls out there who raped innocent girls for pleasure."

"I accept what I did was wrong," Fallon had said.

"Bullshit!" The policewoman was as sensitive as a sea urchin. "You see here?" She prodded a G326 parole profile and stared with undisguised hatred. She had glanced at the overhead camera. "You're not going anywhere."

Fallon collected water in her mouth then squirted it out.

*Raped innocent girls for pleasure.* It wasn't like she had actually done anything. She had only facilitated a transaction for her employer, an American-based company called Dark Video. Dark Video was in the business of supplying suitable escorts to wealthy clients. She picked up the girls at bars and dropped them off at clients' places. It wasn't her who slipped the girls a roofie. She had taken the hit for the real culprits.

But she did not want to retain hatred and resentment. It served no purpose. She placed her hand on the cold copper piping mounted against the wall and traced the grouting between the cracked white tiles.

She had achieved little in prison, had not studied or developed any academic skills. She attended programs on sexual conduct and restorative justice because she was forced to do it. She made an effort at weekly life skills courses because the facilitator was influential on the parole body. That had worked fuck-all.

But she had found a new role to play.

Inmates at Wellington Woman's acquired nicknames based on work they performed. The librarian was Bookie, a loan shark Platsak—empty pocket, a gardener Ho. Fallon's vocation earned her the name Gaaitjie, little hole.

It was not really a choice.

The notion of hiding something up an orifice disgusted her. But as survival became reality, she had little choice. She was a special-needs merchandiser, a fancy description for an inmate who smuggled illicit items between prisoners and cells in their rectum or vagina. The dormitory used a suitably shaped deodorant can to prepare her, a bunch of girls sitting on their bunks, laughing and giggling and conditioning a fellow inmate for her first day on the job. It was uncomfortable and painful, but she learned to relax and appreciate that the passages, the back one especially, was a reliable conduit for smuggling commodities such as SIM cards, Mandrax tablets, currency and cutting knives. She received a miniscule cut of the spoils, but her role bought her protection.

She took a deep breath, looked up at the shower head, and reached for a place of calmness, a sea of blue water sparkling in the sun.

A week ago, she had accepted an interview from a university professor researching female prisoners due for release. His surname was Valentine. He was a funny looking thing with curly hair and sharp pointy features, brown popping eyes, someone from the Cape Flats but without the accent. He did not fit Fallon's stereotype of an educated man.

He had given her a chocolate bar he bought at the prison kiosk. She was only a medium security class offender, but he must have asked for the visit to be non-contact.

"So how's it been in here?" he had asked her from behind a glass panel.

How's it been? Two library books, her watch, no jewelry, no TV or games, a few private clothes, a hand-held radio, an occasional newspaper or out-dated magazine. She had been refused approval to have a laptop.

"Did they work you over?"

She had been surprised by the informality of his questions. *How's it been? Did they work you over?* What did he mean? Who was "they"—the guards, other prisoners? She wondered whether he was getting pleasure from the interview.

"They tried."

Most of his questions were multiple-choice, her answers statistics for some master's thesis. He read from a sheet on his clipboard, but she noticed he only sporadically jotted her response.

"Are your parents alive?"

"No."

"Any siblings?"

"None I know of."

He read her a passage about the importance of family. He said 80% of female prisoners did not have a place to go after their release.

"You've got somewhere to go when you get out?"

"Yes," she said.

"And how did you find the programs in prison?"

"I've learned I'm not my crime."

He frowned. She thought she noticed a small smile hidden behind the frown.

"Did your victims explain the impact of your crimes on their lives?"

She shook her head.

"Are you sure?" He looked at this clipboard. "That's a part of the restorative justice program."

"I don't remember, Professor."

"Please call me Dave." He cleared his throat, looked again at his notes. "Um, OK then, tell me, are you seeing anyone?"

"I don't understand?"

"A doctor?"

"For what?"

He looked up and frowned. "Sometimes there's stuff in our head that we must work out."

"I've got everything worked out."

In her past life, she had played a trust fund bunny, a whore, a criminal lawyer, a girlfriend, a chemist, an undercover detective. She did not say anything about the role-playing. She had learned to keep her mouth shut in front of anyone playing Freud.

Fallon turned off the taps and stepped out of the shower, reached for a towel and dried herself. From a simple plastic bag, she removed a toothbrush and paste. The government provided the soap, toothbrush, toothpaste and sanitary pads; the rest depended on her ingenuity. She brushed her teeth, staring into the peeling mirror. She thought she looked like a witch, hair so dark, eyes so green, skin so pale. Her eyebrows had grown back at least. She twisted back and forth to examine her body. The three years had sharpened her curves. Except for a jagged scar on her right ass cheek, her body was a temple.

She emptied the remaining toothpaste into the basin, broke her toothbrush, and threw the pieces onto the concrete floor.

A rattle of conversations and activity was audible from outside the ablution block. She imagined the other prisoners, another morning, another day, scraping their shoes in the dust. Staring once more into the mirror and reaching beyond the green eyes and into her mind, she was thinking about freedom and did not hear anyone enter until she felt a hand on her shoulder. She spun around and let out a yelp. She did not like frights.

It was an inmate called Corinne, tall and wiry. Corinne should have been out in the yard with the other prisoners.

"What do you want?" Fallon backed away towards the showers.

"You *know* what I want." Corinne's grin revealed a piece of gum in her crooked yellow teeth.

A squat prison warden stood in the doorway. She checked the passage then closed the door and wedged a baton into the handle.

Fallon's heart sank. Corinne reached out with a hand. Fallon slapped it away and raised her fist, backed into the shower area.

"Come on, Gaaitjie. You don't want the warden dirtying your papers on your last day." Corinne grabbed her wrists and pressed against her. "You want to give my tongue a ride, hey?" Her rancid breath made Fallon wince.

"Hey!" The warden called out. "We do what we came here for!" The warden sat on the wooden bench, unfolded Fallon's pants, and extracted her underwear.

Corinne reached into her pocket and removed a surgical glove.

"No. I promise you. I'm not crutching anything."

*I don't want this, not here, not on my last day.*

"Come on now, think of it as a lekker going away present," Corinne whispered into her ear and spat out her gum. She blew into the glove then turned to the warden and winked. "She loves this part."

Corinne raised her right hand and snapped her fingers into the glove. Fallon held her at arm's length.

"Kom, Gaaitjie. The warden thinks you are keeping something from us. Maybe some fat bolletjie of coke to pay for your freedom."

Fallon hesitated. Corinne grimaced impatiently. The warden pressed Fallon's underwear into her face and sucked in her breath.

*Last day. Don't mess it up. Let her stick her fingers inside.*

---

CRACKERJACK

She dropped her arms and closed her eyes, pictured the sea and the sand, how the salt water would feel on her skin. Corinne's fingers wormed inside of her. *It isn't anything, it isn't anything.*

"Mooi and tight," Corinne said. "OK, now turn around bokkie."

She turned. Corinne put her left hand on the back of Fallon's head and pressed down.

"Bend bokkie."

She bent over, felt Corinne's hands part her buttocks.

"Nice apples."

The warden laughed. *One more time, one more, then never again.*

"OK, she's clean."

Fallon straightened up, still facing the wall and the exposed copper piping. Corinne squeezed her left breast.

"Good luck out there, baby shoes," said Corinne and released her. Fallon turned around, her heart beating fast.

"See you soon, Gaaitjie," said the warden, pocketing the underwear. She walked to the door and removed the baton.

Corrine followed her out. Fallon picked up her towel and held it in front of her body.

*Never again will I lose control. Never again.*

She thought about Dave Valentine. Professor Dave Valentine. He had asked for a forwarding address. She made one up. When time came to leave, he had produced a pamphlet from his jacket pocket.

"Here's some useful information."

She took it reluctantly. There was a picture of a young woman striding confidently up a flight of stairs. Fallon Trafford was written in bold on the cover, underneath was his cell phone number and the initials: DV.

**9**

**Carla hooted once.** The wind had turned onshore and the bay resembled an oily harbor. Le Fleur was waiting on bench no.56 overlooking Bali Bay, holding a laptop case, listening to Aqualung complaining about the European crisis.

"World War 3 will be fought with banknotes not panzers."

Le Fleur sprung to his feet and crossed the road before a rush of traffic. "Hold that thought, Freddy," he called back.

Carla was wearing a leopard print romper with spaghetti straps. He hopped in the passenger side.

She smiled and looked in the rearview mirror. "Oh shit."

Across the road, Aqualung held up his arms to part the traffic on Victoria Road. He looked biblical with his flowing gray hair. Carla zipped the window, but he reached over the open roof and touched the top of her head.

"What the hell—" She ducked and accelerated into the traffic. "What's wrong with that guy?"

"He only wants to smell you."

"What the fuck? Smell me? Is he insane?"

She checked in the rearview mirror and adjusted where Aqualung had touched her hair.

"He's different. Don't worry about him. He doesn't mean any harm."

She sped along the coastal route towards Hout Bay, impatient, blasting the horn, flashing lights, riding the tail of slow moving vehicles. From the car speakers, complimenting music rattled the dashboard, seemed to synchronize with her frenzied foot pedal movement.

"So why'd you change your mind?" she asked. "Has Brexit fucked up your trading plan?"

He did not reply. He was not even sure of the answer himself. He examined his fingernails. Despite the turpentine, there was still paint under them.

Carla braked. She was almost against the bumper of the car in front. "Jesus, Granny, we're not in the afterlife series here." She hooted twice at a tan Volvo. It moved aside and she sped past.

"You've got some data for me?" he asked.

She reached into her bag and flipped him a flash drive. She lowered the volume of the music. He inserted the flash into a slim model laptop. The flash drive contained four directories labeled dockets, evidence, statement, and suspect. He transferred the data and eyed the directory labeled "suspect." Its sub-directories were names of people.

"Bruno Pittman," he said, recognizing a name. "I saw him on TV."

He glanced sideways at Carla. One hand gripped the wheel, the other shifted gears, her body tense.

"He was talking about the benefits of the merger between Supertech and GALI," he continued.

"GALI think they can send out some heavy Eastern European bullshitter to take over our company. Fuck them."

"He's got unusual eyebrows."

"Eyebrows?"

"One is dark and the other is light."

"You noticed that?"

*One eyebrow that lies, the other tells the truth*, Le Fleur thought.

"There was someone called Gavin Marx on TV too," he said.

"Gavin is Nial's oldest and closest friend. From school days. They started Supertech. Gavin's a lawyer, he isn't involved in daily operations, but he attends board meetings and strategic stuff. He's stepped up since Nial disappeared."

The copy of data ended.

"So one of these characters on your suspect list knocked off your boss?"

"That's not funny."

"I'm being serious. You think someone close to Nial is implicated?"

She hit the bend at Suikerbossie with screeching wheels. "It must be someone who knows about Nial and Supertech and how we operate."

Fifteen minutes after leaving Camps Bay, Carla paid forty bucks and sped through the tollgates onto Chapman's, a snake-like pass built by convicts shortly after World War 1.

"Did Nial ever disappear before?" He glanced at Carla. The wind whipped at her hair. She did not have a single line on her brow.

She shook her head.

"No midlife crisis. No unusual travel behavior?"

The road hugged the side of the mountain.

"Last year after the divorce came through, there was all the shit with Sophie wanting to take Gregory to London."

"Gregory's the son?"

"Yes. After the court case, he took a holiday with Ynez. He was burned out. The Venezuelan stress didn't help either, but he could handle it. Nial's a fighter."

A suspect sub-directory labeled "Ynez Abarca" contained jpegs: A dark

---

haired woman in a red bikini on a towel, body like a tight spring, another on a boat in a white frock, a third snorkeling in the red bikini.

"What's Ynez like?" he asked.

"How do you mean?"

"Is she clever?"

"Clever or devious?

"Either."

"I think if you stuck her brain in a bird, it'd fly backwards."

Le Fleur looked at her with curiosity. He was not sure how to interpret that comment. He knew how Carla felt about Townley. Was she jealous of his girlfriend?

"OK then. So let me guess? Nial took her to South America. The countries of the bank transfers: Venezuela, Uruguay..."

"I know what you're thinking. They didn't go to *those* places. They went to Brazil. I've seen all the pictures. He sat on the beach reading company correspondence on his cell, and she frolicked topless on the beach."

He checked the sub-directory to see if he had missed any images.

"Listen, Daniel, I don't have to tell you about Nial."

"Yes."

He knew what she would say. Nial Townley is an honorable man who loves his son and would never steal. He wondered how having a Columbian stripper as a girlfriend fit that thumbnail character sketch.

"Nial never went anywhere unless it was work. He didn't like traveling, didn't get it at all, not the culture nor the art. He didn't like lying about on beaches or swimming in water looking at rocks and fish. He especially hated Europe, all the old buildings and museums. He said his ancestors came to Africa precisely to escape the dreariness of that place. If he wasn't working, he'd be home watching sport or occasionally mountain biking, surfing, sailing. Since I've known him, other than the trip with Ynez to Brazil, he never traveled outside of Africa unless it was for business. We made lots of trips to South America, obviously. You can check his passport. There's a digitized copy in the file."

"Oh, so you have his passport?"

"Yes."

"What did the cops say about that?"

"Parks from the Hawks told me you can buy a passport for a grand or less on the Grand Parade."

They had ascended from sea level for five kilometers to the lookout point overlooking the Hout Bay sentinel.

"So Nial would've entered the pass from the Hout Bay side?"

"His car did."

"No clear shot from the CCTV cameras?"

"The driver of the car is indistinct. They've tried enhancing the pictures."

"But it was a lone driver?"

"That's what it looks like. Someone could've been lying on the back seat."

"Could it have been him?"

"Yes, it was a man. Like I guess there are two million of them in the Cape."

Carla reduced speed as the slope of the mountain on the seaward side became a sheer drop into turquoise blue sea, a hundred feet below.

"I feel like Chicken Little," she said, glancing up. "You can either catch a boulder on the roof or helter-skelter over the side."

She eased around another curve.

"A hundred-and-fourteen," he said.

"What?"

"That's how many curves there are."

She glanced at him. "No ways, you counted them?"

"It was in a TV advert. A guy in a Mercedes Benz drove over the edge and lived. For the advert, they jettisoned a W123 with a camera inside to film the journey."

She tapped her head. "You have a memory."

She pulled into a parking space and pointed to a barrier of white painted stones. He exited the car with his laptop, stopped, and peered over the edge. Carla joined him.

"If Nial's car hadn't lodged in a gully, we wouldn't have known about it until the next cleanup." She removed a tissue from the pocket, blew her nose. "They pulled out thirteen other wrecks by helicopter."

Shielding his laptop from the sun, he examined photographs of Townley's mangled Land Cruiser. The roof had concertinaed. He imagined the driver would have been crushed, belt or no belt. The assessment report stated the seat belt was unfastened but operational; the air bags were deployed, front and back; the car was in second gear; the keys were in the ignition; the lock was not set; the front driver's side door was open.

"Where's the car now?"

"At the police scrap yard in Tokai." She stuffed the tissue in her pocket.

"Did they check the SatNav? Some models use bread crumbing technology which leaves co-ordinate markers for off road situations."

"Nial never used SatNav. He wasn't big on tech. Anyway, the front deck was bashed up."

"Tracker?"

"He'd canceled the subscription a year ago."

"Was there blood?"

"No. His fingerprints were all over the car. But it was strange. I'm not a fingerprint expert by any means, but his prints on the wheel were smeared."

She paused and stared at him.

"The expert said it may have been that someone wearing gloves had driven the car after Nial. Anyway... We got independent crash insurance experts to examine the car after the police were finished. We asked them to assess if someone was inside the car when it went over the cliff. They concluded the front driver door was open."

"Open? Like someone pushed it over?"

Carla took the laptop. "Yes. I shot these from a helicopter. You can see..." She zoomed in and indicated with her finger "... where the car hit. There. There. You have these fucking experts. One report says the door could've come open on its own, the other says it's impossible."

"But someone going over the edge may have opened the door as an involuntary act?"

"So then where's the body? We had sea rescue, navy divers. Everything."

"And the police report?" he asked.

"They concluded the scene was staged. Our expert showed Nial could've been thrown into the water as the car hit the gully. The sea was enormous, a real Cape of Storms, all along the Southern coast from the Monday that week."

Without a body, Le Fleur understood why the police doubted this was how Nial Townley met his end.

Carla toggled to the next picture.

"That's a shoe. It was washed up on Noordhoek Beach. Someone found it on the high tide mark. The forensic guy reckoned it had been in the sea for two weeks."

"And the relevance?"

"They're an unusual make. Crockett & Jones. Nial had a pair."

"Only one shoe?"

Carla nodded.

Le Fleur flipped the permutations.

It would have been a lot easier for Nial Townley to leave the Land Cruiser in the parking lot at Cape Town International.

But then they would know for sure he was alive.

## 10

**"Any drugs, debt, shady pals, enemies?" he asked.**

Half an hour later, Carla's Mini wound around the horseshoe bend of a road called Ou Kaapse Weg. A boy skateboarding on his backside wobbled precariously close to the oncoming traffic.

"No."

Le Fleur shut his laptop and canvassed the panorama as the road bisected the two entrances to Silvermine Nature Reserve. Left and right were mountain peaks, behind the Atlantic Ocean and before them the bay named False Bay with its warmer Indian Ocean water.

At the bottom of the pass, they swung left, slipping past Steenberg Estate, the American Embassy, and Polsmoor Prison—incongruous landmarks of wealth, power, and shame on the same road.

She rounded the Tokai traffic circle. "Can we talk about your fee?"

"OK."

"You must let me know how much."

"OK."

"You have any idea?"

"I'm not sure yet."

He was concentrating on not-so-inconspicuous license plate recognition cameras hanging from trees and poles in Constantia.

"Nial never came home that Friday?"

"There's evidence of him leaving for work on Friday morning but nothing later."

She turned into a leafy avenue and braked behind two horse riders. One rider turned and waved at her to reduce speed.

"Mink and manure." She took both hands off the wheel. "Horses rule in this suburb."

He put his hand on hers to prevent her blasting the hooter.

A few moments later they turned into a short driveway blocked by a tall metal gate. An auction notice was posted outside. A CCTV camera recorded their arrival. Carla pressed a remote and the gate opened. She disabled security and they crossed the driveway, entered through the front door. It was a ranch style house, single story. Their entry triggered a high-pitched alarm which Carla disabled at a keypad.

Le Fleur entered the foyer and looked about. After the shriek of the alarm, a cold silence emanated from the house, the ceiling and walls seemed to bear on them as if seeking a reason for their intrusion.

---

"I don't understand the point of this security," said Carla. "The alarm goes off and a security company phones. You're supposed to give them some secret word so they know you're safe."

He was not listening. He was absorbed in the surroundings, the inanimate objects that witnessed unseen events, the imperturbable vaults of information. He spotted the first internal camera.

"So what if there's a guy with a gun? Who's going to give a false password if there's a gun pointed at your kid's head?" she asked.

She opened the curtains in the lounge, revealing a stunning green garden stretching downhill to an electric fence and a backdrop of the east side of Table Mountain above Cecelia Forest. Against the tennis court fence stood a neat wooden clubhouse. The lawn was mowed and an aquamarine pool sparkled as if waiting for swimmers.

He hesitated, unprepared for his feelings of unease. It was one thing snooping about the digital world, another experiencing the sights and smells of a real home: family pictures on the wall, an Africana book collection, wine cellar, floor polish, the air stagnant from being trapped inside sealed windows.

Something had happened here. Was this where Nial Townley planned his great escape from the world?

Carla had been surprised he wanted to see the house. *I like to see what I'm dealing with. It makes it feel real.*

A framed picture caught his eye: Townley and a young boy about eight years old, fair hair, red lips and pale blue eyes. Gregory. Smooth round features, skin easily sun-burned.

*Who's going to give a false password if there's a gun pointed at your kid's head?*

"What were you saying?" he asked.

He turned to look at Carla. She raised her hands to her face and turned away from him.

"You OK?"

Her shoulders were hunched. She shook her head.

"I'm sorry." She wiped her eyes and walked into the passageway.

He followed a trail of surveillance cameras disguised as smoke detectors and night-lights.

There were four large en-suite bedrooms, a lounge, a living room with table tennis set, a study, and a farm styled kitchen.

The boy's bedroom wall was painted blue. On the wall were photographs of mountains, sea and landscapes. A bookcase was filled with books. Le Fleur browsed the titles: the *Harry Potter* series, *Spud, Animal Kingdom* picture books. Model airplanes hung from the ceiling. A picture of Nial and Gregory was gummed to the mirror. Underneath was written: "To the best boy a father could ever wish for."

He stared at the note. He thought about his father Jake. Was he the best boy his father had ever hoped for? Probably not. His father was not the best father he could have hoped for.

Next to the boy's bedside was a framed picture of Winnie the Pooh and Piglet examining prints in the snow. The accompanying message read: *If ever there is a tomorrow when we're not together. There is something you must always remember. You are braver than you believe, stronger than you seem, smarter than you think. But the most important thing is even if we are apart I'll always be with you.*

His throat was dry. He swallowed and looked back at the picture of Gregory and his father. *Even if we are apart I'll always be with you.* Quite a promise to make a young boy... He took a deep breath and left the room before the emotion clouded his thoughts.

The main bedroom was obvious by its volume and the king size bed with ornate brass headboard in center space. Le Fleur inspected the artwork, original oils by local painters, a contemporary piece of Constantia Valley, a commissioned portrait of Townley and Gregory, an abstract landscape. He opened and closed his eyes in front of each work as if taking a picture.

He heard a noise and looked about. Carla had entered the bedroom and was standing at the window gazing out across the sweeping lawn, her back towards him.

"No dogs?" he asked.

She shook her head. He thought she looked vulnerable, reflecting back on something, as if she had been in this room before and it held memories. He wondered if, despite what she had told him, she had been on the brass bed.

Leaving the bedroom, he retraced his steps, continued the exercise outside, inspecting angles and the view on every lens he located.

In the garage, one side was an empty space where the Land Cruiser had been. The other contained a spotless Porsche Cayenne, a surf ski mounted on its racks. A jet-ski stood in the far corner. Two brand new mountain bikes were fastened to brackets on the wall. He spun a tire on the first bike then the next. They were clean, polished. He thought a bike stored in the back of the Land Cruiser would be an effective means of exiting Chapman's without detection.

His feet squeaked on the spotless linoleum floor. If Nial Townley liked to be at home, he did not spend time in the garage.

He returned to the house. He had counted twelve cameras. He found Carla seated in the lounge.

"Where's his safe?"

She seemed to snap back to reality at his question. "No safe."

"No gun?"

"No."

"Can I look at his workstation?"

In the study, Carla unlocked a steel cabinet, booted a desk side computer. A large book case adorned one wall, books on photography, travel, fashion. They were books for decoration, not reading, sorted by sizes.

"His housekeeper is Maria," said Carla. "She saw him Friday morning. She's a sleep-in during the week, but she has weekends off. It was Nial's weekend to have Gregory. He was supposed to fetch him from school. They had a hike planned. Gregory is crazy about nature and it was Nial's way of spending time with him."

They waited while the computer booted.

"Maria made snack packs before she left. She only arrived at eleven on Monday because of some funeral thingy. The police worked her over. She told me they'd made her feel like she'd done something wrong. Her report's in the docket."

"Did Nial like nature, the outdoors? I mean, everything in the garage looks brand new. Unused mountain bikes, jet skis . . ."

Carla face looked pained. "He wanted to do it, Daniel. He was that classic guy you read about. He worked too hard. He spent ninety-nine percent of his time at the office and Supertech. He bought all the toys, but he never had time to use them."

Carla logged onto Townley's computer system.

"Another toy I don't think he used. Gregory played games on it."

Le Fleur assumed control of the keyboard, his fingers moving independently of his eyes. He checked the system configuration and confirmed it was a gaming PC then located the surveillance software, opened a directory and scanned its contents.

He identified the surveillance product as a software system supplied by the company Digital Eye. He browsed through some configuration files.

"Digital Eye monitors most of the southern suburb LPR's and up-market homes," he said. "I remember they had a problem with hackers breaking into their system and posting embarrassing pictures of their clients on the internet. So they implemented AlphaGuard to keep the script kiddies out."

"What's a script kiddie?"

"Like they call a learner surfer a grom or grommet. We call a learner hacker a script kiddie."

"And AlphaGuard?"

"It's considered a virtually impenetrable firewall. AlphaGuard encourages hackers to try. They offer a reward to anyone who can break it."

He continued to examine the system. Surveillance data was stored in a separate directory for each day. There was six months data on disk. He selected the day before Townley's disappearance, a Thursday, and pressed play. Images from the twelve cameras were interwoven into a single viewable file.

On screen, Townley appeared in his underpants on camera no.7, the recording triggered by his movement in the passage leading from his bedroom. The timestamp was Thursday 6:05.

Carla watched over his shoulder. He was aware of her closeness, an intimate blend of perfume and perspiration.

On screen, Townley exuded a masculine sexiness, a physique of broad shoulders, powerful arms, a strong jaw line.

*I would have in a heartbeat.*

"I've been through them all," she said. "He doesn't always wear the boxers."

He fast forwarded through Thursday's recording: Townley emerging dressed from his bedroom, newspaper delivery triggering an outside camera no.12, Maria collecting the newspaper—captured by camera no.11, Townley in the kitchen eating breakfast, in the garage—camera no.9, departing in his Land Cruiser on camera no.11 and no.12.

He rewound and compared the image of the garage with the image in his head. Everything was in place.

"Did SAPS do forensics *in* the house?"

"We hired a private company called Forensic DNA. There were traces of blood in the basin as if he'd cut himself shaving, otherwise nothing, no strange prints, no stains."

He selected the Friday backup and pressed play.

The video displayed a similar routine. 6:05 in the jocks in the passage, 6:15 newspaper delivered, 6:30 Maria collecting it, Townley in the kitchen, 7:05 Townley speaking to Maria in kitchen, 7:30 Townley driving out front gate.

"Then he arrived at work? He was completely normal? You saw him?"

"He spoke about GALI. We shared a stand with them at the Convention Centre. Then Nial left to fetch Gregory and vanished into thin air."

He suddenly thought about the girlfriend.

"What about Ynez? Where was she?"

"She didn't stay at the house on weekends when it was Nial's turn with Gregory. She's got her own apartment in Green Point."

He returned to the surveillance.

Between 8:00 and 11:00 on the Friday, the cameras captured Maria moving around the house, collecting laundry, preparing sandwiches, closing windows. At 11:30, the front gate camera no.11 and no.12 captured her departure.

The surveillance software generated a time stamp photograph every hour from each device. Besides the presence of these images, the motion detector was triggered from time to time by wind in the garden or false movement in the house.

"So you say there's nothing from 11:30 on Friday until Monday morning?"

"There's nothing relevant. I seem to remember a few cars, horses..."

He loaded Saturday's surveillance. The gate camera was triggered a number of times by joggers passing the house. At 10:15, a car drove up to the gate and was caught on camera no.12, number plate visible. It reversed and drove away. He rewound.

She placed her hand lightly on his shoulder.

"We checked every car. People browsing the neighborhood for show houses, wrong turn."

She removed her hand and stepped back.

Le Fleur scanned the surveillance for Sunday and Monday. At 6:15 on Monday, the newspaper was delivered. Camera no.12 showed Maria arriving at the gate at 11:15 and camera no.11 showed her collecting the newspaper and post.

"Maria thought some of Nial's clothes were missing. And a suitcase from the garage. The police loved that. It supported their theory that he ducked. But there's nothing on surveillance."

Carla opened the French doors to the garden and walked onto the smooth lawn.

He made copies of the surveillance videos, browsed the system's hard drive, checked the registry. No favorites, no history, Internet browser prompting as if being used for the first time, updates hopelessly outdated with hundreds of security fixes queued. He could have hacked this computer with his hands tied behind his back.

When he was finished, he powered down the computer and stood. Carla was staring towards the mountain. He watched her until she turned around and walked inside and locked the doors. He was interested to know what she was thinking, but it was not his way to ask.

"Are we done here?"

She shrugged. Her eyes were red.

## 11

**"See you soon," the warden had said to Fallon.**

She arrived at a storage unit in Parow Industria and supplied false identification documents to the security personnel. The documents had been arranged by an inmate nicknamed Groenboekie—"small Green Book," after the familiar South African ID book.

She had rented a 1600cc Chevy Spark from Avis using identification she shared with a woman named Patricia Fitzsimmons who lived in Pinetown, a thousand kilometers away.

Her release from prison was filled with strange sensations. Drawing money from an ATM was liberating. Driving a car filled her with an amazing sense of freedom. She felt like an individual again.

Yesterday she spent her first night at the Town Lodge in Bellville, ordered in a cheeseburger and, though she did not generally enjoy fiction, watched Matt Damon in *Bourne Identity*. She had discovered, with some surprise, that Damon's character turned her on. In privacy, with the right dose of visual stimulation, she admitted, touching one's own body was hard to beat. She was unable to sleep for an hour thereafter.

After clearing security, she drove into the storage complex, located unit 177, and parked her car directly in front of the container. She opened the lock with her security pin and looked inside.

Inside the container was a jumble of suitcases, packed and empty, furniture, computer equipment, crates, plastic bins and black bags.

She rummaged through a selection of handbags stored in an apple box. She discarded a black gothic bag adorned with silver chains and safety pins—too many bad memories. So too a bright red purse in the shape of a vampire coffin. She settled on a black handbag with bullet shaped studs and flat rivets on the gussets. It looked heavy enough to make a mess of someone's head.

She slipped a jangle of silver bracelets onto her arm and filled an empty suitcase with musty clothing from a plastic bin, loaded it into the Chevy.

She returned to the lock up and pulled three crates of shoes towards the exit. She turned the crates over then filled one with the best shoes from the pile—boots, sandals, tennis shoes, and stilettos.

Next she loaded a metal casket with a range of tools and equipment, some new, some used.

Behind the casket was a wooden cabinet sealed with a combination lock. Lining up four numbers on the lock, she slipped it off and opened the cover. In a false compartment on the top side of the cabinet was a hard cover book. The main body of the cabinet contained an array of wooden slots, each filled with a plastic zip-lock bag. At the bottom was a tray of medical supplies—bandages, cotton wool, syringes. She removed a bag from its slot. Inside was a test tube containing a powdery substance. She wondered whether the sample had lost any of its potency.

Without opening it, she replaced the packet in its slot and locked the cabinet, dragged it to her car and loaded it into the hatchback.

She opened a small safe and checked the contents. It contained a Taurus pistol with a threaded barrel, magazine, a silencer, a belt holster, a shoulder strap and a hundred rounds of ammunition. The safe also contained an envelope of currency—USD, Sterling, and some local notes. She did not open the envelope. The currency amounted to about 4,000 USD, if she remembered correctly.

By the time she had finished, the Chevy was packed to capacity with clothing and linen, the metal casket, safe, a laptop, a cabinet, a Hush Puppy shoebox containing papers and correspondence including a valid European passport, a hair dressing kit, and assorted toiletries.

The drive to Sea View Holiday Flats on Beach Road in Mouille Point took thirty minutes. The apartment was registered to a Ms. Fitzsimmons and had been attracting rental income via a pool system for the last three years.

She parked in a side road behind the flats and unpacked her car. A Congolese national called Fabrice acted as Sea View's doorman, security guard, and receptionist. Fabrice helped carry her possessions to the seventh floor.

After offloading, she tipped Fabrice and changed, pulling a loose white blouse and khaki pants over a black one-piece swimsuit. She was hot but did not shower.

She returned to the Chevy.

After she climbed inside and started the engine, she had a strange feeling, something she had not experienced before. It was a feeling that this time she would make it big. Real big. And she would achieve her ambition of escaping this African hellhole and settle in some timeless village somewhere in Europe with lots of money in her bank account.

She drove through Sea Point along the edge of the ocean. She left the radio off and hummed the theme song from *Bourne Identity*. As she drove along the marine, she imagined, like Jason Bourne, she had returned from the dead, unloaded her storage unit, and would ultimately discover her destiny with the future.

She needed money to achieve her goals. Revenge was a luxury. She once had a doctor-boyfriend who called her a money fiend. She did not like to remember what else he had called her.

She continued along the coastal road, eventually twisting off and snaking down to a car park at the sea.

On a white sandy beach, she rolled out a towel, peeled off her shorts and blouse, and leaned back on her elbows, looking out at the sea. She sniffed the cold, rich aroma of the air moving off the ocean and wiggled her toes in the heated sand.

Two boys in black shorts were playing a game of beach bats at the water's edge. A pack of wet-suited surfers jockeyed for positions in the choppy surf at the right end of the enclosed bay.

Fallon felt the warmth of the sun ease through the material of her swimsuit and she relived flashes of the pleasure she experienced with Matt Damon at the Town Lodge. She slipped off the straps of her swimsuit and rolled down the top to reveal pale white breasts.

To her left, a middle-aged man she had noticed earlier admired her as she disrobed.

Fallon cleansed her thoughts. She shut out any concern about her future or past. She focused on present senses: the fine silky sand, the translucent blue sea, the golden sun on her body, the man's gaze, the surfers' antics. She thought about when she would enter the icy water, each step leading deeper into the gasping waves, jumping and resisting until cold fingers reached to her waist and she would dive into her blue future.

She glanced left, over the voyeur's head, towards Little Lion's Head. He wore a short sleeve collared shirt, a sun visor, white shorts, and slipslops. She held his gaze for a few seconds. He lifted his towel and shifted in beside her.

"Hello there."

His face was red and bloated beneath the visor. She imagined he would still smell of whatever he last ate or drank. She did not return the greeting.

"What's your name?"

"Fallon," she said, then looked back at the sea, did not cover her breasts.

"Fallon? That's an unusual name."

He extended his hand, but she ignored him.

"You come here often?"

"No." She shook out her hair then stroked it behind her back. Considering the effort of maintaining her hair during incarceration, it was unfortunate she would not have it much longer.

"So where do you go, hey?" His voice rose.

She did not reply. She could sense the man's stare running over her body like a tongue.

"What a day," he said. "Nearly winter, that's Cape Town for you, hey."

He followed her gaze towards the sea.

She assumed the man was wealthy, the boss of his own company, divorced, kids with ex-wife. He would be forty, thinking he was thirty, knew she was out of his league but because she was pale, out of place, maybe he would be lucky.

A goofy-footer in a black and orange wet suit took off on a right hander. The swell surged and closed out on his head.

"Eina. Crunched. That must've hurt. Are you a surfer?"

She shook her head.

"Is your boyfriend out there, hey?"

"No." She jangled the silver bangles on her left wrist. "Listen, what do you want?"

The man laughed and cleared his throat.

"Uh, I don't...want...anything." He kept his voice low.

"You sure?"

"Why'd you ask?"

"You're sitting here looking at me. What'd you want?"

The man laughed again, looked around. "I'm not sure I understand what you're getting at. I—"

"Do you want to fuck me?" She looked towards the rocky promontory at the end of the beach.

The man snorted. He spun around as if afraid a nearby cluster of sunbathers might overhear. His voice dropped to a complicit whisper. "Are you always so, like, forward, hey?"

"So you don't want to?"

"Hey, like, um, wow, but come on, you're not serious?"

She stood and stared at him, her pupils like pin-pricks in her green eyes. He did not move. His mouth opened, but no sound came out.

She pulled up the straps of her bathing costume, and walked to the water's edge, tested the temperature with a foot. It was ice-cream-headache cold. She waded into the shallows and dived into the first wave, kicking forward, opening her eyes and gasping as the cold struck and sought to paralyze her.

Sometimes reality is nothing like you imagine.

She pushed hard off the sandy floor, bursting into the sunlight, her arms raised above her head. Three years of being hot and sweaty or cold and damp, of sores between the toes and rashes in her crotch. She stayed in the water until she was freezing and her fingers would not close.

As she exited the water, she spotted the middle-aged man with his arm around the shoulder of a slim wet-suited boy who was emerging from the water, clutching a boogie board.

She returned to her towel and smiled to herself. She had never been a good judge of people.

Seven floors up, she sipped an iced Jack Daniels and ginger ale on the balcony of her apartment. With a slice of lime, it was her favorite drink.

She leaned on the edge of her balcony.

She had stocked up on groceries—essentials like chips and sushi and chocolate bars. At a nearby bottle store, she had filled a shopping trolley with bottles of booze and ginger ale.

She watched silently as cars arrived: Range Rovers, ML's, Beamers, Prado Land Cruisers, Porsche Cayenne's. She watched the people emerge, couples hand-in-hand. She imagined they were glamorous men and women with throw away money, out to eat and drink and be seen.

For a moment, she imagined being one of those people, laughing, eating, breeding, happy without care.

She swirled a mouthful of her drink before swallowing.

She had planned to stroll to a nearby nightclub and hook up with an energetic random, but after a third Jack and ginger ale, she fell asleep on the lounger and spent her second night of freedom alone.

## 12

**Le Fleur woke on his back, staring at the ceiling.** His body felt cool beneath the cotton sheets. It was 8:00 Sunday morning. The scent of iodine from the kelp drifted through his open window. He knew the wind was blowing onshore. The sea rumbled like it was inside his room.

Nial Townley. Father and workaholic. An ex-wife and a dodgy girlfriend. Was he dead or alive?

Events of the previous day lined up like objects on a conveyor belt. He jumped out of bed before the strange sensations twisted his thoughts.

He showered, dressed, and made his bed.

Unlocking his bedroom door, he hummed Portishead's "Give Me A Reason To Love You," realized he was happy. In the living room, he swept away an incomplete game of backgammon and slammed shut the wooden container set.

He had made a commitment to obtain cell phone and internet browsing records of the individuals on Carla's suspect list.

He mixed muesli and raisins into a bowl, added milk, then picked up the remote and raised the metal door to the Chrome Room.

The *Wheatfield* was drying on an easel.

He booted the Omega server and scrolled through a list of contacts.

```
THEDUKE - ✝
ZAPPER
SUPERCHARGER
$CENE$TER
WARLORD - ✝
NETWORX
```

The pseudonyms were identities of physical people with special skills.

THEDUKE and WARLORD, denoted with the symbol ✝ for R.I.P, could never be accessed again; their physical masters were dead.

The other four—ZAPPER, SUPERCHARGER, $CENE$TER, and NETWORX—were listed as unavailable.

He dipped a spoon into his muesli and started his SearchMe routine. His first target was NETWORX.

NETWORX's real identity was Richard Chinkanda, a Malawian citizen sometimes known as Charles Richard. He had studied photography at Vega, his mother worked as a domestic servant for a family in Kenilworth.

---

Richard took a classy picture, but his real talent was infiltrating cellular networks.

Le Fleur compiled a list of IP addresses previously used by NETWORX and followed each one into the systems of relevant service providers (ISP's). Cracking ISP lists was becoming harder and harder. But they all ran automated backups to cloud based servers and this was his target. Once inside the ISP's customer database, he could use the IP address to link the user's billing information—name and physical address. Fortunately, an ISP retained details of every click, every illicit connection to the internet.

It took him fifteen minutes to hook a record for C. Richard. There was nothing illegal about his access history: chatlines, links to the gaming sites Hawken and Black Mesa, regular access to mukuru.com, a site facilitating money transfer to Malawi. The history was enough to convince him C. Richard was his man.

Charles Richard aka Richard Chinkanda had not been discreet about his internet activity. He had not even protected his browser against online tracking. Le Fleur requested a connection on Chat Step, everything encrypted, everything deleted when you left the chat.

```
NETWORX     His royal leetness
            CRACKERJACK is back, no way!
LE FLEUR    We do not talk about it
NETWORX     Sheesh, you got some heat
            I went underground
            You clean now?
LE FLEUR    I'm back
            Have you heard from the old crew?
NETWORX     SUPERCHARGER's running
            a software company, I hear
            And you?
LE FLEUR    I see a bit of $CENE$TER
NETWORX     Ooh!
            Send pics or it didn't happen
LE FLEUR    What about ZAPPER?
```

There was a pause in the communication. Le Fleur swallowed a spoon of muesli.

```
NETWORX     ZAPPER?
            That black hat's not living
```

|            | with his mom, for sure |
|            | Last I heard he was working on |
|            | the dark web with the Honker Union |
|            | He's probably in jail in China |
| LE FLEUR   | Are you still building contraptions? |
| NETWORX    | Ah, we must talk |
|            | I have made many breakthroughs |
|            | Call me Alexander Graham |
|            | But hey, what's with the contact? |
| LE FLEUR   | I need some cell records |
| NETWORX    | I knew it wasn't social |
| LE FLEUR   | You can access? |
| NETWORX    | Am I the new cyber inspector now? |
|            | Appointed by the DG ☺ |
|            | Why don't you go direct? |
|            | Lost your nerve? |
| LE FLEUR   | I figured you'd still have the exploits |
|            | You used to own those servers |
| NETWORX    | Exploits! |
|            | Who me? |
|            | The telco's bout as vulnerable |
|            | as Chuck Norris's ass |
|            | They patch those servers more often |
|            | than I've gone backdoor |
|            | Which networks are we talking? |
| LE FLEUR   | MTN, Vodacom, whatever |
| NETWORX    | $#&%@!! |
| LE FLEUR   | ☺ |
| NETWORX    | There's new security in the cages |
|            | You must see the flipping audit systems!! |
|            | You look at the data and it kicks out |
|            | an exception |
|            | I'd have to turn it off first and |
|            | that's a ball ache |
| LE FLEUR   | Are you in marketing now? |
|            | Pushing up the price? |
| NETWORX    | Hahaha |
|            | The more beautiful and pure a thing is — |
|            | the more satisfying to corrupt it |
|            | Are we talking current data? |

```
LE FLEUR    Three months back
NETWORX     *bangs head against wall*
LE FLEUR    Come on!
            You won't have to go into the cage
NETWORX     I know a guy who knows a guy
            who's got a shell
LE FLEUR    I thought you might
NETWORX     What's the urgency?
LE FLEUR    Sooner than impossible
NETWORX     $$$!!
LE FLEUR    I'll pay
NETWORX     WOOT, the leets are back!
            This calls for some masturbatage
```

After the call ended, he sent NETWORX an encrypted list of cell numbers, closed the connection, and spooned in a mouthful of cereal.

It had been a long time since he had made contact with his old world.

CRACKERJACK. No one had referred to his handle in many years.

He smiled at the unique lingo connecting the inhabitants of the deep net.

Rule #32: *Pics or it didn't happen*, NETWORX joking that he wanted picture proof of Le Fleur's meeting with $CEN$TER.

Rule #43: *The more beautiful and pure a thing is—the more satisfying to corrupt it*, NETWORX expressing his joy at being able to defeat the network companies' attempts to block his hacks.

There was order to the Internet, a set of sacred protocols and conventions, contradicted by rule #42: *Nothing is sacred.*

He finished his cereal, washed and dried the bowl, and stored it away. The code of conversation shared with NETWORX was first language to tens of thousands of hackers. Some of the words he had not used for years: woot—a hacker's cry of ecstasy.

The elite or leets as NETWORX wrote. Nighttime inhabitants of a secret place, a virtual world that did not exist but with power, power to humiliate corporate businesses, to amass fortunes, to topple governments.

Le Fleur returned to the Chrome Room, connected to Interpol, and scanned public announcements of missing people called Yellow Notices. He found nothing of interest.

For the next half hour, he browsed the net for information on Nial Townley, his history buried by reports on his disappearance. Forty-four years old. Born in Zimbabwe, educated Prince Edward, studied engineering at the University of Cape Town. There were many repeats of one particular picture: Townley aboard a game vehicle in the African bush, khaki shirt, muscular arms and tanned skin. He could not imagine Townley out of control or anyone's victim.

He closed his eyes and pictured Carla's slim hands, the gold band on her finger, the silver ID bracelet.

*I would have in a heartbeat.*

## 13

**Nial Townley said: "I'm fine, thanks, Fred, and you?"**

After a leisurely run along Victoria Road to Mouille Point and back, Le Fleur showered and dressed warmly then located the recording of Nial Townley's fund transfer, a file called GOLDMAN SACHS LONDON: NIAL TOWNLEY/FRED GOLDSMITH FRIDAY 14:35.

The call had taken place two hours after Carla last spoke to Nial Townley.

He sipped a glass of iced water and replayed Townley's opening words. *I'm fine, thanks, Fred, and you?* The voice was calm and rational. Carla's associated notes read: "Like ice down my spine. First impression: this is Nial. It's him. He sounds completely normal."

```
GOLDSMITH  No bonuses.
           But we carry on rewardless.
```

Nice one, Goldsmith from Goldman's, Le Fleur mused, the same company reported a multi-billion dollar profit less than a year after the world's financial system looked destined to destroy the artificial hopes of the human race.

```
TOWNLEY    Come on, Fred.
           You can miss a season at Livigno.
GOLDSMITH  Where? Italy? You've got to be joking.
```

He read Carla's note: "This is weird. Why would Nial say Livigno? Fred is an ex-pat. He grew up in Johannesburg. He skis in Austria or Switzerland. You wouldn't catch him dead skiing with the South Africans in Italy. I mentioned this to Fred. He remembers wondering why, since he doesn't ski in Italy. He said he thought Nial was confused."

Le Fleur played with the word Livigno in his head. Living? Live and go? He googled it: the word meant avalanche. He let the recording run.

```
TOWNLEY    You received the transaction from Carla?
GOLDSMITH  Yes. Are you buying a fucking island?
TOWNLEY    It's the Venezuelan deal.
           We're going to build another structure
           off Caracas.
GOLDSMITH  What about the other cash?
TOWNLEY    We'll get that back.
```

```
GOLDSMITH   And how is the delectable Carla?
TOWNLEY     She's fine.
GOLDSMITH   Fine?! If she were my P.A.,
            I'd come in my pants every morning.
```

Le Fleur glanced at Carla's annotation. She had not commented. He took a pen and circled the words: *delectable Carla.*

```
GOLDSMITH   Hello?
TOWNLEY     Yes.
GOLDSMITH   I thought I'd lost you there.
            Have they sorted out the
            connectivity shit?
TOWNLEY     Still the most expensive calls
            in the world, but it's getting better.
            Listen, Fred, I'm in a bit of a hurry.
GOLDSMITH   Sure. I'll send confirmation back
            via email. Can you give me the code,
            Nial? It was not included on the
            document you signed.
TOWNLEY     It's Sophie. The code is Sophie.
```

Le Fleur heard Goldsmith chuckle. Carla's notes stated Nial seldom added the code to the document; he thought it a bad idea.

```
GOLDSMITH   We should change that.

(pause)

TOWNLEY     You're probably right.
GOLDSMITH   OK.
            Fifteen-point-eight million sterling
            to Bank West, Caracas for immediate
            settlement, benefactor Supertech slash
            Jorge Ramos. That correct?
TOWNLEY     Yes.
GOLDSMITH   Right-e-o. It'll be valued for
            Monday morning.
```

Carla remarked on the beneficiary: "Supertech accounts were held at

---

ABN AMRO. Fred never questioned why we were using a new account number at a different bank."

```
TOWNLEY    Thank you.
GOLDSMITH  I'll be out in November.
           The exchange rate is too good to be true.
           Is it safe?
TOWNLEY    Safe?
GOLDSMITH  The country. South Africa. Azania.
           That mining protest shit is spooking
           the markets.
TOWNLEY    I'm sure you'll be fine.
GOLDSMITH  Well. Nial. Nice talking to you.
           I'll give you a call. We'll have dinner.
TOWNLEY    Thank you, Fred. Goodbye.
```

Carla had underlined Townley's *I'm sure you'll be fine* comment. She wrote: "Nial is fiercely passionate about the country. He would have said something like—safe as houses."

He listened to the conversation again.

Goldman's hired a voice recognition expert to compare the conversation to previous ones and found no discrepancy. The expert stated Townley's voice sounded stressed but not unduly so compared to his other calls.

Le Fleur increased the volume and played the conversation for a third time, listening for any unusual sounds, as if the ambient noise in the background might carry some message. Triangulation of Townley's cell placed the Goldman call in the vicinity of Cape Town International. Even if he were inside his Land Cruiser, Le Fleur imagined there would be sounds of the surroundings, a plane's engine, traffic, or voices.

Next he logged onto Cape Town airport's flight arrival and departure website. Flights from Comair, Etihad, and Air France landed at exactly 14:35.

He wrote a note to himself: "Use Audacity to remove the talking and boost the background sound" at the bottom of the transcript and circled it.

He dialed Carla. When she answered, the background noise sounded like she was at a party.

"Let me go somewhere I can talk," she said.

The murmur gradually reduced.

"That's better," she said, the sound of a door closing. "You must see where I am. Flipping red curtains, Charlotte Rhys luxury soaps, this is the toilet I'm talking about. You can eat in here."

He imagined that his late father Jake would have an immediate response to her comment. He did not like people who made smart ass jokes so he said nothing.

"There's a Malaysian woman singing like she's on Prozac. And the ceiling looks like the Louvre. So what's up?"

"I've listened to the transcript. I want to ask you a question."

"Go ahead."

"What's the panic code at Nial's residence?"

There was a silence.

"That's a good question," she answered. "You're thinking 'Livigno' was a distress code? I'll check it out. But Nial could've given Goldsmith the wrong code if he'd wanted."

"Not if someone had a gun to his head." There was a brief silence then he continued. "Those were your words, weren't they, I remember, when we were at Nial's house?"

"Yes."

"OK, tell me again about the other money. Goldsmith said, 'What about the other cash?' and Nial said he'd get that back too."

"That's the money the Venezuelan Government was withholding," she answered.

"How much?"

"About fifteen million USD."

He whistled. $20m plus $15m.

"How serious was their claim?"

"What mattered is that they had it. It was like the Nigerian scams. To get it back, we would've had to pay more with no guarantees."

"You could've walked away."

"It would've sunk us. And that would be the end of our South American venture."

"Take them to court."

"The Venezuelan Government? You must be kidding."

"I see Goldsmith's not on your suspect list?"

"He's a fifty-five-year-old banker in London."

"This script doesn't need an international banker?"

"Sorry?"

"Never mind. Where can I find a copy of the email sent to Goldman's?"

"Look in the Transactions directory."

"He said you sent it."

"Yes, Nial did say that. But I didn't. Obviously, I didn't. Captain Parks, the Hawks guy, took a copy of the email. It was analyzed by some digital expert character. They concluded it was sent off our network by someone who'd logged in as me."

"Could he have sent it? Did he have your login password?"

"No. I highly doubt it. Nial was not a technology guy. I know his password. And I sometimes write his emails."

There was a silence. He waited for her to say something more, but she did not.

"So someone else created the email in your name. Someone who knew your password, knew the business, and the format of the transaction details."

"Apparently my password was weak. I use my initials then the month and the year and change it every month. I thought that was pretty good but apparently not."

"What did Parks think?"

"Well, he speculated that I was in cahoots with Nial. But essentially they think Nial wrote it."

"OK."

"OK what?"

"OK, you can go back to whatever you were doing," he said.

"I was making a wee."

He ended the call and moved onto his next task: Where did the money go?

## 14

**Everyone has secrets.** Le Fleur imagined Carla had a wide circle of friends. On the basis of looks alone, there would be a lot of men chasing her.

Mr. Delivery arrived with pizza from Panarottis—a gourmet Carnivore with double mozzarella and a large Al Capone for the fridge.

He stored the Capone, picked the chorizo off the Carnivore, put it on a plate, and opened the Chrome Room.

On the Omega Server, he kicked off a SearchMe scan on his networks and sampled a slice of pizza as sites and directories flashed on the screen.

He opened Facebook and searched for Carla Vitale. He considered social media a vanity chamber, the echo of one's best life moments bounced back and forth in a hollow attempt for attention. He reckoned his old man would have liked it.

Carla's selected profile picture was a monochrome of her standing on a rig, in jeans, boots and t-shirt, hard yellow hat. In his opinion, choice of profile picture was a tell-tale character trait—it was the image you pedaled, how you wanted the world to perceive you.

He ate another slice of pizza.

The timeline provided clues to her life—parents living on the South Coast of Kwazulu-Natal; one brother, could only find one, living in Australia; she had grown up in Durban and moved to the Cape five years ago. A hundred-or-so friends. Posts were infrequent: birthday wishes for a Capricorn, a picture at a wedding on a wine farm—she looked elegant in a black dress and high heeled shoes, a couple of shots playing beach volleyball in a one-piece bathing costume, her expression focused and competitive. There were a few men, happy to be photographed with her but none with the smug face of a consistent boyfriend.

She was more than simply pretty, he thought, her looks on par with intelligence.

*Screw them. They can have their fucking job. I'd rather be poor.*

*I'll exhaust every resource I have to get to the truth.*

There was something he admired about her. Was that why he had accepted the job? He felt an uneasy tinge. What if he had her wrong? He closed her Facebook page.

If she looked him up on Facebook, she would not find anything.

He finished a third slice of pizza. He was full. He returned the rest to the fridge.

He supposed most secrets started with money. He opened a forensic report performed by Deloitte.

Within fifteen minutes of the electronic transfer to Bank West in Caracas, Venezuela, the funds sent from Goldman's were converted to dollars, split into five parcels of $4 million, and transferred to some of the world's dodgiest banks.

It seemed a good strategy. Move fast to avoid risk of recall. Divide the loot to lessen the impact of discovery.

The Forex dealer at Bank West, a Juan Perez, an employee of some eight years, was no longer in Bank West's employ. He searched the dealer's name on the White pages. He got 3,830,000 results.

One million dollars remained in Venezuela and was transferred to seven regional banks. Jorge Ramos, the Supertech agent, worked with local police to trace this tranche to the beneficiary banks. Only one local bank would confirm the account and transfer, but stated the funds had been withdrawn. There were no working cameras in the branch at Wachovia Bank.

Le Fleur grinned, his imagination working as he read the report. He pictured some Mexican guy on a donkey, wearing a panama hat and pitching into a wooden-building bank and asking to withdraw $100,000.

Not all his thoughts were helpful.

He knew the money would disappear into the pseudonymous and irreversible transactions of new digital currencies.

He wrote a list of the countries of the first five recipient banks mentioned in the Deloitte report:

COSTA RICA
LATVIA
NORTH KOREA
PAKISTAN
URUGUAY

Not exactly destinations on Thompson Travel's hot summer holiday list, the cash traveled the dirt freeways of global banking, the roads without traffic lights.

He flicked to a map of the world and examined the destination countries. There seemed to be no link.

Attached to each offshore transfer was a contract signed by Nial Townley. The contract authorized the payment of $4 million to the account holder at the foreign bank for consulting services rendered.

This act legitimized the transactions.

He scanned the list of offshore beneficiary banks. Supertech had hired ITA, an international tracing company, to assist with the recovery.

At Parex Bank in Riga, Latvia, the four million dollars was immediately split into four transactions then wired out again.

The signed contract with Townley's authorization effectively blocked attempts to retrieve Supertech's money from the beneficiary banks. Goldman's needed Bank West to play ball, and Bank West, even if they were cooperative, would have to fight a contractual dispute with clients at other remote banks.

He scanned a list of the second tier banks involved in the transfers. In some cases, they were small regional banks operating current accounts off a larger bank. It made it impossible to trace the cash. It was not like the account could be frozen.

The dead end was consolidated accounts: pension funds, deposit funds, money market and second tier clients.

ITA had submitted letters to each of these terminating accounts requesting client details relating to the respective deposit reference numbers. There were no responses on file.

The money was gone.

He took a deep breath. It was a sophisticated laundry of a large amount of cash.

He examined Townley's signature on the contracts. Like his signature on the fax authorizing the original transfer, it appeared authentic, impossible to judge as a forgery.

He pushed his chair back and drummed his fingers on the desk table. For a moment he felt annoyed, that with all the technology available, the world depended on a signature dating back to Muhammad in Medina.

It was a brilliant scheme.

A shipwreck of cash, flotsam traveling currents, washed up at remote banks around the world.

Someone knew where the money ended up. Someone knew the cipher of how to access it.

He had seen something like this before.

This was the work of someone special, a mastermind.

**Fallon ran her hands over her body and squeezed her breasts together.** The hour of weak sun yesterday had brushed her skin with a light golden hue. Staring at her image in the full-length mirror in the bathroom at Sea View Holiday Flats, she touched her head and considered the result of her "do-it-yourself" blonde job.

She had begun with a shower—much needed—and a good conditioner. Afterwards she had dried her hair then cropped—no, hacked—it short without emotion. Luckily her mane was in mint condition, never been screwed with before. She had applied bleach to her hair and eyebrows and, over the course of the day, watched her hair transform through shades brown and red before turning bright as sunshine. She did not panic. At 4:00—she could not sleep, maybe there was emotion attached to hair— she applied violet intensifier to remove the yellow hue. Then she cut off another inch and did her eyebrows again.

The hair felt dry and detached from her person. She tested a set of hazel colored eye lenses she had used before, but decided to keep something of her identity intact.

She stared at herself for a long time. The nude eyebrows were especially dramatic.

She was someone else.

Earlier, she had phoned Professor Dave Valentine. Duh, what the fuck? DV. Dark Video. It was no coincidence. She had called the local Universities anyway. Professor Valentine did not exist.

Valentine was her link. Three years ago, she was working as an operative for an illicit internet business called Dark Video. She made lots of money hooking up wealthy Dark Video clients with young, drugged women sourced from local bars. Then a computer hacker called JACKER had discovered the identity of U.S.-based Carlos De Palma, her boss and the king-pin of Dark Video, and shopped him to the Feds. She had not heard anything from Carlos or Dark Video for three years. They owed her big time for her silence and loyalty.

She tried Valentine again, but got no response. Impatient, she connected to a channel she previously used to contact Dark Video and posted a message:

    DV operative Africa South for Carlos.

If Carlos De Palma checked the channel, he would understand her message and know she was available for immediate action.

She had decided long ago to leave South Africa. The country had reached a tipping point of corruption and lawlessness and she did not hold much hope for the future. She had set her sights on Europe. Somewhere she could find high class decadence among the refined and cultured. But the living costs were shockingly high in Europe. She needed a nest egg.

She tried Valentine once more.

She *had* to make contact with Dark Video. She had a strong feeling that revenge would feature high on their priority list. Carlos De Palma's revenge would be her financial gain.

She opened the wooden cabinet and removed an address book containing details of her former customers, powerful men who ordered takeaway pleasure from local bars. In those days, she had been known as Diva. She paged through the book, typing names into Google on her laptop. A few searches were hits. A businessman, a sex scandal, a suicide. She did not feel inclined to approach clients directly. She had been out of the business too long. Their tastes may have changed.

She closed the book and walked naked into the living area of the flat. The curtains were open. Through gaps in the building opposite, she could see all the way to Victoria Wharf.

She checked her phone again for any missed calls or messages then placed it on the lounge table, walked onto the patio. She had thrown musty clothes into the sun to air. The patio resembled an outlet for second-hand garments.

She was thinking about the sea and how it changed its mood from alluring to foreboding with only subtle changes of time and nature. This morning it was a lake, the sun reflecting off a glassy surface. Now it was still flat, but the light was gone and wind whipped across a barren desert of oily water. She wondered what sea life still existed in the cold waters of Table Bay.

She pulled a recliner onto the patio and dozed off in the sun to be woken by a ringing noise. She realized it was the apartment phone. She walked across the apartment, and lifted the portable receiver off a narrow tea table.

"Madam, it is Fabrice. I have a call holding for you. The man isn't sure of your apartment number, he said seventh floor between the North Tower and the central column. And..."

"Put it through."

A change of background noise indicated she had been connected.

"Can I help you?" she said.

"I'm sure you can," a man's voice replied. "I'm in the building directly adjacent across the road."

She hesitated. "Yes?"

"What's going on there? It looks like a bazaar on your balcony."

She considered ending the call. Some asshole with nothing better to do than complain. But she had nothing better to do.

"All those clothes but none on you, I thought we could meet?"

Her interest piqued. Did he know her?

"I wasn't spying, seriously, I happened to be on my deck and looking across and I...Wow! I hope you don't mind?"

She walked to the door of the balcony and looked across the divide. A man in a flat two streets away waved. She could barely make him out.

"Do you know me?" She wondered whether the caller could be Dave Valentine.

"No, but I would like to. This may sound crazy. I have a bottle of champagne, would you like to share it?"

She narrowed her eyes.

"You've got binoculars?"

"Nikon."

She turned around.

"I'm sorry," he said. "You're gorgeous."

"I only drink Moët." She pronounced it mow-wee and stretched her arms above her head. If it was Valentine, she would give him something to think about.

"Moët? OK, you're a classy chick. I can get some."

"Who are you?"

She wiggled her finger into her belly button and tested the small scar tissue inside. She thought it was perhaps time to reopen the piercing.

"Does it matter?" he asked.

"I like to know who I'm fucking."

The man chuckled. "Wow!"

"You like that?"

"I do. I sure do."

"So what's the problem?"

"There's no problem. I'll bring champagne over, and we can get to know each other."

"You've been looking at me through your Nikons. If you like what you see, what's there to get to know?"

She stood with her back to the patio door. The sun's heat beamed onto her back like a second admirer.

"OK. All action, baby, I like it. What's the room number?"

"726."

"I'll be right over."

"With Moët?"

"Uh, OK, sure. I'm not sure if I actually have Moët at the flat. It may take a bit longer. But how about the bubbles I've got? It's seriously stellar stuff, are you sure?"

"No."

"Are you serious?"

She did not answer.

"OK, sure thing then. Do you know if there's a bottle store nearby?"

She ignored his question.

"Come on, what's the difference? What say I come over and we can save time?"

She said nothing. She knew every man wanted to fuck her. Some women too. Only the approach differed.

"Is this Dave?" she asked.

It did not sound like her visitor in prison.

"I can be Dave if you want." He laughed.

She closed her eyes then opened them.

"Look here, if you come here and it's not Moët, I'll break the bottle over your head and stick the jagged neck in your throat."

There was a shocked silence. "What did you say?"

"You heard me."

"Hell, man, what the fuck?"

"I'm not kidding."

"Listen, baby, no one talks—"

She ended the call and closed the patio door.

Predatory men did not excite or threaten her. *She* was the predator.

# 16

**Le Fleur could have asked Carla for her address.** Instead he sourced it from a long-forgotten cloud backup of Supertech's company database.

The glass entrance door to the Harbor Heights apartment block was ajar. He stepped inside and tested the door. The lock seemed to be broken. When he eased the door back, it snapped closed. He paused briefly and scanned the entrance hall. A guard was lounging behind a desk reading a book. He spotted no cameras.

*I've watched too many movies*, he thought and took the stairs to the third floor, pushed open the fire escape, and strolled along the corridor until he stopped in front of 319.

He knocked once and waited. He put his ear to the door, heard no sound, so he knocked again, louder.

After five minutes, Carla's voice: "Who is it?"

"Daniel Le Fleur. Be quick, there's a crazy hobo out here."

He regretted the words as they came out of his mouth. The inexplicable urge again. *You're not a funny guy,* he told himself, *so why try?*

The door opened. Carla wore a white camisole and pajama shorts, her hair tousled.

"Is it a bad time?"

"No, no, it's OK." She did not open the door. "Uh, I would ask you in, but shit, my flat is such a mess."

He smiled. *She's not alone*, he thought. Maybe he was wrong and there was a smug boyfriend.

"I'll come back then?" He stepped back from the door.

"Wait!" She stepped outside and closed the door, made an attempt to correct her hair. "What is it, Daniel?"

"I don't want to talk in the corridor. Can I come back when you're ready?"

She paused. "OK, hey, do you know the Italian café in Point Road? Give me fifteen minutes and I'll meet you there."

At the café, a short drive from her apartment, fifteen minutes became thirty. Le Fleur waited on a stool alongside a narrow coffee bar, sipping reluctantly on an espresso beneath the camouflaged CCTV dome camera. He amused himself by identifying European flags hanging from the bar. He got them all except Liechtenstein courtesy of years playing online Sporcle.

Thirty minutes became forty-five. He watched the languid movement of society in the Italian styled café and listened to the click-clack of the cash register. A couple at the bar was holding hands, engrossed in tender conversation. Le Fleur wondered what it would be like to be involved in such a relationship. He barely knew Carla and already he was irritated by her time management.

Carla eventually arrived with wet hair.

"I'm so sorry. My cleaner hasn't been for a week. My place is unforgiveable."

Dark glasses, no bra, nothing like a ball-breaking engineer running international construction projects, nothing like her Facebook profile. He wondered how the macho men in the pits and on the rigs coped.

She sat alongside him, facing across the bar towards the road. Under a green awning, a production crew with foreign clients had their backs to the road, talking about the light and the low cost of the beer. A few locals were sitting opposite, men in vests, sunglasses, caps, two male cyclists in matching gear. A gray-haired man who looked like an aging movie star browsed a magazine.

She dipped her sunglasses and showed her red eyes.

"Ouch," he said.

A balding barista was operating without stress in the tight space restrictions. He lit up when he spotted Carla. "My beautiful Carla. What can I get you, baby?"

"The usual, Mario. And a big orange juice too, no ice."

A waitress with a plastic shower cap on her head reacted to Mario's signal and hurried off to fetch the order. Carla scanned the cafe as if looking for friends then turned and faced him.

"You should've called first."

"I did. It said: Subscriber unavailable."

She fished her cell from her handbag and fiddled with it. "Fuck! Those assholes at GALI have cut it off." She banged it on the counter.

Le Fleur leaned back against the wooden backrest of his stool.

The barista delivered an Americano and an orange juice. She drained the orange juice. Across the bar, the cyclists engaged the barista in a conversation about riding in Sicily.

"Well, at least the bank won't be able to repossess my car now. They don't have a number to call." She placed the empty glass on the counter.

A guy wearing a nutria-colored vest seemed to be watching them. He wore a baseball cap with curly hair pushed out the sides, dark glasses. Le Fleur sipped his cooling espresso. He had not noticed the guy before Carla arrived.

"What will you do if you leave GALI?"

She frowned. "I've got money, if that's what you're wondering."

---

"I wasn't. I read about the shortage of qualified engineers. Importing Cubans. You'll find a new job easily?"

"I don't care about a job. I'm going to find out who did this to Nial. That's all I care about."

He paused in contemplation. What did he care about? What was all he cared about? Not day trading. Not copying the masters.

"You're not bailing on me, are you?"

He shook his head and smiled.

"How's the wrist?"

He tapped his cast. "Better every day."

"I keep looking at those blue crosses on your good wrist. There's a story there?"

He nodded.

The waitress returned with Carla's order. She gripped the bagel in both hands and took a bite. "You're not eating anything?"

He slipped her a paper serviette. "Were you alone this morning?"

She wiped her mouth. "How do you mean?"

"When I knocked on your door, were you alone?"

She paused, wiped her mouth again. "Yes. Why?"

He scanned the bar. The guy in the nutria vest was texting on his cell.

"Are you checking on me?" She was faintly amused.

He changed the subject. "I've ordered the cell records."

"Ordered? That's more like it. Any idea of the cost?"

"A friend owes me a favor. I'll let you know."

The plastic-capped waitress was mopping the floor around their legs.

"So you listened to the Goldman's transcript," she said. "The cash trail ends in black market schemes and companies running current accounts off larger banks in dodgy countries. Seriously, in this day and age, how does that happen? What about the money laundering filters, the *Know-Your-Client*?"

"Five percent of the global economy is laundered funds. Twenty million dollars is peanuts within that context."

"So what do you think?"

"I don't like to speculate."

"OK, sure, but give me a version, if you had to take a flyer."

"A flyer?" He did not like opinion, did not like to receive them and did not care to share them. "They hired some tech guys to login as you and set up the transfer. Some even cleverer ones to distribute the cash. Then someone shoved Nial's car over Chapman's, tossed his shoes in the sea, made it look like he'd had an accident or killed himself. And he skipped the country."

Carla put down the remnant of her bagel and stared angrily across the table.

"You said he was burned out," he added quickly. "Supertech's remaining funds were threatened by Venezuela. Maybe it was the only way out."

"That's not what happened."

"He made the transfer?"

"Yes, but someone forced him to make the transfer."

*How do you force someone to make a transfer,* he thought, but did not respond.

"Someone *did* this to Nial. I'm going to find out who it was."

The street was filled with moving traffic in both directions.

He pulled out his cell and read.

> Nial Townley didn't arrive at work on Monday
> morning. I contacted him at 8:15 am. His cell
> was off. I tried again fifteen minutes later
> and also tried the home number, which was on auto
> answer. I then called his ex-wife Sophie Townley.
> She said Nial didn't fetch their son Gregory
> after school on Friday and she'd been trying
> all weekend to contact him.

"Gregory was in aftercare," she said. "The school contacted Sophie and she went to the Prep and picked him up."

"Was that the first indication something was wrong?"

"Yes. But I didn't know it then."

"His relationship with Sophie was rocky?"

She made a wavy motion with her hand. "Sophie's a classic rag royalty, princess type, you know how they are? The whole world owes them a living. She spends her life in hair salons and shopping malls. She was pregnant at twenty-one with Gregory. Nial thought marrying her was the right thing to do. He isn't the cleverest in the EQ department. She only cares about Nial insofar as it affects her. She wanted to take Gregory overseas and nothing was going to stop her. Fuck the father and his feelings. Nial had to go to the courts to prevent her. She's a determined bitch."

Le Fleur rubbed his cheek. The barista was cleaning his reading glasses under the steam from the coffee machine. The production crew departed, clearing a view to the giant football stadium across the road.

She leaned back in her chair.

"She got a boyfriend?"

"There were a few men, I heard, one a doctor in Kenilworth. It was quite serious, he wanted to marry her. She broke it off. I think she hoped her and Nial would reunite. But it must be her way, on her terms. She didn't like his long working hours, but she sure enjoyed the benefits."

Le Fleur was silent. Kenilworth doctors were not exactly mastermind criminal types. He returned to Carla's statement.

> I contacted Gavin Marx. The police at
> Wynberg wanted us to wait for 24 hours
> before we filed missing person. Gavin and
> I received the transcript of the call to
> Goldman's—but it was already Monday and
> after listening we both thought it was
> Nial and he sounded normal. We were unsure
> what was happening. Gavin escalated to the
> station commander at Wynberg Police
> station. He requested the police urgently
> access Nial's cell records from Vodacom so
> we could trace his movements. Police could
> not requisition the records because no
> crime had been committed. Gavin drafted an
> urgent affidavit stating we believed the
> client was in danger.

He pictured Gavin Marx in the TV interview, the handsome man annoyed by the questions. "He's not on the suspect list?"

She smiled. "Gregory's middle name is Gavin. He's the godfather."

"I added his cell number to the list anyway."

"OK," she said and nodded slowly.

"Does Gavin share your dislike of Bruno Pittman and GALI?"

"Absolutely. He hates them. But he's practical. We didn't have much choice."

He continued to read her statement.

"So the triangulation of Nial's movements on Friday confirmed he was at Supertech offices until midday. Then he drove to the school to fetch his son. Where's the school?"

"Rondebosch. Some parents remembered his car outside the school. My call to Nial and the catalyst call were answered at that location. Then he left. For what reason, God only knows. He tried to call Sophie. Then his cell went off. Ten minutes before Fred Goldsmith's call, his cell reappeared on the network at the airport. That's it."

"No camera capture of the Land Cruiser?"

"There's nothing until a week later at Chapman's."

The barista checked they were OK. Carla ordered another Americano and a Portuguese tart.

"The catalyst call was a trigger, I'm sure. Then according to the cops, and to you it seems, after the call to Goldman's, he gets on a plane and disappears."

The barista delivered coffee and a tart. He looked concerned. "Are you all right, my darling?"

Carla nodded and the barista left. The movie guy handed in a yellow slip for his meal.

"It's such bullshit. Why would he transact at the airport? He wasn't acting of his own choice. Someone had a gun at his head. Nial wasn't an idiot. If he had stolen the money, he wouldn't have dumped his car over Chapman's or gone online at an escape route. It didn't fool anybody."

"Did you find out his home panic code?"

"Yes."

He studied her expression. "It wasn't Livigno?"

"No. Take a guess."

He did not like guessing or gambling. "Sophie."

"Spot on. Christ, can you believe it?"

"Any other reason he would transact at an airport?" he asked.

"No, other than the obvious one. There's no evidence Nial boarded a flight. I spent hours viewing airport surveillance, looking for him, his car."

"He could have—"

"I know," Carla interrupted. "He could have had a disguise. And a fake name. Jesus Christ, this was Nial Townley, not fucking Carlos the Jackal. We must stop considering Nial planned this and start looking at the alternatives."

There was activity at the entrance to the café. The movie guy was leaving, another customer entering. The guy in the nutria vest was sipping a drink.

"Why would Nial go to Gregory's school if he was about to embark on either paying the Venezuelan government a massive bribe or stealing the money?" she asked. "Every indication was he intended to spend the weekend with Gregory. There were sandwiches in the fridge, for God's sake." Her expression hardened. "I've heard this same shit from everyone. I'll send you a video of Nial and his son. Then you can tell me whether you *still* think he'd do this."

---

He felt the prick of her emphasized irritation. Was it impatience? She had obviously considered and been asked these questions many times. Or was it single mindedness? He decided to change the subject.

"So, tell me about the sightings."

She shook her head and pushed her stool back. For a moment, he thought she might leave. He reached out and gripped her wrist.

"I'm serious," he said. "If someone wanted it to look like Nial ducked, they may have deliberately posted false sightings to add to the subterfuge."

She relaxed. He released her wrist.

"Good luck. He's been spotted more than Elvis. There's a fucking five million rand reward. Namibia, Mozambique, you name the destination, he's been there."

Afterwards, he paid the barista following a brief contest over the bill.

On the pavement outside the café, a nip of wind chased packets along the sidewalk. He was watching the guy in the nutria colored vest. He thought the guy was watching them. But he always thought someone was watching. And this was the real world. He could not test it with code.

"Thank you for helping me," she said.

She looked at her feet then stepped forward and put her arms around his waist. She smelled of sweet perfume and shampoo and coffee and Napoli salami. She released him and stepped back, embarrassed, as if she had done something inappropriate. "I'm sorry I got angry."

He put his hands in his pockets and stared at the stadium, built for the Soccer World Cup in 2010, in his opinion a big monolithic reminder of man's folly. "We'll discover what happened."

"Are you sure?" Her blue eyes drilled into his.

"Yes, I'm certain," he said.

## 17

**How to disappear completely and never be found.** The downloaded text was a definitive guide on pseudocide, the science of faking your own death.

Drowning was the preferred method: no body.

Le Fleur thought about Osama Bin Laden. Then he thought about Chapman's Peak Drive and the deep blue water at the bottom.

He settled back on the couch. The TV was on, the chatter of Sheldon and Howard in *The Big Bang Theory* provided a background comfort.

There was the curious case of John Darwin who got into financial trouble. He paddled into the sea to fake his death so his wife could claim on insurance. It was a comedy. The deceased Darwin was actually living in a house next door to his wife. He was spotted by a friend who asked, "Aren't you supposed to be dead?" To which Darwin replied, "Don't tell anyone about this." Another friend overheard a conversation between Darwin and his wife and reported them. On holiday in Panama, the deceased Darwin and his wife were photographed. The picture appeared on social media. But despite this, Darwin's demise was at his own hands. He returned to England feigning amnesia to obtain a police clearance and was arrested.

Then there was Rozeena Butt who faked death by dehydration in 2001. Her motive was a life insurance policy. Unlike Darwin, who was not found until he reappeared, Butt's fake body was: in a remote hospital in Pakistan with a death certificate signed by the British High command. Her error: not allowing enough time to lapse after taking out the policy. The insurance company suspicion led to her arrest.

Not so comical was the German businessman who went missing the day he arrived in South Africa. Prior to departure, he had filed for bankruptcy and installed his mother as the CEO of his new company. Speculation was rife he had fled to Luanda to avoid creditors. His body was found eight months later.

Could Townley's body have been thrown out of the Land Cruiser and washed out to sea? He checked the weather patterns for that week. There was a mother of a storm, shipping warnings, numerous reports of boats wrecked and in trouble along the coast.

He stood and stretched. In his bedroom he stripped his sheets, deposited them into the washing machine. He washed and dried the dishes manually and stored the leftovers of an Asian take-out lunch for Aqualung.

When he returned to the Chrome Room, he located a digital copy of Nial Townley's passports on his laptop and flipped through the pages. Namibia,

Botswana, and Mauritius were stamps in his SA passport, Venezuela and Brazil in his British.

He thought that regardless of whether Townley departed voluntarily or not, the act required substantial planning. If the Hawks focused on "finding" Townley, perhaps not enough attention was paid to activities in the lead-up to the event.

He browsed Townley's social media, his bank and credit card statements, expense claims, and cell phone accounts. Townley's American Express statements validated his South American trip with Ynez. They traveled separately. Townley flew Cape Town to London connecting to São Paulo and Ynez direct to São Paulo from Johannesburg. Townley had flown three days earlier.

He flicked back to the card statement. There was a GBP expense for three nights at the Regency Hotel in London and a cash withdrawal at an ATM in Piccadilly. The cost of dinner at Brasserie Zedel was five hundred Sterling; it seemed expensive for one.

There was another entry with the same date. The description said IL LAGO and the amount was in Euros. He googled IL LAGO. It was an Italian restaurant in Geneva.

Townley went on a day trip to Geneva?

How had he got there? There were no airfare bookings.

He searched Townley's inbox for Geneva, found nothing.

What had Carla said? He hated Europe. He only went if he had to.

Maybe he did have secrets?

Le Fleur felt hungry. He left the Chrome Room. The noise of early evening traffic on Victoria Road signaled an upbeat mood. There was leftover pizza and Asian food in the fridge, but he was not in the mood. He checked outside to see whether Aqualung was around—he was not—and made himself a peanut butter sandwich on rye. Not so healthy, but it tasted good.

*We must stop considering Nial planned this and start looking at the alternatives.*

What were the alternatives?

What about Carla? As Townley's close confidante, and last to speak to him, he considered her fortunate the South African Police Service had not focused on her as a person of interest. In her own words, she was the one who understood the requirements of transacting with Goldman's.

He could not imagine it though. He had no illusions of being Sherlock Holmes, but, to his mind, she had neither the skills to commit the crime nor the "motive of a devil." She clearly adored Townley, seemed disinterested in financial gain, had no shady friends, and was prepared to sacrifice her career to discover the truth of what happened to him.

But women could be villains too.

He opened the suspect directory and located a picture of Sophie Townley in her sub-directory.

She was slim and pretty, a woman not easily ignored on Cape Town's vibrant second-hand social markets. She had long blonde hair, dry as if it were dyed too often. She reminded him of someone, a Hollywood actress, maybe Kate Bosworth. He reckoned his father would have gone crazy over her.

Sophie had motive. With Nial missing, she was able to move to London with her son.

On Sophie's affidavit, she stated she received a call from the school querying why Gregory had not been collected.

Nial's cell records proved he had attempted to call Sophie a few minutes before she received the call from the school, but he had got voice mail.

Why had he called her? To say he could not fetch Gregory?

Why had she not answered?

According to Sophie, Townley left no message.

Le Fleur disabled caller-id and dialed Sophie. Her number rang seven times then went onto message. Her silky voice said:

> Hello, this is Sophie. Leave a message
> and I'll get back to you.

He presumed she had a new UK-based number.

Sophie's affidavit also stated *she* called Nial after hearing from the school, but he did not answer. No one had physically checked that she had made that call. But according to his cell records, he was offline at the time she had given.

He realized why Carla was interested in Sophie's cell records.

Would they reveal that Sophie had received a call from the same number as Carla's so-called catalyst call? That would be answered when NETWORX delivered the cell data.

He made another sandwich, this time with ham and cheese. Online health sites were advocating stay away from bread, but he had no problem with weight, and considered most advice about food fabricated to suit someone's opinion.

According to transcripts of the Townley's custody battle, Sophie wanted to leave because of "the perilous state of safety and security in the country."

He located a travel agreement for Gregory. In the case of a consenting parent being unable to give permission within forty-eight hours, the request would be relayed to their respective attorneys. One month after Nial's disappearance, Gavin Marx signed a conditional consent allowing Sophie to take Gregory overseas for an eight-week period. This consent was subsequently extended for six months.

Le Fleur paused. Marx was Townley's best friend. Considering the courtroom battle to keep Gregory in Cape Town, it must have been difficult for Marx to give consent.

He searched for communication between Townley and Marx. Townley called Marx "George." The majority of emails were business issues regarding South America. The personal discourse covered social and sporting including rugby, mountain biking, and yachting. It appeared they met twice a week for drinks at Constantia Nek. There was no mention of Sophie or Ynez. Or any clue to Marx's romantic interests.

The ex-wife and the best friend. That would make a scandalous story. He was sure there was precedence.

Surely Sophie could not deprive her son of a father?

And best friends were normally bankable. Marx did not appear to be a person influenced by the heart.

He cleared his throat and magnified an image of Nial Townley with his son. He stared into Townley's blue eyes. Livigno. What had Townley meant, perhaps nothing?

Something happened that Friday.

Le Fleur turned his attention to the video surveillance at Townley's Constantia home. He connected his laptop to the overhead screen and settled back on the couch. First he dissected all the system files, the installation logs. Then he scanned each day's surveillance for a week before the incident.

Carla was right: Townley did not always wear the boxers.

He watched the video from the Friday of Townley's disappearance through to the Monday when Carla reported his absence. Then he watched it again.

By the time he turned away from the screen, it was nearly 2:00 am.

# 18

**The ringtone of his cell jangled him out of a deep sleep.** It was 6:45. Carla had a new cell phone. Le Fleur rolled over and groaned.

"You still sleeping?" she said, with the misguided surprise of someone who he had woken much later the day before.

He had sent her a message in the early hours, expected her to read it about midday.

"I'll call you back," he said.

He rolled out of bed and stretched before the mirror, naked except for striped boxers, his hair flat on one side, straight up on the other. He thought he looked like a cartoon character.

He pulled on a sweater. The apartment was in darkness. The under floor heating was on. He walked barefoot to the Chrome Room, pressed the remote, and waited for the metal door to open. Inside, he booted Omega and connected to Carla on Skype. On screen, her video image was clear. She was wearing a white T-shirt.

"I can't see you."

"Wait a moment." He enabled his camera. "How's that."

She was sitting on a bed. He watched as she examined the screen then smiled as his image displayed.

"Nice hair," she said.

He smoothed it down.

Without breaking concentration on the discussion, he hacked a route to her laptop, created a dynamic port, and burrowed through the connection onto her machine. That was why he never used commercial messaging systems.

"Did you watch the video I sent?" she asked.

She had sent him a home video of Nial interacting with his son Gregory. He nodded.

"So do you agree?"

"He puts Steve Biddulph in the shade."

"Steve who?"

Le Fleur ran an elementary test on her system. It spewed out a horror list of infections: Malware, adware, Trojans, key loggers, dialers, bots, worms and hijackers.

"Biddulph. He's a worldwide authority on parenting."

He checked when she last ran a virus check: never. Her laptop was a zombie.

"Oh. And you know this why, exactly?" she asked.

He paused and looked at her screen image. Her face was glowing, she tossed her hair carelessly. He removed his hands from the keyboard and raised them above his head as if reaching for the answer.

"Why do I know about him? Hmmm. OK. I wanted to understand the deal I got on *my* childhood."

"And?"

He smiled. "Nial Townley looks like he's a helluva good father."

"You're a guarded one, Daniel. So what's with your urgent message?"

He uploaded LapRadar, a tracking application, onto her laptop.

"Nial went to Geneva."

"Geneva?"

"You know that funny country with the white flag and red cross. You said he hated traveling Europe."

"I don't know about a trip to Geneva. Maybe it was before my time?"

"It was a year ago."

She shook her head. "I don't recall him making any trip to Switzerland. We don't have any business there. Are you sure?"

"He paid for lunch with his credit card. Two people, maybe three."

"That's strange. I'll ask around at Supertech."

He was not sure if that was a good idea, but did not say anything.

"I've got something else. Check this out—"

He streamed footage from the surveillance taken at Townley's house. Captured from camera no.12, a postman approached the gate on a red motorbike, moving out of view as he hopped off the bike and delivered the post into a slit in the pillar supporting the gate. In the right hand corner, the time counter showed 11:00.

"I reviewed every day for a month leading to *that* Friday."

"No wonder you're tired. Did you like Ynez's sleepwear?"

He ignored her comment. On Camera no.7, when Ynez waltzed down the passage to fetch coffee in the morning, she had no sleepwear.

"Look at the screen. Postman Pat delivers between 10:30 and 11:30, Monday to Friday."

"Unless there's no post," she said.

"Correct."

He split the screen and streamed another output.

"Camera no.11 is inside the gates," he said. "It covers the front gate, also the mail box."

On the second screen, Maria approached the mailbox, opened the wooden door, and removed the day's post. As she turned, the contents held in her right hand were visible. Le Fleur paused the output and created a still shot, magnified it by two hundred percent.

"It starts to distort at higher resolution, but you get a good idea of what she took out the mailbox. And also..." He restarted the video. "The mailbox is empty after she removes the post."

He cleared the screen and started a new stream. It was camera no.12, the Friday of Nial's disappearance. The postman delivered the post and rode away.

"So if we move forward a bit. Camera no.11 . . ."

At 11:15, Maria opened the wooden door and removed the post.

"There're a few envelopes and some advertisement flyers. You see the mailbox is empty," he said.

"Maria's not involved, is she?"

"Let's look at Monday. Maria arrives late for work. A funeral meeting?"

"Yes."

The time showed 10:45. On entering the gate, camera no.11 captured Maria checking for mail. She removed some objects from the mailbox. Le Fleur paused the playback.

"So she's getting the mail," said Carla.

"Except—"

He prompted her response. She said nothing.

"Postman Pat hasn't arrived yet."

He enlarged the frozen image and zoomed in on the contents in Maria's hand.

"What is it?" said Carla, squinting.

"You ever receive a note from a job seeker in your mail box? It's a handwritten request for employment on a torn off strip of paper. Good painters, houseboys, drivers, gardeners, honest, reliable." He stopped the video. He was about to push his chair back before remembering he was wearing striped boxers.

"I don't get it," she said. "So some Malawian shoved a piece of paper in his mailbox."

She was staring at the screen, at his image. He nodded his head slowly back and forward.

"But when—" She paused in mid-sentence.

"There's no video record of any person putting anything in the letterbox between 11:30 Friday morning and 10:45 Monday morning."

"How can that be possible?"

"Someone's got past AlphaGuard and edited out movement on the surveillance footage."

---

## 19

**Le Fleur looked behind him then entered through the automatic doors.** A bell chimed.

"Ian Coulson," he said into a microphone at the unmanned reception desk.

The windows were dirty, gray paint peeled off the walls. A sign behind reception read: "CAN'T TAKE MY EYES OFF OF YOU." He counted three visible cameras. Well-paged computer manuals were stacked on low tables. A single door behind the reception desk had a small window at eye level.

After a minute or two, the door opened.

Other than the rimless glasses, Coulson looked identical to his picture on the internet. He wore jeans and an open necked shirt. His long graying hair flowed over his collar. He might have been a jockey in his youth, music or equine.

"I love it when my hackers come through the front door," said Coulson. He was chewing vigorously. "Come in, Daniel."

A narrow passage wound past sealed doors with access control protection. He followed Coulson into an office strewn with gadget circuitry, wiring, and tools. He looked about the chaos, couldn't help but compare it to his immaculate Chrome Room.

Coulson settled into a faux leather reclining chair behind a long glass desk. A fan struggled manfully above his head. The office smelled of smoke and air freshener. Through the lenses of his glasses, Coulson's eyes appeared massive.

"So what lures you to my dungeon, Daniel?"

A framed University degree and various industry awards hung on the wall. Le Fleur inspected the degree—BA LLB University of Cape Town— and an award from the Minister of Technology before settling in a chair across the desk from Coulson.

"Wait, let me guess," Coulson continued. "You've come to see me for a job? You're hired!"

Le Fleur shuffled on his seat.

"Your chair is lower than mine by the way." Coulson laughed loudly and ran his tongue across his mustache. He ditched his gum and removed the wrapping from a new piece.

A portrait on his desk showed Coulson in a suit with a young woman in a white dress.

"That's my new wife." Coulson lifted the frame. "Three months now. I should've invited you to the ceremony. Two hundred people at the wine farm Vergelegen. Not too shabby, huh? She wanted it. Her old man's a pound millionaire."

Coulson replaced the frame and looked quizzically across the desk.

"How long ago was it, Daniel? Two years? I'm sure the memories aren't so sweet for you, but if you hadn't done what you did then Cybercrime wouldn't own your ass to bust the bad guys. You've been a great investment for us."

Le Fleur nodded. He did not like being considered as anyone's investment.

"You ready for a new assignment?"

"I wanted to ask about your message that Fallon Trafford was getting out."

"Oh, so that's it? It was only a heads up. I keep in contact with the old cases. Some cop woman who ran the case called me. I thought you should know about it, that's all. Are you worried?"

"No. I wondered why you alerted me."

Coulson tweaked his mustache.

"No big deal. I sent a text to all my acolytes. Some of the guys had a relationship, you see." He sucked in air across his mustache. "Did you know her?"

"I knew of her."

"Did you actually meet her?"

"No."

"You know what she looks like?"

Coulson twisted his screen to show Le Fleur a full-size image of Fallon, her green eyes burning.

"Yes."

Coulson tapped his screen and whistled. "I can't be sure if I'd like to fuck her or kill her."

Le Fleur glanced at the photograph of Coulson's new wife. It was definitely his second, maybe a third. He wondered if there were any children.

"Fallon wasn't the reason I came here."

"OK?"

"I was thinking of updating my skills. There's some new technology."

Coulson chuckled. "You want to do a course?"

"Well, I thought you could point me in the right direction."

Since Coulson had explicitly warned him against meeting with Carla Vitale, he could not let on what he was doing.

"I haven't much time for anything. You'd be amazed the time trading takes up. One market closes, another opens. And I'm only following a dozen equities."

"That's pleasing to hear, Daniel. Perhaps you can give me a few tips. I admire you financial types. I am more of a gadget guy myself."

Le Fleur did not respond or correct him. Coulson tossed his gum and produced a box of cigarettes.

"You don't smoke?"

"No."

It was not quite true. Occasionally he smoked weed.

"Never? I'm surprised. It's the lonely man's best friend."

Coulson lit up and pointed across the desk at Le Fleur's cast.

"Lucky you're not left-handed, pal." He jiggled his left fist. "When's that coming off?"

"I'm seeing the Doc this afternoon."

"Hell, man, a scary ordeal. Do you know what type of gun it was?"

"It was a revolver."

Coulson nodded with interest. "You don't have a gun?"

"No."

"It's an essential appendage. I'm a police reservist." Coulson inhaled. He indicated a no-smoking sign on the wall and his eyes twinkled. "Good to be the boss, hey?"

Le Fleur smiled. His mother had smoked. The smell of tobacco had a reassuring memory, especially the first scent after the crack of a match.

"So Daniel, if it isn't the vampire and you're busy as hell, what is it I can do for you?"

"What's your thinking on security these days?"

"Oh God. Security? Don't use cell phones, or the new Windows, or public WiFi, Internet Explorer. Don't ever connect automatically to anything."

"I was reading about some tech called AlphaGuard. They say it's impenetrable. The company's offering a reward to anyone who can hack it."

"And?"

"I thought I'd try my hand."

Coulson sucked deeply and expelled a circle of smoke. "You want to break AlphaGuard?"

"It's not for any devious reason. I think it'll be a challenge. Maybe you know something bigger and better? I hear VaultMaster is something special."

Coulson snorted. "VaultMaster is piss easy. AlphaGuard have done a hundred plus installations in under a year in this country alone." He made a circle with his thumb and index finger. "Nought. Not one break-in. It's fucking Stalingrad. No one can break through the outer layer. And if they do, there're so many booby traps inside, you'd think you were at Houdini's Xmas party. The illicit hacking business has turned so down they'll soon have to look up their own asses. AlphaGuard offers $10,000 if you can break through."

They sat in silence for a moment.

"So it's impossible."

Coulson grinned. "I didn't say that. I know a guy who's been working on a script for a year. He hasn't achieved anything, obviously because the reward is still standing. Give him a call."

Coulson wrote a number on a piece of paper. "Don't say you got it from me," he said and stubbed out his cigarette.

Le Fleur glanced around the windowless office—the ashtray piled with ash and butts, the shelves of microprocessor and casings, the soulless awards and credentials in frames on the walls. The only item of any personal nature was the wedding photograph. It faced away from Coulson.

"How did you get into this business, Ian?"

Coulson picked up his cigarette pack and flipped it in his hand. He seemed to think before answering the question.

"I always liked the tech. My old man brought home an old Apple and I used to play on it. I studied law, but I didn't fit in. I could fix computers not argue semantics. Eventually I realized that tech was my calling. I don't regret the learning." He pointed to his qualification. "Hey, I got the badge. I fucking hate lawyers, but the skills are useful in our business. There's always some cunt trying to ram the law down my throat and get the crooks off the hook."

He waited for Coulson to reciprocate the question. Coulson didn't. Le Fleur surmised Coulson already knew everything about him that he wanted to know.

"How many people work for Cybercrime?" he asked.

"Shit, Daniel. What's with the questions? Have you resorted to social network hacking?"

Le Fleur lifted his hands. "You don't have to tell me."

Coulson tapped out another cigarette but did not light it. "I'm only kidding." He looked up at the rotating fan above his head. "There's me and then there's me."

"You're the organization?"

Coulson grinned. "Then I've got about fifty hacker heads on the payroll. Some are reprobates, some are fucking nerds. Some work from the office down the passage and some work from their palaces in Bali Bay like you.

Hey, did anyone contact you about Nial Townley?"

Le Fleur shrugged and shook his head.

"Five foot eight, short blonde hair, tits popping out and trying to convince everyone she's a qualified rocket science engineer?"

Le Fleur feigned ignorance.

"You heard about Townley?" Coulson asked.

Le Fleur tightened his lips and nodded. "That's the guy who went missing with money."

"Yeah, and every amateur detective in Cape Town is after the reward. This demanding little bitch comes here looking for tech help. Jesus, we've got big shit to deal with, Chinese, Russians, I don't need her sad little story in my life."

Coulson's computer beeped. He eyeballed the screen, swiveled the mouse.

"The fucking Honker Union chinks are at it again." He looked up from the screen. "The Chinese are the new colonialists, mark my words. They've got hackers with skills like you can't imagine. Not that they need much to infiltrate our Government systems. It's one big leak."

"You should contact ZAPPER. Do you know him?"

"I've heard of him. How do you know him?" Coulson asked. His eyebrows drew together.

"I worked with ZAPPER. He was a wizard with language. German, Mandarin, Portuguese."

Coulson looked back at his screen. "Shit." He stood and held out his hand. "Sorry, Daniel. Parliament's servers have been hacked. I've got the Minister of Science and Tech on my bloody back. Can you show yourself out? Back the same way down the passageway."

Le Fleur accepted the handshake. He felt bad lying to Coulson about his involvement with Carla. But Coulson would want to know what he was doing and would oppose the illegal access of cell phone records. He examined the AlphaGuard contact number. He knew the number. He'd phoned it before.

# 20

**Fallon paced back and forth in the living room of her apartment.** She did not understand why Dark Video had not made contact. She tried the number for Dave Valentine again. No answer. Had Dark Video decided she was no longer of value? She replayed the conversation with Valentine at the Worcester prison and considered her responses for any sign that might disqualify her from being a Dark Video operative. Perhaps Valentine had not passed on the message. Carlos De Palma would remember and recognize her qualities.

She sat at the dining room table and rested her bare feet on top of the safe. She had made no effort to unpack her belongings.

At times during the long sleepless nights in Worcester, she remembered the people she had killed, the lives terminated directly by her actions. Yet she did not consider herself an assassin.

She opened the safe, removed the Taurus, and clipped on the empty magazine. There were so many ways to kill a person. But it was hard to beat a gun for effect—the sight, noise, smell, the reaction on impact. She pointed it towards the sea. It was an intimidating weapon, the largest she had owned.

Bang. *Never again will I lose control. Never again.*

She had bought it off a former client, an ex-policeman who liked young girls and had come into money—surprise, surprise—by selling off surrendered weapons intended for destruction. It still had its serial number.

Fallon had killed six people in her life.

She did not intend the first two. They were passengers in a Peugeot she crashed in Harare, Zimbabwe a year after finishing school. That was the worst because everyone knew it was her to blame. People pointed fingers and said she had been drinking and should go to prison. No-one seemed to care about the extent of her injuries, the cranial damage that caused her pupils to be permanently constricted like the eyes of a heroin addict. It was a reminder. Every time she looked in a mirror.

The third was a drunken old man she had shot in the head with his own gun.

Four and five were contract killings. She had been paid to do a job.

The last of the six, she could not explain. They were in a relationship of sorts. The guy was an aggressive asshole and he was pissing her off so she shot him.

When she thought about her victims, the perspective was imagined from their side. The two contract victims knew what was coming their way. She was not sure what was better. If you did not know, you had no chance to arrange your thoughts, to make one last curse or say a final prayer. If you knew, there was the anticipation of pain.

She returned the gun to the safe, cracked a tray of ice and poured a neat Jack.

She was onto a second when the landline rang.

It was Fabrice.

"Madam, there's a—"

"Put it through."

She heard a click.

"Hello?"

"OK, listen to me and listen closely." She recognized Dave Valentine's voice from the visit in prison.

"Dave, I'm so glad you called. Do you know how to contact Carlos De Palma? I—"

"I'll only say this once and afterwards we'll never speak again. I've got a message for you. Do you know how to access a private channel on Whisper?"

"Yes."

"We've got work for you."

"What sort of work? Where's Carlos?"

"Go to the channel."

He ended the call.

She went straight onto Whisper. A handle called DEPALMA was lurking. There was no foreplay. A message transmitted over a voice enabled line.

"Are you able to assist?"

The voice was electronic, monosyllabic, a bland interpretation of words. It was something Carlos De Palma often did. She adjusted her microphone and spoke.

"It depends," she said. She picked up a bottle of scent and sprayed it on her wrist. The vanilla essence triggered memories of times gone by. "What sort of work are we talking?"

"Revenge."

There was no familiarity, no explanation of the business climate, and no appreciation for what she had endured.

"Can you do that?"

"I can do that. What's the deal?"

"I'll give you the target's details and . . ."

"Yes, yes, how much?"

"We'll pay two thousand ZAR up front and ten to fifteen thousand extra if we choose to continue and the job's done."

"What's the business?"

"Don't ask."

The voice provided her with a name, an ID photograph, a car type and registration number, a cell phone number and a list of hang-outs for the target.

"I want five grand upfront," she said. "And then twenty to complete whatever you decide . . ."

There was a silence. She had never dared to negotiate with De Palma before.

"We have a deal."

She was surprised. De Palma was an ego. He was not someone to show any flexibility. And what work was this? Before her arrest, she had been responsible for procuring young pussy for rich old men.

"So when I find him, then what?"

She thought perhaps De Palma wanted to test her.

"When you find him," the voice said, "we want to know about his online activity. We want you to confirm his pseudonym. Make it a meet and greet."

"Is he JACKER? How will I know?" She rubbed her wrists.

"Look at his profiles, make a copy of everything you can get your hands on. Don't worry, you'll find a way."

Normally De Palma liked to go online with video. He liked to look at her. There was no enthusiasm, no innuendo, no flirting. She battled to assess the character of a computer-generated voice.

"Welcome back, Operative Fallon."

She lifted her wrist to her face, took a deep breath. "It's good to be back."

# 21

**In the shadow of the mountain buttress known as the Twelve Apostles, Le Fleur looked on as Carla hopped off a Vespa scooter and shook her hair.** She strode across the marine drive to join him at an outside table of a small café.

"Mini gone?" he asked as she unhooked a blue satchel.

"The bank couldn't wait any longer."

"I'm sorry. Did Aqualung give you the message?"

"He sure did."

She sat with pursed lips. He suppressed a smile.

"Oh my God, this day! Everything's gone wrong. Bruno Pittman virtually attacked me in the parking lot outside Supertech this afternoon. You should've seen his face. It looked like he'd had boiling water thrown into it. If there wasn't a parking guard nearby, I'm not sure what would've happened."

"Why?"

"I'll show you. Right now I need something strong to drink." She raised her hand and tried to attract a waiter. "Hey, you're out of the cast. How's it feeling?"

Le Fleur massaged his left wrist then tapped it on the table. "It's titanium." He had been for a haircut too, but she did not comment.

A waitress arrived.

"You have Tequila?"

"No ma'am."

"What've you got for frazzled nerves?"

The waitress wiggled her tray. She did not know.

"Some sweet tea works," Le Fleur suggested.

"Screw that. Bring me a shot of whatever you have."

The waitress left, confused. Carla removed her coat and tossed it on a chair.

"I can't stop thinking about someone erasing the video surveillance at Nial's house," she said. "Why?"

Her question hung in the air, the implication obvious. Someone got rid of something terrible.

"Either it's an inside job or someone has cracked that system. I've got a contact for an AlphaGuard expert."

She rubbed her face and gazed into the space over his shoulder. The backdrop was a beach fringed with palms. The other outside tables were taken by tourists. Inside the café was empty.

The waitress returned and broke their trance. She brought a shot of Kahlua. Carla threw back her head and swallowed it. "Now bring me another and an Americano." She turned to Le Fleur. "I think we should go to the police."

He nodded. "Should we wait for the cell records first?"

NETWORX had been in touch. His message, COMING SOON TO A SCREEN NEAR YOU, was typed in capitals. Rule #39: CAPSLOCK IS CRUISE CONTROL FOR COOL.

Le Fleur sipped on a cup of tea. It was one of those strange places that thought a client would enjoy brewing their own tea over a small paraffin flame. Carla tapped her hand lightly on the metal table.

"How do they do it? How do they break through the security system?"

"Hacking's like breaking into a house. There are beams and alarms and keys and doors and windows. They're trying to keep you out. You're trying to get in. The hacker has tools like a burglar has a crowbar and torch and gloves."

He thought about Nial's surveillance. Someone was watching Nial on the day of his disappearance.

"The weak point is usually inside the organization. And there's always someone listening. Someone with a big mouth . . ."

Carla shook her head slowly. The waitress returned with her order.

"I've had one fuck of a meeting with GALI today." She reached in her backpack and pulled out her iPad. She turned the screen towards him. "Take a look at this."

She shifted closer. The screen showed mostly men and a few women around a large boardroom table.

She pointed out three gray-suited individuals and paused the video. "That's Schroeder, Straud, and Heinemann. They're the GALI executives responsible for foreign operations and acquisitions. They flew over in the company Gulfstream."

The men were uncannily similar: shiny egg-shaped heads with little hair, silver glasses, and smooth faces.

"I met those goons before with Nial. They thought I was his secretary, gave me their jackets to hang up. The one guy stared at my tits."

"Which one?" he asked.

"I think both."

He smiled. "I'm sorry. I meant which was the one who stared."

She pointed at the screen then resumed play.

Le Fleur recognized Bruno Pittman from his Summit TV clip. "I see

Mr. Eyebrows."

"I found out today he had a custom built mahogany desk shipped over from Munich. The whole office is talking. Can you believe it? They unscrewed the entrance doors to fit it through."

At the meeting on screen, Gavin Marx was speaking. His suit was buttoned and tie perfectly knotted. His impeccable graying hair was brushed in a side parting. Le Fleur thought he looked like an American presidential candidate.

"Gavin didn't have a single gray hair. It happened overnight," she said.

"His nickname is George?" He wondered if she found Marx attractive.

She laughed. "That's Nial's nickname for him. George Hamilton because of the tan. He spends most weekends on his yacht."

Le Fleur had not heard of George Hamilton.

"He owns a yacht?"

"Yes. He has raced it Cape to Rio. I've been on it, cruised around Table Bay. *George's Escape*. It's Gavin's great love."

There was an empty chair. A framed picture of a khaki clad, suntanned Townley in the African bush hung on the wall behind. Next to his picture, the GALI logo—a prowling leopard—seemed like an omen.

There were others, backs to the camera.

"There's Sophie's lawyer. Olive Dlovu is the staff trust. Another lawyer, the secretary."

"Is Marx married?" he asked. He was still thinking about whether there was any chemistry between them.

She shook her head. He wondered if Marx had hit on her.

A GALI executive briefed the meeting on competition boards and shareholder approvals.

"Willie Schroder is head of Foreign Operations. The other two are Finance and Legal."

"How did you obtain this video?" he asked.

"I still have some friends in the IT department."

Schroeder was chairing a lengthy discourse, something about "outstanding conditions."

"What are they going on about?"

"They're discussing plans to merge our Venezuelan business into GALI's South American business unit. Isn't it amazing? A month in charge and our Venezuelan unit has turned the corner. That's the power we lacked as a smaller company. GALI deposited five million Euros into the petty cash tin. You can only imagine which Government officials are getting paid. Oh, here, we're getting to the highlight."

---

>   -   Carla enters and scans the room. She's wearing
>         a ruffled white blouse, white pants tight
>         on her slim hips, a crisscross-strapped
>         blue satchel on her back.

"You were invited to the meeting?" he asked. He looked about to see if anyone was listening in.

  "No."

>   -   "Helloooo, everybody. So sorry I'm late."
>         Bruno Pittman halts mid-sentence.
>   -   Carla scours the room slowly, nodding:
>         "This is good. Real good. Welcome, welcome.
>         So pleased you could make it.
>         Nial would be proud."
>   -   Bruno Pittman stands and grips her arm.
>         "Come now."
>   -   "Don't touch me!" Carla rips her arm away.
>         "Nial would oppose this meeting with
>         everything in his power."
>   -   "You're probably right, Carla," Sophie's lawyer
>         answers. "Unfortunately, that power is no
>         longer around. And unless you have a clever idea
>         to cough up twenty million USD..."
>         He holds Carla's gaze with a joyless smirk.
>   -   Someone coughs. Bruno Pittman glances across
>         the table at Willie Schroeder.
>   -   "Sorry, Willie," Pittman says.
>         Schroeder raises a hand.
>   -   "Carla," says Willie Schroeder, icy blue eyes
>         staring at her. His control is immediate.
>         "Can we not have this discussion at some later
>         stage? This is a shareholder's meeting."
>   -   "And I'm a shareholder."
>   -   "Yes," Schroeder replies. "I know this. And
>         your interests are represented by Mrs. Ndlovu
>         here. I am sure—"
>   -   "I don't give a shit about my shares, or my
>         interest here," Carla cuts in. "I was meant
>         to run this company. Nial wanted that. If I can

> do one last thing for him, I'll do what he wanted."
> - Pittman shakes his head and interjects,
>   Schroeder waves him away.
> - Schroeder adjusts his glasses. He doesn't take
>   his eyes off Carla. "What Nial would have
>   wanted, we now can only presume," he said.
>   "I find it hard to believe—"
> - "Hard to believe Nial Townley wanted me to run
>   his company. Just say it! Because he wants to
>   fuck me, he gives me this great job."
> - "I never said that."
> - "Listen, Willie." Carla emphasized the V in
>   Willie. "I design control systems that'll make
>   you wet your pants. We build bridges not pipes.
>   I can work anywhere in the world and earn
>   twice what Nial paid me. I work with him
>   because I believe in his vision."

Le Fleur shifted uncomfortably. He could feel Carla's emotion, the intense and personal nature of the confrontation.

The video caught Pittman and Schroeder trading glances. Schroeder took a deep breath as if deciding the next course of action.

"Now watch them shit themselves," said Carla.

> - "I've got something for you," Carla says,
>   unhooking her satchel.

Le Fleur concentrated on the screen, recognizing the expressions of those around the table. Their wide eyes indicated, in the recesses of their consciousness, that they had feared a day like this, that their last day on earth would come at the hands of some crazed employee.

> - Sophie's lawyer pushes back his chair.
>   "Carla, please. This is neither the time nor
>   the place. We all feel the way you do.
>   We've got to do the right thing under the
>   circumstances."
> - "Bullshit," Carla shoots back.
>   She unzips the satchel.
> - Nobody moves.

> - She points her finger at the three gray-suits
>   seated at the table. "It's a setup. These
>   gestapo have orchestrated the whole thing."
> - There is an audible gasp. Bruno Pittman
>   reaches out.
> - "Carla," Marx says. "You can't go around
>   calling people—"
> - "Don't touch me."
> - Bruno Pittman grabs her arm forcibly.
>   With his other hand, he gets a hold on her
>   satchel. Carla tries to shake loose, but
>   his grip tightens.

Le Fleur was transfixed by the tension on the screen. He leaned closer.

> - "Let me go!" Carla screams, hanging onto the
>   satchel and sliding to the floor as Pittman
>   tries to drag her towards the door.
> - Willie Schroeder commands something to
>   no one in particular.

"What'd he say?" asked Le Fleur.

"I think he said *Call Security.*" She laughed. "Gavin thought I was going to pull a gun out the satchel."

On screen, Carla kicked out at Pittman. Gavin Marx jumped from his seat.

> - "Let her go!" Marx moves surprisingly quickly
>   around the table. Pittman releases her.
> - "Carla, a word outside," Marx says.
> - Carla stands and removes an envelope from her
>   satchel. "Screw you, Gavin!" She tosses the
>   envelope on the desk.
> - Pittman attempts to move forward, but Marx
>   blocks his access.
> - "That's my resignation," Carla says. "I hope you
>   assholes rot in hell."
> - Pittman lunges at her, but Marx restrains him.
>   Carla meets his approach with her knee.

"Jesus Christ," said Le Fleur. "Not the balls?"
She nodded.

- Pittman groans and doubles over, clutching his
  crotch. Everyone in the room is on their feet.
- Sophie's lawyer shakes his head. The GALI execs
  display horror, amazement, awe. Only Olive
  Ndlovu remains seated, unfazed by the fracas,
  like this happens everyday.
- "That's my house warming present," Carla states
  calmly, fixing the GALI executives in an icy
  stare. "This isn't over."
- She shoulders her satchel, turns, and slams the
  door behind her.

The video ended, the screen frozen on the remaining executives in the room. They sat for a moment in silence.

Across the road, a band of seagulls were vying for some discarded chips. The beach was empty.

"And after that, he confronted you in the parking lot?"

"It was damn scary. He was like a madman, frothing from the mouth."

She pointed at the GALI suits on screen.

"These are the people responsible," she stated icily. "Schroder and Pittman and those GALI suits. They had him murdered as sure as I sit here. All we need is proof."

Her voice quivered. He reached over and touched her hand. He wanted to say *I believe you*, but he did not say anything. He neither believed nor disbelieved her. There was no proof of anything except that someone had erased Townley's surveillance. It may have even been Townley.

Le Fleur closed his eyes and allowed his vision to drift around the boardroom video as if he were a camera. Schroeder, Straud, and Heinemann. He focused on their shiny egg-shaped heads and silver glasses. Gone were the days when people believed educated men in tailored suits could not be guilty of heinous crime.

"Who knows about us, Carla?"

The waiter arrived with her spritzer. She took a sip.

"How do you mean?"

"Who knows the arrangement that I'm getting cell and internet records?"

"It's only Gavin and me. I had to tell Gavin since he pays the bills. He asked me about your charge. You must let me know, Daniel, we don't want you out of pocket."

He said nothing. He felt a sudden urge to reach out and confide in Carla, to tell her about his life and his childhood and the road he walked. But he did not. What would it serve? She was a client. She wanted to pay him. He was her hacker. She wanted him to do a job.

## 22

**Le Fleur walked back to Bali Beach.** Joggers, strollers, and dog walkers filled the narrow pavement. In the online world, he was always cautious. He used his program SearchMe to identify potential threats. Out in the real world, it was different. There was so much space.

Aqualung was lounging on bench no.57.

"No rain," said Le Fleur.

Aqualung did not answer. His jaw ruminated. Le Fleur repeated his comment about the lack of rain.

"I'm not a cucumber," Aqualung replied grumpily. "Are you having sex with the sugar?"

"Freddy," he laughed. "Why would you ask that?"

"Men have sex with women. Women have sex with men. She buzzes over with her legs around that scooter?"

"You have sex with someone who rides a scooter?"

"When they smell like she does." Aqualung offered his hand to Le Fleur.

"No thanks."

Aqualung held his hand to his nose. "Lemons and cherries."

"I'll take your word." He looked back across the road at Crystal Place. "Everything OK?"

Aqualung pulled an old cigarette box out the pocket of his coat. He handed it over. On the back, he had written a registration number.

"She's got friends? Was it the same car?" Le Fleur asked.

Aqualung shook his head. "It was a red rice rocket with tinted windows."

"You sure they were following her?"

"What am I sure of? You ask this of me?" Aqualung stared at him with a strange expression. "I am sure of this day and this bench and you, Monsieur Le Fleur sitting here and talking to me. Other than that I know nothing."

Le Fleur took the cigarette box and returned to his apartment. He restored the surveillance backup and forwarded until Carla arrived on her scooter. He watched as she rang the bell and waited. She turned and saw Aqualung on bench no.56, called to him from across the road. Next she crossed the road and stood a meter behind him. Then she sat on the bench and reached out her arm. Aqualung turned and looked at her, lowered his head, and smelled her from hand to armpit.

In the background, a red Hyundai pulled onto the pavement. She patted Aqualung on the shoulder, crossed the road, and mounted her scooter. She looked about before riding away. Moments later, the red Hyundai followed in her direction. Aqualung's record of the registration was correct.

*She's got friends.*

Outside, the sun slipped below the horizon, a rare Atlantic evening with a warm offshore canceling the chill off the ocean. Aqualung had gone. He closed the glass doors and locked them.

He reached for his cell phone, dialed the AlphaGuard contact recommended by Ian Coulson, and introduced himself.

"Daniel Le Fleur," a voice answered. "Well, well, well, CRACKERJACK, the hacker who lost his anonymity."

"Yes."

Le Fleur's bust, the indiscretion which led to his community service at Cybercrime, had exposed his handle to every hacker in the 650-milllion-server internet universe.

"Anonymous does not forgive," the voice continued. "What the hell do you want?"

Le Fleur considered his approach. With most hackers, it was vanity. "You're the best AlphaGuard hacker around."

"I don't hack systems. Is someone taping this call? I run a software company."

"I've heard it isn't possible. Nobody has claimed the reward."

"You've heard right."

"But it's not right."

"What are you saying, CRACKERJACK?"

"Somebody has done it and is claiming the reward. They got through AlphaGuard into a client's surveillance system and scrubbed the record."

There was a silence. Then: "Who's claiming the reward?"

"I am."

The silence was longer.

"I slim-jimmed Digital Eye's surveillance system," said Le Fleur. "I've got footage of Constantia mommies cavorting naked in their pools with their lovers."

"You're lying. That's impossible. The only person to crack AlphaGuard has been the installer of the system."

Le Fleur smiled. "That's what I thought you'd say, Jeremy Freeman. And you know what? Some people are so vain they stick their handle into the install log. You're SUPERCHARGER. It's been a long time. And I know why you can't claim Alpha's reward? Because you had root privilege to the software and that would be cheating. And secondly, of course, whoever paid you to erase Nial Townley's surveillance paid you a lot more than AlphaGuard's reward."

"I don't know what your deal is, Le Fleur, but you're sticking your nose in a heap full of shit."

"Who are you working for, Jeremy? Tell me and you'll never hear from me again."

"Go fuck yourself."

The call went dead.

Le Fleur held the cell to his face and replayed the conversation. Jeremy Freeman, aka SUPERCHARGER, had been part of his elite group.

He paced around the room then glanced towards the open patio doors. Outside, the night was inky black. He eyed the Van Gogh on the easel, crows hovering, a troubled sky, the road leading nowhere.

He turned on the TV. Sky News and CNN were covering the story of some North African migrant who had left a suitcase of explosives in Piccadilly Circus. It seemed the world was in conflict. He hoped the Southern tip of Africa would be the safest place.

He went to the kitchen, opened a tin of tuna, and mixed it with lettuce and olive oil. It was 20:00, the first time he had eaten. He considered taking a nap, but his mind was racing.

He rubbed his hands.

Each of the elite hackers had specialized skills. He thought about the elaborate system used to disperse Townley's cash. He knew someone who had previously moved a big stash of money. That financial guru went by the handle of $CENE$TER, a friend, his real name Sean Coppis. He texted Coppis:

Friday at Bar Rack. 22:00

An hour later, cell phone data for Carla's suspect list arrived. First, he received a phishing email reporting a problem on a non-existent NTT Telecoms account then a second email a minute later, another phishing message directing him to a form on a Blogger site. Enabling the form kicked off a video of an avatar with meshed eyes mouthing a cipher key, an address for finding the cell phone data, and details for settling the fee. The video ended with an icon of a manacled oenophile wearing a black hat.

Le Fleur downloaded the data and settled NETWORX's account with the transfer of half a bitcoin.

Then he stretched, unlocked the balcony, and stepped into the darkness. He removed his clothes and slipped into his plunge pool. The cold water was a slap in the face. He blew out his air and sank to the bottom of the pool, stayed there until his lungs were burning.

When he got out of the pool, he wrapped himself in a fluffy white robe and looked over the balcony. The sea was calm. He wondered when the weather would turn.

The rain could not stay away forever.

## 23

**Carla waved at Aqualung on Bench no.57.** *New best friends*, he thought with amusement. With less than an hour's sleep, Le Fleur was watching from the balcony. The sky was cloudless, the weather cold but dry. He wondered if she would survive a winter on her scooter.

He still could not help wondering if Carla Vitale was all she said she was.

*I design control systems that would make you wet your pants.*

The red Hyundai spotted by Aqualung was a problem. It had different number plates back and front and neither fitted that car's description on the National Car Registration database.

*Sugar will make your teeth ache.*

When the bell sounded, he buzzed her in. The front door was open. She walked straight into the Chrome Room, rolled her helmet on the floor, and slipped into the seat next to him.

"What've we got?"

Projected on an overhead screen was a map of Cape Town crisscrossed by color coded lines.

"Each colored line on the map represents the movement, based on tower triangulation, of one of your suspects over a specified period," he said.

She stared at the screen.

"The screen currently shows the physical movement associated with all the cell phones on the Friday of Nial's disappearance."

He clicked on an amber icon and all the colored patterns except amber disappeared.

"Clicking a specific color isolates one person's movement. Amber is yours." He changed the time frame. "This is last Saturday's movement."

Using the mouse, he traced the amber lines with the cursor, the path tracing Carla's movement map on the day they had visited the accident scene at Chapman's and Nial's home in Constantia.

"You got my cell records as well?"

He changed the date selection and clicked on a violet icon. "Nial Townley is violet," he said. "So we have amber and violet. One week before his disappearance, it shows how *your* movement crisscrossed with his."

At the intersection of amber and violet lines, Le Fleur zoomed in. The co-ordinates belonged to the Alphen Hotel in Constantia.

Carla frowned. Then she nodded. "Yes, we had dinner there. It was probably a week before he went missing." She did not add any detail or explanation.

"Obviously a cell needs to be turned on to register movement. The software allows us to map everyone's movement over time. So let's see where you went next," he continued. "OK, he goes home and she goes home."

She looked at him. Her cheeks were flushed. "It was nothing sinister, I promise you. Nial and I had dinner often."

He said nothing and swapped keyboards. A second screen was projected onto the overhead screen.

"Then this function shows the relationships between actual calls," he said.

He selected amber and violet again with the same date.

"There was only one call between you and Nial on the day of your Alphen dinner? At 19:30."

She considered this for a moment. "I was late."

He clicked out the amber icon and a cluster of violet lines projected out like tentacles.

"These are calls made and received by Nial Townley on the same day. It shows where and with whom. If the call was one of our suspect numbers then a colored box appears at the end of the line, otherwise it's a blank box."

She scanned the screen.

"Why don't you play around with it?" He shifted his chair away and left Carla to query the system.

He walked to the patio and checked the weather conditions. A low cloud had moved in from the mountain side. He thought about his missing mountain bike. Was it time to purchase a new one?

"Can I make you an Americano?" he asked when he returned.

She twirled on her chair. "You can make one of those?"

"As good as Sicily with real cream."

"You're a man of many talents, Daniel."

He did not tell her he had recently bought an Espresso machine, a hundred coffee capsules from Mario at the Italian café and a supply of fresh cream. Found the recipe on the Net. He did not even like coffee much.

When he returned with coffee, she was reviewing movement and calls on the day of Nial's disappearance.

He worked on his laptop and kept an eye on her searches.

"This system is amazing," she said. She examined the call relationship between Townley and Gavin Marx. There were numerous calls in the week preceding Friday. Then a few on the Monday.

"Gavin was obviously trying to contact Nial," she said. She swapped Townley for her own cell number. Le Fleur had already checked it. "Look at how the lines run out like a spider."

"Does Gavin Marx have a girlfriend?" he asked.

There were no calls between Marx and Sophie Townley prior to Nial's disappearance. More recently there were a few from her to him, probably relating to the consent for Gregory's travel.

"A few."

"He's a player?"

"I wouldn't say that. But he has never settled."

"Never married, no family?"

"No. You cannot believe the physical change in him in the last few months." She reached for her cell and flicked through her gallery. She showed Le Fleur before and after pictures of Marx. He looked like he had aged ten years.

Carla moved onto Sophie Townley's call list. She had been at home on the Friday of Nial's disappearance. She had not received a call from Nial, though she had tried to phone him many times over the weekend.

"How can it be possible there's a call from Nial to Sophie shortly after twelve, but on her record there's no call from him?" she asked.

He shrugged. "Perhaps his call did not register on the network."

There were no links to the phone number of the catalyst call.

Carla pushed back her chair and clapped her hands. She covered her face with her hands. "I was so sure there'd be something."

He resisted the impulse to provide hope.

"I'll load the analytics and data onto a flash drive and you can take it home and keep going through it," he said. "Maybe something will turn up."

She sipped her coffee and rocked back and forth.

The data had no other references to the fateful 12:02 catalyst call.

There was no interaction between Sophie and any of the others in the period leading to Nial's disappearance. There were no suspicious calls to the Digital Eye surveillance company. He had also checked Jeremy Freeman's number.

Calls made by Carla and Supertech offices to Sophie and Ynez after the disappearance were understandable.

Carla sighed and closed her eyes.

"I did find something," he said. "I'm not sure if it's important."

He clicked on Ynez's turquoise icon and zoomed into her location.

"Some of her triangulations show she's been hanging around Buitenkant Street. Isn't that the strip club, Gorky Park?"

Carla stared at the screen.

He adjusted the parameters to display all calls made to and from Ynez's cell. "I didn't see this at first because I was focused on the calls made before and directly after Nial's disappearance. Look at the calls she made in the last week."

On the list of Ynez's incoming calls, one of the numbers displayed with a purple icon.

"Who's purple?" she asked.

"It's Mr. Eyebrows, Bruno Pittman."

# 24

**An hour before midnight at Bar Rack in Somerset Road.**

Sean Coppis, aka $CENE$TER, a twenty-seven-year-old hedge fund trader. He wore green skinny jeans, a burgundy flannel shirt, classic Reeboks, and eyeglasses without lenses. He had shameless attention seeker written all over him. Le Fleur thought he looked like an eggplant.

"I'll be right back, order me another."

Le Fleur eased from behind a steel table, ran his knuckles along the flaking wall as he stepped through the bar in the direction of the outside toilets. The rundown look was part of the vibe at Bar Rack, a carefully cultivated aura of seediness and risk. An hour earlier, in this same moldy alley, he had smoked weed with Coppis. Coppis had a dealer for indoor weed and a dealer for outdoor weed, and dealers for a host of other substances too.

He stopped and waited in a queue outside the unisex toilets.

No body. No murder. No money. At least the money had a trail. Nial Townley seemed to have stepped off the planet.

A door opened, two guys came out. A trio in front of him scurried inside and locked it, leaving him alone in a tiny waiting area with a basin.

He gazed at a painting of an amorphous female nude with silver disks for nipples on a hairless body. Her crotch was dark and hidden and except for the lumps of breast, she could have been either sex.

A low moan emanated from the adjacent toilet. He could not distinguish whether it was male or female, pleasure or pain, real or acted? In those private rooms, rituals of coke and sex were playing out. Half a gram of Buddha had made him feel remote, detached from reality, separate from his species.

The second door opened and a slender woman in a black dress stepped out. Her eyes were red and she peered intensely at him. "Do I know you?"

For a moment he thought she may be someone he had dated. A long time ago... A relationship that started but never progressed to the next level. Like all his relationships.

"No." He stepped around her and into the cubicle, closed and locked the door. He ran his hand lightly along the toilet bowl and checked it for remnants of white powder.

His phone rang mid-piss. He managed to answer: "What's it now?"

"Ynez is back at Gorky Park," said Carla.

He zipped his pants and tucked in his shirt. Carla was at Shimmy Beach

Club. She had been invited to dinner with Gavin Marx and the ex-Supertech management. She said they wanted to talk some sense into her.

"Gavin has seen her," she said. "She's desperate and using emotional blackmail, like 'What would Nial have thought about us prostituting her life?'"

Outside, the other cubicles were locked, voices and giggling coming from both.

"Did you tell Gavin about the calls from Pittman?"

"No. What do you think? Should I tell him?"

"No." Rule #1 of the Internet: *Anything you say can and will be used against you.*

"What are we going to do about it?"

"Let's see what Pittman browses on the Internet. I searched his story in the media. He's a bit of a ghost. Either he walks lightly, or someone's been clever about erasing his footprints."

Back inside Bar Rack, he slid onto a cushioned bench, lifted a fresh brown bottle of Jack Black. He did not drink often and, when he did, he drank beer, not the mass-produced stuff. He preferred the funk of new craft brands.

"To easy living," toasted Coppis.

Bitcoin was up thirty percent. He had not made a single trade, raised his glass anyway.

Bar Rack was packed with bubbling hipsters. Its patrons, in flea market clothes, were its identity. He felt he was odd man out in blue jeans and T-shirt, hoped the ironic slogan on his shirt—Out On Bail—made up for his low-key gear.

"What do you know about Nial Townley?"

Coppis reached up and touched his expertly spiked hair. He looked about. "Not much."

"That's not like you, Sean. No theories?"

"Ah, there's a world wide web of theories. He's in Brazil with his model girlfriend. Why do you care?"

"He did it and skipped, that's what you think?"

"Maybe, you've got a better idea?"

"Well, for one, I know his model girlfriend is not in Brazil."

"So where is she, maestro?"

"She's straddling laps at Gorky Park."

Coppis narrowed his eyes and stared at Le Fleur. "Fuck, I know what's going on." He thumped his forehead. "Jesus, I should've known. The smooth haircut and the sudden call for a meeting. I know, I know. You're fucking that, what's her name, Carla?"

"It's a professional arrangement."

"Ha! Rule eleven, baby. All your carefully picked arguments can easily be ignored. When your heart starts beating, Daniel, you can't be professional for shit. You're probably in love with her already."

"How do you know her?"

Coppis sipped his drink and looked across the rim of his glass. "I don't know her."

"About her?"

"Everyone knows she's looking for Nial Townley."

"She asked you?"

"Maybe."

They stared at one another. Le Fleur looked at his watch. "Come, I want you to meet someone."

## 25

**Gorky Park Revue Bar, Cape Town's most exclusive strip club.** Rumor was you could buy anything from a hand job to full sex.

Le Fleur paid VIP entrance fees for two.

"Jesus," said Sean Coppis as they entered the ground floor lounge. He stared at his cell then scanned the room expectantly. "Grindr's going ape shit in here." He flashed pictures of gay barmen in a twenty meter radius.

Upstairs in the platinum section, they sat at a low silver table. Strippers cruised by, subtle as chainsaws. The hostess swooped in, gave them a menu with cocktails and services.

"Does someone called Ynez work here?" he asked. He had never been inside a strip club.

"Ynez?"

"That's the one."

"You sure her name is Ynez?"

"I'm sure."

"Let me check."

"No, she's Colombian," interjected Coppis. "You get it? Czech?"

Nobody did.

"Do you want to order anything?" the hostess asked.

"No thanks. If you can call Ynez?"

"I'll come back."

The club reeked of decades of cigarettes, booze, and cheap perfume. It was ingrained in the carpets, the walls, on the menus. Coppis jumped up and gyrated in mock appreciation of the music, the studs in his eyebrow glistening in the blue light. "How do I look?"

"Like Billy Idol."

Coppis jerked him the middle finger. Le Fleur scanned the room, picking out cameras disguised as smoke detectors.

"Oh my God, they're playing Motley Crüe," Coppis said. "Do they know what century it is?"

"Girls, Girls, Girls" pumped over the club speakers. The floor crawled with skin and lingerie. A stripper with small breasts twirled on a pole, a group of men watching her like hungry lions at a watering hole. A dark-haired woman carrying a shiny handbag approached their small table. He recognized her from pictures in the suspect directory. She was dressed in blue lingerie.

"I'm ee-Nez," she said with no enthusiasm.

He stood to greet her.

"I'm Daniel. This is Sean."

He could sense her computations—a quick assessment of whether they owned anything worth having. He opened his wallet and removed a wad of notes. She looked at it disdainfully then slipped in alongside, stroked his leg right up to the crotch.

"You have a nice an unusual name," he said. He'd looked it up—meant chaste in Spanish. Coppis pretended to vomit at his opening line.

He'd seen naked footage of Ynez on Townley's surveillance. In the video, she looked like a thin, sleepy woman. Tonight, she was something else. He felt a tremor of fascination, understood Townley's attraction.

"How much for a lap dance?" he asked.

"Downstairs, no touching, it's R500. Or there's upstairs—"

She smiled and stroked his leg. Her false eyelashes fluttered.

"What's upstairs?"

"Three songs in private, you can touch me for two grand."

Coppis picked up the menu and showed where it said one grand for three songs upstairs.

"That's without extras," Ynez said.

"Ah, what a rip. Three songs? I'll call them. Something by Def Leppard for starters. Then that milkshake song, who sings that? And at the business end of your ten minutes—definitely AC/DC."

Le Fleur made up his mind. Upstairs was private. He grasped Coppis's arm and pointed to the camera with his index finger. "I want the video."

"Cool."

He followed Ynez across the red carpet. His late father would approve of Gorky Park and the easy choice of transactional sex. *Hey, Jake, look what I'm doing? That's my boy.* She led him up a flight of stairs and into a private booth. He sat and she pulled the velvet curtains.

"Cherry Pie" came on. Coppis had been close.

She placed her handbag alongside him.

"What do you keep in that bag?" he asked for something to say.

"My attitude," she said, picked up the bag, and opened it. It was filled with crumpled cash.

"Let's get rid of this." She unhooked her bra and pressed a pointy breast into his face. She smelled like candy floss. She turned and rolled her ass on his lap. He closed his eyes. If he could just let go . . . He placed his hands on her hips and held her firmly.

"Listen, Ynez, I want to talk to you."

Her rhythm slowed. "What?"

"Talk."

"It'll still be three songs. We talk what?"

"Nial Townley."

The grinding ceased immediately. "Who are you? Are you a cop?" she hissed.

"Do I look like a cop?"

She detached his hands from her hips, hopped off his lap, and faced him. "What do you want? I told them everything I know." She reached for her bra.

"I'll pay you double to answer a few questions. That's all."

She fastened her bra. "Double? OK, we can talk down there with your gay boyfriend."

He patted the cushioned seat and removed his wallet, placed it on the table. "This is fine."

She adjusted her bra, removed a pack of cigarettes from her bag, and lit up.

"What do *you* think happened to Nial?"

"How should I know? Who are you?" She sucked the cigarette in her red lips.

"I'm a computer expert. I've been hired to investigate the case."

"Who hired you?"

He ignored her question. "Tell me about Bruno Pittman."

"Who?"

He spun his phone around and showed her a picture of Bruno Pittman. *One eye tells the truth, one eye lies.*

She spat out. "This one! Bruno. This Bruno, did he hire you?"

"No."

She eyed him suspiciously. "He come here with his fat Rottweiler friends and asks for me. He says *he* runs Nial's company now." She leaned forward. "He offered me a lot of money, but I say no. He says I can name my price, still I say no."

"He offered you money for sex?"

"Yes."

"What do you mean by Rottweiler friends?"

She opened her mouth and tapped her teeth. "They've gold teeth."

"I'm not sure what you mean. Does he come in here often?"

"Often."

"He phoned you."

"Yes."

"How long after you met him, did he phone you?"

"The next day."

"What did he say?"

She appeared to think this over.

"He wants to fuck me. What else must he say? I tell you, Mister Computer Expert. I leave this life for Nial. I never wanted to come back. This is for young girls. Russia. Moldovia. Romania. They rub their cuca on your pants and make money, lots of money, no tax, more than all these people in Cape Town. It's a joke for them. Not for me."

"But you are receiving money from Gavin Marx?"

A cleft cut her forehead. "Gavin. The big boss?"

Le Fleur frowned. "What do you mean big boss?"

She opened her arms and shrugged.

"Of this place?" he asked.

"So they say." She closed her arms and indicated a small gap between two fingers. "He's a careverga. I get such a little bit from him."

She checked her watch. The song changed. "It's Raining Men." He imagined, downstairs, $CENE$TER would not react well.

"Did Nial do or say anything to make you think he was planning to disappear?"

She thought for a moment. "No."

"Think about the weeks leading up to his disappearance?"

"I didn't see him much. He's always busy. Gavin and him. I say to him he should fuck Gavin then. Always business. South America. He was always working."

He gave her time to think some more. "No travel plans?"

"Nial said he was going to take me away on holiday."

"When did he say that?"

She squeezed her lips. "Maybe, two months before he go."

"Did he say where?"

"He said it was a big surprise. An island."

Le Fleur drew a deep breath. He was glad he was not a full-time detective. He reckoned he sucked at it.

"What about Carla? Do you know her?"

"Oh yes, this Carla."

Her expression tightened and her mouth curled into a sneer. He did not feel it was the right time to share Carla's opinion of how her brain would affect the flight of a bird.

"Carla this, Carla that. She's all over him."

"How do you mean?"

She fluttered her eyelids. "In this business, you see through a man like glass. Inside Nial, there is stuff for her. The police say he stole the money. Maybe him and her?"

"Do you think that?"

She shrugged and reconsidered. "I don't know. I don't know what happened." She patted his thigh then took his hand and placed it between her legs.

"Your time's nearly up. You want to buy an extension?" She touched his face lightly as if she were an adoring lover. "You have a kind face."

He did not move for a polite interval then withdrew his hand.

"Some other time . . ."

He imagined his father laughing—*Can't even get laid by a hooker. Fussy doesn't fuck.*

Back at Bar Rack, he ordered another Jack Black, Coppis a double whiskey.

"*Anonymous is legion,*" Coppis quoted #4 and flashed the screen of his iPhone with a black and white image from the camera at Gorky Park's entrance.

"Good work, Sean."

Magicians and hackers never reveal their tricks— unless they're Sean Coppis.

"OK, you know the cute barman, the one in the faded jeans with rainbow yarn? The one that calls his cock Mercury . . ."

"Because it's silver? Sadly, I don't know that one."

Coppis pulled a face. "Is that supposed to be funny? Not a romantic bone in your body, Daniel. Anyway, he had a password to the server. Tada! Probably so he can balance his stock theft." He fumbled in his pocket, tossed a till slip on the table. "I wrote the details on the slip. You owe me. I bought the barman a shooter or two."

Le Fleur looked at the slip. A URL address and password were written on the bottom.

"Is this the right slip? The printed bit doesn't say Gorky Park. It says Apollo."

Coppis shrugged. "Apollo, Acme, these places hide the truth from jealous spouses. Why'd you want to hack their server anyway?"

Le Fleur put the till slip in his wallet. "I'm going to download pictures of strippers, what else?"

"You're not a funny guy, Daniel. You shouldn't try."

Coppis reached for his Bells, shook the ice in the tumbler. He tasted the drink with his tongue, made a face, shook the ice again.

---

"What do you know about Townley's cash?" asked Le Fleur.

Coppis added some more ice and tested the drink again.

"Did you hear me, Sean?"

"With all three ears. His cash took a holiday. What should I know?"

"The cash went all over. Latvia, Uruguay . . . An elaborate scheme. Something you could've done."

Coppis sipped his drink and smiled. "What's it to you?"

"I want to bring the cash back."

Coppis looked up, mouth tight and small. He looked left and right. "Listen, Daniel, I know nothing. I want to know nothing. I'm a day trader. So are you. Wine her, dine her, 69 her. But don't get involved in this shit."

"Why not? What happened to Mister You-only-live-once, the incredible $CENE$TER?"

Coppis looked away, shook his head. "Stay out of it. That's all I'm telling you."

"Have you had contact with any of the others? NETWORX, SUPERCHARGER, ZAPPER?"

"No. I'm out of that world."

They sat for a moment without speaking. Coppis whistled through his teeth. "*He wants to bring the cash back!* Everybody's after the five million ZAR reward but not you. No, Daniel Le Fleur is after the twenty bars U-ES-DEE. You're insane."

Le Fleur stretched his arms above his head in false relaxation. Like awareness of an oncoming car approaching silently from behind, he sensed danger. Rule #45 of the Internet: *When one sees a lion, one must get into the car.* Is there an instant when you could jump out its way, when you see it bearing down? It's too late.

## 26

**Fallon located the target at the Wakkancluri Argentinean Polo Bar.** The clincher was his red Porsche parked in the street outside with the matching registration number. Inside the club, the target was dressed like a young millionaire—designer jeans, striped lounge shirt with lots of open buttons, biker boots.

*We want you to confirm his pseudonym. Make it a meet and greet.*

She was sure this was JACKER. And five grand for a meet and greet! She wished she had asked for more. Dollar was religion.

She was dressed for her part: no panties beneath a single piece black cocktail dress, top like a strapless bandage.

A barman brought a Jack and Ginger and she avoided looking in the direction of the target. She knew he was looking at her. Everyone in the bar was looking at her. They were only waiting to see if she was alone or with another man and then the bravest would sidle up with their weak conversation and pathetic hopes. She lifted her right hand and sniffed. There was no remnant of cordite. She smiled secretly. How would these patrons react if they knew she had spent the day at the Milnerton shooting range blasting targets with her Taurus?

She took to the dance floor, put her hands in the air, and felt the heat of the room. She eyed the target. He was looking directly at her. She looked away.

He approached her ten minutes later as she was returning from the ladies room. He was tall and wiry, long-haired with a lopsided smile.

"Are you looking for one of these?" He slipped her a yellow tablet with a smiley face.

"Do I know you?" she asked and looked over his shoulder to the bar counter. Many Cape Town bartenders had known her. None of the bartenders were watching. She assumed her blonde disguise was working.

"I'm Jeremy."

She smelled the tablet. It smelled of aniseed.

"You got some trust issues?" he said, the easy smile, real easy. He showed her another tablet, popped it in his mouth and swallowed. "Come."

He pointed to the bar counter and she slid onto a silver bar stool.

"What can I get you?"

She ordered a Jack and ginger ale. The bar was throbbing with late night revelry, young executives with their wives asleep at home, out-of-towners, playboys, bachelors, party girls, divorcees, a high energy meeting space for the restless and unlovable.

"What's your name?" he asked.

"Tricia."

"Tricia as in Patricia?"

"Tricia as in Tricia."

"Nice," he said and touched the silver bracelets on her left wrist.

The drinks arrived.

"Cheers."

She placed the Ecstasy tablet on her tongue, tasted its bitterness then chased it with a shot of Jack. Jeremy rubbed his hand along the studs on her handbag.

"Where's your boyfriend?"

She rolled her eyes. "He's fucking your sister, I don't know, what sort of a question is that? Where's your wife?"

He laughed. "I have a wife?"

She shrugged and sipped her Jack. She had screwed up her last two encounters. This one had cash riding on it. She thought it ironic she was being paid to pick up a guy, the easiest assignment on earth. She reckoned after midnight she could fuck any guy in this bar, young, old, rich, poor, married or not.

"So what are you good at?" he asked.

"If these are your best opening lines, maybe you should shut up."

He laughed. "No, I'm serious."

She knew her weaknesses. She had no friends, no interest in social media or sports or arts. She did not particularly like food and drink, and she hated domesticity. What was she good at? She was not bad at technology. She was ambitious. She was a fucking crack shot.

"Look, I'm in the mood to be wild tonight. Are you with me?" she said.

He widened his lazy eyes and lifted her off the stool. Even with heels, she barely reached his neck. He followed her to the dance floor. The beat was repetitive and mindless. Still she felt there was something magical about swaying in a hot crowd. It almost felt real. The five grand in her account was real and felt even better.

She recognized the next song. It had a sinister opening with a rattle like a snake. Then cymbals crashed and the beat kicked in. "Sweet Emotion." She did not remember the artist's name, but the rhythm grabbed her. She put her arm around Jeremy's waist and rubbed against him. Within a few minutes, he was grabbing her ass.

When they returned to their seats at the bar, there were new drinks. Jeremy gave a thumbs-up to the barman and joined her on a silver stool.

She placed her hand on his crotch, located his penis, and stroked it through the jeans.

"Want to take it further?" she said.

Before he could answer, she kissed him, tongue in deep, tasting the cigarettes, beer, garlic.

"You got some drugs?" she asked.

He smiled. "Some base."

"Base heroin?"

"No, fucking base rocket fuel. Of course, Missy. Have you got vinegar?"

He felt under her dress, traced the slit of her vagina with a finger. She felt like she had been shocked.

"Or lemon juice. We can put on our tackies and chase some dragons."

# 27

**Fallon removed keys from her studded handbag and unlocked the entrance door at Sea View Holiday Flats.**

The reception was empty. No Fabrice.

They took the lift to the seventh floor.

Inside her apartment, Jeremy opened a pack of diabetic syringes and got to work on rigging their shoot. She found bandages in a tray inside a wooden cabinet and wrapped it around her forearm. She had injected cocaine before but never heroin.

"OK, Missy."

He applied the needle at an angle and sucked air.

"Fuck sake!" She sank her nails into his arm.

He registered again with the needle flat. This time she saw the blood as he plunged the drug into her vein.

"Gotcha, Missy, there . . ."

She loosened the tie, closed her eyes, and felt the warmth rush into her like a tide. She lay on the floor.

"How's that orgasm?" he said.

She opened one eye and he was busy with his own shot.

"Ace, ace, ace," he crooned, leaning back, looking at the ceiling with his arms outstretched.

She closed her eyes and imagined she was in a room with a big fire, children opening Christmas presents. She felt safe and comfortable, as if wrapped in a giant blanket.

She heard a noise. In the darkness, Jeremy tripped over a box. "What the fuck's going on here? This place is a wreck." He picked up clothes and held them to his face. "Boxes of shit, dirty clothes, fuck me."

"It's my cousin's place," she said drowsily and closed her eyes again.

There was Christmas music, *Santa Claus is coming to town*, a woman, was it her mother? She tried to focus and see the woman's face.

She thought she heard Jeremy vomiting.

She tried to shake off the dreamlike euphoria. Jeremy was mumbling some mantra over and over again.

"Hey," she said.

She got up and he pulled her against his bare chest. The roughness of his hold sent a thrill through her body. She opened the buckle of his jeans and ripped out the belt. His pants slipped down his legs. She cupped his balls, but he pushed her away, kicked off his jeans, and sauntered naked about the apartment. He stopped and turned.

"Show me what you got, Missy, I-I want to...Missy..." His dialogue fluctuated between clarity and incoherence.

"Stop calling me Missy."

"What's your name again?"

She told her real name. She wanted him to remember it. Remember it for eternity.

She pulled up her dress, revealing a flat stomach and spiky crotch. He crossed the room, put one arm around her waist, pressed his thumb against the nub of her clitoris.

"It's a nice little thing."

She lifted the dress higher. He stopped her.

"Don't take it off."

In the bedroom, he fell horizontally across her bed on his back, his head hung over the edge and his arms outstretched like a trapeze catcher. She hoisted her dress and straddled his face, reached out to stroke his flaccid penis.

"Heaven is a dancer." He licked her core with his open tongue, meeting the rasp of her sex with his stubble, his hands pumping her ass.

She closed her eyes and pressed against the source of her ecstasy. His tongue slotted into her. She shuddered, the high, the anticipation, the excitement of real flesh inside. Her body tensed, cramp spasms spreading from her calves to her feet. She faked an orgasm and raised her ass.

"You alive?" she asked. He must be breathing through his ears.

He pulled her down, eating at her core with a drunken ferocity. A warm sensation coursed through her body, it was relief, a release of tension. She went with it.

"Sweet Jesus."

She had not expected that. She stepped off him and staggered to the center of the room. It was not the first time, but it was the first in a long time.

"Hey, come back here, Missy." Jeremy stood and shook his limp member. "Shit. I'm too high."

She went to the kitchen and poured two Jacks. When she returned, he was fumbling in his wallet. He held up a blue pill in his fingers. She gave him a glass and he swallowed it.

"So what do you get up to?" he said.

"I'm just using up spare time. What do you do?"

"I run a software security business."

"Any openings?"

He laughed and wiggled his cock. "You have come to the right place."

She got him talking about his business. It was tedious propeller head stuff and he drifted in and out of lucidity. He went on about the Web and evil like he was some off-kilter philosopher.

Ten minutes later, he fell back onto her bed.

She pulled her dress over her head and mounted him. She rubbed his goatee and rode him, holding her pelvis tightly against his and sliding up and down on a horizontal axis. After a minute, the friction was starting to become unpleasant.

"Are you getting there?"

He was rock hard, showed no sign of an impending orgasm. She pulled his hands onto her breasts, but they slipped off. She thought he may have fallen asleep. She continued for another minute then rolled off, took his wallet to the bathroom.

*Look at his profiles, make a copy of everything you can get your hands on.*

She checked through his wallet, Jeremy Freeman, a number of cards and sales slips. Could this be JACKER? She expected to find JACKER's signature picture, the elusive joker card. She did not take the cash in his wallet.

When she returned, he was smoking a joint, his face shrouded in a cloud of smoke. His cock was still rigid. She was not on the pill and he had not used a condom.

"This Wild Cherry shit is so dank," he said.

He rolled onto the pillow and laughed hysterically.

She got on top of him, took the joint, and pressed it between her lips, stroked his hair. She inhaled deeply, held it, and looked at him lying there with that stupid look on his face.

The look reminded her of the old man she had killed in Harare all those years ago. What was his name again? He had been civil at first. Driven her to a deserted spot on the outskirts of the town and she had given him a blowjob in the car. He wanted to smoke and talk and she wanted her money. Earlier he had shown her a revolver in the cubby hole and the money in his wallet. She was not scared. She only wanted her money and a lift home. Eventually he asked how much and when she told him, he said it was too much, the last blowjob was better and cost half. She did not remember the amount, but it was not much. She knew he was rich, he had a fancy car. When she argued, he slapped her and kicked her out his car. She remembered it so clearly. He opened the passenger door then leaned back and booted her with the heels of his shoes. She had grabbed the gun out the glove compartment. She only wanted her money. When she saw the drool on his lips, his quivering mouth, his red eyes, she pulled the trigger like she had seen in the movies. Afterwards she took the money he owed her, wiped her prints, placed the gun in his hand, and pulled his dick out his zipper. She had walked five miles home in the dark. She was nineteen.

"What you thinking about?" he said.

"You'd love to know."

She sucked on the weed and admired his lean body, rock star hair, small bony ass, horse-like dick. Why the fuck was she thinking about the old punter she had shot in Harare all those years ago?

He slapped her leg.

"What?"

"Get off. I have to take a dump."

She waited for the bathroom door to shut then reached for his cell phone. She heard the toilet seat go down. She scrolled through his applications. His email account was password protected. She flicked through his picture gallery—lots of porn, no personal stuff. There were a number of messaging applications: WhatsApp, WeChat, RedPhone. She went for RedPhone first, couldn't access the messages. WeChat contained business communication from clients.

"What you doing out there, Missy?" he called.

She didn't answer. She gave up on WeChat and opened WhatsApp.

"I hope you're not being a naughty girl."

She heard the toilet flush.

All messages on WhatsApp were deleted. The only item of interest was the icon on Jeremy Freeman's profile. It was a charging stallion, a SUPERCHARGER.

## 28

**Le Fleur stood on his patio and looked back through the glass windows at his Van Gogh rendition.** Something on the canvas was bugging him. He closed one eye. The problem was movement. His copy lacked the original's impression of high winds.

The outside temperature was cool, a mist over the sea but clear inland. A red city sight-seeing bus rumbled along Victoria Road, tourists raised glasses on the open upper deck.

Earlier he wrote a list to order his thoughts.

Clues and Postulations.

1. SUPERCHARGER involved in cracking
   AlphaGuard to erase surveillance at
   Townley's house. And also LPR cameras
   in Constantia(?)
2. $CENE$TER assisted with laundering
   the missing cash (?)
3. Bruno Pittman in contact with Ynez.
4. Carla is being followed.
5. Gun-at-the-head theory.

The gun-at-the-head theory was based on Carla's view that Townley was coerced. He added a No.6 and No.7.

6. What was Townley doing in Geneva?
7. What does Livigno mean?

Last night he extracted internet usage for Carla's suspects, including Carla and Gavin Marx. Then he slept for two hours and woke without an alarm. This morning he analyzed the background noise on Townley's transfer call with Goldman's and made an unexpected discovery. He added two items to the list.

8. Background noise at the airport?
9. Apollo till slip??

He liked to have ten points on a list. He thought for a minute, but couldn't come up with a tenth item. Eventually he added one.

```
10. Townley and Ynez to an island?
```

He phoned Carla at 11:00.

"How's your health and wellness? I think we need some outdoor activity."

"Activity? As in exercise?" Her voice was croaky.

"It's an epic day for a hike up Table Mountain. And we've got matters to discuss."

"What about the muggings?"

"Don't worry. On a day like this, there'll be lots of hikers on the footpaths. Law of averages says we'll be fine."

He looked back at the Van Gogh, opened and closed his eyes. The trodden grass on the side of the road differed, sap green, probably not the best choice of color.

"OK, you're on. I've got a wine farm to sweat out," she said.

Half an hour later, outside Harbor Heights, Carla appeared in a sleeveless tank top, short white skirt and slip slops, and a handbag. He stared at her bare legs.

"Why are you staring at me?"

He cut the ignition.

"We're not going shopping. We're hiking straight up Plattekloof Gorge." With his right hand, he imitated an airplane taking off. "It's a steep path. There'll be people underneath you looking up." He paused to see if she understood. "You need sensible clothing."

"This isn't sensible?"

"It is if you want people staring at your underwear."

She checked him out: knee length shorts, well-worn boots, and a no-sweat white collared T-shirt. When she returned, she had khaki shorts and running shoes.

The drive took ten minutes. She told him how, the previous night at Shimmy, Gavin Marx asked her to reconsider her position on working for GALI. He felt she was throwing away her career.

"And he asked me about your fee again?"

Le Fleur parked at the side of Tafelberg Road. Beneath them, the energy of the city bowl sparkled in brilliant sunshine. She poked him in the ribs.

"Gavin wants to meet you. Are you OK with that?"

They got out of the car. She placed her foot against the curb and stretched.

"Why does he want to meet me?"

---

He mentally tallied his direct expenses: half a bitcoin to NETWORX, four grand to Ynez. He doubted Marx knew how to settle in bitcoin.

"I don't think he trusts someone who won't take our money."

"I never said I wouldn't take your money."

He led the way up the path, ascending steadily with wide steps into the opening of the ravine. His backpack was loaded with water, a spare sweater and anorak, apples and suntan lotion. He had a pepper spray canister in his pocket. There was no shade; the sun blazed down.

"You got a girlfriend, Daniel?"

"Nope."

"Boyfriend?"

He shook his head, did not look back.

"It's no big deal," she said.

Le Fleur stopped and looked up the gorge. Rugged granite rocks created a timeless staircase to the summit. The sky was a blue desert, the absence of running water, a reminder of the drought. He stepped aside and allowed her to pass, trying not to follow the movement of her backside inside her khaki shorts. A thin line of perspiration trickled down her lower back.

"I've downloaded the internet history and sent it to you."

Last night after his meeting with Coppis at Bar Rack, he had fired an exploit onto GALI Africa's corporate ISP, his target the internet sites accessed by Carla's suspect list prior to Nial's disappearance. He hoped it would turn up a Google search for something like: "How to make someone disappear." It amused him how most people thought that deleting their browser history would erase fingerprints of their dodgy access. Every web access was recorded in saved logs on ISP servers. But he already knew he was not dealing with "*most people.*"

"Anything interesting?"

"You'll have to tell me. Buoyweather, WindGuru, Sailnet, the Seychelles, Scorpus.com and eFunda. Nial spent a lot of time researching GALI."

Carla placed her hand on her knee, negotiated an upward step.

"Does it surprise you?" he asked.

"We were already in discussions with GALI. I would expect him to do his homework."

She stopped and peered up the ravine, face wet with perspiration. Three descending hikers slipped past with wry smiles.

"*Your* browser history is curious."

She looked back, hands on her hips.

"What?"

He nodded.

She frowned then raised her hands to her face.

"Oh shit! I can only imagine. My last boyfriend was a porn addict and he used to surf that shit on my laptop."

He said nothing. Something about her having a porn addict boyfriend kicked him in the stomach. He imagined his father laughing.

"You don't believe me?" she said.

"I believe you."

He overtook her and they climbed in silence for a few minutes.

"What about Bruno Pittman?" she asked.

"His access records date from his arrival in Cape Town. Before, who knows? I didn't find anything particularly exciting. Some sport—European football, world news, some pornography, the usual sites men visit."

He stopped and looked back. She was peering up at the distance to the summit and breathing hard.

"My calves are burning," she said.

"Let's take a break."

They rested on opposite rocks bisected by the path.

"Did you say anything to the Supertech team yesterday?" he asked.

"About Pittman's call to Ynez? No. We spoke about Ynez. Nial wouldn't want her destitute. What are we going to do about Pittman?"

He did not tell her he visited Ynez last night at Gorky Park.

"Not much we can do right now. Moving in on the ex-chairman's stripper is not a crime. You think he's a crook?"

"He's an asshole."

"There's a difference between a crook and an asshole."

"He's an asshole crook."

They continued the ascent. At the summit, they turned away from the tourist choked cable station, found a spot on the craggy rocks near the edge with a 360° view over the city. Cool air dried the perspiration on their bodies.

"You look down there," she said, biting into an apple. "And realize in that shadow somewhere below, someone knows what happened to Nial."

He passed her the water bottle. She spoke about the positive turnaround in South America.

"Ironic, isn't it," she said. "GALI takes over our business and suddenly the Venezuelans are playing ball. It seems so unfair. Big corporations have the financial muscle to buy off anyone, even a government."

He agreed. South Africa was choking in corruption scandals.

They stood and continued across the upper table in the direction of Maclear's Beacon.

"How far are we going?" she asked.

"We follow the path and those little yellow feet they use for trail marking."

She stuffed the water bottle into his rucksack.

"Someone stirred trouble for us with the Venezuelans. Nial knew that. They wouldn't release our payments. And we didn't have the contacts. With big deals, it's all about political power."

"Who's the someone?"

"I don't know. Some politician, another contractor..."

She stopped, put her hands on her hips, looked back along the route they'd come.

"Put one foot in front of the other? I haven't seen one fucking yellow foot." Her face was red from exertion.

They reached Maclear's Beacon, the highest point on Table Mountain. She crouched then sat on the ground. He took a moment to discuss links with astronomy and the curvature of the earth, told her Thomas Maclear was a friend of Livingstone, the famous African explorer. For an engineer, he thought her particularly disinterested in his lecture.

"You like it up here?" she asked.

"It's like being on the moon. No cars or noise. If you come here during the week, there're no people."

"You don't like people."

"I'm never sure."

He picked up a stone and tossed it into a cairn of rocks. She stood slowly, brushed the dust off her pants. Back on the path, they set off in the direction of Skeleton Gorge. Behind him, he heard her take a deep breath.

"You mustn't think about the end," he said. "One step at a time. If you think about the end, you'll crack."

"Crack? I thought that was a hacker term?"

"It's also an old schoolboy term meaning to breakdown, give up."

"Well, I'm not going to crack, that's for sure."

They reached Skeleton Gorge. Nestled at the bottom of the gorge was Kirstenbosch Gardens with restaurant and refreshments. He did not tell her. Instead he followed the curve right towards Constantia Nek, slowed for her to catch up.

"Aqualung told me you're an orphan."

"Of sorts," he replied.

"What happened?"

"My mother got breast cancer and didn't get help in time."

"I'm sorry."

"It was long ago." He knew his answer was both true and false.

"Did your father take it badly?"

"I'm not sure he cared."

The old man was what he was. Over time, Le Fleur had come to accept it. No excuses.

"That's pretty harsh."

"He was a player with women even when my mother was still alive."

She said nothing and he continued.

"He used women to feel good about himself. That's what did him in."

It seemed easier to talk about his father, his failings. He could not talk about his mother, the abuse she had taken. He never understood why she kept coming back.

"A woman killed him?"

"No. Vanity did. A hair dye gave him skin cancer."

"Why didn't your mother leave him?"

"I don't think she knew where to go, what to do."

"Perhaps it was you she was worried about. You have any siblings?"

"No."

He stopped. A dead baby bird, a white-eye, lay in their path. His mother stayed because of him. What Carla said made sense. But it also made it harder to bear. He crouched and picked up the bird, placed its body in a clump of Fynbos.

They walked in silence for five minutes.

"Aqualung said he met you on the street a year ago. He was hassling for money and you ignored him. He said he told you one day he would save your life."

A group of hikers passed in the opposite direction and offered greetings. Thick Fynbos edged the paths, diverse species of flora, flaming Watsonias, pin cushions, bell shaped Ericas, more species than in the entire United Kingdom.

Carla continued: "Then a week later you came looking for him and placed him in the Somerset Road shelter and organized a job at Bali Bay."

A sugar bird needled a Protea with its long beak.

"Why did you do that?" she asked.

"He said he'd save my life."

"Has he?"

He thought about the yellow tea-pot, the red rice rocket. "Not yet."

She was beginning to slip behind. They passed two reservoirs and swung left along a well-defined jeep track, passing the small beach at the end of Victoria Reservoir and reaching the gates of a small cottage. She sat on a low wall. He filled the water bottle.

---

"You cracking?"

"My legs are jelly. What's this place?" She sounded hopeful.

He explained it was the overseer's cottage, not a restaurant, and checked his cell for a signal.

"Have you ever heard of a Stingray?" he asked.

"As in Steve Irwin?"

"As in FBI."

"No."

"I've been thinking about your gun-at-the-head theory. If Townley believed he was in danger. Or someone close to him."

"Like Gregory?"

"Or Sophie. Or Ynez. Or you."

She nibbled on her bottom lip and stared out at the pristine vegetation.

"If he thought that, what would he do?" Le Fleur asked.

"He'd phone someone."

"What if his phone had been compromised?"

"I don't understand."

"I'll explain. Nial receives the catalyst call and believes someone close to him is in mortal danger. He's ordered to turn off his cell and drive somewhere, ostensibly to meet someone or receive further instruction. He tries to tell Sophie that he's not able to fetch Gregory, but he can't make contact. They, the perpetrators, direct him to return home. There is no record of this because the LPR surveillance has been doctored."

Two mountain trail runners ambled past and waved.

"To pull off the deception, they had to control his phone. A Stingray would allow them to detect cell phone signals and manipulate the use of the phone. It's a portable cell phone tower, no bigger than a suitcase. The FBI uses Stingrays to locate criminals and record conversations. And it appears normally on the cell network, or not."

Carla reached down and massaged her calves. "It sounds a bit far-fetched, even by my standards." She forced a narrow smile.

More hikers were passing. The jeep track was becoming a hiking highway.

"Come, let's move away from here."

She looked up, wiped the sweat from her face, and squinted into the sun behind his head. Then she stood slowly and followed him.

"So what I'm saying is if Nial believed Gregory had been kidnapped, the bad guys couldn't let Nial phone the school. Or Sophie." He walked backwards as he spoke, undeterred by her skepticism. Carla's eyes were at her feet.

At a rusted iron cross, they left the main path, and stopped at the edge of another reservoir. He sat on a boulder and took off his back pack. She sat next to him.

"We've got all these possibilities, Daniel. We know they tampered with his surveillance. We know Bruno Pittman and Ynez have some connection. Shouldn't we take this and your Stingray theory to the police? To Parks Phakatini. Let's see what the Hawks make of it."

He did not reply. He did not think they had enough proof. If they exposed their hand, their adversary would be alerted. His eyes swept across the water to a dam wall in the distance. The reservoir was less than half full, boulders he had never seen before protruding above the water line. Carla stood and stretched, reached towards her toes.

"So hiking and biking, this is how you clear your head of ones and zeros?" she said from between her legs.

She straightened and grinned at him.

"You'll find this hard to believe, but I also did some cage fighting." He looked at his right wrist and rubbed the three crosses. "About the same time I got these."

"Oh my God, with those delicate hands! Whatever did you do that for?"

He shrugged. Why had he told her that? He imagined Jake Le Fleur: *Putting your best foot forward, son?*

"I didn't last a month. I'd get so wholly fucked up, I couldn't think straight for a week."

She also stared out at the expanse of water. "Can you swim here?"

"No. It's not allowed."

She pulled her tank top over her head. "Oh really?"

She unbuttoned her khaki shorts, stripped to her underwear. He looked away. Above, the sky was smoky blue and seemed to be on top of his head. When he looked back, she had taken off her bra and was tip-toeing towards the water's edge.

"Oh my God, that's so good." The water reached her midriff. She rolled onto her back, her breasts invisible below the stained water.

When she emerged, he threw her his spare sweater to use as a towel. He filled the water bottles, returned as she was stuffing her wet panties into her pocket.

"Don't act so shocked. You've seen a topless girl before?"

"Only on YouPorn."

He felt his face redden, thinking his reply ranked with his lamest. He repacked the rucksack and sat on a boulder. Carla squeezed the water from her hair.

"That was so worth it." She sat alongside, her leg touched his. "What made you come around to this gun-at-the-head theory, Daniel? When I first suggested it, you didn't believe me."

"And now I might believe it, you don't?" He pulled out his cell phone. "This is why."

He selected an audio clip and played it, held his cell to her ear.

"It's Nial's conversation with Goldman's. From the airport."

She nodded. He pulled the phone away and started another audio.

"What do you hear now?"

She frowned and pressed his hand and the cell against her ear.

"I don't know," she said. She shook her head. "It sounds like...What is it?" He held the phone to his ear.

"Airports are noisy places. There was no background sound. I removed the conversation's audio and left only the ambient noise. Then I boosted that volume by a hundred percent."

He held the phone against her ear again.

"Clip-clop, clip-clop," he said. "Constantia mink and manure..."

Her eyes widened.

"Don't they say it's the *thunder* of horse hooves? Nial was nowhere near the airport when he made that call. He was at home. And that's why they scrubbed the surveillance."

## 29

**Fallon woke with a blinding headache, strung out by last night's binge.** Her eyes were bloodshot and cheeks chafed with the friction from Jeremy's beard.

After Jeremy departed, she left a message for Dark Video on Whisper. She confirmed Jeremy was SUPERCHARGER and owned a computer security business. Then she fell into a dead sleep and, at some stage of the morning, dreamed about the old man she had shot in Harare. It was like watching a movie. A bald man in a gray suit with his top button open and tie loose, a teenage Goth in fishnet stockings and steel toed boots nestled alongside on the shiny red seats of his car. She could smell the oil in the man's hair, the sweat in his groin, his smoky breath. He was kicking her, shouting at her: Get out, get out. Then the Goth reached into the cubbyhole and pulled out a gun. She aimed it at the old man. But suddenly, in the dream, it was not the old man, but her, looking into the wild, green eyes of the enraged Goth. She stared at the gun in the teenager's hand then the barrel flashed silver and her nose filled with cordite.

She gulped a glass of water and thought about the dream.

A bottle of eye drops and a green tube of effervescent vitamin boosters rested on the telephone table in her apartment. The curtains were closed. She was naked and had not showered. She felt like her feet were above the floor. Not like she was floating, like she was balancing on a different surface a foot above the ground. Ridiculously, she felt like she was in love. She filled another glass of water and downed it.

When she checked the channel, there were numerous messages.

```
Good work, Operative Fallon

You will check your account—ZAR 5,000
has been deposited
```

She created another tab on her laptop and logged onto her overseas account. There was a deposit. It was marked DV Seattle. Five grand was a measly three-fifty Euros. She should have asked for ten. She could make more money as a hooker.

```
It's not like it was. Things have changed
```

She picked up an empty bottle of Jack and squeezed the last drops into her mouth. What did he mean by that?

The stakes are much bigger

In prison, she had considered what would be waiting for her when she got out. She feared Carlos De Palma had been destroyed and Dark Video's empire dismantled. She thought she would have to start from scratch. The news on the channel was exciting, better than her expectation. Bigger stakes meant more money.

The next channel entries described her assignment. She felt a twist in her stomach as the instructions sunk in. She rubbed the back of her hand over her crotch then held it to her nose. She could still smell him on her.

ZAR 20K was the agreed remuneration on successful fulfillment of the objective.

The final note on the channel read:

Revenge will be most satisfying

She stared at the blinking message for a long time. But there could be no doubt about the decision to be made. She pulled on blue jeans and a tight-fitting T-shirt and grabbed the keys of her Chevy.

## 30

**Marx's secretary was blonde and petite.** She wore white pants with a thong visible underneath. What would his father say? *Get her number.*

"Gavin will be right with you," she said in a sing-song voice. "You can take a seat over there."

He did not feel like sitting. He reviewed the magazines on the table, a cross section of recent sporting, legal, sailing and financial. He picked up a magazine called Super Lawyers. Marx was on the cover. He put it down and opened the Business Day. On Page 3, Bruno Pittman of GALI Africa reported Supertech's Venezuelan problems were largely resolved, the Venezuelan Government had released Supertech's blocked funds, and GALI planned to merge offshore business into GALI's American operation with immediate effect.

He thought the article was sure to piss off Carla.

A second article on GALI caught his eye. He was reading it when the secretary announced he could go through to Marx's office.

"Thank you," he said but she didn't look up. *You see*, he could hear his father, *you wait and wait and wait. Fussy doesn't fuck.* Le Fleur shook his head to erase the voice.

Marx was waiting at the door when he entered. He was dressed casually, an open neck shirt and gray slacks. He smelled of a powerful aftershave.

"You must be Daniel. Carla has told me so much about you. We are extremely grateful."

Marx reached out and shook Le Fleur's hand warmly. In that moment Le Fleur considered that Marx was probably fucking his secretary and how embarrassing it would be if he had asked for her number. He felt a tinge of annoyance. All these years gone by, and his father's misdemeanors still taunted him.

He was offered a seat at an oak table on the window side of the office. The view swept across the harbor into Table Bay. It was hard not to contrast Marx's office with Cybercrime's Ian Coulson's. He thought lawyers obviously invested more money in image.

"Thank you for coming to see me. I wanted to make sure we have compensated your efforts."

The secretary appeared at the door. She did not say anything.

"Would you like anything?" Marx asked. "Tea, coffee. We make a fine cappuccino."

He declined. The secretary disappeared.

"Look, I've specifically asked Carla not to over inform me, unless of course, she turns up something. I don't want to know exactly what it is you're doing except to say I fully support it. I trust Carla implicitly. You know Nial was priming her to run Supertech?"

He nodded.

Imitation concrete wallpaper covered the extent of the office. On the walls were pictures of yachts and a framed copy of Marx's qualifications.

"It was a trick Nial learned from the Anglo-American Corporation, no less—hire the brightest young graduate, make them your PA, and teach them the business by observing their boss in action."

"I'm glad Carla has your support," he said.

Marx smiled.

"She showed you the video of the boardroom fiasco? She's a tiger, that's for sure. She doesn't have much time for GALI. Can't say I have either, but what can we do? Look, it's no secret we were in trouble. Nial knew it. I am not sure how much Carla told you, but we were involved in a construction project, a subsea structure off the coast near Caracas. The Venezuelan Government was making some ominous threats, ones that could place a company the size of Supertech in serious trouble."

"Yes."

"But you know, no amount of pressure affected Nial. I've known him since I was a kid. He would never have bowed."

Marx stopped and cleared his throat. He looked out the window. Behind the cranes and tug boats in a busy harbor, Robben Island, where Nelson Mandela was imprisoned for eighteen of his twenty-seven years, was visible.

"Three months and more have gone by and it doesn't get easier. There's a little boy in London pining for his father. You don't know how that makes me feel."

Le Fleur said nothing. Marx's outlook was consistent with Carla. They spoke of Townley with deep compassion.

"Now about payment . . . I would understand if you're reluctant to supply an invoice. I won't need one. I can pay you directly."

He looked intently at Le Fleur. Le Fleur put his fist in front of his mouth and coughed. "I wanted to finish everything up, you know, first. There's no hurry."

Marx frowned. "As I understood it, you have completed your assignment. Cell records. Internet access."

"There are a few loose ends."

"Ah." Marx stood and walked behind his desk. There was a model of a

---

yacht on it. He poured a glass of water. "Would you like some?"

He declined. "That's your yacht." He pointed to the desk.

"Yes." Marx passed the model to Le Fleur. *George's Escape* was written on the boat's hull in blue lettering. "Are you a sailing man?"

He looked at the yacht then passed it back. "No, not at all. Carla said you raced the yacht to Brazil."

"Yes. Not an ideal yacht for long distance." He paused. "Not ideal."

"What's the range?" Le Fleur asked.

"How do mean?"

"You said it's not ideal for long distance. But you made it to Brazil. Could you make it to say Mauritius, the Seychelles?"

Marx shook his head.

"I wouldn't advise that." He chuckled. "The Southern Ocean is an unpredictable beast. They don't call this the Cape of Storms for nothing."

He replaced the model, returned to the table but remained standing. "I'll take you for a sail in the bay if you'd like."

"I get seasick."

Marx chuckled.

"So you mentioned a few loose ends? I don't want to be, well, a lawyer, but we unfortunately don't have an open-ended check book. How much are we talking?"

He had not considered the amount. Check books? Did they still use them? A couple of bitcoin, maybe?

"I'll send you an account next week."

"And these loose ends?" Marx adjusted his belt and trousers. He looked a person who was not easily rattled, calm, confident, probably well versed in dealing with characters from all walks of life.

"We are still analyzing the call patterns. Would you mind if I asked you a few questions?"

Le Fleur paused. What would Marx say if he told him Nial never made the calls from the airport, that Townley's home's surveillance footage was compromised? Would he still be so calm? He wondered what Townley and Marx spoke about, meeting twice a week at Constantia Nek.

"Of course."

"Why do you think the pressure in Venezuela decreased since GALI took over?"

Marx rubbed his cheek and narrowed his eyes.

"Mmm. A probing question. GALI takes the reins and suddenly everything changed. It's maybe more complicated. Of course, the GALI oomph makes a difference. How does this relate to the cell calls?"

---

Le Fleur skipped the question.

"Bruno Pittman," he said. "What's your view on him?"

Marx smiled and took a deep breath.

"I see Carla has got to you. Look, I don't like Pittman. I'm not sure what Carla told you, but the man's typical of these corporate movers and shakers. He knows everything but nothing. He depends on head office and they rely on his loyalty. But Carla has a whole GALI conspiracy theory which I don't discount, but there is no evidence. Bring me some evidence, Daniel. Then we can talk."

Marx smiled and looked at his watch. "Is there anything else?"

Ynez had called Marx "the big boss." He wanted to ask Marx what they were paying her and how he felt about Pittman wanting to screw his best friend's girlfriend. He wanted to know whether Marx and Carla had ever been romantically involved. But he did not ask. He stood and glanced at Marx's qualifications. Marx walked him to the door.

"I want Nial back, Daniel. I would give anything. Perhaps it is not possible."

They shook hands. Le Fleur considered that Marx was everything he thought he would be. Controlled, direct, and business-like. There was Marx's comment about Nial Townley's son. A little boy in London... As if he were showing just enough concern. Le Fleur hadn't expected Marx to share his grief. He had expected a lawyer and got one.

He left the office. Marx's secretary looked up and smiled.

"Thank you," he said to her.

"It's a pleasure."

She looked back at her screen. He hesitated. "Excuse me?"

She looked back, eyebrows raised.

He pointed to the Business Day. "Do you mind if I take the newspaper?"

She nodded. He did not ask for her number.

# 31

**Fallon wiped a film of perspiration from her upper lip.** She was standing on the balcony of her apartment with a bottle of Jack. Below her, a steady stream of cars whizzed along Beach Road in both directions.

Long before the early morning traffic, she had been in the northern suburb of Durbanville watching the home of Jeremy Freeman aka SUPERCHARGER. The prick *was* married. She followed him when he left for work then returned to watch his bitch wife leave the house with two kids. No wall around their property, was that not insanity? By lunchtime the kids were home, playing in the sloping front garden, banging about on black push tricycles. What sort of screw-head owned a big mansion without walls and electric fencing?

She stared out at the sea.

She suddenly remembered the name of the old man she had shot in Harare. It was Monty. Monty. The name sounded jolly. He was still breathing when she left him, gun in hand, cock hanging out. The same day, she left for South Africa and never returned or bothered to confirm Monty's fate.

She emptied her glass and took a deep breath.

Why was she thinking and dreaming about Monty? It had been triggered by the stupid look on Jeremy's face after sex.

At 16:30, she returned to Durbanville on the N1 highway. She parked at a junction Jeremy passed on his way to work earlier in the day. She figured he would take the same route home. Of course he could have already passed and she was wasting her time. Her assignment had no timeframe or method, but she wanted to get it over. She had already established there were no LPR cameras on the route and there would be no reason for anyone to remember a nondescript white Chevy Spark parked in a quiet suburban side road.

Twenty grand. It was better than nothing.

To pass time, she listened to the radio, switching between stations, stopping on Good Hope FM because they were playing a song by UB40.

After the incident with Monty, Fallon did not kill anyone for many years.

Times were tough after she fled Zimbabwe. To survive, she spent the first years as an escort in Johannesburg. Young, new meat, she would have raked in money, if it were not for a pimp who sapped her earnings. She wished she had killed him.

Then she met the boyfriend.

Depravity could be washed away. Dressed up, she could accompany a company chairman to a ball and stir the room to envy.

The boyfriend was private-school and clean cut, blue eyes, sharp brain. He was all ambition.

No.

She paused as if recognizing the point at which she could have reserved a life of pampered privilege. Was it a happy time? She could not remember.

The boyfriend was studying medicine. He had dug into his student loan and loaned her the money to enroll for a diploma in Pharmacy. She never opened the course material. He thought she was studying, but she was earning fast cash as an exclusive escort to a group of married executives. She got used to fucking older men with gray haired chests and withering muscles.

If there was a role, she could play it. Why was real life, normal life, so fucking impossible to follow?

The boyfriend found out. The perfect doctor-to-be and boyfriend who spent all day working, nights on call, was too tired to go out at night, found out she was fucking geriatrics for money. He was so shocked, so utterly disbelieving.

"How could you do this to me?" he had said.

She had not thought she was doing anything *to him*. She was doing it *for them*, so they had money to buy luxury items, to go out to restaurants. The suffering was all hers.

Why did people always think of themselves?

"Not only that you're lazy and dishonest," he said. "You're a money fiend with the soul of a criminal."

She did not see how they differed. They were ambitious, he wanted to be rich and successful, so did she. He was not studying medicine to help people and be poor? Everyone played a role to achieve what they wanted. *The soul of a criminal?* His words stuck in her head.

She took the Taurus from her bag and screwed on the silencer. She clipped in a full magazine. The extended length of the weapon enhanced its threatening appearance. Shooting at the range had fine-tuned her confidence, the 5-8 yard drill yielding every shot in the same hole.

She had tried to win him back, the boyfriend, unable to relinquish the false dream of a role in normality. She threatened and cajoled and pleaded. It taught her a vagina was bait, not a net. The boyfriend was over her, the draw of her sex a worthless currency. She imagined her doctor married a pretty graduate who did not work and drove their three kids around in a Range Rover.

Could have been her.

She put the gun back in her bag, rubbed her thighs, and looked at her reflection in the mirror. She wondered how long before the dark roots would show through her blonde hair.

She was looking in the mirror when Jeremy's Porsche drove past her vantage point.

Her heart jumped. She turned off the music and inserted ear plugs. She started the car and followed at a safe distance.

The distance to his house was five kilometers. Her stomach was churning. She thought about Jeremy's lean, bony body, his dexterous tongue, his lopsided smile, his laugh. *Revenge will be most satisfying.* It was not *her* revenge. She did not care if he was SUPERCHARGER or JACKER.

She accelerated and closed the gap when he reached his street. If there were people around, if his family were outside? She had not considered a set of conditions for aborting the job.

The road was empty. He turned into his driveway and she pulled in behind. By the time he opened his car door, she was rushing towards him. He looked up as she appeared in his peripheral vision.

From a distance of fifteen feet, she raised the Taurus and fired one shot. The bullet hit him between the eyes on the bridge of his nose. He raised his right hand defensively and his left hand towards his face.

No words were uttered as he staggered forward then away from her.

She reached into the car and grabbed his wallet from the front seat.

When she turned, he was on his knees, hands over his face, a low animal-like gurgle emanating from his throat.

She picked up his cell and looked towards the house. The curtains were closed. She walked to her car and drove away.

## 32

**"Ah, the sour mash of Tennessee," Aqualung rasped, homeless for a night due to a renovation at the shelter.** He was spread across the couch, showered and dressed in an oilskin, swigging from a bottle of Johnny Walker and ready for a winter that would not come.

"It's like the bite of oak soaked gasoline."

He liked to tell a story about a guy who went blind drinking Johnny—he was stabbed in the eye with the bottle.

Le Fleur ignored him and checked his LPR surveillance system. Point no.4 on his list: *Carla was being followed.* The output files were empty, no new visits from the red Hyundai.

His mind wandered, an uneasy feeling growing in his gut, a warning flashing in his head. He did not like the message. He was convinced that SUPERCHARGER had erased the surveillance at Townley's home. SUPERCHARGER was involved with the installation at Digital Eye and he knew no other hacker who could have penetrated the AlphaGuard firewall. And based on the modus operandi used, he strongly suspected $CENE$TER had aided the dissemination of missing cash.

Now he had a new consideration: the criminals used a Stingray.

So the school could not contact Townley, so Sophie never received a call from her husband and no subsequent calls from her or anyone else were relayed to Townley.

And later, so it appeared Townley was phoning from the airport when he was actually at his home.

He heard Aqualung turn on the TV and walked into the Chrome Room. He opened a private conversation on Chat Step. NETWORX responded immediately.

```
Le Fleur    Did you get your half coin?
NETWORX     Thanks. Why do you want those
            cell phone records?
LE FLEUR    It's not like you to ask questions
NETWORX     I don't want to get into any shit.
            How do I know you not doing a SABU?
```

SABU was a famous black hat hacker who surrendered his identity to the FBI.

```
LE FLEUR    All girls are men and all kids are
            under cover FBI agents. What's eating you?
NETWORX     I gotta be careful, you know
```

Le Fleur knew Richard Chinkanda had not been careful. He was active on too many IRC chats, using the same name, sharing personal details, posting searchable advertisements for cell phone tracking services. Even his browser's fingerprint was unique.

```
NETWORX     Is this about Nial Townley?
LE FLEUR    I think you know it is
```

NETWORX was typing, erasing, typing again, but there was no further activity on the screen. In contrast to their last conversation and banter about leets and masturbation, there was no witty repartee.

```
LE FLEUR    Have you done any new work on
            the Stingray?
```

No response.

A few years back, NETWORX had asked questions about building a device. He called it a "contraption." Based on the components and circuitry, Le Fleur now knew it was a Stingray. NETWORX's aim was to acquire free call time and data by bypassing cell networks. He had helped NETWORX with the design, but they had never managed to get it operational.

```
LE FLEUR    Are you still there, Alexander Graham?
```

NETWORX began typing a new message but did not send it. After a delay, his message appeared.

```
NETWORX     That shit doesn't work.
            The design was screwed up
LE FLEUR    OK. Maybe you can send me your
            last design? I think someone
            could be tracking my friend's
            cell phone with a Stingray.
            Every time she visits,
            some shark comes cruising by.
NETWORX     I don't know anything about that.
```

Le Fleur waited for a response but received no further communication. The Chat Step session ended, all communication erased forever.

He tried to reconnect then stuck his head out the Chrome Room door. "Are you hungry?"

Aqualung was asleep. He went back to work.

The same Stingray used to manipulate Townley's cell could be used to track his or Carla's cell phone. He scanned through the source code of his LPR software. It was one thing capturing the image of a suspicious car and translating the plates, another being able to establish who was in the car. He downloaded code segments from the Net and adapted the source to read the geo-locations of connected cell phones in the vicinity. Next time the red Hyundai passed Crystal Place, his LPR system would capture all active cell phones in the area including the occupants.

Afterwards he locked the Chrome Room and fixed ham and cheese rolls in the kitchen. He looked at his watch: two hours spent modifying the LPR system.

Aqualung was awake. On TV, a young man was sitting in front of a computer.

"Computers are taking over the world," said Aqualung. "Soon it'll be over. No car chases, no nests of spies, no fusillade."

"What are you talking about?" He passed Aqualung a plate.

"Look at this, the action is two boys banging keyboards in opposing chambers." Aqualung pointed to the Chrome Room. "Like that chamber. Shiny computers flickering in a dark room. No shaven-headed condamnes loading munitions into automatic fusillades, nerds, these hackers, stick in flash drives and whirring machines hurl information at one another." Aqualung banged his hand against his thigh. "Take this command. Bam. No, you take this one. Bam."

"You're funny, Freddy. So keyboards will come out with designer cartouches? They'll have filed down serial numbers. It'll be so exciting."

Aqualung bit into the roll, mouth churning dough like a concrete mixer.

"At least nobody dies."

Carla phoned at 21:00. A light rain, no more than a wet mist, was falling outside.

"I swear, every muscle hurts, even my brain," she said.

"Take an anti-inflammatory."

"I think I'm going to take one of those and a sleeping pill. How was your meeting with Gavin? Has he organized payment?"

He opened the Business Day from Marx's reception. He was not concentrating on her questions. "Yes." He found the article on GALI.

"You know you've done your job, Daniel. You've got the cell records and the internet usage."

He looked at his phone. "I can go now? So you pay me and I go away?"

"You can. You can do it. It's not your battle."

He wanted to say *Lady, you don't know me very well*, but that was his father's style, not his.

"What about the reward?" he asked.

She laughed. "Oh, are you after the reward now?"

"Maybe... Listen to this..."

He read from the Business Day:

> *Griesser Arnold Loidl Ingenieurswerk Ag (GALI), the international engineering firm listed on German and Austrian stock exchanges, is in big green trouble in Nigeria. GALI was founded in 1935 in Linz, Austria, a family business supplying structures and electronics to Krupp during the Second World War. After the fall of the Third Reich, they profiteered from the reconstruction of post-war Europe. In the late 1950's due to corruption and bad management, and shortly after the death of founder Kurt Griesser, GALI went bankrupt and sold off its assets. Two decades of dormancy followed before GALI re-emerged in the 70's, under the guidance of co-founder Willem Loidl's son Martin, and grew from a regional Bavarian company to an international powerhouse with a set of professional managers that would do an investment bank proud. Head office is now in Munich, but the management team work out of Linz.*

"I see they built the La Linea tunnel in Columbia," he said. "So they were in South America already."

"They bid against us in Venezuela."

"They must've been secretly glad you won."

"You're so right."

"And they are being sued in Nigeria."

"GALI is desperate to crack Africa. All the big players are already in— Bechtel from the States are involved with Kabila, Black & Veitch with Eskom. GALI had a false start in Nigeria and had to walk away from a major oil project. But then we fell into their lap. After Nial's disappearance, GALI greased a lot of palms to push through a life raft deal. We had plenty of well-fed public servants in fancy suits on our doorstep."

"Eighty-eight acquisitions in eight years. That's nearly one a month."

"Schroeder, Straud, and Heineman. They're the guys you saw in the boardroom video. They're GALI's heavyweight acquisition team."

He pictured the trio of executives with their shiny egg heads, silver glasses, and smooth faces.

"What about Pittman? Where does he come from?"

"He was running a GALI subsidiary in . . . someplace I can't remember . . . Poland, Slovakia, somewhere in Eastern Europe. Apparently, he was involved in a previous integration in some tough place and, because he had local knowledge, they thought him suitable for Africa."

Le Fleur looked at the window. The drizzle had stopped.

"His appointment wasn't discussed, agreed with the Supertech management team?"

"Well, at least Willie Schroeder seemed to think we'd be pleased about Pittman's appointment. As if we'd instigated it. God, now he's chasing strippers at Gorky Park." He heard her sigh. "Where's this going, Daniel? I was sure the cell phones or the Internet access would provide some major revelation."

He said nothing.

"What's next?"

"We keep on keeping on. Layer upon layer until a story develops."

"And the truth emerges."

"Yes."

"Does it work like that?" she asked. He thought he heard a little desperation in her voice.

"Sometimes."

Afterwards he showered and dressed warmly. He looked forward to a first full night's sleep in a week. He spent an hour on his bed reading about Emily Roebling, the nineteenth century woman engineer who completed the Brooklyn Bridge when her husband, the principal engineer, became disabled.

There was something about strong women that he admired.

"Good night, Freddy," he said to Aqualung at midnight. "You OK on the couch?"

Aqualung pushed himself upright and drained the bottle of Johnny.

"Tell me, Monsieur, if you don't give the sugar sex, why does she come here?"

"Not that it's any of your business, but I'm helping her with a problem."

"A problem? She's a nut case?"

"No."

"There's danger?"

"I am not sure, Freddy."

His heartbeat quickened, chest tightened. He checked the output from his LPR camera again. This was not a quiet country. At some point, he knew, he would stick his fingers into a place someone did not want them to be.

He recalled Aqualung's words on the first day he met Carla. *"Like you have this place, money, this life, but what is it you looking for?"*

"Why are you doing this?" Aqualung asked.

So he would solve the case and Carla would fall in love with him?

"For the money," he said.

It seemed the easy answer.

## 33

**When her head hit the pillow, Carla was asleep.** She did not wake when the lock fell out of her apartment door, or when the door was pushed opened and Quinton "Lolly" Fortuin entered her darkened Green Point apartment. His face was covered by a stocking; he had an Adidas rucksack and a headlamp. He wore motorcycle gloves, and leather shoes his friends called "brothel creepers." He had gained access to the underground parking in the blind spot of an incoming resident's vehicle then slept until midnight between two cars.

He had removed the lock of apartment 319 with a cordless drill.

Inside the warm apartment he stood and listened, tuned for movement, eyes acclimatizing to the dark. The headlamp was off. He closed the door, inspected the un-deployed dead bolt, and accepted his good fortune without emotion. The curtains were open, no moon. The apartment's view looked over the Eastern Boulevard to Duncan Dock and across Table Bay to Robben Island.

They had offered him a lock pick gun, but he had never used one. Last night he had taped the cordless drill's casing to muffle the sound and practiced his skills on a similar lock.

Fortuin had spent roughly two thirds of his adult life in Polsmoor Prison, mainly for larceny, but his most recent misdemeanor was more ominous: rape and assault of a passing jogger. He was the beneficiary of a recent pardon granted by the President.

Surprisingly, he had avoided having his face tainted with crude blue scribbled tattoos, named Chappies after the writing on wrappers of bubblegum with the same name. That way he still looked decent enough to land a gardening job two days a week at a rich foreigner's house.

He waved his hands and invoked a red flicker from the eye of a security laser. It was not armed. If it were, he did not care. But now he would have more time.

He packed the cordless drill into its casing, closed it, and returned the tool to the bottom of his rucksack.

Tonight's work, courtesy of a friend of a friend, suited him fine. He was recruited at his brother's auto electrical shop in Delft where he worked the rest of his week. The rich foreigner paid well, but this kind of money beat a day in the hot sun cutting grass and hedges. It was a grand in advance and another two when the job was done. Anything he took from the flat was a bonus. He had already spent the deposit on a week of high living.

Fortuin felt like his career was progressing. This was a planned job. He was given information. He had cased Harbor Heights the day before, discovering he could penetrate the security via the faulty front entrance or via the garage boom when a car came or left the compound. Yesterday he had used the fire escape to the third floor to check the lock type on the door. Tonight he had used the lift.

He flicked on his headlamp and followed its beam up the stairs.

The bedroom door was open. No one moved when he entered and aimed the light across the room onto a sleeping form in bed. Fortuin paused as a thrill vibrated through his body. The sheets were thrown back, and the woman was naked except for blue panties. Moving his head, Fortuin dragged the light across her body and instinctively rubbed his groin.

He knew she was attractive—he had a picture in his pocket.

He paused, listened to the sound of her breathing, mesmerized by the rise and fall of her chest, the small round white breasts like cupcakes. This was more like it, he considered. No more kicking down doors to grab a laptop or a handbag in the five minutes before the security company arrived.

She whimpered and shifted her right arm.

It amazed him how deeply humans slept. So vulnerable, all instinct disabled. From prior experience, he knew sleeping people were not easily awakened in the first hours of REM sleep. She would be shocked when he woke her.

*Make it look like a robbery.* Make it look like? It was going to be a fucking robbery. He briefly darted the light around the room, a laptop, her bag, some jewelry on the dressing table. He could not see a cell phone.

Under his coat, he had a half-meter steel cord wound around his waist like a belt. No knife. No gun. At five-foot-seven and a hundred and fifty pounds, Fortuin had been fucked up more times than he had done the fucking up. But his hands were like metal claws and his head was as hard as a coconut.

He wondered what such a beautiful woman had done to piss someone off so much.

He picked up her handbag, tipped it onto the floor, and rummaged through the contents, glancing up intermittently to check she was not waking. He opened her purse and removed the notes: three hundred rand, not much. He paused before discarding the purse then changed his mind, unhitched the rucksack, and inserted it. He added the laptop then examined her jewelry. It was costume jewelry, but Fortuin was neither informed nor discerning. He scooped up bracelets, chains, and rings and shoveled them into a pouch in his rucksack.

Lifting the stocking, he sucked in a mouthful of fresh air. The room was heated and he was perspiring. He rolled the stocking above his nose, could smell her perfume. Sexual resolve was not one of Fortuin's strong points, his predilection exasperated by smoking a variant of crystal meth called tik. If his employer had known about his previous rape conviction, he might not have been assigned.

A box of aspirin, sleeping tablets, and a half full glass of water were on a bedside table. He spotted her cell phone and pocketed it. He had strict instructions not to touch anything with his bare hands. He had watched a bit of CSI and understood the issues.

Reaching under his coat, he removed the steel cable and wound an end around each hand. He tested the grip then dropped one side of the cable and reached forward, aimed the light into her groin.

She did not move.

What a waste to kill her. But he did not have a rubber and he knew about semen and its telltale DNA. Whoever hired him had a specific plan, and if he wanted his next two grand, he could not fuck it up.

He leaned forward. If he reached out, he could touch the soft fabric of her panties.

The gloves irritated him, made him feel clumsy. He placed the cable by his feet and removed the gloves.

The lust growled at him like a hungry dog.

He pointed the light towards the bathroom. He could use tissue paper and clean up without leaving a mess.

He took a deep breath and unzipped his fly.

Then he heard her move and, when he shone his light on her face, her eyes were huge as she looked right at him.

## 34

**Carla sprang upright on top of her bed in one movement.** Fortuin lunged forward, his right hand hooking between her legs. Carla raised her left leg instinctively, her knee catching Fortuin in the socket of his eye.

She screamed, terror heightened by the outline of her camouflaged attacker in the dim light.

Fortuin tightened his grip on her crotch. She was temporarily paralyzed by the pain, lashed out with her hands, scratching, tearing at the stocking on his head.

The headlamp came off. The room plunged into blackness.

Fortuin reached behind her back with his other arm and pulled her towards him. She screamed again and fell forward against him, tearing at his face and sinking her teeth into the soft skin around his neck.

Fortuin groaned, released his grip, and grabbed her hair, ripped her off him like a doll.

She crashed to the floor, sliding across the smooth surface. She bounced up like a cat, on her haunches and crawling. Fortuin rubbed his neck, his cock sticking out his fly like a baton. He tried to grab her, but he was off balance, his soft shoes slipping on the shiny floor. She got inside the bathroom, slammed the door and set the lock, screamed as loudly as she could.

Fortuin groped for the headlamp and strapped it around his head. He bent his cock into his pants and zipped up. His stocking was ripped. The woman continued to scream.

He did not panic.

He replaced his gloves and looked around the room. Anything he had missed? Carrying the steel cord, he walked to the bathroom door and wiggled the handle.

"Help me, someone please help," she screamed.

Fortuin turned around and aimed a backward kick at the wooden door, cursed the shoes he had chosen for stealth. He did not want to unpack his cordless drill.

He attempted another backward kick, the woman's scream like a sharp pain in his head. *Jusses*, he thought, suddenly more urgent, *with this sort of noise I could be wearing my vokking Timberlands.*

He put his shoulder to the door and tested it. It was solid. Not like those pine cheapies in his house. He heard glass breaking. The woman had stopped screaming. *Vok.*

---

Fortuin put his ear to the door. There must be a window in the bathroom? He was unaware of an exit route on the third floor. He paused and considered the predicament. No, there was not a window large enough for her to climb out. She was clever. She had broken a mirror, was waiting behind the door ready to stick him in the eye. He took a breath. The bite on his neck ached. Everything was fucked up. A moment earlier, he'd been in control. Then the maniac in his pants had started crowing.

The bathroom was silent.

Fortuin groped for the light switch on the wall. He tried to orient himself. Perhaps he had looked at the wrong bathroom. Maybe this bathroom had a larger window, a window facing into the courtyard. Which way was that?

He considered whether to take out the cordless and drill out the lock. It would mean unpacking all his loot.

What if she had got out?

Fortuin hurried down the stairs leading from the bedroom into the living room. He opened the front door and peered cautiously along the corridor. Empty. He looked up. The window to the upstairs bathroom would be on the east side of the building, a sheer three floor drop to the ground.

She was still in the bathroom.

With no activity on the corridor of the third floor, Fortuin grinned to himself and closed the door. At least she had stopped screaming. He scanned the living area in the light thrown from the bedroom above.

He picked up a bronze statue and clumped up the stairs.

It was not too late.

With two hard bangs of the statue, he smashed a cavity in the bathroom door, tentatively put his hand through the hole.

She had already bitten him, he was not going to let her stab him too.

He pulled his hand back and aimed the bronze at the lock. One, two, three. The lock buckled.

Sweating profusely, he tried to lever the lock. A section of the door splintered and he looked through the gap. He could not see or hear anything. He rammed the statue again, created a wider gap, got his hand on the lock and pulled it towards him. It came away and he kicked open the door.

He wondered why she had stopped screaming.

The broken pieces of the mirror lay on the tiled floor.

A small window at the far end was open.

There was no one in the bathroom.

# 35

**Fortuin stared into the empty bathroom.** She must be a gymnast. She must have scaled the drainpipes. He hurried down the bedroom steps and exited the front door. With a bit of luck, she would be lying on the cement at the bottom of the building. He descended the fire escape, ran into the parking arcade, and peered up the east facing wall.

No way she could have climbed out the window.

Fortuin paused. She *must* be up there. Lights were turning on above. She must have raised the alarm.

He cursed and sank to his haunches. *Nee, man. This was kak.* The devil got into his head the moment he saw her naked body.

Now he was trapped. He had planned to use the woman's keys to exit the apartment block.

He straightened and adjusted the straps of his rucksack. He needed to keep his head.

Carla sprinted along the third floor corridor, banging on doors, screaming. A door opened gingerly.

"Please help me, help me."

A startled man allowed her to enter. A woman was on the phone. "We have a crisis. Please send them now!"

"Lock the door. Lock it, lock it, please!" screamed Carla.

The man locked and double bolted the door. "Are you OK? What happened?"

"There was a man in my flat."

The woman replaced the phone and stared at the semi-naked woman, scanning her body as if expecting to see terrible injuries.

"For God's Sake, get her a jacket," the woman said and eyed the door nervously. Her voice dropped to a whisper. "Is he still in your flat?"

Carla crisscrossed her arms across her breasts. She walked to the window and looked down on the street.

"I think he's down there."

The man returned with a suit jacket, slipped it over Carla's shoulders.

Outside there was the sound of glass breaking.

"What's that?" said the man, rushing to the window. The woman joined him. "Jesus Christ, we are under fucking attack here—"

Blood dripped down Carla's leg.

"Are you OK? Are you hurt? Get her a towel." The woman put her arm around Carla's shoulder.

Down below, the activity continued—a security guard running in the street, residents with heads stuck out of windows, someone shouting to the guard: *There he goes.*

Carla stood at the window and watched. The man brought a towel. The woman took it and dabbed Carla's face. She tried to work out where it came from.

"You're bleeding from the mouth."

"I think it's his blood," said Carla. "I bit him."

She dribbled into the towel then rubbed her mouth vigorously. The man brought her a glass of water.

"Go wash your mouth out at the basin."

The woman led Carla to the kitchen sink. Carla opened the tap, took in a mouthful of water and spat it out.

"What happened?" The woman gave Carla the towel.

"I woke up and...there was someone in my flat. At my bedside, I—"

Carla's face was white. The woman held Carla's arm, buttoned the jacket. Carla leaned forward and inspected her bloodied legs.

"Did he . . . rape you?"

Carla pressed the towel between her legs. "Can I use your phone?"

# 36

**Carla's face was ashen, her body convulsed.**

She was sitting on his bed wearing tracksuit pants and his oversized painting shirt, her hair damp, right hand bandaged. She jumped up and hurried to his bathroom. Le Fleur heard retching.

When he had arrived at Carla's apartment shortly after 1:00, the police were already on the scene. She was struggling to walk, would not explain exactly where she was injured, and did not want to see a doctor.

Captain Roly Phakatini aka Parks of "drain-the-dam" notoriety was running the show. A finger print technician, miraculously available, was dusting for prints.

Le Fleur told Parks about the red Hyundai with false plates.

"So you're helping in the investigation? And who are you exactly, chief?" He looked early thirties, spoke in a posh accent.

"I'm Carla's friend."

Parks noted his name, cell number, and address.

He had convinced Carla she could not stay overnight at Harbor Heights. She had asked him to pack an overnight bag. She could not face her bedroom, the bloodied bed, the smashed bathroom door. He had tossed a tracksuit, jeans, a few tops, tackies and socks, toiletries and some underwear into a blue carry bag.

When she arrived at Crystal Place, she had showered immediately. He feared she had been raped, despite her statement otherwise to the police.

"Are you OK in there?"

She returned from the bathroom, flopped onto his bed, and buried her face in the pillow.

"I can run you over to Christiaan Barnard."

The hospital named in memory of the country's famous heart surgeon was a ten minute drive away.

She shook her head.

He walked over and touched her shoulder. Three years in this apartment, and nobody else had lain on his bed.

"I'll get you something to drink." He went to the kitchen, filled the kettle, and boiled water. He returned with two mugs of sweet tea. "Sugar helps."

She sat up. Her face was patchy and streaked with tears. He sat at the base of the bed. She wanted to talk, kept repeating she had heard nothing until sensing someone in the room.

"He drilled out my lock." She hugged her shoulders. "Are you sure we're safe here?" Some color returned to her cheeks.

"I've locked the lift and the fire escape only opens from the inside. Those are the only ways in. I have cameras at both ends. If someone comes in, we'll know. And we can always seal in behind the lock downs. Then Aqualung's gone downstairs and is keeping guard. He's very concerned about you."

Carla held her hands to her face. "Shit, I can still smell his sweat." She gritted her teeth, stared at him, and placed her tea mug on the bedroom table. Then she looked around. "I don't even have a phone to call someone."

"You can stay here. It's fine. Are you warm enough?"

He used the remote to check the room temperature.

She sipped her tea. "I'm sorry I got you into this."

He looked at Carla's bare feet. It flashed a memory. Long ago. His mother. Cold, bare feet. At that age, what memories stick, what never goes away? Her voice. An old song about rain and summer and lost love. But more the aftermath, the impossible longing for the cold bare feet. The digital world was his secret place, it made time disappear. Maybe Aqualung was wrong about purpose. He was longing for reality.

"This wasn't a random incident," she said.

He snapped out of his thoughts. He felt guilty for the information he had withheld from her. Forty-four people had been murdered in Cape Town last week, nothing in the local paper except the ongoing shit about crooked politicians. Residents lived in a cross fire of violence, never believing it would hit them. He should have made a bigger issue of the red Hyundai.

"We've had petty theft in the building before, but no one's been attacked." She grimaced.

"Are you in pain?"

She nodded, looked at the ceiling, tears held back. He wanted to know where, did not ask. He fetched a box of pain killers from the bathroom, put his hand on her brow, and checked her temperature. She was cool.

"Take two."

Easy to blame the attack on random violence: wrong time, wrong place. The security at her apartment was lax. She set an alarm when she went out but not when she was home.

He did not think it was random either. Why go upstairs when you have no idea what's up there? A thief would have stayed on the lower level—her expensive sound system was untouched.

"They killed Nial, now they're after me."

He stared at her, did not respond.

She was scared, the first time he had thought that. And out of her depth.

"Something's changed," he said.

"What do you mean?"

"They could've acted months ago."

"Maybe it's something we've hit on?" Her eyes focused into executive mode, fear gone. "Nial's video security? What if someone knows of your discovery? That the footage is compromised?"

"Who could know that?" said Le Fleur.

"I haven't told anyone," she said.

He thought there were numerous possibilities—his reconnection with the hacker gang, the visit to Gorky Park and Ynez, the mention of a Stingray to NETWORX, the discussion with $CENE$TER about the missing money, his call to SUPERCHARGER about AlphaGuard. In the computer world, the problem with applying a number of fixes at the same time, you never knew which one worked.

Was it caused by something he had done, or Carla?

He rubbed the face of his cell. Parks and his men would go through the motions at Harbor Heights. Another day, another crime. No urgency, no rush to run fingerprints or view freeway CCTV's. The enforcement gang were weary, disillusioned, a sand bag dropped in the path of relentless tide.

"It happened so quickly. It was over before I realized what happened. A few seconds. But then hiding in the room and hearing him smashing down the bathroom door. That felt like hours."

"You held your nerve. It saved your life."

She had broken the bathroom mirror, tricking her attacker into thinking she had escaped through the bathroom window. It worked. When he went downstairs to check the external passage, she had gambled, left the bathroom, and hid in a built-in cupboard in her bedroom, a long shard of mirror in her right hand. The bathroom door was unlocked when her attacker smashed through it.

Le Fleur made her a toasted sandwich, brought fresh tea. Later he dimmed the light and covered her with a blanket.

He did not feel tired.

In the Chrome Room, he booted Omega. Carla's attacker had stolen her cell phone and laptop. But he had installed LapRadar onto her laptop during their previous Skype session.

He opened the LapRadar menu and her laptop appeared with the identification SUGAR. The agent software emitted no warnings so the thief would be unaware that the device was advertising its proximity as obviously as a street hooker.

On Google Earth he drilled to continent, country, city then suburb.

Delft.

He checked the configuration details and refreshed the map. There was no change.

Delft was a crime-infested suburb on the Cape Flats; houses inhabited by gangsters and drug merchants had recently been marked with red crosses by police. Dixie Boys, Jesters, Sexy Boys—not exactly names associated with corporate crime.

He zoomed in. The location of Carla's laptop indicated an abandoned landfill.

Whoever took her laptop was not interested in the data.

He turned off the under floor heating and looked into the bedroom. Beneath the cotton sheets, Carla slept soundlessly.

Returning to the Chrome Room, he clipped on headphones and tuned to Pearl Jam, a favorite album *Vitalogy*.

He took a deep breath and concentrated.

The frantic nature of the song contrasted with the calmness of his thoughts.

He chose an activity he thought may have triggered a reaction from an anonymous adversary: his lap dance with Ynez at Gorky Park.

Ynez said acting GALI Africa MD Bruno Pittman *had fat Rottweiler friends. With gold teeth.* What did she mean?

Pittman had called Ynez.

And Carla had kicked Pittman in the balls.

He used his analytic software to check the date of the call from Pittman to Ynez.

On the headphones, Eddie Vedder was warming into "Nothingman."

Next he hacked Gorky Park's web server using the password Sean Coppis scored from the barman with a cock called Mercury. He located the files containing video from the club's CCTV cameras.

The video downloaded; he checked on Carla again. She was still sleeping. He removed the empty cups and plates and took them to the kitchen.

Back in the Chrome Room, the Gorky Park CCTV surveillance had downloaded. He located backup from the day before Pittman's call to Ynez and viewed jerky black and white footage from the monitor at the front entrance. It took ten minutes to find the shot he wanted.

The screen time displayed 23:45. A clear shot showed Pittman arriving at the club. The eyebrow man . . .

Scrolling forward using footage from cameras inside the club, he spotted

Pittman seated at a round silver table. He zoomed in for a better view.

*Rottweilers.*

It was Pittman's companions that interested him most.

## 37

**The next morning, Le Fleur removed a silver attaché case and an envelope of cash from a hidden panel in the Chrome Room.** He had catnapped for two hours on the couch. He threw a change of clothes and his laptop into a rucksack then had a short discussion with Aqualung on bench no.57. Afterwards he woke Carla, called a taxi, and waited while she dressed. The taxi transferred them to a car hire at Cape Town airport where he paid for a rental car with his credit card.

By the time they reached Somerset West, Carla was asleep again on the passenger seat. His cell phone lay in the well between the seats with its battery removed.

Three hours later, he steered the rental off the N2. Carla sensed the deceleration, opened her eyes, and massaged her neck.

Inside a white picket fence, a board at the edge of a lush green lawn advertised the Garden Route Lodge.

"What's this place?" she asked and continued to massage her neck.

The rental ducked under a roofed gateway and turned into a tarred parking lot. If not for a South African flag hooked to the signboard, it could have been a motel straight out of an American movie, somewhere on Route 66.

There were three cars in the parking lot, a Castle lager sign hoisted on two poles alongside lettering advertising a cash liquor store.

He circled the parking lot, leaned forward in his seat, and looked up at the flat roof of the building, eventually parked alongside a curtained window, beneath an air conditioner box.

The receptionist, a young male who said his name was Stefan, appeared on the second ring of the bell.

Le Fleur used their real names to check in, paid cash for the room, breakfast excluded.

After settling into a musky en-suite double and setting the fan to full throttle, they left the room and walked along a dirt road towards the edge of a river.

"You sure you're OK?" he checked, his hands thrust deep into his jeans pockets, staring ahead, the cold, fresh air like a tonic. Any doubts about the size of the stakes were gone.

He was stepping through the sequence of events, a drumbeat in his chest increasing tempo like a warning, like something he had been ignoring, like something he thought impossible but now seemed obvious.

"I haven't even phoned my parents," she said. "Probably best not to worry them. My dad would want to fly down and sort everything out."

"I left your key with Aqualung. And I called a company I use for spring cleaning and maintenance. They'll sort out your apartment."

She shook her head. "I don't think I can ever go back there."

He looked down at the road, their two sets of feet walking in time.

"And I've lost all my pictures and personal documents."

"You don't have a backup?"

"I did, but it was on a portable hard drive in my laptop bag."

When he secretly installed LapRadar on her laptop during a previous online conversation, he had also made a backup of her data. He didn't mention it. At the right time, her data could miraculously reappear. Now was not the right time to update her on his transgressions.

"The cell phone data was on the laptop," she said. "Aren't you worried about it falling into the wrong hands?"

"No."

"But it's illegal data. They have access to it? And if the police recover the laptop, they'll know that the network was hacked."

He tightened his lips and put his hands behind his back. "The phone data is encrypted. It can only be read by my analytics program. The program syncs permission on the Internet. When I change the permission, which I have, the data cannot be read."

The simple encryption worked with all his data. Without his consent, his data was meaningless, every email, every text, every document, picture, video.

An icy wind whipped along the valley. They walked in silence to the white fence.

She stepped gingerly over, grimaced. "I'm not sure which is worse—my calves and quads from Table Mountain or my, uh, lower extremities from last night."

They continued to walk on alternate sides of the fence.

"Or my flipping hair. He nearly ripped my scalp off. I'm just lucky he didn't have a weapon. If he had a knife or something..."

"How're you inside?" Le Fleur stepped over the fence, and continued to walk beside her.

She looked at him sideways. "I'm numb."

He dug his hands deeper into his pockets. Why had he withheld evidence of Bruno Pittman's Gorky Park visit? Didn't she deserve to know everything and decide on the course of action? She was the client, after all. Deep down, he knew that, to solve the puzzle of Townley's disappearance, he needed to be in control, to do it his way. But in doing so, he was placing their lives in danger. And his motives? You are troubled by your purpose, Aqualung had told him. An obsessive drive to discover an answer? Certainly that was his way, in his make-up. But in this case, perhaps there was more. He knew there was more. It was more than the money for certain. Maybe it was about being a hero. Carla's hero.

"Have you got a gun, Daniel?"

"No."

"That's not good."

He shrugged. "Nobody knows we're here. And when they do, we won't be here anymore."

Something had changed. Something caused the change. Something they had discovered or gotten close to.

Bruno Pittman kept suspicious company.

"You're going to tell me the plan?" she asked.

"We have a plan?"

"I'm too sore to laugh or cry."

There was a nip in the air. They could be a couple on a late afternoon stroll along the river, absorbing the silent nature, so much of the Southern Cape pristine and undeveloped.

Carla stepped off the path into a bog on the river's edge. "Oh shit."

The water squelched into her shoes. He held out a hand and guided her onto firm ground.

"I hope it's not a bad omen or something," she said.

She did not complain about the shared room with one bathroom and two single beds. She dried her shoes with a hair dryer and he went on a mission for food. When he returned, she was asleep in her clothes, pain killers on the bedside table. He covered her with a blanket.

He ate a dubious burger and shriveled salad then hacked the Inn's pay-for-access network and connected to the Internet.

His cell phone battery remained out.

From his silver attaché case, he selected three inkpots of paint, a paintbrush, contact adhesive and a number of small devices.

He left the room, locked the door, and went to work.

When he returned, two hours later, Carla was still asleep.

He repacked his attaché, separated the single beds, and pushed his bed close to the window. He removed his shirt and shoes, lay on top of the narrow bed, and tried to sleep.

Sleep refused to come.

He wrestled with limp pillows, plumped them up, then turned onto his side. Through the dusty window, a dim light outlined the Lodge's unkempt garden.

The room smelled stale, as if something remained of everyone who had ever stayed in it.

On the N2 highway, as a truck thundered by and the floor vibrated, he considered the properties of sound waves.

If someone came for them here, he knew they had no defense.

He got up and removed a fire extinguisher from the wall and placed it behind the patio door. Then he returned to his narrow bed and tried again to sleep.

## 38

**The silence was broken by the hissing noise of a big truck dropping gears as it descended into the Klein Brak valley.**

Le Fleur lay awake staring at the ceiling, behind his eyes a vivid image of the crows in the wheat field. He tried counting them, got confused between the number of crows in the original image and his copy.

It was often in the early hours of a morning that he considered what may lie ahead in the day. He knew there was a day that would be his last, as there was for everyone. It may be a heart attack, a head on collision, an unexpected fall, a violent attack. It could be the result of destiny, error, nature, or external force. But what he always wondered was whether there would be a telltale indication, a subtle hint from the most anonymous of them all.

*When one sees a lion, one must get into the car.*

What if he didn't see the lion?

Carla's shallow breathing resonated from the bed alongside. It had been a long time since he had slept in the same room as another person. The room smelled like meat and onion.

A half-hour before first light, he shook her. She opened her eyes and grimaced in pain.

"What's the matter?" she asked, suddenly aware of the circumstances, the terror of the previous night.

"We're leaving."

His hair was slicked back. He flashed his cell, battery in, screen illuminated. She struggled out of bed and ran her hands across her body as if checking everything was in place. She rubbed her crotch.

"It feels like I've been raped by a thousand camels. Did you even sleep?"

He nodded grimly. She pulled back the sheet and stared briefly at the cold hamburger on the bedside table.

"It's breakfast on the go. I'll wait for you at the car."

He shouldered his rucksack and lifted the attaché. Outside, he placed a *Do Not Disturb* label on the doorknob.

Shortly afterwards, Carla emerged with her carry bag, looking cold and miserable. She had not showered or changed, her hair was tousled. He opened the door and she climbed inside.

"Are you going to tell me what we're doing?"

He walked over to a metal dumpster, muted his cell, and tossed it over the edge. Then he climbed into the rental, reversed, and drove under the roofed gate of the Inn, down the avenues, and back towards the national road.

At George airport, they ditched the rental and got into a mini bus.

The driver's bushy gray sideburns poked out from under a tartan driving cap. He did not smile. Daybreak was daybreak.

The taxi drove them back to the N2 then took an easterly route along the coast, past the Wilderness and Sedgefield, around the lagoon into the small town of Knysna. The trip took an hour. He paid the driver and watched him drive away.

"Are you hungry?" he asked.

They crossed to the other side of the road. Kentucky Fried Chicken was closed. Further along the road, they found an early morning café and ordered toasted sandwiches which they ate down a side street.

"Give me a moment," he said.

He walked back to the Main Road and negotiated a new ride in a taxi. They stopped for Carla in the side street, gospel music blaring through the speakers. He was fortunate to be seated against the window, Carla crushed between two large women in bright orange clothing, the uniform of their Zionist Church.

*Go away devil, go away devil, go away*, the women sang softly.

The taxi rattled up the hill out of Knysna and continued east towards the next town. It turned off the N2 into Plettenberg Bay. Opposite a petrol garage, at a carousel decked café, he paid the driver and they got out with their belongings.

"Now what?" she asked with a wry smile.

"You OK to walk a bit?"

A steep gradient descended to the ocean. Every five minutes, Carla dropped her carry bag and pressed her hand against her crotch. At the bottom of the street was a boutique hotel—once a hangout for teenagers to drink beer and make noise, now a member of some luxury hospitality chain.

He wiped his face and presented them at reception as newlyweds Mark and Sarah Parker. After an awkward discussion—he explained their wallets and cards had been stolen in Cape Town—the hotel accepted cash in advance for a premier suite for one night.

A porter showed them to their third floor room. The hotel was quiet, no sign of other guests. He took the key and tipped the porter.

"I should probably make some calls at some stage," she said. "I'm worried someone will be looking for me."

He closed the door.

"I'm going to tell you what we're doing, I promise," he said.

The suite consisted of a lounge and bedroom. Carla went to the bathroom. He opened the French terrace doors, stepped onto the narrow balcony, and looked over. If someone came in through the front door, the only escape was to jump.

Beyond the perimeter wall, a tangle of milkwoods encircled the hotel. He stared east across the bay. A thin mist coated the horizon, no wind, the sea moving powerfully, the surf roaring. A pack of gulls worked relentlessly in the thermals. The blue sky and ocean contrasted against the graph-like mountain range background. He thought of Bali Bay, the Van Gogh drying, and wondered when he would be home again.

He wandered through to the bedroom.

"Did you make up the newlywed business or was it part of the plan?" she asked. Her jeans were unbuttoned.

"What plan?"

"You see how the receptionist looked at us when I limped in? They must reckon this marriage is doomed."

The bedroom view was a panorama sweeping across the lagoon to the Outeniqua Mountains.

"Look at this." She pulled down her jeans. Her red striped panties looked like candy. "What do you think?"

He saw the blue bruises on her inside thighs.

"Not exactly the epitome of a willing bride. What was my name again? Sarah Parker? Isn't she the *Sex and the City* woman? Well, flipping good luck to you on your honeymoon."

He shook his head and looked away. She pulled up her pants.

He opened his laptop and accessed the hotel's WiFi. After a few clicks, he stepped back and turned the monitor towards Carla.

"Jesus," she said.

The screen was divided into three views of the Garden Route Lodge: the parking lot, the reception, and the inside of a room.

He adjusted the room's air conditioning then fell back on the white linen bed and, for the first time, looked relaxed.

"Now we wait."

## 39

**Opening the door of her rented Chevy, Fallon loosened the buttons of her tunic to enjoy the morning sunshine on her chest.** A light breeze shimmied through the leaves of newly planted trees on the sidewalk.

Target #2's front door was visible from her vantage point, the house address painted in white on a black bin in the driveway.

She had already established there were no dogs, no maid, and the target was a black man who exited the house at 8:45, departing in a shiny Audi which had been parked under a carport behind a solid gate. She had followed him to a Sunset Beach abode where he embraced a white man with a thin mustache and wispy hair on his chin.

She felt a sense of calm, knew it would not last. She smoothed out her stiff blue skirt. Her legs were sticking to the seat.

Money for the elimination of SUPERCHARGER had been deposited.

She was aware of the risk, shooting him in daylight. Had she been spotted? She considered ditching the Chevy. After the shooting, she escaped along a route of side streets, crossed onto the West Coast Road, and spent the night dozing in her car on a dirt road near Langebaan before returning to Cape Town.

Her new instructions on the channel from Dark Video were more complicated. There was no response to her request for a fee increase. She accepted the offer, but this wet work had a shelf life. It needed to be more lucrative if she were to expand the nest egg required to immigrate to Europe.

She had earned thirty thousand rand this month to date including five in advance for this surveillance. Not nearly enough. The rand was weak. A month's rent on a flat in Europe would cost a lot more. Her earnings would not even afford a case of her favorite Champagne.

By 11:00, the target had not returned and she was bored. She turned on the radio. The DJ was a prick, complaining about the lack of rain. Was there nothing else to discuss? The curbs of the suburb of Tableview were dry as yellow straw. She opened her car door and kicked off her sandals, rubbed her bare feet on the pavement.

A truck carrying building supplies drove past.

Tab-la-view, she pronounced, rolling her tongue over the pronunciation. Tableview, the fastest growing white suburb in Africa.

Last night, SUPERCHARGER's cell was off network until she reached Atlantis, a lost suburb of poverty and gangsterism. The cops would probably start searching there. During the long, cold night alone in her car, she had thought about Jeremy's last moments. He must have looked up and registered her presence as she approached. She did not dwell on his family without a father, a suburb thrown into horror and turmoil. She reasoned these were implications Jeremy Freeman should have considered when he set out on the activities that led to her action.

It was not as if she escaped all guilty feelings. In junior school, a classmate had created an incredible picture of intersecting geometric shapes. Each shape was perfectly scaled and drawn in a different color. It must have taken days to produce. When the class came in from break-time, the picture was in pieces on the floor, someone had torn it up. Fallon was innocent, but felt so guilty that she owned up. She told the teacher later that she had taken responsibility so the real perpetrator would feel guilty about an innocent person taking the blame. No one else confessed.

SUPERCHARGER was her third contract killing. She thought about her first and an image of a Russian stripper crept into her head and she shivered despite the warmth of the car.

She did not want to think about it. Last night in the car, she could not stop thinking about her.

The stripper crossed the wrong people at Dark Video. With a contract, if *you* did not carry it out, someone else would. It was not on her initiative that someone must die; it was someone else's bidding. It was business. That was her rationale.

Before she could distract herself, the stripper's voice was in her head again, pleading: *please, please, I never meant it, I'm sorry, it won't happen again, I'll pay back the money.* A shudder rippled through her body. She knew what was coming—the flash of a long silver blade and blood spurting from the stripper's throat like a fountain. She leaned forward and almost gagged. In prison, she had dwelt on her sordid back-story. Now she was free, the memories continued to haunt her.

Hungry and thirsty, she drove to the Bayside Mall and bought a flame grilled burger with chips and a coke and consumed them in the shop. The shiny floors and glass windows of the shop fronts looked to her like a crystal palace where princesses with money could linger and choose their prizes. She caught a glimpse of her reflection, her smart blouse and skirt, short blonde hair. She thought she looked more like an airline hostess than a realtor.

Outside a property agency, she stopped and browsed their portfolio. An ugly four-bedroom home with patchy front lawn was selling for two million rand. How many people would she have to kill to afford that hovel? She took a business card and wrote the name TRISHA FITZSIMMONS and her cell number neatly on the back.

Afterwards she returned to the Tableview address of the target. The Audi was parked under the carport.

The burger and coke had restored her confidence. Killing on contract was not the same as killing because you could not control your temper, or because you were a crazy psychopath. It was a job. Like a hooker, a housewife, a home appliance salesman. Everyone had a role, a job to do.

She approached the pedestrian gate, a distance of five meters from the front door. A vibracrete wall around the garden perimeter provided a level of protection. The Taurus, some cable ties, a bottle of chloroform, and a syringe containing ten grams of liquid pentobarbital were hidden in her handbag. The gate box housed a standard doorbell with no camera attached. She pressed the doorbell. After a short interval, a soft voice answered.

"Hello. Sorry to disturb," she said. "My name is Trish Fitzsimmons. I'm an estate agent from the Property Agency. I've got a client who's mad about your place."

The owner peered through a side window. She waved with her card.

"It's an overseas buyer."

"It's not for sale."

She laughed. "Come on. I have a killer deal for you."

"Sorry."

Perhaps the front door was unlocked. She could vault the wall and be inside in seconds.

"You don't want to know how much?"

There was a pause.

"OK. I'll put my card in your post box and if you're curious, give me a call."

There was a silence. She placed the card in the letterbox.

She knew he would open the door next time she came.

# 40

**Carla showered and emerged from the bathroom in a towel.** She reached into her carry bag and held up a lacy, impractical brassiere.

"That's the last time I get you to pack for me."

She laughed and returned the bra. He left the room so she could change. Five minutes later, she emerged in a tracksuit, a towel wrapped around her head.

"How do you do it?" She examined the images on his laptop. A view of the lodge's reception was current, Camera No.2 as if looking through the eyes of receptionist Stefan.

"I installed a whole bunch of digital video camcorders."

Each one weighed about as much as a matchbox, was thinner than a cell phone battery.

"Won't they be spotted?"

"I painted them."

She shook her head then removed the towel, shook her hair.

"Have you ever done anything like this before?" she asked.

"No."

That was untrue, he thought. He had used cameras as a secret eye on many occasions. And if she were referring to his overall plan, he had thousands of hours of practice practice outwitting opponents in online games. As long as there was no real life contact, he was in control.

"It's like you're a pro."

He turned on the TV and news headlines floated across the screen: ten people dead in a bomb blast in Brussels, it used to be Kabul or Baghdad, perhaps the little corner of Africa was not such a bad place to be after all. He switched to local news: ANC voter clashes in Polokwane, service delivery unrest in De Doorns, a businessman had been murdered in a drive-by shooting in Durbanville. He turned it off. He was aware of her eyes on him.

"You've never told me about the trouble you were in."

His eyes remained on the blank TV screen.

"Was it spamming?"

"You mean like ABSA sending out those annoying messages trying to trick customers into logging in and exposing their account details?"

She laughed. "Or telling me I'd won a million pounds on the FIFA Coca Cola lottery."

"I didn't do that."

---

"Do people actually fall for it? The authors can't even spell. Like *Congradulation.*"

"It used to be about twenty hits in a spam blast of a thousand messages."

She shook her head incredulously. "Is it easy to do?"

He shrugged. "Sure."

"How?"

"You really want to know?"

"I did Information Technology as part of my engineering course. I know the lingo."

"OK. You fire off botnets from compromised computers to spam millions of users. Then you write HTML with a form requesting details and send the result to a designated email address."

She laughed. "I suppose I asked for that. Why can't they trace the spammer's email address?"

"They use bogus addresses. Sometimes the IP addresses in the header details provide clues. It's big business. There's a top ten list of wanted spammers. International organizations like the Spamhaus project are dedicated to stopping these guys."

"So what did you do?"

He paused. "Have you heard of denial of service?"

"Sure," she said. "Like what Anonymous does when they want to shut someone up. They bomb the site with incessant traffic?"

He smiled. "Hey, you're quite good."

"So who did you shut down?"

He hadn't spoken of this in many years. Why was he telling her? He wanted to tell her. If he didn't understand himself, maybe she could.

"I shut down the big five banks."

"Jesus!"

"It was stupid. And a long time ago . . ."

"Is that when you got the X's tattooed on your wrist?"

He nodded.

"Why?"

He thought about this. Time had passed and perhaps now his understanding of what he had done was different. "Banks rip off their clients. Banks manage names and numbers in a database, but they have this hold over society. I wanted to be heard."

"A guy with principles. Nial warned me about your type. Was it worth it?"

"No."

"Why not?"

"Nothing changed."

---

He had never had this conversation with anyone else.

"Did you go to jail?"

He shook his head. "A guy called Ian Coulson heard about my problem and convinced the prosecution I could be more use to the Cybercrime organization than a prison kitchen." He paused. "I traded jail time for servitude."

"Did you say Ian Coulson? His name rings a bell," she said.

"He's the head of Cybercrime. He told me you approached him for assistance."

*Five foot eight, short blonde hair, tits popping out.* The description was stuck in his head.

"Oh, yes. I remember him. A short guy with a big mustache and roving eyes. He said he wasn't able to help."

"So how'd you get my number? What did you call me? The top cyber professional in the country?"

She frowned and thought for a moment.

"I got a message soon after I'd approached him. An SMS, I think. I thought it was him, but I guess it may not have been."

"Coulson warned me to stay out of it. Your problem, I mean." He looked at the screen of his laptop.

"Well, I think it's pretty cool to protest about something you believe in," she said and touched his arm.

He didn't move. Pretty cool, huh. His father was in his head. I think she likes you, kid. You better make a move. Her hand remained on his arm. He felt a light perspiration on his brow. This wasn't his game. He had no feel for real life moves or clever pick up lines. He imagined turning towards her, reaching out, a mistake, her shock, her pulling away. What are you doing?

She removed her hand as Stefan, the reception at the Garden Route Lodge, came into focus on the laptop.

"Christ, it's like a morgue there," she said. "We must've been their only clients in weeks. Are you sure this is going to work? What if my attack was a coincidence? It's not the first intruder we've had in our block."

He shrugged. "Then no one will come and tomorrow or the day after, we'll fetch my cameras and go back to Cape Town."

For lunch, they ordered room service. Carla chose sirloin and chips and he went for the famous Cape Malay bobotie.

Ten minutes later there was a knock at the door.

"That was quick," she said.

He froze. No defense. No escape. He crept to the door. "Who is it?"

"Room service."

*Too many movies*, he chided himself, *too many flipping movies.*

He met the steward at the door, tipped him, and took the tray.

They ate in the lounge at a narrow table with a vase of porcelain roses, his laptop strategically positioned above the second TV.

The speedy arrival of lunch had rattled him. He did not want to be surprised in this room—there was nowhere to go. He mentally retraced their movements to make sure he had not missed anything. His cell was in a dumpster outside the Garden Route Lodge, and he had not used a credit card since Avis. No one could link him to this hotel.

Not yet anyway.

He had used his laptop on the Garden Route Lodge WiFi and again in Plettenberg Bay. The open connection was accessible to an eavesdropper. An expert could isolate the device and trace his location. Not any expert, but an elite hacker who could break impenetrable firewalls, launder money across the world, build and deploy a Stingray.

Someone like him...

"If nothing else, this is making me feel a whole lot better," she said, waving greasy hands.

He agreed. The bobotie was a smooth curried lamb mince with a thick crust of custard and yellow rice.

Halfway through the meal, his laptop beeped. He stood and toggled each of the hidden cameras. On Camera No.1, a car had pulled up to the cash bar.

False alarm.

## 41

**Le Fleur stared out at the vista sweeping from the sea to the lagoon and the island between.** "If this was the French Riviera, they'd stick up a Nikki Beach on the sand island and make millions in season."

"I like the sound of it," she said. "You've been to France?"

"I've watched the travel channel."

At 16:15, a white panel van drove into the parking lot and triggered the surveillance alarm on his laptop.

They came in off the balcony and into the lounge.

The occupant remained in the car and the angle of the sun prevented a clear view on Camera No.1.

Ten minutes later, the driver exited the panel van. He had a beard, shoes without socks, a shirt with alternating gray and green panels. He stretched and yawned, gazed at the entrance to the Lodge, checked his watch, then returned to the panel van.

"Is he a person of interest?" she asked.

"He looks like a local waiting for his skelm to arrive."

He picked up the lunch tray and placed it outside the door. He checked the passage. There was no sign of other guests on their floor.

When he returned, the driver of the panel van was visible through the windscreen. He looked like he was eating a pie.

Le Fleur was restless. He walked onto the balcony. An offshore wind muffled the noise of the sea, smoothed the surface into rows of swells.

At 16:35 his laptop beeped again. Two men entered the revolving doors of the Garden Route Lodge. Camera No.2 above the reception desk detected their movement.

On Camera No.1, the panel van driver looked like he was sleeping. His head tilted to the passenger's side.

He toggled between Camera No.1, covering the parking lot, and Camera No.2, the reception. The panel van had fallen into shadow. A red Hyundai was parked at an angle beneath the trees in the distance.

His heartbeat accelerated immediately.

"Here we go."

The two men had entered through the vendor's entrance and avoided Camera No.1.

"How do you know?"

He magnified the Hyundai's rear license plate and captured a still image.

"My LPR cameras in Bantry Bay captured this Hyundai. It has false plates. I told Captain Parks."

He shifted from the car to the men.

"This is like watching a damn scary movie." She pressed closer. "How far away from them are we?"

"We're fine here, don't worry. It's over an hour's drive."

The men approached the reception desk. One wore a black leather jacket, open and flapping. The other had a blue V-neck jersey. Both were short and stocky. Except for skin complexion, they could have been brothers.

"Recognize them?" he asked.

She shook her head. "What's he's carrying?" She tapped the screen, indicating an object in the hand of the man in the leather jacket, held below the counter.

He zoomed in on their faces and captured still pictures, saved them in jpegs. Leather-Jacket had a shaved head, V-Neck tight peppercorn locks. Their hardened faces were grim. They looked like men who would only be stopped by an automatic rifle.

In jerky motion, Leather-Jacket reached into his pocket and produced a document. He handed it to an unseen receptionist, probably Stefan who had received them yesterday.

After a short interlude, Leather-Jacket recovered the document and pointed across the hallway then turned back to the receptionist for confirmation.

"He's given them directions to our room," she said in a hushed tone. She put her fingers in her mouth.

V-Neck pulled out a cell, flipped back the lid, fingered the keys, then spoke into the receiver. Even the way he spoke looked brutal.

Le Fleur clenched his fists. He knew his plan was working.

"What's he holding?" repeated Carla.

He zoomed in on the object, a yellow bar that looked like a device for locking the steering wheel of a car.

"What the fuck is that thing?"

"It's a cattle prod," he said.

## 42

**On Camera No.3, inside the room Le Fleur and Carla had rented, the door exploded and the two men they had seen at the reception of the Garden Route Lodge stood behind the debris.**

"Oh my God!" Carla screamed.

They were a hundred and twenty kilometers east, watching the act via three concealed mini-cams.

Carla flinched and squeezed Le Fleur's arm. She glanced towards the door of their hotel room then back at the screen of his laptop.

Leather-Jacket had destroyed the hotel door with a single kick. It crashed to the ground, a hole where his boot had made contact, the hinges and lock still in the doorframe.

"Room service." Le Fleur tried to be cool, but adrenaline surged through his veins.

"Jesus. Do you think there could have been two in my apartment?"

"Modus operandi." He pointed at the smashed door in picture. "These guys use Merrel Razorbacks not lock drills."

The cattle prod in Leather-Jacket's right arm projected a robotic appearance. V-Neck's arms extended outwards as if carrying poles under them. The camera aimed directly into their faces as they stared through the doorway at the empty room.

"Can you imagine, *imagine*, if we were still there." She shivered and hugged her shoulders. Le Fleur touched her arm. He felt the same fear she was experiencing. Like watching your own murder. Except...it was evolving exactly as he had planned.

V-Neck stepped inside and rounded the unmade bed, disappeared from view into the bathroom.

"What's on the bedside table?" asked Carla.

"It's the burger I bought you last night."

V-Neck reappeared with an expression of disappointment and resentment, spoke to his accomplice, arms open in a gesture of failure and anger. Leather-Jacket scanned the passage as if anticipating someone's arrival.

Carla held out her hand. "Look how I'm shaking."

V-Neck bent and checked under the bed, threw open the cupboard, pulled out empty drawers.

"That guy's face...Oh my God...He's a killer." Carla's voice was a whisper. "We must call the police."

Leather-Jacket scowled in the direction of the cam. Le Fleur held his breath, hoped he would not spot the thin device gummed above the curtain rail.

V-Neck pulled out his cell. He flipped back the lid. It was an unusual phone. Like a Motorola or a Sharp. V-neck spoke into it like he was addressing a walkie-talkie. After a brief discussion, he snapped it shut and tightened his lips.

"We can trace it?" Carla said, half question, half statement.

Le Fleur nodded.

V-Neck pulled the sheets off the bed, lifted the pillows. He smelled the sheets. His face was devoid of emotion, as if he could never experience happiness. He stepped away from the bed and conversed with his partner in the doorway. Then they turned and walked away from the chalet.

"What about Stefan?" she said. "Shouldn't we warn him?"

Camera No.2 recorded their reappearance at reception. Without hesitating, V-Neck removed a weapon from under his shirt and pointed it towards the camera.

"Oh my God!" she screamed, held her hands to her head. "He's going to shoot him. He's going to shoot him."

Le Fleur froze. The terror of the on-screen violence was worse than any movie he had seen. This was real, this was live.

In his free hand, V-Neck waved what looked like a photograph. There was cold malice etched into his face, mouth barely moving as he berated the receptionist.

Le Fleur wished there was sound to the video. He captured a still of the screen.

"That's the picture he showed when they came in. He's trying to determine where we went," he said.

"Jesus! Please don't shoot him."

V-Neck pocketed the photograph and waved the gun threateningly. His head bobbed as he spoke, increasingly urgent. Then he advanced under the camera, seemed to lean over the counter and grab something.

Leather-Jacket was busy too. Camera No.1 activated as he emerged from the Lodge and sauntered across to the pie eater in the white panel van.

"Doesn't look friendly," said Le Fleur.

"What's he doing?"

"They're making it look like a robbery."

Leather-Jacket transferred the cattle prod to his left hand and pulled an object from his jacket pocket and held it to the driver's window of the van. The window exploded with broken glass.

"Oh no, no, no..." Carla moaned softly and covered her eyes.

## 43

**The video continued to stream.** In the parking lot of the Garden Route Lodge near Mossel Bay, a leather-jacketed gangster smashed the window of a panel van, pulled the driver out, attacked him with a cattle prod, and robbed him. The gangster was joined by his partner and they sped off in a Red Hyundai.

Carla opened a gap between her fingers to create a safe window of vision. "What's happening?"

Camera No.3 displayed a frozen image of the room they had slept in last night, a broken door kicked in by the gangster's razorback.

On Camera No.2, a dazed looking Stefan, the Lodge's receptionist, ventured out from behind his counter and peered through a window into the parking lot. He retreated and disappeared from view behind the reception counter.

On Camera No.1, nothing and no one moved. It looked like a scene from a cheap movie, a forlorn dusty car park and a prostate man beside an open car door.

"Is he dead?" she asked.

"He's moving."

Reducing the live window, Le Fleur scanned back through the footage, isolating identification shots: faces, car registration, cell phone calls. He created two clear mug shots of the attackers.

Carla paced back and forth, clenching and unclenching her fists.

"This is madness. Is this what happened to Nial?" She brought her hands to her heart. "Did you think this would happen?"

He stepped back from the laptop and stared through the windows at the Outeniqua Mountains.

He had set a honey trap and the hoods had come stumbling in.

"I've got him," he said quietly.

"What?" said Carla.

"Look at these guys." He referred to the digital images of the gangsters.

"I don't need to look. I'll never forget those faces."

"Now look at this."

On screen, he displayed a sharpened black and white picture, three men seated around a silver circular table. The place was Gorky Park. The man on the right with the dark and light eyebrows and intense expression: Bruno Pittman.

"Where'd you get this?"

---

He tapped the screen indicating the character on the left most side of the table. Carla stared in disbelief.

"Oh my God, that's the guy with the cattle prod."

"Ynez told me Pittman was hanging with gangsters at Gorky Park. She called them gold-toothed Rottweilers. These are shots from the club's cameras."

"They're with Bruno Pittman! I can't believe it."

She breathed in and out. Her face was flushed with shock.

A tap on the door startled them. Le Fleur sat upright. Carla clutched his arm.

"What's that?"

He placed a finger on his lips and walked into the lounge. Carla followed, tiptoeing behind. The French doors were open, the sunset casting a golden hue over the ocean.

Another knock.

"Who is it?" he called out.

"It's room service."

Carla put one hand to her mouth, grabbed him with the other, her nails digging into his arm.

"Shit, Daniel. I'm so scared."

Could someone have traced his laptop on the hotel's WiFi network? A cracker would have to poll every hotel and internet café within a three to five hour radius. He reckoned forty-eight hours minimum.

"Go onto the terrace," he whispered. "If something happens, jump over."

She glanced out the window, shook her head vigorously. "Are you crazy?"

He pressed against the door frame. The gangsters made short work of the chalet door at the Garden Route Lodge, but this was solid teak.

"We didn't order room service," he called out.

"It's a turn down service, Mr. Parker. And I have a bottle of sparkling wine for the newlyweds."

He exhaled. "Sorry, uh, we're not dressed. Can you leave it outside?"

"Certainly, Mr. Parker."

He listened for departing footsteps. Carla's hands were on her hips, face blotched with anxiety, body trembling.

"This is a fucking nightmare. Let's call the police."

He retrieved the sparkling wine and placed it on the lounge table. Carla was still shaking. He went to the bedroom, fetched his jersey, and gave it to her. She pulled it on. "Did you hear me?"

"We can call the police. But that'll be the end of it."

"What do you mean?"

"Those guys are gangsters. It's likely they're wanted for a dozen other crimes. They're probably out on bail. They'll get locked up and their trial will run in six months."

She swallowed hard. "If we go to the police with what you have found out, they'll find these guys are working with Pittman."

"Yes, then in six months' time, you'll be a witness saying how they followed you and they broke the door of a room we'd been staying in."

She stared at him.

"The video won't be admissible. Two gangsters may or may not be convicted. Pittman will go to ground and we'll never know what happened to Nial."

She frowned. "You've seen what these people do. You'd risk your life for this?"

"I don't think of it like that."

She hugged her knees beneath her chin. "I'm not sure I can handle this." Her eyes brimmed with tears.

"Do you trust me?"

"Of course I do. But I'm so shit scared."

On Camera No.3, a local police van pulled into the parking lot. He checked his watch: an hour and fifteen minutes since the gangsters departed. The driver of the white panel van was semi-conscious beside his vehicle. A motel staffer had laid a blanket over him, and put a pillow under his head.

"I'm so freaked out."

"You can call the cops. I'm not going to stop you. You're the boss. If you want out, then—"

*I'll exhaust every resource I have to get to the truth.*

"It's not about wanting out."

She could not look at the screen, what was seen could never be unseen. He continued to monitor activities at the lodge. An ambulance arrived and medical orderlies attended to the injured driver.

"It's too dangerous, Daniel. At what cost? Our lives? We don't know how deep it goes. Is it Pittman? Or the whole of GALI? It's not worth it."

*I will never give up searching for the truth.*

"Look, someone with the ability to break through AlphaGuard compromised Nial's surveillance. Someone manipulated his cell phone reception with a Stingray device. Those are highly specialized skills. Pittman did not act alone."

She clutched her head.

"Jesus, I sat in meetings with that murderer."

---

He went to the bathroom. Carla's discarded clothes were on the floor, jeans, t-shirt, and candy-striped panties. When he returned, she was standing in the bedroom.

"Are we safe here? Can they trace us?"

He was suddenly exhausted: four nights, no sleep. He removed his shirt and collapsed on the edge of the bed.

"They don't know we recorded the attack. That's our advantage."

"But what if they find us? Jesus, you saw what that guy did."

He stared at the light on the ceiling. "We're safe tonight, I promise. We'll move tomorrow."

She stared at him, bit her fingernails.

# 44

**No moon. The bay was in darkness.** The crashing waves were a constant reminder of a powerful unseen force. He pulled the balcony door shut and flicked on the kettle, his thoughts clouded by fatigue.

"I can't stop thinking about the cattle prod," said Carla.

"There will always be even more fucked up shit than what you just saw."

"What's that supposed to mean?"

"It's rule thirty-six of the Internet. Do you watch *South Park*?"

"No. I don't get it at all. What's the catch? It's a bunch of vulgar cartoon characters debating American crap. I hate that show." She lay on one side of the bed. "Why'd you ask?"

"I was thinking about it. There's an episode in Season 3 when Eric Cartman gets poked with a cattle prod while singing Christmas carols."

"I don't want to hear it. I don't want to think about it. I'm trying to delete it from my head. Jesus, what kind of animal is that, who are these people we live with in this country?"

Le Fleur decided not to show her Cartman's rendition of *O Holy Night* on YouTube. He had watched every program for the first fifteen seasons. Then he stopped. About the same time he called time on online gaming. He turned his wrist and looked at the pale blue crosses.

Carla shifted her position and grimaced in pain, reached for the painkillers. The kettle boiled and he filled the cups. He placed the tea by her bedside and looked at her. He felt a sudden desire to hold her, to feel her body against his. He bit his bottom lip. Sleep. It was sleep he needed. Sleep until his thoughts were clear.

If there was a choice between solving the case or being with Carla?

He sat on the bed, wished he was here in different circumstances, with time to indulge. He lifted his teacup and rubbed the rim.

"There is something I must tell you." He took a deep breath. Stored and boxed in compartments of his memory, there was a story he never intended to tell anyone. She looked at him intently.

"You're scaring me."

"A long time ago, I was involved in a group called JACKER. We met on the 4chan random bulletin board. It's a completely anonymous, untraceable online space. Our target was a crook by the name of Carlos De Palma. He was selling sick videos over the internet."

His voice was low and monotone. He ran his hand along the stubble on his chin.

"I was an idealist. The internet is mankind's most important invention. People like De Palma shouldn't be allowed to subvert it. We wanted to bust him, wipe him off the Net because conventional justice was impotent when it came to getting rid of filth like him."

Carla stared at him.

"There were seven of us, originally. We knew De Palma was a deviant running an online site called Dark Video."

Lack of sleep, the shock of events at the Garden Route Lodge. For a moment, he hesitated, wondering if he should proceed.

"I don't understand. Does this relate to Nial?"

"We were a consortium of hackers that wanted to make a positive difference. But the members had different agendas. One guy, THEDUKE, started being cagey with information and acting strangely, like he was the ringleader. It was THEDUKE who established that Dark Video was Carlos De Palma and that he was hiding out in a place called Yarrow Point in the USA. THEDUKE even started doing business with him, making videos."

"What sort of videos?"

"Sex and death and violence. Bad stuff, believe me. A deep, dark web. Then THEDUKE disappeared. We suspected he was murdered by a Dark Video hitman. That was five or more years ago. We went underground. I mean, we were clever kids, but we weren't used to dealing with killers."

"Murdered?"

Carla shifted her pillows and he touched her leg briefly.

"We were reduced to five because another guy, Richard Walker— WARLORD—died mysteriously before THEDUKE disappeared."

"How?"

"He overdosed in a crack house in Salt River."

Carla frowned. "Cape Town?"

"Yes. JACKER was Cape Town based. We've got some of the best IT skills in the world. Google and Microsoft have software development departments in the city."

"What happened to this De Palma?"

"De Palma was running an international network of wealthy clients. He never kept physical records. We hunted him day and night. We pulled billions and billions of bytes of internet transactions searching for patterns his software sent out. We played along with him, writing his code, assisting with technical matters, but all along we were outing his clients and screwing up his business."

"Did you get him?" she asked.

He rapped the back of his hand into the palm of the other.

"We destroyed him. We created a list of his clients and got our hands on his cash."

He paused as if waiting for Carla to ask him about the money. She did not.

"Why are you telling me this? What's Nial's disappearance got to do with him?"

"After we destroyed De Palma and Dark Video, there was dissent. A hacker called ZAPPER wanted to take over the Dark Video client network for commercial gain."

She narrowed her eyes.

"I walked away. I exited the group and removed every trace to Dark Video."

"I still don't understand."

"These hackers have the skills to achieve a sting of this nature. SUPERCHARGER can break through any firewall, NETWORX owns the cell networks. The transfer of Supertech's money is similar to how $CENE$TER shifted De Palma's cash from Dark Video's offshore accounts."

"You stole De Palma's money?"

"We repatriated it."

"To yourselves?"

"Yes."

Carla paused, stared intensely at Le Fleur.

"That's why you've never been too interested in claiming your fee from us?"

He did not answer.

"And it's not really the paranoid Swiss who own your apartment?"

"No." He rubbed his hand over his unshaven face.

"And what was your handle in this...gang?"

There was an edge of disapproval in her voice. But the overriding tone was disbelief.

"CRACKERJACK."

"What does it mean?"

He sighed. "I was known as a master hacker. I can break codes, control hidden cameras..."

"Do *you* have the skills to have done this?" Her voice shook as she asked him.

He imagined how she must feel. Attacked in her flat, now alone and isolated with him, until recently a stranger, but someone she trusted.

He reached forward, put his hand on her upper leg, and looked into her eyes.

"I guess I do."

# 45

**In his consciousness, morning did not arrive, it was always there.** His first thought was fragments of dreams and nightmares, about fields and crows, of cartoon characters, of Carla and warmth and companionship. He remembered waking once, aware of her closeness, her arm resting across his hip.

When he woke and adjusted to the bright light shining through the window, the first thing he noticed was the silence in the room.

"Carla?"

He reached across and knocked a glass of water off the bedroom table.

"Shit."

He rubbed his face, the safety in dreams replaced by reality. The gangsters' attack at the lodge. His revelation to Carla about JACKER.

He checked the bathroom. Empty.

"Carla?"

He unlocked the patio door and stepped onto the balcony in his boxers. The grass embankment was empty. Had she gone to breakfast? In the distance, low tide strollers were hunting for pansy shells in the shallow water. He could not identify anyone resembling her.

She would not go anywhere without telling him.

It was 9:30. He could not believe he had slept so long. Or so deeply he had not heard her leave.

He dialed the restaurant on the hotel phone and enquired whether Mrs. Parker was at breakfast. She was not.

Opening the room door, he checked the empty passage.

He closed the door. The unopened bottle of sparkling wine stood on the table. He returned to the bathroom. Carla's discarded clothes were still on the floor. The shower was dry.

He pulled on his T-shirt and picked up his laptop. The webcams at the Garden Route Lodge were intact. The broken door had been removed but not replaced.

He phoned reception. It rang and rang.

*Relax*, he told himself. *Any minute now she'll bounce through the door.* Any minute.

An ominous beat filled his head like a concert of dread.

Last night, she was terrified. He did not believe she would leave the room without waking him.

He tried to dismiss thoughts of kidnapping as paranoia.

---

It would all be resolved.

In a few minutes.

What if she had panicked as a result of the story he told her last night? Perhaps she was with the cops now, telling them the story, about Carlos De Palma and JACKER, identifying him as a suspect in Nial's disappearance.

*Do you have the skills to have done this?*

He took a deep breath, bit on his lip, and evaluated his choices.

He connected to the hotel's WiFi. The router was weakly protected; he used its settings to hack back into the server. The server's security log showed no obvious breaches. They did not have any visual surveillance software and he had not noticed a camera at reception. When he opened the hotel's incoming email box, his eye spotted an email delivered at 2:50 from SATSA, the South African Tourism Services Association. The header said: SAFETY ALERT. HAVE YOU SEEN THESE PEOPLE?

Heart pounding, he opened the email and scanned the text.

```
Hotel management is requested to keep
a look out for the two people in the attached
photograph. They are wanted for questioning
by police in Cape Town. They are believed to be
traveling between Cape Town and Port Elizabeth
and may have checked in under false names.
SAPS request they be detained by hotel security.
Anyone spotting them should contact the below
number, quoting case 464.
```

He opened the attachment, a picture lifted from a CCTV camera at Cape Town airport, taken as they left the rental offices. He suspected the email had been sent to every hotel on the SATSA database.

He phoned reception again without success.

He checked the email status. It had been read at 8:15.

He identified the hotel's telephone management software and searched the log for outgoing calls. There was no record of anyone phoning the bogus email contact number from a hotel phone.

He transferred the email onto his laptop and deleted it off the hotel's server then returned to the bedroom and picked up his jeans.

He went out into the passage and checked the front parking lot through windows in the passage. There were only three cars in front, no movement.

Returning to the room, he looked up a list of local shuttle services then called Dolphin Shuttle on the hotel phone.

He had to hurry.

"I need a shuttle."

"Yes, sir. Where to?"

"Uh. What's the next town, holiday spot east of here?"

"Excuse me, sir?"

Le Fleur zoomed in on a Google map. "St Francis Bay. How far is that?"

"Yes, sir. It's about an hour and a half."

"That's perfect. Can you fetch me now?"

"Now?"

"Yes."

"Let me check availability. Can you give me a moment?"

The voice returned promptly. "We can send someone in fifteen minutes."

He gathered Carla's clothes and toiletries from the bathroom and bundled them into her carry bag.

If the front reception was blocked, the only way out was over the patio railing.

He checked his watch. It would take an hour to reach him from Mossel Bay, the closest town to the Garden Route Lodge.

He got back onto the net and burrowed through a number of proxy servers. He had wanted to solve the Nial Townley case without the authorities. He zipped the video footage from the lodge together with the still pictures of the red Hyundai and clear impressions of the two gangsters. He added the pictures lifted from Gorky Park, linking Bruno Pittman. He attached a note to Ian Coulson from Cybercrime.

> Ian, I may be in trouble. I've been helping
> Carla Vitale track Townley. She was attacked in her
> apartment. These guys tried to kill us at the
> Garden Route Lodge. Can you notify Captain Parks
> at Hawks urgently? Carla's disappeared and I am
> very worried. Will make contact again soonest.

Coulson would be disappointed he had gone against his word. But he would help immediately.

He sheathed his laptop and slipped it into his rucksack.

He walked back onto the balcony. Seven layers—sea, sand, lagoon, land, mountain, cloud, and sky. His eye traced the line between them, some layers distinct, some melting into one another. He felt the panic. If he ran, was he leaving Carla in the lurch? How could he best help her? Perhaps if he drew their pursuers onto him?

He used the hotel phone to dial the contact number on the fake email. It rang twice and was answered by a machine. A robotic voice said:

```
Please leave a number and message where you
can be contacted.
```

He waited for the beep then killed the call. He left Carla's carry bag in the bedroom. He lifted his rucksack and attaché case. He slung the rucksack over his shoulder and exited onto the balcony.

The last time he had gone over a precipice he broke his wrist. This drop was steeper, but he was prepared.

He climbed onto the railing.

He was about to jump the three meters onto the grass below when the door opened and Carla walked in.

# 46

**Fallon had target #2 tethered, his hands and feet bound with cable ties to the posts of his bed.** She unbuttoned his shirt and ran her nails lightly along the smooth brown skin on his chest.

"What's going on?"

"Welcome back," she said. "I thought I'd lost you to sudden sniffer death."

Richard Chinkanda coughed and exhaled abruptly from his nose.

"What have you done to me? Who are you?"

She had arrived early. Morning was for optimists, a least expected time for crime.

When he opened the door to Trish Fitzsimmons from the Property Agency, she had bashed him on the head with the butt of the Taurus then used chloroform to knock him out. She had dragged him to his room—he was surprisingly light, she estimated a little more than a hundred pounds—and strapped him to the bed with cable ties.

She looked at her watch. She had only applied a drop or two, but he was behaving like she had driven a truck over his head.

While he was unconscious, she had moved her car inside the solid gate behind his Audi and hidden from road view. She had searched the house looking for a safe, had not found one. On his laptop, she found an open spreadsheet with four individual sheets. Each sheet was labeled with a name and cell phone number and contained rows of dates, times, cell numbers and co-ordinates.

But what caught her attention was "R5M REWARD," the title of the spreadsheet. So she photographed each sheet with her cell phone and waited for Chinkanda to rouse.

"Are you JACKER?" she asked and examined her fingernails.

"I don't know what you're talking about. I'm a photographer. You can check my portfolio."

His cell rang. The ringtone was "Drunken Sailor." She checked the screen. The caller was Damien.

"It's Damien."

Chinkanda struggled against the ties. "He'll be looking for me."

"Tough on Damien." She wiggled her fingers. "Is he the guy with the Vandyke on his chin?" She went to the window, raised the blind, and peered through. She had no Plan B. If anyone came to the house, she would shoot them. The cell stopped ringing.

---

"You've got the wrong guy. I don't know what you want with me. Take my money, my wallet's in the lounge."

She ran her hand along a large poster featuring a meshed network of connected globes.

"Who do you work for?" she asked.

"Nobody. I work for myself."

Her instruction was to retrieve some gear called a Stingray and terminate the target. Fallon was never one to follow instructions to the letter. She had already spotted a locked black briefcase she suspected housed the Stingray.

She returned to the chair alongside the bed, removed the Taurus from her studded bag. He sucked in his breath when he saw the weapon.

"No, no, please—"

"I didn't come here to play Tetris. There are some things I know and some things I don't. I'm going to ask only once, OK?"

Chinkanda moaned softly.

"I don't know what you want from me. I don't know, please."

She cocked the gun.

"I'm sure you've heard the story about the guy trying to find his way to heaven. He comes to a junction where he has a choice of two identical paths. One leads to heaven, the other to hell. He doesn't know which to take."

She ran the nozzle of the silencer along his lip.

"There's an angel standing at each path. One only tells the truth, the other only lies. He can ask only one question. You get it? So, I know some things and I don't know others. Here's your problem. I'm not a fucking angel. You tell the truth every time. Then you'll live. You'll see Damien again and suck his cock like a dummy. You want that. Don't you?"

She pressed the Taurus lightly into his crotch.

"Who are you working for?"

Chinkanda closed his eyes. "I don't work for anyone specific. I have clients."

She twirled the half-cocked Taurus. "Are you sure, Richard? Are you sure? This game ends with the wrong answer."

Chinkanda pulled at the cable ties binding him to the bed post.

"Who orders cell phone records from you? Give me names."

"I-I get lots of orders. I promise. I don't...I swear to God, I swear. Clients contact me for information about cell phone calls and I get the data. I d-don't ask questions."

She breathed in and out slowly. An update in last night's Argus newpaper reported robbery as the motive for the Jeremy Freeman drive-by. It was believed his assailants followed him in a car. *Assailants.* That was good news.

She jammed the silencer against Chinkanda's top lip, the hard metal pressing through the flesh against his upper teeth. He twisted on the bed in terror.

"No prizes for you, Richard. Think of Damien. You don't come through and he's going to be bending over for some other dude's cock."

"I don't know what you want, I swear. I work for lots of people."

He took a deep breath through his nose.

"In the next thirty seconds, when your brains are leaking onto the perfumed pillow beneath your head, don't think whoever you're protecting is going to be grateful."

She moved the gun nozzle over his face like she was performing some facial procedure, alternating the pressure. Chinkanda closed his eyes and whimpered.

"Do we understand each other?"

He nodded. She slipped the weapon into the back of her skirt and fetched his laptop. She sat on the bed alongside.

"I need you to explain something to me."

The four sheets of the spreadsheet were labeled:

```
LE FLEUR
CARLA VITALE
LE FLEUR'S LIST
TOWNLEY
```

She clicked on the latest coordinates of the LE FLEUR sheet and a map of the South West coast appeared, a flashing star illustrated some hotel near Mossel Bay.

"Who is this Le Fleur?"

"Look, I don't know what you want, but I'll pay you. I haven't done anything wrong, I—"

She leaned over and thumped her fist on his chest.

"Will you shut the fuck up, you sniveling little freak. Shut up and listen. I ask the questions and you answer, do you get it?"

He nodded.

"So tell me, Richard, who is Le Fleur?"

"He's a f-friend, a hacker. He's somebody I know."

"A cyborg? What's his handle?"

---

"It's, uh, CRACKERJACK."

"Is he also known as JACKER?"

"J-J-JACKER? What are you talking about?"

"You heard exactly what I said. Who is JACKER?"

Chinkanda's body heaved. He grimaced and coughed.

"Look, I...whatever you want. J-JACKER is not a person. It's an organization."

Fallon lit up. "An organization? What does that mean?"

"There were number of hackers involved in JACKER."

Fallon frowned. If Chinkanda had not known who she was, mention of JACKER must have alerted him. That JACKER was many hackers was a revelation. She wondered if Dark Video knew.

"Was there someone called SUPERCHARGER in JACKER?"

Chinkanda closed his eyes tightly. He gritted his teeth. "Yes."

"And you're NETWORX?"

He nodded feebly.

SUPERCHARGER, NETWORX...Fallon looked back at the meshed poster on the wall. She suddenly got it. Her assignment was deleting the group of hackers who had acted against Dark Video in the name of JACKER.

"You said 'a number of hackers involved in JACKER.'"

"I-I don't know how...how many exactly."

"Is Le Fleur, CRACKERJACK, one?"

"Yes."

Fallon pulled a face. She did not fancy knocking off hundreds of nerds.

"Careless of you to leave this spreadsheet open, Richard."

Chinkanda was struggling to breathe.

"What does it mean? I gather this coordinate under LE FLEUR, Lat S 33.57, Long E 18.22. That's his residence. What work do you do for him?"

"He wanted phone records. Look at the sheet called LE FLEUR'S LIST, you'll see. He asked for those numbers. It has nothing to do with me."

"Why did he want the numbers?"

"He didn't say."

"I don't care what he said. Why?" Her voice sharpened.

"I think it's something to do with Nial Townley."

"Who's he?"

"He's a missing person."

"Missing person? Is Le Fleur some fucking detective?"

"There's a reward out. Five million."

She whistled. So that was the meaning of the name of the worksheet. Five million would buy her a new life faster than killing hackers.

"Are you looking for him? Townley?" she asked.

"No. I swear. I get the information and pass it on."

"So why are you following Le Fleur?" She tapped the pages of coordinates. "This is his cell, his movement."

Chinkanda paused.

"Think carefully before you lie to me, Richard. Someone's going to be heartbroken when the money stops arriving in Llilongwe."

"A client wanted a trace on Le Fleur. And on Carla Vitale."

Fallon tabbed between the four sheets."So Le Fleur is both hunter and prey? That's dishonest."

None of this interrogation was in her instructions.

Under the TOWNLEY sheet, she had noticed a set of emboldened coordinates. A linked comment had the words "No.12" written alongside. She held the laptop in front of his face.

"What's this?"

Chinkanda made an effort to examine the page.

"Why's it in bold? No.12. Why's it important? What's it mean?"

"I-I-It's the number of a flat."

"What's the address?"

"They're coordinates."

"And so?"

"It's an address from which I got a number of calls from a client. I thought maybe the . . . the client—"

"The client tracing Le Fleur?"

He nodded.

Fallon bared her teeth. "And you circled the 12. It's important. No?"

"I don't know?"

She banged the Taurus lightly against his temple. He screamed.

"I don't know."

"Listen, Richard, I know you may be scared about what your other boss can do to you. But look at me, and believe me when I tell you, there's nothing scarier than this. When I let you go, you can run away with your boyfriend and hide. If I let you go. So why'd you circle it?"

"I-I sometimes like to know who I'm dealing with."

"That's not good enough for me, Richie-Rich."

"I thought...maybe something happened to Nial Townley at that location. There was activity in the week he disappeared."

She grinned. "So you do ask questions?"

She replaced the laptop, walked to the window and checked outside. Everything was quiet. She pointed to a black briefcase behind a chair. "Is the equipment in the briefcase?"

Chinkanda was shaking, sobbing softly.

"What's the code for the lock?"

He recited the sequence. She unclipped the latches simultaneously and looked inside. "Jesus, this is a Stingray? What does it do?"

"It tracks calls." He paused. "It's recording your cell phone right now."

She smiled at him. His eyes were wide, wild.

"Tracking me, huh? There are agents waiting outside and ready to pounce? So I better not do anything naughty? I'm not a fool, it's turned off."

She examined the device, a number of boards with indicator lights, some attached devices, a pop up aerial. She assumed the device marked WD was a hard drive. There was a USB port, probably for connecting a monitor or downloading information. Her instruction was to deposit the device into a safety box in Roggebaai.

"Tell me more about Nial Townley."

"I—" Chinkanda hesitated.

Fallon raked her nails down his chest.

"Don't think, Richard. When you think then I think. And I think you're lying to me. Talk! Talk, talk, talk!"

"I-I didn't know it at the time, I swear. I was paid to tap a line. I didn't know it was Townley's phone. I never listened to the conversations. I only passed them onto the client."

"And the client was Le Fleur?"

"I... No...I don't know. I don't know who the client was, I swear. They used an anonymous channel and all communication was encrypted."

"Carry on. You tapped Townley's line?"

"I only found out later it was his. Nobody told me, I promise you. I worked it out from the reports. I don't get involved in the client's matters. I can't afford to."

"You've said that. Is Townley dead?"

"I don't know."

She banged the Taurus against his forehead and he screamed.

"Tell me, Richard. Tell me everything. Talk until I tell you to stop."

"I don't know, I swear. I-I am...was required to tap his line for about a month. On the...on the day he... disappeared, I blocked calls to his line. I diverted a call to his cell to another cell."

"Why?"

Chinkanda took a deep breath.

"I-I think they wanted to make it look like he was somewhere else. And they didn't want him getting through to someone. I think his wife."

"You did all that using this contraption?" she asked in amazement.

"I'm not the only one, I swear," he said. "There are other Stingrays. There are others involved—"

"You know where Nial Townley is." She said it as a fact.

"No."

"Le Fleur knows?"

He paused momentarily.

"No...Yes...Maybe he does. He requested the cell phone records."

She strolled into the ensuite bathroom, dropped the toilet seat, and urinated. For a moment, she considered her course of action. Could Chinkanda be an ally? Could he help her find Townley and share the reward? She watched Chinkanda raise his head, struggle against the cable ties.

She flushed and returned to the room.

"What are you going to do to me?" he asked, voice shaking with terror.

She pulled out a pair of gloves from her bag. Then she removed a syringe, held it to the light, and flicked at the point of the needle.

She did not want to share the reward with him.

## 47

**"You look like you've seen a ghost," said Carla.** He appeared from the balcony with his rucksack and attaché case, and rubbed his hand against his heart.

"Where were you going?" she asked incredulously. She had a brown paper packet in her hand.

He closed his eyes and breathed in, disbelief turning into relief as he realized that Carla was safe.

"What's the matter, Daniel? What's going on?"

"I thought...I'm not sure what I thought. I thought you'd been taken."

"Taken? Oh my God." She closed the door. "I couldn't sleep with the pain. As soon as it got light, I walked into the village to find a pharmacist. I left a message for you by the bed."

He looked at her.

"You didn't get it?" she said. He shook his head.

She walked through to the bedroom and returned holding a piece of wet paper.

"It must've been knocked off the table. I'm so sorry. I was in agony."

"We must get away from here," he said.

They slipped out the hotel and waited for the shuttle at the edge of a fisherman's path cut between thick Milkwoods. He told her about his SOS to Ian Coulson and the fake email from SATSA.

"I don't think it's a bad outcome," Carla spoke in a hushed tone. "We had to involve the police. Pittman must be stopped."

He looked at the time on his watch. What if the shuttle failed to arrive? Other than going back into the hotel, he had no way of contacting the service. He knew that calling the number on the fake email would have triggered a reaction. How quickly would they move?

Eventually the shuttle arrived, half an hour later.

"I need cash up front, boss," the driver said.

He paid and tossed their luggage into the vehicle.

"Where're we going?" asked Carla.

"Away from here."

The shuttle chugged up the hill towards Main Road. He looked at her and shook his head slowly. She patted his leg.

As the shuttle reached Main Road, a red Hyundai, wheels screaming, turned down the hill.

---

"Oh my fucking God," said Carla.

Le Fleur closed his eyes momentarily. Next they would trace the shuttle service from his call on the hotel phone. He tapped the driver on the shoulder.

"Stop here."

The driver slowed and pulled to the side, spun around in surprise.

He peeled off five R200 notes.

He said to Carla: "Is there anything important in your carry bag?"

She shook her head.

"Leave it here," he said and turned to the driver: "We're getting out. You must take our bag to the hotel in St. Francis Bay. Don't stop for anyone."

The driver looked at him as if he was crazy.

"Which hotel, boss?"

He looked at Carla.

"The St. Francis Hotel," she said.

They boarded a nineteen-seater Baz Bus traveling west on the national road, in the opposite direction to the Dolphin Shuttle. Carla was pale. Her pain killers were in her carry bag in the Dolphin Shuttle. Le Fleur rested his head against the window.

Outside it was hot and sunny. Eager young travelers on the bus, a hop-on, hop-off culture, operated within their own social bubble.

In Knysna, the bus stopped for passenger interchange. Two guys in khaki pants boarded, faces glowing from a recent bungee jump. Chewing gum, they walked down the aisle, high fiving fellow backpackers.

"God, it's hot in here." Carla flapped her tracksuit top. "I can't take it off, I've got nothing underneath."

He sniffed an armpit, had not showered or changed clothes since they left Cape Town.

She looked at him and smiled: "Hell of a honeymoon, hey?"

Shuttling across the Knysna lagoon, the khaki pants brigade attracted attention, pointing out the defunct site of Crabs Creek, reminiscing over drunken memories.

"What the fuck do we do now?" said Carla. "We can't keep running."

Le Fleur pointed ahead in the direction the bus was driving.

"Let's give Ian Coulson another hour. If I know Ian, he'll already have a tail on those gangster's phones. Once we know they're in custody—"

"What about Pittman?"

He shook his head.

"I imagine Parks will take him in for questioning and that'll end his ability to direct the gangsters. How is it possible that Pittman ended up in Cape Town?"

"I think it's obvious. GALI put him here. They must've had Pittman up their sleeve from the start. I remember months before Nial and I met Schroeder and his team and Pittman didn't seem to fit in at all. Shouldn't I phone Gavin? When he hears what GALI have done, he'll bring in the fucking army."

"I don't think it's a good idea."

"You don't trust Gavin?"

"I didn't say that. Let's wait until I've spoken to Ian."

He shuffled in his seat. He had a strange feeling in the pit of his stomach. He could not immediately identify its origin. It was not fear, not excitement, more likely it was disappointment for panicking when he could not find Carla. He had blown the advantage of surprise and lowered the chances of uncovering what happened to Townley and the cash.

A girl across the aisle dropped her water bottle. Carla retrieved it and handed it back. The bus joined a short queue at a stop-go sign for road works near Sedgefield.

"Where are you guys going?" the girl said. She and her female companion were dressed like twins in matching check shirts, faded blue jeans, arms heavy with bracelets, bare feet.

Carla shrugged her shoulders and glanced at Le Fleur.

"It's a surprise," he said.

He unsheathed his laptop and shielded the screen from the sun.

Connecting via 3G, he opened the bogus email sent to the hotel and inspected its metadata for information regarding the source.

He used his sleeve to wipe dust from the screen.

"Nice one of you in your going away outfit for the album." He showed Carla the picture taken outside Avis.

At the back of the bus, the khaki pants guys were in party mood, a bottle of Old Brown sherry going hand to hand. The countryside alternated between forest and agriculture.

The email had passed a spam test, but the return-path—a Gmail address—differed from the sender's name.

He clenched and unclenched his fist.

The bogus email traveled five hops originating from a webmail in New Zealand. A seven-minute delay existed between the first two hops. He inspected the sending system's machine name and compared IP addresses. The details of the second sender machine was fake, the point where the email had been falsely injected, probably from a dial-in account.

The user agent was Roundcube Webmail, the content type text. It was the character set, GB2312, that caught his attention. The GB2312 set was used for representing simplified Chinese characters. Whoever sent the email had encoded it using a non-standard keyboard.

He put his hand over his mouth and blew into it. Carla's eyes were closed, her head resting against his shoulder.

ZAPPER was an expert in Chinese.

Throughout JACKER's campaign against Dark Video, the hacker known as ZAPPER had maintained absolute anonymity. ZAPPER was responsible for making Carlos De Palma believe he was interacting with independent parties—South African hacker, a German software scientist, or a Chinese Defense Council member. There were times when he had thought $CENE$TER or SUPERCHARGER could be doubling as ZAPPER. They probably thought the same about him. After the downfall of Carlos De Palma, ZAPPER wanted to extort the Dark Video client base for financial gain. When he exited JACKER, he never heard from ZAPPER again.

The bus passed an informal township on the side of the road and he looked at his watch.

Pittman did not act alone. Could ZAPPER be the technical mastermind?

The next stop was Fairy Knowe Backpackers in the Wilderness, the national road cut between the town and the sea. Carla stiffened as the bus applied brakes. The khaki pants guys got off, nobody got on. A former Prime Minister once lived in the Wilderness. Le Fleur could not remember the name, maybe Botha.

Raucous laughter erupted behind them. A girl was imitating a demonic dance impression. The girls sitting across the aisle were playing Gin Rummy.

The bus set off again.

"Every time we stop—" said Carla and cut off the sentence. He knew what she meant.

He nibbled on his top lip. The Dolphin Shuttle would be in St. Francis by now. How long before the gangsters realized they were chasing a shadow? How long before Ian Coulson got the police onto them?

A red car flashed past the window, a Toyota.

The girl alongside opened her handbag, removed a tin of deodorant, and sprayed under her arms.

"Do you mind if I borrow that?" asked Carla.

She slipped it under her tracksuit and gave herself a blast then offered it to Le Fleur. He hesitated then took it and gave himself a shot.

"How do you read Ynez?" asked Carla after passing back the deodorant.

"Do you think her story's genuine? That Pittman's pursuing her? Or is there something more to it?"

Le Fleur did not know the answer. He pictured Ynez in her blue lingerie. He liked her, but that was her expertise?

"Like she's involved?"

"I wouldn't put it past GALI," she said. "She had an inside track on Nial."

"Why doesn't she like Gavin Marx?" he asked. He had looked up the word Ynez called Marx. It meant dickhead in Spanish.

She shrugged. "Probably because he won't pay her what she wants. Gavin doesn't like her, that's for sure. He never did. Nial used to act like a naughty boy. I mean, what the hell was he doing with her? She probably knew exactly who Pittman was. She smells money from a mile. If she wasn't already involved with GALI, she probably made the first move on Pittman."

Le Fleur's gaze swept across another settlement of tin shacks without registering, his mind deliberating the possibility that Ynez was involved with Pittman and conspiring with a gang of hackers? They wanted to eliminate Carla because she was getting too close? Possible? Probable? He sighed as he recognized the irony of his thoughts. For a person accustomed to exactness and certainty, his reason was increasingly clouded with emotion and gut feeling.

His eyes returned to focus and he registered the Garden Route Lodge on the left side of the road.

He tapped Carla, but her eyes remained fixed at her feet.

## 48

**Fallon dragged Chinkanda's lifeless body through the house, out the kitchen door, and onto the backseat of her Chevy.** She covered him with a blanket from his house.

She returned and stripped the bed. She remade it with fresh sheets then packed clothes into a duffel bag, leaving some on the floor as if he had been selecting outfits for a holiday. She added a toiletry bag, his wallet, laptop, and the Stingray suitcase to the bag.

Damien called again and left a text message. She read through a history of previous interactions between Chinkanda and Damien then texted back:

> Can't talk now. With a ☺ client. Will call as
> soon as I'm free, probably later this afternoon
> R xxx

She wiped areas she may have touched before putting on gloves. Then she loaded the bag and soiled sheets into the boot of the Chevy and ordered a taxi on Chinkanda's cell phone.

She locked the house. Another twenty grand in the bag and a five million reward to chase. She drove the Chevy out, parked around the block, and waited until Chinkanda's cell registered the taxi arriving.

A few minutes later, the taxi driver called Chinkanda's cell.

She did not answer. She waited until the taxi driver canceled the trip then removed the battery from Chinkanda's cell.

She planned to dump the body at Langebaan, but changed her mind. She reckoned a floater in the lagoon would be sooner identified than one in the bushes. Between the road signs for Grotto Bay and Jakkalsfontein, she pulled onto the dirt road of a remote private nature reserve and hid his body beneath foliage in a thicket.

She was driving back when memories of her second contract killing disturbed her thoughts.

The target was a reformed pedophile who drugged young girls in clubs. She had lured him from the Poseidon Bar and Grill and shot him with a Sigsauer P238 Lady in an abandoned parking garage in Woodstock. Not because she disapproved of his lifestyle choices, but because he was competing in her client's space. When she tried to imagine how he must have felt, lying on the concrete floor of the parking garage, knowing his life was over, she sensed only his sadness; he did not care about dying, there was so much darkness in his life, his death was a mercy.

It made her feel like she'd done him and the world a favor.

On returning to the sea front, Fallon shopped for groceries at the local supermarket. When she arrived at Sea View Holiday Flats, Fabrice was at reception. And a small face peeped from behind the counter.

"And who are you?" Fallon crouched and made eye contact with the little girl in a pink dress, striped ribbon in her hair.

"This is Francine, madam," said Fabrice.

Fallon put down her packet and reached out a hand but Francine shied away, clutched onto Fabrice's leg.

"Francine. Your little girl?"

"Yes," he said. "Say bonjour to Missus Fitzsimmons."

"She's too cute. Where's her mother?"

"She's not around anymore."

"You look after her?"

"My mother does, mostly, when I am at work. But she had to go to the hospital today."

Fallon reached forward and touched the little girl's cheek with the back of her hand, a strange emotion rising from deep inside.

"Francine," Fallon whispered. Then she looked at Fabrice. "She is loved."

Fabrice laughed. "Yes, she is! Her mamie spoils her."

"You're a lucky girl, Francine."

In her apartment on the seventh floor, Fallon took aspirin to quell a pounding headache and updated NETWORX's Facebook status:

SURPRISE. HOME TO MALAWI TONIGHT.

A missing black man who said he was returning home to Malawi. Good luck filing that one with the local cops, Damien.

She closed her eyes and lay on her bed. She thought about Francine downstairs with the pink dress and ribbon, the brown skin, and the wide eyes. Her father answered phones, opened doors. But Francine was cared for. Fabrice loved his daughter. Francine had a mamie that spoiled her.

She dozed for half an hour and when she arose she messaged Dark Video—the job was done, she would deposit the Stingray the following day. Later when she checked her bank account, she had been paid the full tranche for the latest hit.

Next she took a bath. There was a warning message pressed under her door about water restrictions, but it did not mention anything about a bath. She lay in the hot water with a cloth over her face and tried to cleanse her thoughts. She tried to imagine little Francine's life. She pictured Francine running down dusty roads with tens of laughing friends. She pictured her swimming in a nearby river. But her thoughts kept returning to what she had done. There was something about her last assignment that she never wanted to repeat. It was too deliberate, too drawn out. The previous contract killings had been swift, no time for the imprints of horror to set inside her brain. She had earned twenty-five thousand and a lifetime of Richard Chinkanda's terrified eyes to relive in her dreams.

She considered her options.

Her new role at Dark Video was blunt and unsophisticated and did not exploit her special skills. She was a role player with the ability to manipulate people. She had technical computer skills. She was used to dealing with rich executives in the posh suburbs of Bishops Court and Bantry Bay, interfacing between the clients and barmen in Cape Town nightclubs. Popping hackers in Tab-la-view lacked finesse.

And the funds were coming too slowly.

Her goal had not changed. The sooner she could acquire the cash, the sooner she would leave.

She hadn't decided what she would do in Europe, but she thought selling luxury holiday apartments to wealthy tourists was a possibility.

After her bath, she dressed and spent the rest of the day reading about Nial Townley's disappearance and examining Chinkanda's worksheet of coordinates.

Five million ZAR. She realized that this could be her special opportunity.

She unlocked the Stingray's suitcase and carefully inspected the device. She considered turning it on, but was concerned her attempt would register, and Dark Video would identify she had tampered with it.

She fetched her toolbox and carefully unscrewed the hard drive from the casing. She unclipped the cable connecting the drive to the main board.

She figured the hard drive could contain valuable information.

She connected the drive to her computer and downloaded its contents, made a copy on a flash drive.

She then reconnected the drive to the Stingray and locked the briefcase.

The following morning, she delivered the Stingray to the designated safety box in Roggebaai.

Any stress she felt from yesterday's hit had dissipated by the time she cruised slowly along Victoria Road scanning for an address referenced by Chinkanda's coordinates.

The guy called Le Fleur.

She spotted Crystal Place and continued for half a kilometer. She turned into a driveway, reversed and doubled back, arrived on the seaward side of the road. She ramped onto the curb, unwound her window, and peered up at the white building.

This Le Fleur lived in a palatial spot.

She grabbed her handbag and exited the Chevy. There was a strong smell of kelp coming off the sea. She crossed the road and examined Crystal Place's entrance. Four numbered name tags appeared alongside the buzzers. None of the identifying names on the labels said Le Fleur.

She noticed the front door of the apartment block was damaged. She pushed the door with the toe of her foot and it opened.

Inside the foyer, she examined the locking mechanism of the glass door. It looked like there had been a burglary.

She went outside and pressed the buzzer for No.1.

A woman answered.

"Hi, I'm looking for an old friend, uh, Mister Le Fleur. Is this his place?"

"He's No.4," the woman replied curtly.

Fallon pressed No.4.

She waited a few minutes then tried again.

No answer.

She re-entered the building, caught the lift to the fourth floor. As the lift opened, she hesitated. She reached inside her bag and touched the Taurus for reassurance then walked slowly along the carpeted passageway towards the door of No.4.

The front door of No.4 was damaged, the lock broken.

She stepped back.

It looked like a trap.

She turned and took the lift back to the foyer, exited the building, and crossed Victoria Road. Inside her car, she sat and thought.

Both locks broken and doors damaged.

She was startled by a sharp rap on the passenger window. A vagrant flattened his nose against the glass. She touched her heart and breathed out: "Go away."

He did not go, rapped again then lumbered around the front towards the driver's side.

She wound her window and locked the door. "Fuck off."

The tramp ignored her, continued to knock, rolling his hand as encouragement for her to open the window.

She considered flashing the Taurus.

The tramp pressed his face directly against the window.

She patted her handbag, mimicked a gun with thumb and index finger.

---

"I'll fucking shoot you."

The tramp lifted his fist to his mouth, balled his tongue in his cheek in pretended fellatio.

She chose to drive away.

She was cautious when dealing with people who had nothing to lose.

## 49

**Ian Coulson's fat black Lexus was parked on a yellow line, street side parking taken by police and civilian cars.**

He ripped a pink ticket off his window, balled the fine, and tossed it into the road. A pair of Oakley's rested on the dash. Even right outside a police station, Le Fleur thought Coulson was lucky not to have his window smashed.

Coulson wore an oversized blazer wrapped around his waist like a blanket, a white tieless shirt, black jeans, and brown boots with heels. He spat out a piece of gum and removed a pack of Gunston and a silver lighter from his jacket pocket, pressed the pack straight to his lips, and sucked out a cigarette. He lit up and snapped the lighter shut, leaned against his car.

"Ah, that's fucking better," said Coulson.

Le Fleur gazed at the Dutch Reformed Church at the end of the street. He had never needed religion, now he was not sure. The road was clogged with pedestrians and cars, a gateway between the trade on Main Road and the suburbs.

Coulson looked at his watch.

"I've got to fetch wifey in half an hour." He made a wavy hand sign and showed off the fat gold band on his ring finger. His finger nails were long and manicured, definitely not a vegetable gardener. "You know it's my third time. I never learn." He slapped his hand against his forehead. "In the beginning, they're like puppies wagging their fucking vaginas all day long. Who can resist?"

The tip of the Gunston glowed red and the lines around his mouth tightened.

"Then after the honeymoon, they grow up and the puppies become dogs."

Le Fleur rubbed his hands together. His belly was empty and his mind detached from his body.

"I'm guessing you don't mean loyal and dependable," he said.

Coulson blew out a mouthful of smoke, eyes twinkling. "Mean and mangy and always scratching for cash."

"Sounds like you're a candidate for a gender appreciation course, Ian. Are there any women at Cybercrime these days?"

"Not a nipple. Sad that."

Le Fleur looked towards the entrance of the police station. Carla was still inside with Gavin Marx in consultation with Parks and other senior police officers. He looked at his watch: two hours.

"How's that hysterical cunt lawyer of hers? What's his name? Marx?" Coulson fiddled with his blazer. "You see his imported suit? It's got a baton sewed in the pants for anal penetration."

He sucked in, blew out.

"You reckon she's balling him?" he asked.

Le Fleur did not respond. He was replaying what he was told about events of the last two days. Gavin Marx had tried urgently to reach Carla the day after her attack at Harbor Heights. When he could not, he raised the alarm. Captain Parks was in possession of Le Fleur's cell phone and address and when *he* could not contact anyone, the police went ape shit, storming his Crystal Place apartment like it was a hostage stand-off. Meanwhile he was cruising on a slow Baz Bus back to Cape Town with Carla, arriving at Crystal Place to a ransacked apartment with smashed doors.

"What's the damage like?" asked Coulson.

Captain Parks took full responsibility, did not blame anyone. SAPS would pay for repair of the damage. He gave le Fleur his personal cell number and told him to call if he ever had a problem.

"The worst is they threw my security guard in jail for the night."

"Security guard? He's a fucking hobo."

"He works undercover."

Coulson reached forward and squeezed Le Fleur's cheek. "You're a funny guy."

A police transport van rumbled down the hill.

The good news was the two gangsters involved in a robbery at the Garden Route Lodge were in custody courtesy of his photographic evidence.

"Who says the police aren't doing their job?" said Coulson. "How'd you like Parks's accent? He's a little Transkei boy who went to a private white school because he can run fast and catch a rugby ball. Now he's a mover and shaker. He moves goalposts and shakes pockets."

"He seems like a pretty decent guy to me."

"They all do," said Coulson.

"Well, at least they got the gangsters."

"At least."

The gangster with the cattle prod was Sparky Peterson, a notorious Cape Flats gang member. The other one was Short Donkey Martin.

"Rumor has it Sparky killed his cousin in a fight over a cell phone. I hope you've got your passport handy. These guys don't play around."

"Will they get bail?"

"Have sharks got waterproof asses?"

---

"What about the other guy you said they arrested?"

"His name is Fortuin. It looks like he's your little darling's midnight visitor. He tried to sell her cell to an undercover cop. What a fucking bingo. And he happens to work in the garden of one Bruno Pittman, MD or whatever, of GALI Africa. So the police got a double whammy."

Coulson inhaled deeply.

"Has he implicated Pittman?" asked Le Fleur.

"No, but come on, what are the odds? He said he got his instructions from some guy in Delft. Place your bet that guy is Sparky Peterson?"

Coulson mouthed out a slow smoke ring.

"This isn't our circus, Le Fleur. I warned you. You hear about Jeremy Freeman? The best firewall cracker around. Bang, bang. Shot dead outside his home."

Le Fleur's heart jumped. Coulson's eyes met his.

"You hadn't heard?"

"No. I spoke to him last week. About the AlphaGuard. Remember, you gave me his number."

"Sure I remember," said Coulson evenly. "Look, these are some dangerous fuckers. Hell man, you see that beautiful woman...Carla. Then you imagine that animal with a steel cord around her neck. I hope they hang Pittman by his balls."

Le Fleur closed his eyes momentarily.

"What about the email from SATSA?" he asked.

"If I didn't know better, I'd say you wrote it yourself." Coulson laughed. "It hit every hotel in the Cape."

"You telling me they're training cyber thieves on the Cape Flats these days?"

"I'm not telling you anything, my friend. You tell me." Coulson inhaled as if he was trying to absorb the entire nicotine stick in a single gasp. "What do you think of the lawyer's theory?"

Gavin Marx had immediately approached the Commercial Branch with allegations GALI manipulated the Venezuelan government to withhold payment to Supertech to weaken Supertech so they could take them over.

Coulson continued without waiting for an answer to his question.

"I was chatting to colleagues at Commercial. They reckon this could be the biggest case since the Arms Deal. They're apparently already moving on informants in Venezuela who'll testify GALI bribed Government officials. Have you read Karl Lombardy's report?"

Le Fleur pulled on the leaf of a palm tree that hung over the tennis court fencing separating the park from the road. Gavin Marx was accusing GALI of a massive fraud. Ironic GALI would post a reward to solve *their* crime. Perhaps it was part of the subterfuge. They could settle the reward out of the money stolen from Nial Townley. He shook his head.

"You've got to read Lombardy's report," Coulson continued. "He's an investigative journalist who's made a life work researching GALI. GALI have been doing everything they can to shut him up. He's compiled a pretty volume on their shady dealings. Jaw dropping shit."

Le Fleur rubbed his face. Coulson sucked hard.

"I think it's a case of join the dots. GALI wants Townley's empire. So they bust up his business in Venezuela, when it doesn't effect change at the desired rate, they go to Plan B and get rid of him and steal the money. What do you think?"

Le Fleur shrugged. "Where's Pittman?" he asked.

"He's out of the country."

"That's convenient."

"Very. The corporate jet, I bet? I don't even know if we have an extradition policy with Austria. You must read what Lombardy has to say about him. The guy's a psychopath. Don't know how he hasn't been locked up yet."

"So who tipped him off?"

Coulson shrugged. "Not sure if anyone did. He's been gone for a week. It makes sense he's away while Sparky deals with the loose ends."

A car sloshed past. It struck Le Fleur suddenly the road was wet. The sky was overcast, the air thick.

Across the road, they watched Carla and Gavin Marx walk briskly out the police station exit and along the pavement. They hopped into Marx's car, a green Range Rover.

Coulson's eye twinkled. "You get a little bit of that?"

Le Fleur shook his head.

"Sorry to hear it. Tell me again, so you're holed up in a honeymoon pad and you think she's run out on you?"

He looked down and scraped his feet on the pavement. Then looked at Coulson and nodded slowly. "She'd gone to the pharmacy for pain killers."

Coulson laughed. "It probably saved your life. I know you. You go for gold, Le Fleur. You're the prince of virtual reality. You must catch a wake up, this is the real deal."

The Range Rover punched into a stream of traffic and headed up the hill. Coulson patted him on the arm, a thin smile drawn across his face.

"Anyway, lighten up. So the princess says no and you live happily ever after. Drive fast cars, go hunting, fishing, fuck cheerleaders in the ass, drink Captain Morgan. Life is short."

Coulson took a last drag then ground the stompie into the tarmac beneath his boot.

Across the road, two bergies argued over the contents of a black plastic bag.

"Are you going to leave this thing alone now?"

Le Fleur did not respond. Even if he wanted to, he knew it was not going to leave him alone.

The black plastic bag ripped, empty bottles clattered to the pavement, a verbal tirade ensued. A passing cop van noticed the scuffle, sounded a short blast on the siren.

"Let the investigation take its course. I suggest you keep a low profile."

It sounded more like an order than a suggestion.

Coulson beeped the alarm and hoisted himself into the Lexus then held his fist to his mouth like a telephone. "I'll send you Lombardy's report."

## 50

**Le Fleur picked up the dice and juggled them in his right hand.** He leaned over the backgammon set. A pot of baby potatoes was boiling on the stove. The weather was pressing against the windows, but rain was still a tease. It seemed an age since the drama down the coast.

Actually, it was three days.

He rolled the dice and moved the brown counters. He placed the dice on opposite sides of the board so he could remember whose turn it was.

He felt a strange sense of dissatisfaction. He wanted to solve the puzzle. Now there was a formal process to find the truth, but like so often, the process would grind the truth to dust.

Dissatisfaction. Was that all he was feeling? He stood up and stretched, reluctant to confront what he knew was his truth. A sense of purpose. Of being involved in a dangerous assignment on behalf of someone he had feelings for. Feelings. Feelings of companionship. Or more? For three days and three nights, he and Carla had been inseparable, bound by their mutual fear. He had reached out to her and shared his secrets.

He walked across his apartment and checked the front door. The ground floor entrance to Crystal Place was still unsecured. Ditto his apartment door. He kept the remote nearby and wedged a stopper under the door to prevent it being opened from the outside.

He returned to his seat and completed the game. Brown again. On a piece of paper on the table, Brown led White by seven games to three.

He removed the pot of potatoes. Potatoes and butter and salt, famine food but it was all he felt like.

He looked at his new cell. He had received a message sent to Richard Chinkanda's friends from someone called Damien:

> Anyone with information about Richard,
> please contact me urgently.
> Please, please, if anyone hears anything.

*I suggest you keep a low profile.* Ian Coulson had warned him.

Carla phoned while he was eating supper.

"Are you OK?" she asked.

"I'm fine."

"I'm sorry I haven't seen you. We've had a full day with the guys from Commercial on GALI's malfeasance. Gavin is at their throat. I think we're

---

going to go through the night."

He cleared his throat.

"I want you to know how grateful everyone is for your help. None of this was possible without you," she said.

"Many thanks," he said.

She paused. He thought he heard her chuckle.

"'Many thanks' sounds like you're signing off an email. Anyway, we're going to nail those fuckers. We've got teleconferences with government, Reserve Bank officials, Austrian Fraud unit. We're going to take back Supertech."

"That's good."

"Gavin said we've paid your invoice. I wanted to check you got it?"

"I haven't checked. Oh, but a mountain bike was delivered. I assume it was from you?"

"Yes. I hope it's OK? The guy at the shop said it's a bike made of dreams. I thought it seemed fitting. You deserve some dreams."

"Thank you. I . . . . It's very kind of you. You didn't need to."

"I want you to know that what you told me—about the hacking, Dark Video—I won't tell anyone."

Le Fleur remained silent.

"I'm doing this for Nial," she said.

"Yes."

After the call, he checked his front door was wedged. He looked for Aqualung on the benches below, but he was not there.

He was thinking what to do next. Perhaps go away, somewhere far away, lie on a beach in the sun, watch the happy tourists, eat a lot, forget, forget about Carla and Supertech. *You deserve some dreams.* He closed his eyes. Did she have any idea *what* he was dreaming about?

Last night he had dreamed that they were back in Plettenberg Bay, not a dream of gangsters and fear, but of him and her, walking on the beach, hand in hand, bare feet in the shallow water.

He could sense Jake Le Fleur's amusement. *What a joke you are.*

He wandered into the Chrome Room and sat in front of his server. He reached out and touched the keyboard. Twenty years of this reclusive life in a digital world. It had saved him, filled his hours, days, nights.

He connected to the news24 website and read about the murder of Jeremy Freeman aka SUPERCHARGER. He thought about the loss of knowledge, loss of expertise, but it paled to nothing when he read: survived by his wife and two kids. *These guys don't play around.* Ian Coulson warned him.

He opened his email and looked for the message from Coulson. It was titled: KARL LOMBARDY GALI REPORT. The attachment was eighty-five pages and undated:

> In 2009 GALI purchased a 100% stake in a
> family business in Colombia called Estructural
> Ingenieria Colombia. The Arango family had
> managed the firm since 1964. In 2008, EIC was
> plagued by a year of trade union unrest.
> Shortly after the GALI acquisition,
> a paramilitary group infiltrated EIC and
> murdered three union board members.
> Other union members were forced to either
> resign from the union or leave EIC.
> The Arango family claimed GALI management
> influenced trade union unrest prior to
> the acquisition to strengthen their bargaining
> power. Once GALI owned the company, the
> Arangos alleged, they used the paramilitary
> to crush the unrest.

Screw it up, then buy it and fix the screw up. The wrongdoing was similar to Supertech allegations.

> In 2011, GALI purchased ATT Ingenieros with
> 80 employees to broaden services in Chile.
> The majority shareholder Industria de Ingenieros
> had been forced into bankruptcy after the
> Government enforced a collaborative pricing
> judgment. A group of shareholders brought an
> action against GALI for manipulating the market
> and creating negative conditions to reduce
> the purchase price.

Ditto.

Lombardy's report exposed dealings of numerous senior GALI officials, some toxic characters, more fitting of a Sicilian mafia than an international engineering firm.

He scanned the articles for names he recognized. Willie Schroeder was clean, so too the other shiny egg heads.

Then he found Bruno Pittman.

> Pittman was born in Vienna, son of a wealthy
> property baron Julius Pittman who was friends
> with the founder's son Martin Loidl.

Lombardy's research was meticulously recorded with detailed references. He provided feedback from Pittman's school reports. He had been expelled twice for unspecified anti-social behavior.

> According to Pittman's CV, he studied civil
> engineering at The Upper Austrian School of
> Engineering in Wels and graduated in 1991
> [2014/ref 2118]. In the official records at the
> university, there is no record of his attendance
> after 1989.

As Le Fleur read the report, he became increasingly amazed how Pittman could ever have landed such an important job in Africa.

> In 1992, Pittman was investigated after a woman
> went missing in Vienna. Pittman had been dating
> her and was allegedly the last to see her alive.
> A friend of the woman claimed "he (Pittman) had
> a terrible temper and once he banged her head
> into a wall outside a nightclub." No conclusive
> evidence was found and Pittman was never
> charged. [2013/ref 18]

> Pittman joined GALI in 1995 after a failed
> attempt to start his own company selling
> imported liquor. Based on correspondence
> Pittman sent to a colleague [ref 2104/561],
> he found work at GALI "excruciatingly boring"
> and that he felt "they had no job for him,
> other than to honor Loidl's loyalty to
> his father."

The research continued, documenting a litany of poor performance, multiple assignments and re-assignments across Europe. Pittman had married. His wife had filed and dropped a domestic violence claim. He was divorced and remarried. In Austria, he faced tax evasion. He was divorced a second time. Two further cases of reported domestic violence had been unearthed by Lombardy.

```
In both cases, the claimant had been encouraged
to drop charges [ref 2008/262, 2009/112].
```

There was record of a civil case lodged by a neighbor who claimed Pittman had attacked him with a golf club. It was settled out of court. One chilling paragraph read:

```
In 2011, Pittman was arrested by Bulgarian police
while serving as Vice President of a new GALI
subsidiary in Sofia. He was suspected of
association with a Bulgarian underworld boss
who was linked to an assassination attempt
on a senior Government member. Pittman was
released on bail. The police stated they had
insufficient evidence to hold him.
GALI withdrew Pittman from Bulgaria.
```

No wonder Coulson considered him a psychopath. He wondered whether Carla had read the report yet.

He re-read the document. Illuminated under Lombardy's meticulous microscope, the shocking pattern of corporate abuse emerged. Afterwards he googled Karl Lombardy, found an image of a sharp-faced man, a ferret, some hair, small mouth, lived in Geneva.

Geneva.

He recalled the expenses on Townley's credit card, the restaurant, IL LAGO.

He looked at his watch: 22:30. No time difference. He imagined Lombardy would be a studious type.

He dialed the number on the web page, got an answering machine, left his name and number, it was urgent, he was phoning from Cape Town, South Africa, re: Nial Townley and GALI.

He closed his eyes and visualized a movie set of characters. GALI, Pittman, the gangsters in a red Hyundai with a cattle prod. He felt like he was looking at a Photoshopped picture. The shadows were all wrong. *Are you going to leave this thing alone now?* Coulson's question repeated in his head.

---

He returned to backgammon. The door of his bedroom was open. The remote was nearby.

At 23:00 his phone rang. A woman said her name was Helga Lombardy.

"I wanted to speak to Karl," he said. "Are you his wife?"

"Yes."

"Is it possible for me to speak to him?"

There was a long silence.

"It's late," she said. He apologized, but she continued. "I don't usually answer this phone, but I couldn't sleep. Sleep is a stranger to me. These days—"

Her accent was part French, a hint of Flemish.

"There was something in your message. I don't know what. You sounded...sincere. I thought maybe I must speak to you. Something made me think that. I don't know why. I never do."

"Thank you," he said.

"Karl is dead."

He inhaled sharply. "I'm so sorry. I didn't know."

For a moment, he thought she might have hung up.

"How...when...did this happen?"

"Three months ago in a car accident." Her voice was calm, flat, as if she was on medication to remove both the highs and lows of life. "Karl devoted his life to this GALI business. It was his passion. I used to warn him. If you wrestle with darkness, you might never see the sun again."

"You think that it wasn't an accident?"

"His car left the road on the Autoroute Blanche. Karl drove recklessly sometimes, but he'd never had an accident before. Backups of his work have been misplaced. His unpublished work is gone. People ask me..." Pain traveled the line, tightly packaged in small compartments of every sentence. "Ah, I don't want to say. These people are clever. What did you want to ask Karl?"

"I wanted to know if he ever met a person from South Africa. He's a businessman, an engineer, who disappeared."

"Over the last month, I've read every one of Karl's published documents. There are thousands of pages." She paused.

"Did Karl ever mention Nial Townley? Could he have met him? Or had contact?"

She seemed to be thinking. "Townley? I never heard him mention the name. But Karl traveled around a lot."

He waited for more, but there was silence.

"Would you like me to phone you back?" He nibbled on his lip.

"It's a funny thing," she said suddenly. "Funny what the mind remembers. About a year ago, he told me about meeting two South Africans. I remember because we don't meet a lot of people from there. South Africa. You know, I didn't know it was a country, I thought it was a reference to a part of Africa."

"Yes, of course. It's silly," she continued. "Nelson Mandela. I am the wife of a researcher and I know so little. I read about those girls in Nigeria. The ones who went missing."

"Kidnapped by Boko Haram," he said.

"There's so much mystery on the dark continent. Karl had a meeting, I think, and when he came home that night, he spoke about Africa. Lions and elephants and rhinoceros. He loved Animal Planet, National Geographic on TV, anything with the wild animals. He told me he wanted to visit South Africa."

"You said a year ago?"

"I think so."

He reached for his laptop, pulled Townley's case file, checked whether Townley had searched on Geneva, Lombardy, did not find anything.

"Would it be possible for you find out? Is there a backup of his calendar, for example?"

"His electronic record is gone. But he did have a hand diary in which he kept appointments. Last year's may be still at his offices."

"Thank you. That'd be helpful."

"I have to take the train to Bern tomorrow to go to the Registre Centrals des Testements. Karl didn't have much money, but something is better than nothing. I will try and find it. Give me the date."

After ending the call, he continued to sift through case files. When Townley was in Geneva, Carla's schedule contained site meetings with project managers in Gauteng. He searched through the schedules of other managers. None were absent from the country.

He stepped out onto the balcony and clutched the balustrade. In the moonlight, the sea was calm, no wind, a slight drizzle. The sky and sea were merged into a single dark horizon.

He wondered if Coulson and the South African authorities even knew Lombardy was dead.

*Two South Africans.*

What if Nial Townley had met Lombardy? What if Townley was aware of GALI and knew the sinister truth behind their activities?

If Townley was the one South African, who was the other?

---

## 51

**"You had a visitor. Le Joli. A cheveux blonde, dangereux."**

Earlier, there'd been a short burst of rain, now it was dry but threatening. Aqualung on bench no.57 opened a pizza box and considered the contents before selecting a slice. Le Fleur was waiting for Camps Bay Maintenance to arrive and fix his doors. Cars were pacing steadily along Victoria Road. Behind them, the sea belched with the weight of a loaded tide.

"What did she smell like?"

Aqualung pushed the pizza into his mouth.

"I wouldn't want to smell that one," he mumbled.

"When was this?"

"While you were on holiday with your sugar," said Aqualung.

He frowned. A dangerous blonde? Aqualung reached into his pocket, removed a crushed cigarette box and handed it to him. On it, he had written a car registration number.

"A white pug."

Le Fleur frowned. "Did you see who it was?"

"Oui."

"And?"

Aqualung got hold of another slice of droopy pizza.

"Freddy?"

"What?"

"If you accepted a new phone like I offered, you could've taken a picture."

Aqualung looked up. He did not respond.

"Well, can you describe her?"

"Ah, you are so interested? Perhaps competition for the sugar? She had short blonde hair and hungry eyes."

Le Fleur frowned.

"You know someone like this?"

"No."

Aqualung pulled at his throat like a turkey.

"She made the sign of a pistolet. Perhaps she wants sex, perhaps she wants to kill you."

Aqualung turned and looked at him intently.

"And I'll tell you something else about this woman, monsieur. The dots in her eyes, they do not change. I think she does not feel emotion."

"You noticed that?" he said, intrigued. "What color were they?"

"Emerald."

Le Fleur felt a cold chill. SUPERCHARGER was dead. NETWORX was missing. Fallon was out of prison. Was she hunting the surviving members of JACKER?

"And she was coming here? Are you sure?"

Aqualung gestured across the road at Crystal Place.

"She went all the way to the top."

Le Fleur gazed up at his apartment, unfamiliar without the flapping sail shades which he had taken down and stored for the winter. He dialed Camps Bay Maintenance. The doors needed to be fixed without delay.

## 52

**In the public square outside Quay 4, Sean $CENE$TER Coppis was waiting as agreed,** his knees shaking as if he needed the toilet, hands in woolen mittens, peroxided blonde hair hidden under a beanie.

Le Fleur sat and rubbed his hands together, pulled his collar up.

"What's with the clandestine?" asked Coppis.

Le Fleur looked at his watch then scrutinized Coppis.

"You should wipe your nose. Breakfast of champions, snorting cocaine already?"

Coppis rubbed his sleeve across his nose.

"Ah, what's the problem? Some days need a kick start. Who cares? So what's this all about?"

Pregnant clouds hung impatiently in a purple night sky.

"I came to warn you."

"Warn me? Fuck. Warn me about what?"

"SUPERCHARGER is Jeremy Freeman, the guy who was murdered in a drive-by last week."

Coppis lit a cigarette and sucked it intently. "I knew that. I also read the paper."

"Did you also know he hacked video surveillance of Nial Townley's disappearance?"

"I don't care." Coppis stared vacantly at their surroundings, the Victoria & Alfred Waterfront, a man-made conglomeration of shiny shops and presented nature, bustling with shoppers and tourists.

"NETWORX is missing."

"Richard?"

"Yes. He's also involved with Nial Townley. I think he got the Stingray working."

A group of tourists passed them. For a moment he wondered where everyone went before the waterfront existed? Now there was nowhere else. Cape Town's bucket list reduced to a box and a price.

"You've got lots of theories, Daniel. Rule seven, remember? Anonymous is still able to deliver. What're you saying?"

"Are you involved?"

Coppis rubbed his hands together. His exhaled breath condensed into vapor. "Define involved."

"You know exactly what I mean. The splitting of the cash and the international money transfers."

---

Coppis gazed towards the dock, its water black and oily, a foreboding backdrop.

"Sean, these people aren't messing around."

"Don't be so melodramatic. Listen to me, Daniel, I'm flush. I did nothing illegal. I was asked to *consult* on money laundering, how to create accounts. Ask no questions, tell no lies. I had no knowledge of the final use of my advice."

This is why hackers make perfect accomplices, Le Fleur considered. Work secretly, individually, remotely and do not care about the consequence of their brilliance so long as they get paid.

Coppis's phone rang. He pulled it out his pocket and looked at the screen, started to stand. "I must go."

Le Fleur grabbed his arm and pulled him down. "I'm not finished, Sean."

A passerby overheard, stopped, turned around and stared, walked a bit, turned again. Coppis's phone stopped ringing.

"I think I may be involved too."

"Oh really? So what did you do, buddy?" asked Coppis.

"I linked some psychopath GALI employee Pittman to a bunch of gangsters."

"You think gangsters killed Townley?"

"It's possible."

"Well, you always wanted to be a hero, Daniel. We don't all choose our roles. I set up bank accounts for a fictitious money laundering scheme. I didn't know it was Townley until—" He stopped and stared into space.

"Where did you get your instructions?" asked Le Fleur.

"Are you kidding me? Where'd you get yours?"

"Carla Vitale."

"Well, it wasn't her."

"Don't you see, Sean? It's all of us. We're all involved. It's someone who knows about JACKER."

He ran his eyes across the inky black water. There was no activity on any of the tug boats. Not even the seals were around.

"What about ZAPPER?" asked Le Fleur.

"What about him?"

"Where is he? How can we get hold of him?"

"I don't care. Maybe he's at fucking DEF CON. For all I know, he's you. Or Richard. Or whoever. Anonymous can be a horrible, senseless, uncaring monster."

They sat in silence for a minute or two.

"I got a dodgy email," La Fleur said. "It was somebody pretending to be SATSA, the tourist board."

"I get a thousand fucking emails every day, pal."

"This was one trying to track my location. The keyboard used had a Chinese letterset. ZAPPER was involved in the Chinese stuff, even way back, do you remember?"

"What do you want me to do, Daniel? Search the universe for a fucking Chinese keyboard. I don't care about ZAPPER. I hope he's dead too." Coppis rubbed his hands then sat on them. "Jesus, it's cold. When the rain stops, the fucking polar bears come stomping down the mountain."

"Have you got protection?" asked Le Fleur.

"Protection? What do you mean?"

"They're all gone, don't you understand? SUPER-CHARGER, NETWORX, ZAPPER. That leaves you and me. I've read a report on GALI and Pittman. They are ruthless. If you are any danger to them, they won't hesitate."

Coppis thought about it, shook his head, and rubbed his nose.

"I'm no danger to anyone other than myself," he said.

"Fallon visited me." He had traced the Chevy's registration to Patricia Fitzsimmons in Pinetown. He knew it did not belong to Patricia Fitzsimmons.

Coppis leaned forward. "Jesus. I heard she's out." His cell rang again. His eyes rolled, red veins of tension throbbed in his orbs. After five rings, the call died. "Maybe we should report this to Ian Coulson? He'd help us. No ways he'd let anything happen to his best hackerfication guys."

"Why's he phoning you?"

"How'd you know it was him?"

"An evil maid hack," said Le Fleur. "I saw his face on your screen the first time he called."

"I'm so over this Cybercrime shit. All I want is a quiet room with lots of bit coin mining machines whirring away and no worries."

"So what's he want?"

Sean raised his eyebrows. "Am I a wizard? He probably wants me to be his script kiddie and chase some worm that's making online purchases at fucking Makro with his dead uncle's credit card."

"You do that?" asked Le Fleur.

Coppis shook his gloved hands and blew a cloud of vapor into the air. "Whatever it takes, pal, whatever it takes. The more you hate it, the stronger it gets."

# 53

**Fallon followed the hipster kid from Heritage Square to the Cape Town Station and boarded the southbound train.** She did not buy a ticket.

"Anyone sitting here?" she asked a man of Indian descent. He was mid-twenties, business-like. She took the seat before he could answer. The hipster kid stood at the far end of the carriage, staring out the window.

The train accelerated out of Cape Town station, hardly a sound of the wheels on the narrow gauge tracks. She had not ridden the metro for many years, felt strange in the mix of business men and women, students, and pickpockets.

The man was reading on a Kindle, pretended not to notice her. He had an odd smell, something in his hair.

"Better than sitting in traffic," she said.

She had not had sex since Jeremy and the urge was in her head. She thought this Indian fellow would have an appealing slim body underneath the suit.

He lowered the Kindle briefly, raised an eyebrow. "Yes, much better." He carried on reading.

Fuck him. A bottle of chloroform and a sponge was concealed in her bag. She felt like shoving it in his face.

The hipster kid turned and gazed back into the carriage. She looked away, imagined his eyes sweeping over her. When she looked back, he had returned to staring out the window. She wondered what he knew, whether deep inside there was an instinctive light flashing, warning him of danger. Probably not, probably he was thinking about getting home to his computer and a new online game.

She picked up a discarded morning newspaper. A small column speculated the murder of digital security expert Jeremy Freeman could be work related. She wondered whether he had been buried or cremated, thought about his wasted flesh. She flipped through the rest of the newspaper. There was nothing about Richard Chinkanda, nothing newsworthy about a missing Malawian national.

Yesterday her second visit to Crystal Place attracted the attention of the nuisance vagrant again. He had howled like a dog and licked her windscreen. She decided to pop past at night and, if the vagrant was still around, to push him over the edge.

Afterwards she drove past Marlborough Court, a block of flats corresponding to coordinates on NETWORX's worksheet. She assumed the emboldened No.12 referred to a flat in the block. She had tested the bell of No.12, but no one answered. She wondered if Le Fleur was hiding out there and whether the flat would provide clues to finding Nial Townley and claiming the reward.

The train stopped in Woodstock then Salt River. Two women boarded, identities hidden beneath their flowing burkas.

She opened her bag and looked inside. She knew exactly what it contained, but she checked anyway. Chloroform and pills, she had left the Taurus behind.

This morning she had received target #3's work address, routine, and instructions. They called him $CENE$TER.

His life is sad, help him end it. Suicide, no note.

A guy in Converse tackies was watching her. He looked like a wannabe mugger. There was a dangerous edge to his bony face, his leering gaze. She thought maybe she could work with something like that.

She removed her European passport from the back pocket of her jeans. The picture looked nothing like her. After completing her day's work, she planned to find someone at the station to do a Photoshop fix-up for her.

At Observatory, the hipster got off.

She disembarked and waited. He dropped into the subway and out of sight then re-emerged on the other side of the fence. She followed.

An hour later, it was done.

# 54

**The next day, it rained. Storm winds clattered the American shutters at Crystal Place.** Bali Bay resembled a cauldron of boiling witch water. Le Fleur pulled on a woolly cardigan, grabbed a raincoat and umbrella, and merged his Saab into chaotic southbound traffic.

He bought a dozen red roses at Alison's in Wynberg.

The cemetery in Plumstead was deserted, no other vehicles in the parking lot. He sat in the car for a moment and listened to the steady beat of the windscreen wipers as they swept away misty drizzle. What had he got himself into?

He got out of the car and popped the umbrella. The municipality had erected a new signboard with prohibited activities. One depicted a stick figure lying on the ground, a crescent moon above. No dying in here? He looked about for signs of activity. Today it was only him and those below the ground.

He walked to his father's headstone and paused. *Hey, Jake.* It had nothing for him. A gust of wind flayed his umbrella, inverted it. He imagined his father laughing. *Visiting graveyards is a dying pastime, let's go get you laid.*

He fixed the umbrella and moved along the pathway. There were chrysanthemums at his mother's grave, strong and lively in the cold autumn wind. He liked the irony. He read the attached card: "Wake up now, when leaves like corpses fall." It was stamped: The Christina Home for Abused Women. He laid the roses on the granite and stepped back. All those years and still the longing persisted. Maybe his aloneness now had nothing to do with his father.

He aimed his umbrella into the wind and walked slowly back to his car.

No further news from Carla and he had not called her. He felt strangely detached, a persistent feeling he had been used, played his part in a system so vast and elaborate it may never unravel.

He got back in the car and turned on the heater, ran the windscreen wipers.

There were loose ends that his mind refused to settle.

Did Nial Townley know about GALI's criminality from the outset? That was a huge question mark in his head. And if it were so, was it something he wanted to expose? He imagined how the revelation would devastate Carla.

Then there was the Chinese character set in the header data of the SATSA email, circulated when he and Carla were on the run. It was clear

---

to Le Fleur that the mastermind behind the scheme had access to the JACKER hacker group: SUPERCHARGER, $CENE$TER, NETWORX, himself. And the Chinese links to the fake SATSA email pointed at his one-time JACKER associate, the anonymous hacker ZAPPER.

Even if he heeded Coulson's advice to stay away, there was the threat of Fallon.

A car rolled into the lot. A man got out with two Alsatian pups.

His cell beeped. A text from Carla:

> Press briefing on GALI/Supertech matter
> at Table Bay Hotel. Perhaps we can have an
> Americano after.

He read the message twice, a strange buzz of excitement dispelling his gloomy thoughts.

*Hold it, cowboy,* he heard his father comment. *Don't get too excited. An Americano? She probably wants you to write her some code.*

He put the car into reverse and exited the cemetery.

He arrived at the Table Bay Hotel late and dripping. The conference doors were closed. A kind lady allowed him entry after he explained he had come from visiting his dead parents. Inside the room, the South African flag hung from the ceiling and provided backdrop to a long, rectangular table on a podium. Two police officers flanked alternate ends. A sign read National Media Centre Corporate Communication. Pressmen were seated in rows of plastic bucket chairs.

The acting police commissioner, a large black man in SAPS uniform, seemed to be relishing the limelight, spoke without hesitancy.

*Two gangsters arrested...connection with missing engineer Nial Townley ...a coordinated effort...*

He squeezed into a space alongside Ian Coulson. Coulson wore a suit, hair hanging neatly over the collar.

"Ah, Daniel, surprised to see you here. How's my favorite recidivist?" Coulson sipped from a plastic cup of coffee, eyes fixed on the podium.

"A press conference during an investigation, is this normal?" asked Le Fleur.

"This is South Africa. Normality is overrated. And they're so happy to have someone other than the Gupta family in the limelight."

The Gupta family and an alleged corrupt relationship with South Africa's leading politicians and businessmen had been dominating the South

African news landscape.

*Modern age of crime detection...vast arsenal of technological...combat organized crime...Internet anti crime agencies...South African Cybercrime organization...co-operating with FBI Cyber division...*

He spotted Carla on the podium. She looked professional, a young executive in a plain white blouse, hair tied back.

"The commissioner wants us to ask for assistance from America. Fuck that. That's the problem with Africa," said Coulson. "We think anything American has got to be better. They can't even hack their own fucking iPhones."

*Have identified computer hackers involved...Sophisticated cell tracking devices...equipment confiscated...under surveillance...*

"Ian, did you ever make contact with ZAPPER about your Chinese problem?"

"Nope, why?"

"The bogus email from SATSA had Chinese markings. I think it came from ZAPPER."

Coulson raised his eyebrows.

"Do you know who he is?"

"Daniel, even if I knew who he was, would I tell you? I've advised you to leave this thing alone and I'm telling you again. There are some bad apples involved." He pointed to the stage. "Let the professionals do their job."

Le Fleur looked away. Did Coulson know ZAPPER's identity? In his role as head of Cybercrime, Coulson could access a vast network of connections into the dark world of local hackers. Perhaps he had already identified the hackers involved with GALI and was ready to strike. Le Fleur shook his head slowly.

"I'm out of it," he said. "I'm here because Carla invited me for coffee."

If Coulson believed his only interest was Carla, perhaps it was best. And maybe true.

Coulson patted him on the back. "Good man."

*Performing attribution process to establish who is behind cyber attacks... Expect further arrests...*

After the announcement, there were questions from the floor.

Someone sought confirmation as to whether Townley's body had been found. It had not.

*Is it true agents from GALI AG are implicated?*

*We are investigating these allegations.*

The acting police commissioner met the questions with a straight bat. His predecessor had been inclined to shoot from the hip, had called some foreigner a monkey. That's why he was a predecessor.

*Can you comment on speculation that murdered IT executive Jeremy Freeman was involved in the scam?*

*We are interviewing a number of IT persons who may have assisted in this crime.*

"Obviously he won't be interviewing Freeman," Coulson muttered under his breath.

A large man with a hoarse voice put his question forward:

*Who are these IT persons? Do we know who they are?*

*We are busy with sensitive forensic investigation.*

"Don't worry," said Coulson.

"Why would I be worried?" Le Fleur wiggled his toes inside his shoes.

*Was Freeman killed by GALI agents to silence him?*

*We do not discount any theories.*

*Why's the FBI involved?*

*Our current detective services are not equipped to combat sophisticated cyber crime.*

"What a lot of cock," muttered Coulson. He turned to Le Fleur. "There's no FB-fucking-I doing the work. It's us."

*We have specialized agencies like Cybercrime.*

"That's more like it."

*They in turn draw from a network of IT professionals.*

"IT professionals? That's a euphemism for a ragtag bunch of day hackers and computer game addicts. Our friends, huh, Daniel? I think I've seen enough for one day."

Coulson patted him on the shoulder and squeezed out towards the exit.

Next, Gavin Marx rose and gave an update on civil matters. He read directly from his notes:

"GALI AG, a multinational engineering firm with head offices in Munich, is accused of complicity in a number of illegal activities in South America. We expect the first of these trials will commence in Panama later this year. We have recently learned the Policía Nacional Bolivariana, the Venezuelan national police force, have secured reliable evidence that GALI bribed Government officials to prejudice Supertech's business prior to Nial Townley's disappearance."

Le Fleur felt someone squeeze his arm. It was Captain Parks. Le Fleur gestured towards Marx on the stage.

"You had any good tips from a lawyer lately, Captain?"

Parks shook his head and smiled. "Ah, I'm still so sorry, chief. Damn lawyers can be quite persuasive, especially that one. I've learned my lesson.

Next time, huh? I owe you. Has everything been fixed up?"

"I can lock my door now."

Marx continued:

"*We* believe this is no coincidence. Thanks to SAPS forensic division and the Cybercrime organization, we have evidence GALI's locally appointed executive, the MD of GALI Africa, is linked to a criminal element that made an attempt on the life of a Supertech executive."

There was a murmur in the crowd.

"I cannot comment further as this is subject to ongoing investigation. I must commend the police for their exceptional work on the early arrests."

"Nice going," said Le Fleur.

Parks nodded. "Occasionally we bust down the right doors."

Marx cleared his throat.

"The South African Reserve Bank has supported our order and the assets of GALI in South Africa have been frozen. This includes funds previously attached to Supertech's Venezuelan office and repatriated by GALI Africa. As of today, The Townley Trust has assumed management control of Supertech. We are in the process of securing overseas funding to extricate ourselves from GALI and Venezuela and continue Supertech operations in Africa."

The questions came again.

"Who is going to run Supertech?" asked a thin man in a tweed coat.

"That will be decided by the existing executive team," said Marx and gestured to Carla and the rest of the management team. "We will be meeting immediately after this to discuss. It's what Nial would want. We are going to restore SUPERTECH to the business Nial would be proud of."

Nial Townley would be pleased at the outcome. Supertech's blocked Venezuelan funds had been restored, GALI ousted, and management was in the process of securing external funding.

"Who are the overseas investors?" asked a woman with a clipboard and earphones.

"They're a consortium of European investors."

Marx disclosed no more.

Le Fleur looked at the podium. Carla's face shone. Marx had mentioned a meeting to agree Nial's successor. He sent Carla a text:

Thanks for invite. Maybe next time.

He got up and slipped out the exit.

---

## 55

**The scent of blood lingered in her nostrils.** Her right arm was in a bandage sling.

A shade after noon at the Sea View Holiday Flats, Fallon rubbed her burned wrist against her mouth and swallowed a mouthful of Jack straight from the bottle.

She eased onto the sofa. A loose T-shirt covered her knees. The patio door and curtains were closed, the windows rattling like someone was trying to break in.

Yesterday's outfit lay in a heap on the floor. Luckily, they were black so the blood on her clothes didn't show.

She did not think about the hipster kid. Faking someone's suicide was an easy assignment. She would have pushed him off the balcony of his flat, but that seemed cavalier. She sorted him out with chloroform then an overdose of pills, left him foaming in his bedroom. She wondered if anyone had found his body yet.

She had barely raised a sweat completing her assignment for Dark Video. It was what she did afterwards that caused her pain and problems.

After eliminating the hipster, she found someone on the Grand Parade to modify the picture on her passport. Then she visited a small back street electronic store and purchased two battery operated remote controllers. The remotes were for access to No.12, Marlborough Court.

She should have gone home after that, but she was feeling horny and reckless, so she found a bar in a side alley off Long Street and picked up a nobody with tattoos and muscles.

Dangerous sex was like diving with Great White sharks.

What started as smoking crushed Mandrax and energetic foreplay in the toilets ended with Mr. Muscles burning her with a lighter in a locked room in Ravensmead and a line of hopefuls queuing outside. Fucking men. Give them a finger and they'll take an arm.

She had managed to stab the second guy with her box cutter then jump from the window of the double story premise.

A kind taxi driver drove her home to Sea View Holiday Flats, helped her out of the taxi, and escorted her to the entrance, would have probably followed her up to the seventh floor and tried to fuck her had Fabrice not been at his post. The taxi driver settled for R500 payment.

She had injected morphine and reset her shoulder. The trick was waiting long enough for the morphine to take effect but not so long as to fall asleep. She had sat on her bed with her knees pressed to her chest, rocked back and forth, and pulled and stretched until she heard an audible pop.

She hadn't slept well despite a double dose of sleeping tablets.

Now she lay on the couch in the living room. A blast of sea wind battered against her windows. The landline rang.

"Hello madam."

She had already thanked Fabrice with a cash gratuity left in an envelope at reception.

"Thank you for the money," he said. "It was not necessary. I have Francine. She wants to say something to you."

"Madam, merci beaucoup," Francine's little voice whispered. "I hope you are better."

Fallon swallowed, feeling again the rising of emotion, a sour taste in her mouth. Francine safe in her father's arms, the spoiling love of her mamie.

"Thank you," replied Fallon, her voice rasping.

Fallon ended the call and walked to the kitchen, ignoring the unwashed dishes, glasses, the counters strewn with takeaway boxes and wrappers. She opened the fridge and removed a half-eaten chicken wrap, took a bite and put it back.

She returned to the living room, lifted a Hush puppy shoe box of correspondence, and returned to the couch.

In prison, her facilitator had encouraged Fallon to open up about her childhood. *We are what we are because of what we were.* Psychobabble.

*I don't know where I came from and I don't care,* Fallon had said. But it wasn't entirely true.

Fallon opened the shoe box of correspondence. She had accessed it recently to locate her old European passport now updated with a shiny new picture of her blonde self. She rummaged around the shoebox and pulled out a plastic folder. Her heartbeat quickened.

She did know something about her childhood.

They were not *her* memories. She had been given a packet of letters by the orphanage matron when she turned eighteen.

Fallon opened the plastic folder and removed a blue envelope with two Protea stamps, thin paper, the addressee was SAMANTHA BURGH in a scrawling script. The letter was written by someone called Frans; she had read it many times in her youth. The story of Sam and Frans. Poor Frans. Sam was too good for him. He tried so hard.

> Hey my love. I'm in heaven. I can't believe that
> such a beautiful woman is mine. Though I'm far

away, my heart beats with yours. I will love
you forever Samantha. Samantha, I love you.
I love you.

Fallon felt nauseous. It was clear from the letter that Frans and Sam
were separated by distance. Frans spoke about life on the mines and lone-
liness; he counted the days until they would be together. Fallon swallowed
a mouthful of Jack Daniels and opened another letter, a green envelope,
the same address, a 20c Protea affixed to the cover.

Hey my love. All I want is to lie with you and
feel your warm body pressed against mine.

*Hey my love.* Fallon's cheeks burned. His correspondence was dominat-
ed by memories of recent togetherness. The beach, a special trip down the
coast, a dinner at a restaurant called La Perla. Fallon carefully returned
the brittle page to its envelope.
*Lie with you and feel your warm body pressed against mine.*
She opened a third, pink letter. This was the big one. The address was
different.

Hey my love. I'm shaking. I'm so shaking. I can't
believe it's true. I want you to know. It was
meant to be. Maybe we aren't ready, but I am so
ready. I'm so ready for this. Our love, our love.
This is our love. I will marry you. Will you
marry me? I'm asking.

The letter shook in Fallon's hand. The sour taste twisted in her throat.
She swallowed hard.
*Hey my love. Hey my love.*
*This is our love.* That was me. Samantha was pregnant. *It was meant
to be.*
But no, Samantha, Sammy, Sam, believed she deserved better. Better
than a man to love her, to hold her. Better than a man who wished for
nothing more than to lie in the same bed and press his body against her.
To call her up and just say: *Hey my love.*
Fallon felt the urge to ball the pink letter in her hand.
Fuck Samantha Burgh, fuck her to hell with its bloodless shadows. Long
ago she'd torn up Frans's other letters to Samantha. They were responses

to Samantha's requests for money, his pleas for her not to have an abortion.

*This is our love.* Not, this is our baby to be. Even to Frans, she had not been important, not wanted. All he thought of was his love, his feelings. Not her.

But he'd kept her alive.

Frans had kept her alive. Not because he loved her. Not because he wanted her. Because he didn't have the money for an abortion, because he wanted Samantha, because he wanted to fuck her cheating, lying body, the body that carried her. How shameful.

There was one other item of correspondence addressed to Samantha Burgh—a letter from a mine manager in Welkom explaining that Frans van Blerk had gassed himself in his car in the garage of his rented mining residence.

Fallon didn't know what became of Samantha Burgh. There was no record. Fallon imagined Samantha Burgh fucked her way to nothingness and then was stabbed by a drug addict, bled to death on some dirty carpet. Found out the hard way that the best offer was, after all, a warm body to lie with.

She was born to Frans van Blerk and Samantha Burgh. Hell on earth awaited her.

The pink envelope was steady in her hand.

She was Fallon now.

No one would fuck with her. She was a product of her father's cowardice, of her mother's apathy. Did he think about her once, just once, floating in the whore's womb, before he fitted a hose to the car's exhaust pipe?

Fuck him.

Fuck everyone.

She didn't fear death. Death was feared by people scared of losing assets and individuality, scared of leaving loved ones. She had no desire to retain her identity in another world, no loved ones to mourn.

Fallon folded the pink page and returned it carefully to the envelope. She held the envelope briefly to her face then returned it to the shoe box. Her breathing was even.

Frans Van Blerk. *Hey my love...* If only he had seen her, if only he could have held her. She could have been Francine with a father like Fabrice and a mamie that spoiled her. Frans would have realized she was more important than that cheap whore Samantha.

She closed her eyes and squashed out the tears that filled them. Frans van Blerk was no longer a coward. He was too gentle for this world. She wished she had a picture of him. In the imaginary world she'd invented as a teenager, he was stocky with broad shoulders, dark curly hair, a ruddy complexion, a kind face, a throaty laugh. He'd smell of braaied meat and rum. Perhaps like the man on Llundudno beach. People slapped him on the back. His friends laughed with him. He lived life lightly and never expected much. Until he met Samantha Burgh.

Fallon closed the box and took a long sip of her drink.

Did Samantha Burgh ever care for her before giving her up for adoption? Did she look into her baby's eyes and feel anything? Did she leave her to lie in her shit? Fallon remembered nothing. Not a song, a sound, a smell.

She imagined a musky garage in Sea Point, Frans fitting the hose to the exhaust pipe, sitting back and twisting the window tight against the hose, starting the engine and breathing in the fumes.

For Samantha Burgh, the whore?

Why did he not think of her?

His unborn baby...

She put the letters back in the folder and returned the folder to the shoebox. She got up and checked her bruises in the mirror. Her pupils were pinpricks in her green eyes.

The high paying adrenaline job had given her purpose and a home. She'd felt wanted, needed, important. More money than she'd dreamed... It was like being in a movie. Her movie...

Then it came crashing down. Jacker had destroyed that. He'd destroyed her life.

But she had survived.

She returned to the couch, closed her eyes, and tried to find a comfortable position. There were no admonishing voices in her head, no *I told you so*, just a dull acknowledgement that her life was on a roller coaster and if she did not escape soon, she would be dead in Africa before year's end.

She had not checked the bulletin for new messages or her bank account for confirmation of deposit of payment for settling the hipster assignment.

She was not expecting a knock on her door or any visitors. She did not expect him.

## 56

**The woman who answered the door was blonde.** Her green eyes shone in blackened sockets, her arm was in a sling, a gun in her left hand.

"Who the fuck are you?"

He held up his hands as a sign of pacifism. Prior to being mugged, he had never seen a gun in real life and the shock was again a jolt though his body.

"I'm Daniel Le Fleur. May I come in?"

She pushed open the door with her foot then moved aside. He stepped inside. The room was strewn with empty bottles, discarded clothing, fast food wrappers, and pizza boxes. It had an airless, animal scent like someone had been living in it for a long time.

"Turn around. Keep your hands up."

He complied. He could see her in the hallway mirror.

She frisked him with the gun hand, tapped the barrel against his phone in the pocket of his jeans.

"Take it out, slowly."

He removed the phone with his left hand and held it up.

"Put it on the table in front of you."

She kicked the door closed with her foot. In the mirror, he could see the gun pointed in his back.

"How did you get in?"

"I told him downstairs I'm your boyfriend. A small bribe helped too." He lowered his arms and turned slowly.

"You've got a fucking nerve. How did you find me?"

"I should ask the same question. What happened to you?"

"I fell. You need to tell me *very quickly* how you got here?"

He looked straight in her eyes.

"You met my security man? He's the guy with the bad suit and tonsorial issues. So the first time you popped by, he took down your car registration and I entered it into an LPR surveillance system. I wrote an add-on to that system. When it triggers a hit, it also produces a list of every GSM device within a hundred meter radius. When you came back a second time, it was pretty easy to eliminate other cells from the list. Then all I had to do was locate your cell phone's geolocation which was also easy since you hadn't disabled it."

He spoke deliberately slowly, calmly, like he had all the time in the world, like he was sharing technical secrets with a good friend.

"Walk slowly across the room. Keep your hands on your head and sit down."

Only one of three chairs in the room was habitable. She put her gun on the table, picked up his cell phone, and removed the battery. Then she swapped the cell for her gun and walked across the room, looked out over the balcony.

When she returned to the room, she dialed the landline, spoke to someone and asked if her visitor had been alone.

"I'm alone," he said. "Nobody knows I'm here."

He hoped she appreciated he could have exposed her if he had wanted. He adjusted a pillow, locked his fingers behind his head, and leaned back.

"What do you want?" she asked.

"You were looking for me?"

He had never seen her in the flesh. She wore only a big T-shirt. Her injuries did not make her any less dangerous, perhaps more.

"What are you up to, Fallon?"

Her expression told him her mind was racing. In the corner of the room was an open wooden cabinet with rows of test tubes, some type of pharmacy unit. The furniture was reasonably new. There was one picture on the wall, a gaudy blue beach scene. No television set, no books, no magazines. He wondered what she did in her spare time.

"You were part of JACKER. You're the reason I spent three years in prison."

He did not respond. He could have pointed out she was incarcerated because she drugged young women then delivered their pretty asses to wealthy men with perverted minds. He did not say sorry.

She tossed a heap of clothes from a chair and sat opposite, pulled her shirt lower for modesty, her eyes moving over him like a torch. It was impossible to read her thoughts, but he gave it a try.

"You're wondering why I've come here, why I would walk in here when you could probably kill me in a flash."

She shrugged.

He continued. "You don't believe I told no one? There are no blue lights flashing below. I haven't busted you, have I?"

Her eyes flashed anger.

"You've nothing to bust me for. I've done my time. I'm living my life."

"OK."

"And why would I want to kill you?"

"You have three years of revenge? It must have eaten you every day."

"I can't eat revenge. But I don't speak for Carlos De Palma."

He did not shift his position on the chair. He opened and closed his eyes, processing the image before him. She was injured and looked vulnerable. But he knew his eyes were lying. The image was a shell.

"Carlos De Palma from Dark Video?"

She did not respond. He watched her face, her expression. On the table between them was a laptop.

"Can I show you something?" he asked.

She hesitated. The gun was on her lap. She moved her head slightly in a gesture of assent. He leaned forward and lifted the laptop's lid, typed quickly, turned the screen so she could see.

"This is a Canadian police web site for unidentified bodies."

On screen, a black and white picture appeared, a dead man lying in an alley, frozen, face twisted, snow covering a scraggly beard. Underneath the image, someone had written the caption:

```
Carlos De Palma's last resting place.
In death what dreams come?
```

She stared at the picture for a long time. She moved to push the laptop away, but he held it steady. Carlos De Palma's corpse, a grotesque expression immortalized on his frostbitten face, stared back at her.

"You're working for a dead street person."

He made sure his voice contained no malice, no satisfaction. He wanted her to trust him. He closed the lid of the laptop, placed his hands behind his head, and leaned against the cushion.

After a long interval, she said: "Who said I'm working for anyone? It doesn't matter whether he's dead or alive." She closed her eyes and the color drained out her face.

"Are you in pain?"

She opened her eyes. "Why are you here?"

He looked around the room. Every door leading from the lounge was open. He could see the unmade bed in the bedroom, open suitcases, clothes and shoes on the floor. He wondered what type of person lived like this, what had happened to turn her into who she was.

"I told you," he said. "You came to see me. If you're not working for anyone and you didn't come to kill me, then what?"

Her nostrils flared as she inhaled deeply.

"What do you know about Nial Townley?" she asked.

He was surprised by her question. He knew whoever she was actually working for was unlikely to confide in the hired help. Seeing her reaction to De Palma's corpse, he was sure she thought she was working for Dark Video and on a path of vengeance against JACKER.

"I've been helping somebody determine what happened to him," he said.

"I know this. Carla Vitale. Tell me something I don't know."

"Why should I?"

She looked at the gun in her lap. Then she smiled. "I might have some information for you."

He recounted a chronology of events, speaking slowly, sending a message he was unafraid and trusted her. He told her a gang of hackers was involved. He watched her face carefully as he spoke, but she gave nothing away. Inside her head, he felt, was absolute clarity. Unlike her cluttered habitat, her mind was concise and calculating.

He talked about AlphaGuard and the Stingray. He mentioned Bruno Pittman and GALI but simplified how he had linked them to the crime. She listened and said nothing, the only indication of her interest the occasional blinking of her eyes. She did not interrupt once.

When he finished, she got up and fetched a bottle of Jack. She took a sip and offered.

"Sorry, no clean glasses."

"No, thanks."

She sat and swallowed a mouthful. "So this guy—Pittman—you're not sure he did it?"

"I think it may be a set up. It's all too easy. It was such an elaborate plan and perfectly executed with no loose ends. Then to send in a bunch of gangster hit men, it feels like someone wanted me to expose Pittman's link to the gangsters."

"Scary people, those gangsters," she said and changed positions uncomfortably.

He thought about the gangsters, Pittman's gardener with a cord around Carla's neck, Sparky Peterson with the cattle prod. Was the woman in front of him any different? Behind her clipped accent, her beauty, perhaps Fallon had also been an unloved child from a broken home, an outsider, accepted only in a world of violence.

She filled her mouth with Jack and swirled it around before swallowing. It seemed she was drinking for the pain not pleasure.

"Daniel," she said. "Who names anyone Daniel?"

He did not respond.

"What was the Bible story? Daniel and the Lion's Den? I can't remember it. Did it work out well for Daniel?"

"Apparently the lions didn't eat him. Yeah, I guess it worked out. So which character are you named after, Fallon?"

Her eyes glazed. Aqualung's observation about her eyes was accurate. The pupils were fixed and did not dilate or contract as she spoke or listened. The effect made her appear indifferent to anything said.

"I picked a random name from an old TV series. *Dynasty.*"

"I didn't think it was your real name."

She stared at him, her intense gaze like a hot ray.

"You live alone, Le Fleur? In that big fancy place of yours?"

He nodded.

"Do you smoke?" she asked.

"No."

"Me neither. Gamble?"

He shook his head.

"You watch pornography?"

"Not much."

"Strikes me we are the same," she said.

*Except for a few things,* he thought.

She licked her middle finger and rubbed it over her nude eyebrows. He knew she was trying to intimidate him. He had decided before the meeting to avoid the subject of the death of SUPERCHARGER or NETWORX's disappearance. If he confronted her with that, he would have no chance of reaching a truce.

"So, Fallon, what have *you* got?"

Her face remained expressionless.

"You said you had information about Nial Townley."

"I have Hunter's Dry, if you'd like something lighter." Her eyes glinted. He shook his head, did not smile. "You don't drink, Le Fleur?"

"Not much."

She stared at him with her catlike eyes. "You know what they say about people who don't drink."

"What's that?"

"You can't trust them." She pointed at her laptop. "If I open that connection, your name will be on the channel and I'll kill you."

He did not move. His only backup was Aqualung ready to call Captain Parks if he did not return to Bali Bay within three hours. How had he been so nonchalant? It was his problem moving from the virtual to the real. He couldn't just reboot or restart the game when things went wrong.

"I thought you weren't working for anyone. How much?" he asked.

She would know he had some backup. She could not take a chance.

"How much what?"

---

"How much will they pay you?"

"It doesn't matter."

"You'll never achieve the Townley reward without me. I have the connections. Parks from the Hawks is the head of the investigation, Ian Coulson of Cybercrime has the inside track on the tech."

She grimaced and changed positions, tucked her legs in, pulled the T-shirt over her knees.

"What makes you think I'm interested in the reward?"

He paused. "Five million reasons—"

He looked at the tattooed X's on his wrist. Dealing with the devil, what would that be worth?

# 57

**He felt like he had bungee-jumped.** The unnatural act of diving over the edge, trusting the rope will hold, the nagging doubt that if something goes wrong, there's no second chance.

Le Fleur made tea and flicked on the big screen TV.

Fallon had told him she knew where Nial Townley was being held. What could he make of that? Was she lying? Le Fleur did not believe Townley was alive.

Fallon also said she had evidence of calls made on the day of Townley's disappearance. She showed him a picture of a Stingray-like device which she could easily have pulled off the Net.

But what interested him most about the image was that the Stingray had a significant modification, a hard drive attached to the chassis.

He had made her a promise. When he stared into her green eyes, he knew that the promise would cost him more than he could afford. Not a cost in monetary terms, but an irrecoverable loss of virtue. He promised if she produced the evidence he would ensure she received the reward. No more, no less, no questions asked.

On TV, Sky Business crossed to the Bachplatz, GALI's Munich head-quarters in Kaiserstrasse. Press was gathered on drab stairs outside the building to catch GALI executives emerging from a closed door meeting.

"Herr Loidl, Herr Loidl," a voice called above the hubbub.

He recognized Schroeder alongside the founder's son Loidl. They glared at the crowd of news seekers. Loidl looked especially agitated, a public relations liability.

Schroeder shoved someone backwards, took control of proceedings.

"Can you stand back? If you can stand back and give us room?"

A back voice narrated:

> *Bruno Pittman, a GALI AG employee and*
> *until recently Acting CEO of GALI's South African*
> *subsidiary GALI Africa, is wanted for questioning*
> *by Interpol. GALI is trying to facilitate his handover*
> *for questioning. Pittman returned to Europe earlier*
> *this week. At current time, his whereabouts*
> *are uncertain.*

"Do you know where Pittman is?"

"We don't know." Schroeder's head moved like a puppet, next question please.

"What do you say, Herr Loidl, to the accusation that your company orchestrated the abduction and murder of the CEO of a company in South Africa?"

Loidl's mouth moved up and down as if he was chewing. Then his jaw locked and jutted forward, his watery blue eyes flickered.

"It's absurd. It's not true," answered Schroeder.

> The GALI Board has assured stakeholders that
> the company has at no time been involved in
> illegal activities as alleged in reports by the late
> Karl Lombardy. GALI is involved in litigation in
> this regard. GALI is confident all charges will be
> dismissed and their reputation restored.

"Herr Loidl, the photographs of Pittman at a strip club, surely given his past history, GALI must act severely."

Schroeder touched Loidl's arm.

"We can't comment on that," said Schroeder. "We're not in a position to defend Mr. Pittman's private life. The South Africans had a choice of executives for GALI's African venture and they chose Pittman. So let's not prejudge him."

*The South Africans chose Pittman.* Le Fleur narrowed his eyes. They chose him. Who were "they"? Someone who knew what Lombardy's report contained?

"What about allegations that GALI manipulated competitor business in South America?"

"This is preposterous nonsense. GALI will vigorously defend these allegations."

It was clear Schroeder intended to field all the questions.

"Is this not a time, Herr Loidl, to ask you again what your company knows about the death of Karl Lombardy?"

Schroeder pursed his lips. He looked like he was thinking of the best way to say something without saying anything.

"I will not listen to your unsinn," blurted Loidl, stiff, hands trembling. "It's all lies! Lies!"

Schroeder gripped Loidl's arm.

"We cannot take any more questions. Everything is on our website."

"Did GALI know Pittman had convictions for domestic violence?"

Le Fleur knew the questioner was trying his luck. Based on Lombardy's report, Pittman had not been convicted.

Schroeder put his hand up to block the cameras. He whispered to Loidl and the two men turned their backs on their interrogators and stalked back to the building's entrance. Sky reverted to the in-studio presenter.

Le Fleur took his tea cup to the kitchen then walked to the Chrome Room. The metal door was buckled. *Thanks, Parks.* He had ordered a new customized door. The sight of his violated space grated his sense of order; he would have to live with it for a month.

He sat and ran his hand over the Omega processor, thought about what Fallon said.

*She knew where Nial Townley was held?* Did she mean Townley was alive? She had ignored his question.

*She had evidence of calls made?* He had a sinking feeling this knowledge was tied to Richard Chinkanda's disappearance.

It occurred to him that Fallon could have simply heard about the reward and made up a story.

He opened a screen on his laptop and checked the output from the WiFi camera he had sneaked into the foyer of the Sea View Holiday Flats. Unless she had jumped from the seventh floor, she was still there.

He buzzed Sean Coppis but received no answer. He wanted to give Coppis another chance to admit what he had done. Coppis had not looked at his phone since yesterday midday, but that was usual. He would binge on drugs and computer games until dawn then sleep for a day.

He held his hands in front of his mouth and blew.

Shortly after midday, his cell rang. He recognized the sad voice of Helga Lombardy in Geneva.

"The fire at Karl's offices in Bern destroyed his documents. I tried to access backups, but I..."

He stood, opened the balcony doors and stepped out. The sky was dark with heavy clouds and a cold, salty wind stung his face. Aqualung was on bench no.57.

"...but I remember, I have his journal, his diary, you know. Karl kept every one since even before we met. He wrote a lot in those diaries. Personal things: the first time we met, the times we made love..." She laughed. "He'd draw a heart at the top of the page. Not in recent times, you know, in the beginning...there were lots of hearts."

He waited patiently, eyes scanning the cars on the street.

"Everything in pencil, you see, a sharpened pencil. There were always pencil shavings on the floor. I would step on them, barefoot, and shout at him. Then he would come along and sweep them up with this little guilty and magical smile. Like a little imp. Karl was always smiling."

She paused.

"I found last year's diary. There's an entry."

His heartbeat quickened.

She confirmed the correct date.

"What's it say?"

"He's got a reminder to update his SWISS passport."

"OK."

"Then this is what you are probably looking for...At one o'clock."

A sudden squall blew one of the deck chairs to the edge of the balcony.

"Il Lago's a restaurant overlooking Place des Bergues. It's very exclusive. I don't remember going there with Karl. It's too fancy."

He felt a rush of excitement as she mentioned the name of the restaurant. He pressed the cell against his ear. What if that was all?

"Karl didn't like Italian food. He liked his mother's cooking. Rostis and fondues, he was traditional. OK, then there are two names. He's written them in capital letters."

He waited, palms sweaty, heart banging.

"The one name is N. Townley. That's the name you asked after? The missing businessman?"

"Yes. And the other name?"

Helga Lombardy paused. Then: "And the other says: Marx."

## 58

**A cold wind rattled the closed balcony doors of Fallon's apartment.**

She surveyed a collection of items on her bed. Rucksack, bandage, gloves, lock jimmy, head torch, Swiss army knife, petroleum jelly, crowbar, hacksaw, pliers, camera, wet wipes, box cutter, plastic sleeves, two blue remote controls, Taurus with silencer fitted.

Satisfied she had laid out everything, she packed certain items into the water proof black rucksack.

She glanced across at her naked body in the mirror, a human canvas of purple, blue and black bruises. She didn't blame anyone. She had grown up in the jungle. Those afraid of the big bad wolf should stay at home. She wondered how she would handle bumping into Mr. Muscles from Ravensmead. "Thanks, pal." Then shoot him or fuck him again.

Sheets of rain were now pounding against her seventh floor windows.

She thought about Le Fleur. Could she trust him?

The last time she had a partner, it ended badly. His name was Ferdi, a bozo with muscles, bulging abs, quads, everything. She killed him in the same parking lot where the pedophile met his end. He was a scumbag that did not follow instructions. She shot him in the head while simultaneously having one of the best orgasms of her life.

But Le Fleur was different. He was clever and cultured. He was the kind of partner she wanted.

He had showed her Carlos De Palma's dead body and told her Dark Video was defunct. She wondered if he was aware of her activities since leaving prison. He must know, she considered, at least some of it.

After he left, she did not go to the channel. She did not want to know who was next on the list. She could check tomorrow. What was one day?

She closed her eyes and pictured Carlos De Palma as he was when he was alive and in control of Dark Video. She tried not to think about his corpse, his face distorted by some final reckoning for his sins. Who was her new employer? Surely not Dave Valentine, her prison visitor? Perhaps it could even be Le Fleur?

She walked into the living room and removed the telephone directory from a table drawer. The curtains were closed, lights on.

Le Fleur was particularly interested in the design of the Stingray in a picture she had shown him.

She opened the telephone directory. Inside she'd cut a slot in the pages to hide a flash drive. She checked it was safely in place. Le Fleur's reaction to the Stingray picture affirmed that making a backup of its hard drive before returning the device was an inspired decision. It was her collateral.

She returned the telephone directory, pulled a yoga mat from under her bed and rolled it out on the floor. She lay and raised her feet in the air. Her body ached and her back muscles were tense. With her feet in the air, she clenched and unclenched her buttocks. The stretch burned in her core. She lowered her legs and lay motionless, listening to the weather and the drone of traffic. Then she reached for the petroleum jelly and pulled her knees up to her chest.

Tonight she planned to break into Marlborough and find Nial Townley or clues to his whereabouts.

From prior surveillance, she knew the block contained fourteen apartments. She had acquired an idea of who went where, all except for two apartments: No.12 on the ground floor and No.23 on the upper floor.

No.12 was her target, the number emboldened on NETWORX's spreadsheet.

The block's security was average, a camera above the pedestrian access but none at the vehicular entrance. Both access points were electronic. The sharp metal spikes protecting the green perimeter fence were bendy with accessible footholds. The ground floor flats had low balcony walls with burglar bars on the windows and doors.

She rolled off the yoga mat and positioned in front of the mirror. She tightened her buttocks. Her shoulder ached and her ribs were bruised.

It was time to get ready.

First she disguised her blackened eyes with eyeshadow and a cover stick then slipped into a loose shirt, her right arm hanging inside the sleeve. She pulled on a pair of stretchy black leggings. Without panties, they were partially transparent, but modesty was not her concern. She completed her attire with a belt and holster around her waist, an anorak, boots, and a baseball cap—all black—then examined her appearance in the mirror. Faceless, shapeless, she could be one of a thousand looking for easy opportunity in the city.

When the sun slipped away, she hitched the rucksack over her shoulder and tested its weight. The Taurus went into the belt holster at the back of her pants, its muzzle cold in the cleft of her backside and reminding her that surprises often came from places you never expected.

# 59

**Fallon parked at the end of the road and walked the remaining distance to Marlborough Court.** The pavement was damp, but the wind had died. A pervading cold gripped the darkened suburb. She chose a time when residents would be relaxing after dinner, taking in a TV show, but not so late as to attract the attention of a roving security firm.

She buzzed No.12 and stepped out of the light next to the intercom. Nobody answered.

The green fence around Malborough Court stood head high with sharp vertical poles and spikes. She walked along the fence into a shadowy area and pulled off her rucksack, removed a set of pliers, and flattened a number of spikes. After throwing the rucksack over, she cautiously raised her weight onto the fence, and, using her left arm, straightened up and jumped over.

The impact with the ground on the other side sent a spear of pain through her right shoulder.

In the shadows, she crouched and listened. A wave of nausea rose in her throat. She squeezed her eyes shut and fought back the throbbing pain in her shoulder.

She opened her eyes and checked the windows for movement. Satisfied her entry had not drawn attention, she removed a head torch, Swiss army knife, and the blue remotes from her rucksack and crept over to the vehicular entrance.

Security was a figment of imagination. The gates and fences people hid behind could be climbed over, the doors could be opened with a crowbar.

She fitted the head torch and unscrewed the gate controller box and illuminated the contents. Carefully she fitted two tiny jumper switches to the control board and pressed the green button on the remote. An audible beep signaled control of the vehicular access. She repeated the exercise for the second remote.

She shouldered her rucksack, opened the gate with the remote, and walked casually out. She returned to her car then drove it into Marlborough Court.

Inside the Chevy, she pulled on her gloves and stared at the building. There were no beams inside the garden perimeter. She suspected the flat may have an alarm. A sliver of self-doubt crept into her thoughts. She knew she could have died last night in Ravensmead. She did not want to make it two nights in a row.

---

She opened the car door and got out, leaving the keys in the ignition and one blue remote on the passenger seat.

The building's entrance was sealed by a glass door and security gate. She walked along the grass verge until she reached the balcony of No.12. She gripped the balustrade with her left hand, levered her boots against the wall, and pulled herself up and over. She let out a low moan. She could not avoid taking some pressure on her right shoulder.

She stood still and waited for the pain to subside.

No noise.

No new lights.

Aside from a folded deck chair and a rotting clothes horse, the balcony was empty and partially obscured from the road.

A barred gate protected the glass porch door.

She removed the hack saw from her rucksack, sliced through three bars to make squeeze space. The porch door was locked, but the lock jimmy made short work of it.

Inside, she aimed her head torch into the darkness. Her instinct detected no human or animal presence. The musty smell of stagnant air triggered a wave of apprehension.

She listened for electrical sounds indicating an alarm. If an external security firm were alerted, they would be impeded by the vehicular gate. If anyone from inside Marlborough Court responded, she would shoot them.

It was always important to have a plan and stick to it. Not that she normally did.

She fixed the flashlight to her head and scanned the room. A blood red Persian covered the slatted wood floor. The furniture was dark and old fashioned, and the mantelpiece was lined with glass ornaments. There was no television and no light bulbs in the ceiling sockets. A china frog with a gaping mouth perched on a faux fireplace. She picked it up. The mantelpiece was covered in a film of dust.

She replaced the frog and removed the Taurus from her belt holster. Her boots squeaked on the smooth wood flooring as she moved through the lounge, along an empty corridor.

Her heartbeat accelerated. She did not like the anticipation of a sudden surprise or fright.

She opened a door. It was a bathroom, empty except for a dirty white vest lying on the floor. In the light of her head torch, she prodded the garment with her toe and crouched. It looked like it had been used as a cloth to wipe the floor.

Dull noises from other apartments in the block sounded like faraway echoes.

She drew a cheap plastic shower curtain and aimed the torch around the tiled floor, up the walls. The soap dish was empty. The floor was dry and appeared not to have been used in some time. She touched the tap with her gloved hand but did not turn it on.

Moving out the bathroom, she filed silently along a narrow corridor into a bedroom. It contained a single bed with mattress, no sheets or covers. She holstered the Taurus, lifted the mattress, and looked underneath. It was clean and dry. There was a single shoe. A man's shoe, it was dusty but otherwise in good condition. She pouched the shoe in a plastic sleeve and put it in her rucksack.

She crossed the corridor into a second bedroom, also empty.

A loud creak sent a tingle down the back of her neck.

She retraced her path along the corridor and reached a gutted kitchen at the far end.

At the door, she paused and illuminated the room with her torch. There was a faint scent of incense and the electric humming of an appliance. She drew her Taurus and went inside slowly, gun at waist height in her left hand. An aperture gaped where a stove had once been. A narrow passage led into a scullery. The humming intensified. She directed her torch light into the room. A large volume chest freezer stood in the corner.

Shit.

A glow of silver light filtered in through a narrow window on the far wall. She crouched, dimmed her head torch, and listened. Evil had happened here, she could sense it. It was squeezing her, tightening her chest, her breath.

She took a deep breath, straightened up, and reset her head torch. There were bricks on the freezer's counter cover and under the base.

Another loud creak caused her to turn sharply. Her stomach lurched.

She bit hard on her bottom lip.

The torch cast light over the freezer.

It was big enough.

She ran a gloved finger along the edge of the rubber seal and held it to her nose. She sniffed the surface to confirm the smell was ammonia.

Breathing through both mouth and nose, she suppressed a claustrophobic need for fresh air, wondered if her stomach would be strong enough.

She slipped the Taurus into the belt holster.

Carefully she removed the bricks and placed them on the floor.

She took another deep breath and lifted the counter lid.

---

## 60

**Fallon held up the lid and illuminated the freezer in the light of her head torch.**

She was expecting a body.

The bottom of the freezer was covered with a brown jelly-like substance on top of a wet newspaper. There was a crumpled blue towel in the corner. She tested the substance with her finger. There was no smell.

She reached down and pulled out the towel, tucked it into a plastic sleeve. She tore a page from the stained newspaper, folded it carefully and inserted it into another plastic sleeve and dropped both sleeves in her rucksack.

A sudden noise startled her. She straightened up. The sound was behind her, heavy footsteps on the floor. She screamed, dropped the lid and twisted around, reached for the Taurus.

Something hit her like a bus.

She snapped backwards over the freezer, gun clattering to the floor.

Giant hands gripped her by the front of her jacket and ripped her to her feet. Pain from her right shoulder was like an electric shock. In the light of her head torch, a second person kicked the Taurus across the floor. Tall and slim, he reached out and ripped the torch from her head.

She screamed again as a hand pressed against her mouth and slammed her head against the wall. She tried to bite the hand, but the palm was cupped. Her assailant hit her in the stomach. She doubled over. He pressed his knee against her head and pinned her against the wall. Hands were everywhere, up her legs, between them, inside her pants, under her arms, on her head, over her breasts, squeezing hard.

She was spun by her shoulder, face to the wall, her feet kicked open, rucksack ripped away. The man behind leaned against her, his elbow like a baton against the back of her neck, crushing her face into the wall.

There were two. Even uninjured, she stood no chance. She heard the second man make a call on his phone. The first man's elbow was imbedded in the back of her neck.

"Jacky, we had a break in."

She was yanked around. The man gripped her by the throat. A cell phone camera flashed in her face.

"Ja, it's a woman."

The grip slackened, but she knew she could not overcome the force behind it without a weapon. She stood still, compliant, focused on the present and to keep thinking, to stay alive.

"OK."

The second man pushed in behind her. He pulled off her gloves. She screamed as he ripped her hands behind her back and zipped her wrists together.

A dirty cloth, smelling like oil, was pressed against her face. She shut her mouth, tried to resist the rag. A hand tightened on her throat, thumb applying pressure to her larynx. The rag was pushed into her mouth. The first man held her by the hair, the second man rolled duct tape around her head, over her mouth, once, twice, three times.

Relax. Breathe through your nose. She fought the urge to gag.

The man ran his hands down her body, fastened a bind around her ankles.

She was dragged through the kitchen, along the corridor and into the lounge, tipped onto the Persian.

Watch, breathe, think, smell, listen and keep track of time. Lying on her left shoulder, it was all she could do.

"Check her bag."

Dim light from the window illuminated the room. Both men were using their cell phones as torches.

Her rucksack was tipped out. They rifled through it. They removed the battery from her cell phone.

She lay on her left shoulder, completely still.

She focused on the gangsters. The big one had black tracksuit pants with a white stripe, brown fleecy, black beanie, his fat cheeks reminiscent of a youthful bully, a failed rugby player with no discipline, all carbohydrate and Coke. The other was a beanpole in dirty jeans, red Nike T-shirt, rusty hair, face like bubble wrap. She looked away. If she was going to die she did not want their faces to be the last images she saw.

The beanpole opened her wallet and looked at her ID. He smiled at her.

"What now?" the big one asked.

"Jacky kom nou."

The beanpole struck a match. She smelled the sweet aroma of a joint. Dope was good. They would relax.

She wondered what had gone wrong. She imagined a silent alarm system activated and alerted the gangsters of an intrusion at No.12. They must have been inside the property and guarding the flat? She had not expected this.

## 61

**"What the fuck's wrong with the gate?"**

Even before she saw the man in a trench coat and balaclava, Fallon knew it was Professor Dave Valentine, her visitor in prison.

Valentine flicked a laser light towards her then turned his attention to the contents of her rucksack scattered on the floor.

"Is this her stuff?"

"Ja meneer Jacky."

He used his cell as a torch and his foot to shift through the items.

"Are you sure? She didn't come by car?"

"Nee meneer. No car keys."

Valentine bent and examined her cell phone and battery. He used his cell phone to scan her equipment as if trying to ascertain whether any device was transmitting signal. He picked up the blue remote and frowned.

"What's this?"

He pulled a pen knife from his pocket and popped open the transmitter. He dropped it to the floor and crushed it with his boot.

"What the fuck you playing at, Fallon?"

He spotted the plastic sleeve with the torn section of stained newspaper. He lifted it and held it to the light.

She thought about Carlos De Palma and how he dealt with betrayal. If this Valentine was his successor, would he be any less ruthless? In her weakened state, a terrible fear swept over her. She had to get a grip.

Valentine dropped the plastic sleeve then walked over and kicked her in the ribs with the point of his shoe.

"You stupid bitch!"

The impact seemed to shake her out of a state of helplessness and fine tune her instinct for survival. *It doesn't hurt*, she told herself. *He can't hurt me if I don't allow it.*

He kicked her again and turned to the gangsters.

"You guys can take a hike."

The gangsters looked at him, childlike.

"Go on, fuck off and make yourselves useful."

Valentine removed the balaclava, lit a cigarette, and paced the room thoughtfully. His curly hair was longer than when she had seen him at Worcester Women's Prison.

He picked up the Taurus and examined it.

"What are you playing at?" he said.

---

He walked towards her. A cigarette hung from his mouth. She watched the boots that had kicked her like a dog. They had yellow and brown laces.

"A poor man's Beretta," he said and placed the weapon on the windowsill. He stubbed out his cigarette and lifted her beneath her arms. Her right shoulder screamed as he dragged her off the Persian across the dusty wooden floor and propped her against the wall on her knees. They had bound her hands behind her back instead of in front. Normally that was more secure.

He stepped back.

"That's what they call execution position," he said.

She strained at the bind. It was tight, but she could maneuver her fingers. She wondered how much time had passed. She had to act before the gangsters returned. Alone with the three, she had no chance.

He ripped the tape off her mouth and she spat out the cloth.

"Why do they call you Jacky, Professor?"

He kicked her hard against the thigh.

"I ask the questions, you bitch. What are you doing?"

Her thigh throbbed. She thought quickly. She could not say she was chasing after the reward for finding Nial Townley. She calculated that since Valentine set her up with the fake Carlos De Palma, he must work for whoever had taken over Dark Video. So her boss was his boss, whoever it may be.

"I'm on assignment for Dark Video."

"Huh? What assignment? Who sent you *here*?"

She could not think straight. It felt like every part of her body was sending frantic messages to her brain. He lifted his boot.

"No, don't kick me. NETWORX gave me this address."

Valentine stared at her then shook his head and spat on the floor.

"How did you get here?"

"Uber."

She knew he could check, but he would have to reconnect her phone.

He went to the other side of the room, lit another cigarette, and walked back across the wooden floor.

Behind her back, she stretched and wiggled her fingers under the elastic of her black leggings. She struggled to maintain an impassive expression while her right shoulder was throbbing with pain. She flexed her stomach muscles and looked straight at him without blinking her eyes.

He sucked deeply on the cigarette. Her plan relied on timing and proximity. Her only weapon was his underestimation.

"I know Carlos De Palma is dead," she said softly.

---

He blew the smoke towards her and did not answer.

"I don't care," she said. "I am happy to work with you, Jacky."

His cell rang. She listened to the conversation.

*No, she's alone. No. We've checked. She came alone. I don't know. I will ask.*

*She says she came here on Dark Video business. She's got a fucking big gun, fully loaded.*

His eyes were fixed on her and she dared not move.

*Someone called NETWORX. That's what she said. Hey, I'm only the messenger.*

He smirked at her.

*She also said she knows someone called Carlos is dead.*

Fallon closed her eyes. She wished she had not told him that.

*OK. Don't be long.*

She was pleased Valentine neglected to mention the contents of her bag. Maybe she could bluff her way out—she had made a mistake, foolishly listened to NETWORX, came to the wrong address. She wished she had checked the channel to confirm who she was supposed to be knocking off.

"Who did you come here with?" Valentine asked.

"I came alone."

"You were meant to bring someone."

"What? I don't understand. Who was I meant to bring?"

He flicked ash on the floor. "Never mind."

She wanted to keep the conversation going, maintain the distance between them, and distract his attention from her.

"You can tell me, Jacky. We're on the same side."

"You've got everything worked out. I remember what you said in the slammer, huh, baby. Everything worked out. Well, clearly not."

She willed all her skills to maintain a neutral and subservient expression. She had to disguise the concentration required to reverse the situation.

---

Valentine sucked hard on the cigarette. His eyes bored into her. Had he read her? In one movement, he could pick up her Taurus and shoot her. He may have his own weapon. The gangsters could return.

She squeezed her stomach muscles again and the box knife in her rectum shifted.

## 62

**Fallon maintained an impassive expression as she manipulated her core muscles.**

Valentine checked his phone. She knew he was waiting for instruction. Her fingers touched the end of the sheathed box knife. She clenched her stomach again and pushed the knife out.

Valentine's phone beeped. He read the message and looked up.

She froze. It took a concentrated effort of every brain cell to maintain a passive expression while she extracted the box knife with the fingers of her bound hands.

Valentine shook his head to emphasize his regret. She knew immediately what the message was. He stared at her intently. For a moment, she feared he had sensed her movement, but then she recognized the look. She had seen it on the faces of so many men, the pathetic and instinctive hunger. He had instructions to kill her. But he wanted to fuck her first. Perhaps the universe would be on her side.

Valentine ground out his cigarette. He walked back towards her. She held the box cutter behind her back in her bound hands. If he walked behind her or checked the bind, he would spot it and take it off her.

"You're sweating," he said and crouched before her, wiped her brow. He smelled of stale cigarettes. She thought he looked like a fish, a barbel.

She reckoned a half hour had passed since she had been accosted. Every sense was tuned to the sound of the gangsters' return. She had to free her hands before that happened.

But she could not risk moving without attracting his attention.

"I dreamed about you," she said.

"You did?"

He grinned and unzipped her anorak and tested her breasts through the black garment. "Such a waste."

Men never ceased to amaze her. There was zero chance in hell she could have romantic thoughts about him, yet he was taking the bait. She arched forward. She could feel the box cutter's blade against the cable tie holding her wrists together.

He pulled away and straightened up. She pressed the blade of the knife against the cable tie.

He picked up her Swiss army knife, opened the blade and turned back towards her. She froze. He kneeled beside her.

"Who are you, Jacky?" she said seductively.

---

He flicked open the blade and pressed the tip to her throat.

"I follow orders," he said. "Like you should've."

With one hand, he held the tip of her blade against her throat. With the other, he squeezed her left breast.

"What did you think of my work as a professor? Not a bad actor, what do you think? The prison authorities believed me too."

"You were amazing. Jacky, listen, I made a mistake here. We're on the same side."

He closed his eyes and his mouth opened. She saw his nicotine stained teeth. He ran his tongue across his upper lip.

"You came here looking for Nial Townley," he said.

He turned his free hand and pressed it into the front of her pants. She sucked in her stomach to give him room to maneuver. The movement allowed her to press the blade deeper into the cable tie.

"Oh," she sighed erotically.

"No panties. I like that."

She felt the gloved hand slide into her stockings, a finger poke at her. He wiggled the finger inside her pants, tried to force it in.

"Do you know about Nial Townley?" she asked.

She pressed her pelvis forward. He pulled his hand out and removed the glove. His breathing increased. The Swiss army knife was pointing downwards.

"I pushed his car into the sea."

"Oh my God, was he in it?"

He laughed. "No. It was just meant to look like he was."

As he pressed his hand into her pants again, she was able to force the box knife through the cable tie between her wrists.

"What're you doing?" he said.

She moaned as if in ecstasy.

"No, don't stop," she said.

He grinned and wiggled his finger.

She twisted suddenly, raised her left fist, and ripped the box knife across his throat. Valentine screamed and fell backwards. She thrust the point of the cutter into his eye. Valentine stabbed wildly with the Swiss army knife, grazing her shoulder with the first swipe, but she rolled away. He screamed again and raised his hand to his neck, one knee on the floor. Dark black blood squirted from his throat.

"You fucking bitch!"

His second swipe went nowhere. She rolled again and kicked hard with both boots. He fell back onto the seat of his pants. She sliced the cable tie binding her ankles. Valentine clutched his throat and gurgled.

"Help me, please help me," he screamed.

She did not look at him again. She had to escape immediately.

She picked up her Taurus. Training the gun on Valentine, she gathered her items into the rucksack. She slipped the Taurus into the belt holster.

She reached the front door simultaneously with the sound of footsteps in the outside passageway. She double bolted it as the handle turned, heard the impact as the gangsters smashed against the door. It would probably only take two kicks.

She sprinted across the room and exited via the patio door, squeezing though the burglar bars she had hacked earlier and out onto the balcony. She vaulted off her left arm over the balustrade and landed on the grass, was running before she landed.

She got to the Chevy, jumped in, started it. Her hands were slippery with blood. She grabbed the spare blue remote off the passenger seat, pressed the green button, and silently mouthed: *you fucking better work.* The vehicular gate slid open as the thin gangster burst through the front entrance doors of Marlborough Court. She reversed hard, swung out the gate, and pressed the remote again. She did not want any cowboys car-chasing her through the city.

## 63

**At 2:45 the next morning, Carla arrived at Crystal Place looking tired and pale.** She took off her coat. Underneath she was dressed in a pink tracksuit and white sneakers.

"I'm sorry to call you out at this time," Le Fleur said. "I could've come to you."

He adjusted the under floor heating with his remote.

"No, it's better this way," she said. "I'm staying at an apartment in the Waterfront. I don't even know how the boom gates operate."

Moments earlier, he had watched her arrive in a new model BMW.

"You've got yourself a car?"

"It's a rental. It's too fucking cold to drive around on a scooter in winter in Cape Town."

She sat on an ottoman. He remembered her first arrival at Crystal Place, her sadness and determination to find Nial. He felt like he'd known her a long time.

"Does anybody else know you're here?"

She shook her head, looked worried.

He placed a plastic sleeve on the table in front of her. A folded page of stained newspaper was visible inside the plastic.

She reached forward but did not touch it. "It's a page from a newspaper?"

"Can you read the date?"

She leaned forward. "It's a week after Nial disappeared. What's the brown stuff?"

"I think it is blood," he said softly.

She gasped and looked up, her eyes wide.

"Where did you get this?"

"It came from a commercial freezer in a flat in Gardens. There was also a towel."

"Oh my God, you think it's Nial's blood?"

"Yes."

She stared at him. He stood and paced the room.

"I got an anonymous call. The caller knew things about the Stingray, cell numbers, coordinates."

Carla knew nothing of Fallon, not even her existence. He wanted to keep it like that.

She sucked in her breath. "You think Nial's body was stored in the freezer?"

---

He did not respond.

"But we can't be sure until tests are done," she said hopefully.

"Unfortunately, there's something else."

He fiddled with his cell phone then passed it to her. On screen was a picture of a single Crockett & Jones shoe. She stared at the picture then closed her eyes and breathed out.

"This photograph was taken in the same flat."

She opened her eyes again and sat for a long time staring at the picture. Then she handed him back his cell and looked at the newspaper in the sleeve. She shook her head slowly.

"Oh my God, this is so unbelievable. I don't..." Her voice tailed away. She buried her face in her hands. He left her sitting there and walked to the kitchen, turned on the kettle.

Yesterday evening, his micro camera in the foyer at the Sea View Holiday Flats captured Fallon leaving her apartment dressed in black and carrying a rucksack. About two hours later, she returned. A little after midnight she left the apartment again, this time dressed in jeans and a blue jacket, without the rucksack. Ten minutes later his LPR camera picked up her Chevy on Victoria Road below Crystal Place. He had watched her deposit the plastic sleeve in his mailbox.

He heard footsteps behind him in the kitchen.

"Do you have the actual address of the flat?" she asked.

"Yes."

"We must inform the police immediately."

"I've already informed Parks."

She clenched both fists. The color returned to her face.

"We've got those fuckers now. Gavin is going to be so pleased. I swear this, Daniel, when we are finished with Pittman and GALI, they'll wish they never set foot in this country."

He stood with his arms at his side and said nothing. Carla was progressing with the new Supertech and what he was about to contend would devastate those plans. But he needed her support to succeed and bring the real criminals to justice. And he needed to trust her.

The buzzer rang downstairs.

"Who's that?" she said, eyes widening, the events of their garden route mission still fresh.

Le Fleur stepped past her, walked to the monitor, and checked the screen.

"Take the lift to the third floor," he said.

He looked back at Carla and nodded.

"I have a plan," he said. "It's a risky one. But I believe it is the only chance to discover what really happened to Nial."

"Who is it?"

"You know her," Le Fleur said.

There was a knock on the door.

# 64

**At 11:00, later the same day, Fallon arrived at Crystal Place and pressed the buzzer of No.4.** There was no response. She removed the flash drive from her bag and hesitated. She was troubled and confused.

She was troubled because she was acting outside of her instinct. She considered betrayal as misfortune falling on others, not her. That's why she did not trust. To be betrayed, one must have first trusted. Had she made a mistake?

She stretched her neck and her battered body trembled.

Last night Le Fleur told her he needed more proof, the blood on the newspaper and towel and the picture of a shoe was not enough.

He also told her the police were at Marlborough Court. They had found the gate derailed, a significant blood loss in No.12 but no freezer. She reckoned the gangsters—and whoever Valentine was working for—had got rid of Valentine's body and the freezer before the police got there.

The flash drive backup of the Stingray was her collateral.

She took a deep breath and patted the Taurus inside her jacket on a shoulder strap.

The confusion came from what she had read on the Dark Video channel this morning. The new instructions were a shock.

There was a picture of Le Fleur and his home address.

```
He is JACKER. Tell him you have information
regarding Nial Townley.
```

It was almost as if someone were playing a trick on her.

```
Take him to the flat No.12 Marlborough Court
in Gardens.
```

The time showed the instructions had been drafted *before* she had gone to Marlborough Court.

She remembered Valentine asking: *You were meant to bring someone.*

Nothing was making sense.

Without Le Fleur, she had no chance of getting the reward. He had trusted her by coming to her flat. She could have killed him. He must have known. He had trusted her. She had to trust him.

She had not trusted many people in the past. She had previously pro-

---

tected a young varsity student from Dark Video. She was not sure why. The student named Robbie was an honorable person. That was his problem. So honorable, he chose honor before her and shopped her to the police.

It struck her Le Fleur was the same type.

He would choose between his moral obligation and his commitment to her.

She removed the flash drive and inserted it into the mailbox.

As she turned, she noticed two men alight from a black BMW.

Her heart bounced. She turned back to the mailbox. She would have to blow it up to get the flash drive back.

The traffic on Victoria Road was light.

The men were walking towards her, trying to act casual. They wore some type of uniform, not like police, more like gangsters dressed up as municipal workers. She retreated in a steady step towards her Chevy, eyes on the pavement.

The gap was a hundred meters. A sprinter could close it in ten seconds. To her left, the Atlantic Ocean stretched out like a gigantic wasteland.

One. Two.

Her popped shoulder ached. She did not look about. The men were coming for her. Le Fleur had betrayed her.

She maintained a steady step. She slipped her hand inside her jacket to test the weight of the Taurus. Time felt like slow motion. She tensed her body, prepared for crisis.

Three. Four.

Shoes smacked on the road behind her. If they intended to kill her, she knew she would be dead already. They wanted to capture her. She would rather die.

Five. Six.

Someone shouted.

In front of her, two elderly ladies in her path froze, concern etched on their faces.

Seven. Eight.

Fallon gripped the Taurus. She must be sure. First time. One chance only.

Nine. Ten.

She could not wait longer. She spun around and crouched. The figures were blurred, one in front, the other behind. She fired six times in immediate succession, the suppressed blast muted by the sound of the sea and traffic. Both pursuers went down.

She stood and ran towards the prone men, weapon extended. She knew she had not hit them both, was lucky to hit one. One man was not moving. The other wriggled onto his side trying to free his gun from its holster. She fired two more shots. One bullet kicked up tar from the road, the other seemed to sigh as it sunk into his chest.

Someone screamed.

She watched the two men for movement. They had not expected her to shoot on Victoria Road.

More screaming came from multiple sides.

She looked around. The two old ladies cursed loudly, Jewish grannies, not frightened.

A car approaching from the Llundudno side screeched to a halt, reversed frantically.

She sprinted to the Chevy and jumped inside, fired the ignition, spun into the traffic. More cars now halted on both sides of the fallen men. The black BMW detached from the sidewalk.

The Chevy bounced from the pavement with squealing tires as she sped off in the direction of town. The black BMW, engine roaring, pulled in behind her.

She had no time for a seat belt. Inertia pulled her towards the center of the car as she negotiated the first of the curves. A bakkie packed with construction workers slowed her progress. She flicked her lights, leaned on the horn, then swerved blindly onto the other side of the road and overtook. The workers cheered as if they were at a football game.

In her mirror, the BMW had not yet overtaken the *bakkie*.

She swung the wheel left down a one way road towards the sea. She had no idea where the road came out. With some luck, the BMW would miss the turn. She cornered at the bottom of a short hill onto a slip road, prayed it would not be a dead end.

A slide would have taken her through the barrier and over the edge into the Atlantic.

As the road straightened out along the coast, the BMW was still on her tracks, using its larger engine to close the gap. She considered ditching the Chevy and fleeing into one of the apartment blocks, but they all looked like locked up fortresses.

She exited onto Beach Road, a double carriageway. A traffic circle caught her by surprise, she braked hard, went right—a shortcut on the wrong side of the road. A car hurtled head on towards her. The extended pavement of the one-way offered a margin to her left. Holding nerve, she forced the oncoming car to veer onto the pavement and smash against an overhead lamppost. The next car braked furiously and held its line. She ramped the pavement space and sliced past, the Chevy's shocks groaning as the car rebounded onto the road.

There was no sign of the BMW. She expected they would follow the parallel road and try to cut her off at the next intersection.

She reached the merge before the BMW. It pressed in close behind her.

She knew about the pit maneuver, a side swipe to the back of a car that would spin it out of control. She juggled lanes so they had no space.

She tightened her mouth. She had not reloaded the Taurus. One for Jeremy, six plus two now. She reckoned the magazine was empty and she had one shot left.

She spun the wheel and skidded right into a narrow side road. She rounded a truck attempting a parallel park and ramped the pavement, scraping the Chevy driver's door against the wall of an adjoining building. Pausing only temporarily, she shimmied left and right, crossing the busy Main Road before turning towards Lion's Head. A municipal worker stepped into the road to warn it was one way only. He jumped back as she sliced through the space he had seconds before filled.

As she raced up the one way, not knowing what awaited her at the apex, she was calm. Her European passport was in her handbag. And before she left the Sea View Holiday Flats, she had emptied the contents of her purse and given it to Fabrice, nearly three thousand rand.

"Buy that little Francine a golden teddy and a new pair of shoes," she had told him. "And will you give her a message from me? Tell her: *hey my love.*"

"I beg your pardon, madam?"

*Hey my love.*

She clenched her teeth and gripped the wheel.

All that mattered was here and now and there were only two outcomes, life or death, and neither of those mattered. Neither offered any lasting satisfaction. She'd stared at death twice in the last two days—by gang rape in Ravensmead, at the blade of Dave 'Jacky' Valentine in Gardens. She knew if she did not die today, she would die tomorrow or the next day. She promised herself if she got through today, she would finish what must be finished—then run, somewhere far away, lick her wounds, and fight another day.

Ahead she spotted an oncoming car, to her right a one-way sign and red no-entry. Choice was a luxury. The BMW cruised effortlessly behind. She skidded on the curve and scraped another car. Metallic grating filled her ears. An inch more and it would have been game over.

She was going uphill rapidly, Lion's Head growing larger.

These were residential roads. She hoped there would not be children. She did not want to kill a child as her last act on earth.

She came out of the one-way and turned left onto Kloof. She wondered how many people were in the black BMW.

On Kloof Road, a robot hanging over the road signaled green. She raced through it. Directly ahead a junction, decision time again: cul-de-sac right towards the mountain, two no-entry signs blocking continued direction, the road arced left and back into Main Road.

The robot was red. She steered onto the right hand side, hooted, and shot across Main Road, dodging between a car at the opposite robots and one going in her direction. The short road led her back to the sea and Beach Road.

She was hemmed between the Atlantic and the mountain. The BMW was undeterred; it was two cars back, emergency lights flashing.

She could smell the heat from her car's 1600 engine, the burning rubber of the tires.

On Beach Road's thinner traffic, she was able to weave around slower cars. The BMW was unshakeable.

She was now less than a kilometer from her home.

Spinning into the inside lane to avoid a right turning car, she sideswiped another vehicle, felt the passenger door of the Chevy concertina, lucky not to blow a tire.

The BMW was flush behind her. She shimmied the steering wheel to prevent them pulling a pit maneuver.

At Rocklands, the robot flashed orange and two cars in front stopped for the pedestrian light. She slowed. In her rearview mirror, she spotted the passenger door of the BMW open. She jammed her foot on the accelerator and mounted the center curb then over onto the other side of the road. She braked and spun the wheel, skidding back onto the right side of the road but beyond the robots.

Then she accelerated. The sun was overhead, the sea to her left. Beach Road widened into four lanes. She checked her rear view; the BMW was closing in.

She sped forward, straight on towards Green Point. The BMW pulled up alongside. She could see nothing through the darkened windows. She imagined the barrel of a gun pointed at her head.

She hit brakes and swerved left, off the road and onto the grass embankment, narrowly missing a palm tree as she bounced over the uneven terrain and onto the road behind the Point Health Club. Nothing emerged from the dust behind her. Her pursuers would have to make a U-turn and

double back. She hit an immediate hard left.
    She was clear.

## 65

**16:00 Friday afternoon at Gorky Park Revue Bar.**

Le Fleur was seated on a scotch-guarded couch in the Common Room. The collar of his shirt was torn and he had a red welt on his neck. He was silently contemplating the wisdom of his decision to come to Gorky Park. His plan was in action. He wanted to prove a theory. But if his theory was right, he could be in great danger.

He had argued with a stripper—Ynez—in one of the VIP booths and attracted the attention of a bouncer. Ynez told the bouncer he was making wild accusations. The bouncer escorted him to the Common Room, a space usually reserved as a fantasy chamber for the ultra-rich, but out of season it served as a board room with benefits. The bouncer spoke to the manager who decided to make a call to one of the co-owners.

"He asked for you twice," he overheard the manager say on his cell while eyeballing him. "Yes, I'm sure."

Clubs like Gorky Park preferred to resolve its issues in-house. Clients were a valuable commodity and sometimes strippers were a little too eager to take their money.

A woman's voice shouted: "You tell Gavin to come here right now!!"

"I think you should speak to him, Gavin," the manager insisted. "Yes. Mister fucking Le Fleur. That's the name he gave me."

The Common Room had padded walls, silver poles, a lush red carpet and life size sculptures. There were couches, leather chairs, a wide wooden bar space and framed black and white photographs of nude beauty queens on the walls. A door opened to a bathroom on the far side. Le Fleur imagined the room had seen a lot of powerful men with their pants down. He slouched lower on the couch, closed his eyes, and pretended to doze off. The bouncer remained at the open door.

He heard Gavin Marx arrive thirty minutes later.

"Where is she?" asked Marx.

"She's in my office." It was the manager's voice.

"Bring her along, won't you."

"Do you need me?"

"I can handle it," said Marx. "Where's he?"

"Inside. Says he's waiting for the 'big boss.' I think he's had too much to drink."

The bouncer at the door stepped aside and Marx entered. He was casually dressed in blue jeans, turquoise Polo shirt, dark glasses on his head.

"Hello, Mr. Le Fleur?" said Marx tentatively as if uncertain who he was greeting.

Le Fleur opened an eye and lifted his hand feebly. He cleared his throat and straightened up. The manager appeared with Ynez in tow. She rushed up to Marx and hugged him. Her mascara had run down below her eyes, giving her a demonic appearance. Marx touched her shoulder as if he were avoiding contracting a disease. The manager gestured to the bouncer and they closed the Common Room door and departed.

Ynez sat, Marx remained standing.

"What's happened here?" asked Marx. He looked rattled, his hair slightly out of place as if he were having an afternoon sleep when called.

Ynez spoke excitedly. "First he asks for a private dance and he's grabbing me all over." Ynez waved her hands expressively. "Then when I slap his hands, he accuses me of killing Nial."

"What? He said *you* killed Nial?" Marx looked from Ynez to Le Fleur in amazement.

"He said it. Ask him, ask him!"

Marx raised his hands. He seemed unprepared. Le Fleur wondered what Marx had expected, what he had thought about on the drive over.

A man in a well-fitted black suit entered and nodded towards Marx. Marx did not speak or introduce him. Le Fleur sat up. The man was in his mid-twenties with a bony face some might consider handsome. He was not physically imposing, but he had an air of someone who could handle most situations. He had a cell phone device in his hand. Le Fleur guessed he was sniffing for spy type devices. The man walked around the room, checking the device. He went into the bathroom. When he came out, he looked Le Fleur over but did not approach. He nodded to Marx and left the room.

"Charming fellow," said Le Fleur with a slight slur.

Marx cleared his throat. "OK. Can we resolve this dispute? We all say things we don't mean when we've had too much to drink."

"He hasn't paid me," said Ynez.

"I'll sort it out," said Marx. "Don't worry, you'll be paid."

Ynez removed a beige makeup purse from her handbag and applied lip gloss. Marx fixed his eyes on Le Fleur.

"Would you like a drink, Daniel?" he offered, then appeared to regret it. Le Fleur shook his head. Marx turned to Ynez. She shook her head too. Marx pressed his toe on a white button switch on the floor.

"Mary," said Marx. "Could you bring me a rock shandy?"

"I need to use the ladies." Ynez stood and went to bathroom.

Marx stared ahead. Marx waved his hand irritably. His jaw was set, lips tight, as if he intended to end the discussion quickly and go home.

"What about that ass, Gavin?"

Marx did not comment.

"Thank you for coming to sort things out."

Marx remained silent. Ynez returned from the bathroom.

"Must I stay? I want to clean myself up." Her shoulders were down. She did not look at Le Fleur.

"You may go," said Marx.

She shouldered her handbag and walked to the door of the Common Room and knocked. The bouncer opened it and she walked out without looking back.

"Cash for gash, she's a champion," said Le Fleur. "Nial Townley's girlfriend being fingered by everyone in Cape Town, aren't you proud?"

Marx reacted like he had been hit in the face. His face reddened.

"I don't know where you get off saying things like that. What's your problem? You've clearly overdone it. I suggest you go home and sleep it off."

The door opened and Mary arrived with a drink on a tray. She was pretty, perhaps not tall enough to be a dancer at the club so she served drinks. Marx took the drink and she bowed slightly and left the room.

"You're a co-owner of Gorky Park?" said Le Fleur.

Marx sipped his drink. Le Fleur could see Marx's legal impatience rising.

"It's not common knowledge, no?" Le Fleur added.

He waited, but Marx did not respond.

"And Nial Townley too."

Marx sipped his drink and tightened his mouth.

"You did a lot of things together."

Marx swallowed his drink and banged the glass on the bar counter.

"I have no idea what your game is, but I suggest we close up here before someone says something they regret. What's eating you? You've been paid? Is it not enough?"

"It's not enough," said Le Fleur.

Marx placed his hands on his hips. His face was burning.

"I paid the amount Carla told me."

"I want the GALI reward."

## 66

**"The reward? Why on earth would we pay you the reward?"**

"I found out what happened to Nial Townley."

"Daniel, I am trying hard to understand where you are coming from. That was a reward offered by GALI. When a killer offers a reward for his own capture, you can generally bet he won't honor the payment."

"He was your best friend, Gavin."

Marx visibly flinched. His shoulders tightened and he clenched his teeth. He looked like he was ready to storm out the room.

"You should sit," said Le Fleur calmly, but as an order.

Marx narrowed his eyes. His mouth was tight and small. He looked like an adversary assessing his opponent, realizing suddenly he was more substantial than first thought. Marx adjusted his jeans and sat opposite.

"What *is* this about?"

"What's it about?" Le Fleur looked up at the ceiling. "What's it about? It's about money, I guess."

"You want us to pay you R5m for the work you did for us? That's absurd."

"It's a drop in the ocean compared to what you've saved for Supertech and Nial."

"What's that got to do with anything?" He raised his voice. "You provided a service and we paid you. What don't you understand? Where's Carla? I want to phone her." He pulled out his cell phone. "Does she know about this?"

Le Fleur put up his hand.

"No."

Marx fiddled with his cell.

"You and Nial went to Geneva," said Le Fleur.

Marx pressed a button on his cell and looked up.

"What did you say?"

"You heard me."

"I don't understand. Why is that relevant?" Marx glanced up at the camera disguised as a smoke detector.

"You know why."

"What are you talking about?"

"You met with Karl Lombardy, the expert on all things GALI."

Marx placed his hand over his mouth and rubbed it back and forth. He stared at Le Fleur. Then he stood up. "Sorry, I must organize something." He toed the switch. "Mary, could you send Zaheer to the Common Room."

Marx sat down and folded his arms. Le Fleur felt the stakes had been raised. The energy inside was bubbling, a mix of adrenaline and determination.

"Who's Zaheer? He's the guy in the black suit? Is he going to fuck me up?"

Marx said nothing.

"Are you interested in how I found out that you and Nial are co-owners of this establishment?"

"Not particularly."

"I'm a bit slow, you see. I'm not great at puzzles. That's odd, don't you think, when I've played more hours of computer games than most?" He tapped his head. "There's so much information. And that's my game. I think to be good at puzzles you must take in less not more. Don't you think?"

Marx feigned disinterest.

"A few weeks ago, I had a visitor from a yellow teapot. A car registered to a company called Apollo Financial Services. I didn't think much of it. I thought perhaps someone was having Carla followed. For all I know, you were the driver of the teapot."

Le Fleur wriggled forward, pulled his wallet from his back pocket, and removed a sales slip. "Here it is." He waved the slip in Marx's direction. "This doesn't say Gorky Park. No, we can't have the client's wives spotting this when they go through their husband's pockets in the morning, can we now?" He held the slip close to his eyes. "It says Apollo. Apollo."

Marx shrugged.

"So I checked the company registry for Gorky Park aka Apollo Financial Services and what did I find?"

He looked across at Marx.

"Five owners. And well, I've already told you this. N. Townley and G. Marx."

The door opened and the man in the black suit entered. Marx rose immediately and spoke to Zaheer in a hushed tone.

Le Fleur breathed in and out.

Marx pointed towards the concealed camera. Zaheer departed and Marx returned to his seat.

"You turning off the cameras?" asked Le Fleur. "I don't know why you bother. You can ask your guys to erase the footage afterwards."

## 67

**"Why would you accuse Ynez of killing Nial?** Do you think you can coerce the reward out of us? You've got a fat chance, my friend."

"Oh, I only did that to make you come to Gorky Park."

"Who do you think I am? Some fucking stupid dick?"

"You're the lawyer, not me. I'm getting quite thirsty. Could you ask Mary to bring me a beer? What type of beer do you serve here, Gavin? Do you have any craft beer?"

Marx expanded his cheeks like a frog. He toed the switch.

"Speak."

"Hi Mary, I'm Daniel, could you bring me a craft beer, any craft."

He looked at Marx as he waited for a reply.

"I'm sorry, we don't serve craft." Her tone was friendly, contrasted with what he knew was ahead. He did not relish confrontation, but saw no other way.

"What do you have?"

"Heineken, Peroni, Castle, Amstel."

"Do you have Black Label?"

"Yes."

"That would be great."

He gave Marx a satisfied look. Marx adjusted his pants and returned to his seat. He leaned forward.

"Daniel," he said. "Listen to me. I don't know what you are trying to achieve. But if you're thinking of making trouble, you'll get a nasty surprise. If it's more money you're after, let's talk. Come over to my office on Monday and I'm sure we can work something out. Not five million though."

Mary entered with a beer on a tray. Marx sat back on his chair. She placed the tray on the bar counter and filled a glass. She brought the glass to Le Fleur.

"Thank you, Mary," he said.

She turned and left with the tray and empty bottle.

Le Fleur sipped the froth off the glass and wiped his mouth. He raised his glass to Marx. Marx's mouth was downturned.

"So you went to Geneva with Nial?"

"I've been to a lot of places."

"That's when you thought about it, isn't it? That's where the plan originated. Someone was screwing Supertech in Venezuela. It was GALI. You learned from Karl Lombardy how GALI roll and that's when the hallelujah moment occurred. How to put Supertech's resources beyond the reach of the Venezuelan government? A fake kidnapping. Whose idea was it? Yours or Nial's?"

"You tell me. You seem to know everything. But before you go on, Daniel, think about it. Do you want to swim in these waters? You have seen what GALI can do. They are ruthless."

"Pittman? Who you and Nial handpicked for GALI Africa? Oh, I think GALI will be overjoyed with what I've got to tell them. I think they'll hand over the reward without delay."

"You've got it all worked out."

"Let's go back to Geneva. Maybe Nial didn't go for the plan. We call it the gun-at-the-head plan. Nial believed someone close to him was in danger. Did you plan it together then you crossed him? You could get rid of Nial, grab the millions, and pin the blame on GALI."

Marx closed his eyes. Le Fleur knew his ability to read Marx's reaction was crucial. He had to push him over an edge. But where was the edge?

"Livigno," said Le Fleur.

He paused, allowing the word to sink in. Marx did not open his eyes.

"I thought about it for so long. I am prime with straight arithmetic and games, but riddles? I suck at figuring those out. I suck at puzzles. What did Livigno mean? Avalanche. A risky valley. I went over and over it. I thought it could be an SOS to Goldman's. Then I thought it was irrelevant banter. Now I realize. Livigno is a town in the province of Lombardy. Karl Lombardy. Livigno was a code, a special message to you. Was it so you'd know GALI were extorting him to transfer the funds? Or was it simply a gesture between two friends who'd planned an elaborate and risky scheme?"

Marx seemed to be in a trance.

"Carla always asked me what I thought. Take a flyer, she'd say. I don't like that. I don't gamble. My world is exact. One byte wrong in a billion and nothing will work. That's why I'm not good at this detective stuff. I look at what's in front of me and it seems like half the bytes are wrong. He was your best friend. You are the godfather to his son. How *could* you have done this?"

It seemed like the room had closed in around them. Marx's eyes opened and fluttered. It was a good two minutes before he spoke.

"You don't think that goes through my head every minute of every waking hour."

He stopped and stared at the wall.

"Something went wrong?" said Le Fleur.

---

Marx's cell beeped. He read the message and typed a response. A sentence.

"Who sanctioned the hit on Carla?" asked Le Fleur.

Marx did not answer.

"Whoever you are working with is a killer, Gavin. There's a hacker dead and two others unaccounted. They're the tech skills that made it possible for you. Your accomplice is silencing anyone who knows anything about what happened."

Marx's cell beeped again and he read the message and responded immediately. A short message. One word. *Yes, no, maybe?*

"Carla took me to Nial's house. I went into Gregory's room. I'm sure you did too. You must've stood at his bedside and seen the picture frame."

Marx's lip trembled. A third beep on his cell. This time he read it and stared at the screen without responding.

"The picture of Winnie the Pooh with a quote. Do you know the one I mean? It starts: *If ever there is a tomorrow when we're not together.*"

Marx looked up from his cell and breathed in deeply. His nostrils flared.

"You can still do the right thing, Gavin."

"It's way too late for that," he said and rose, walked to the door of the Common Room.

## 68

**The man in the dark suit entered as Marx left the Common Room.**

He approached Le Fleur and stopped a yard in front of him, his legs slightly parted and his hands behind his back. Was he going to beat him up, kill him? Le Fleur had no idea. He squeezed his left wrist. How strong was titanium?

"I'll be on my way now. Sorry about this." He stood.

"Can you pass me your cell phone?"

"You want to make a call?" he said. "Sure."

He handed it over, took a step to the left. Zaheer pressed his right hand lightly against Le Fleur's chest.

"Can you sit down, sir?"

"I'm going to leave now. When you've finished with my phone, that is."

Zaheer increased the pressure on Le Fleur's chest. Le Fleur sensed something terrifying from Zaheer's calmness, the neatness of his suit, his slicked black hair.

"Can you please sit?"

"But I'm happy standing. I know the door is locked. Don't worry."

Zaheer removed his hand and placed the cell on the bar counter.

"Could I please ask you, sir, to hold your hands up above your head?"

"Am I under arrest?"

"Please sir."

He had a sense of déjà vu as he raised his hands. First the muggers, then Fallon, now this. Three times. In spite of his predicament, he refused to show any fear.

"May I call a lawyer? Oh, I forgot the lawyer left the room."

Zaheer patted him and removed his wallet and keys and placed them on the bar counter. "I'm sorry, sir, but I need you to remove your watch and clothes."

"You've got to be joking?"

Zaheer smiled politely and shook his head.

For a moment, he flashed on the seriousness of the situation. He was not a gambler. *The inexplicable urge.* He had trusted Gavin Marx was a reasonable man and would not allow something to happen to him in this room. Already he knew he was wrong. He took off his watch and handed it to Zaheer.

"I've got nothing else on me." He patted his own chest, the legs of his jeans.

"I'm sorry, sir."

He hesitated and glanced at the smoke detector housing the camera. "You're forcing me to undress?"

"Mr. Marx has ordered surveillance off in the Common Room," Zaheer replied as if he believed Le Fleur was concerned about his privacy.

"I don't believe this."

He unbuckled his belt and removed his jeans, shoes and socks, T-shirt. Down to his boxers.

"Everything?"

"That is OK, sir," said Zaheer. "Please could you raise your hands?" He patted the area around Le Fleur's crotch. "Could you turn around, sir?" He pressed his hands down the inside of his legs. "You may sit down now, sir."

He sat and watched Zaheer examine his clothing. Zaheer turned out the jean pockets and tapped the soles of the shoes.

"You've done this before?" he asked.

"Once or twice, sir."

Zaheer removed the battery from his phone and inspected it closely. It looked the same as a normal battery to the naked eye. Le Fleur looked at his watch. Disconnecting his cell phone had started a process. A shred of confidence returned.

Zaheer took his phone, wallet, keys, bundled the clothes together, walked to the door and knocked. The door opened and he stepped out.

Le Fleur looked at his bare legs still scabbed from his fall at the King's Blockhouse. He contemplated his strategy. Marx had arrived as per plan. Had he done enough to provoke Marx into action? Sitting in the Common Room in boxers, he knew he had.

Ten minutes later, he heard the door open. He looked up.

Ian Coulson stood in the doorway.

## 69

**Le Fleur stared at Ian Coulson in the doorway of the Common Room.** He had a bottle of red wine and a glass in one hand, a narrow laptop under the other arm.

"Let's bring this weekend forward!" Coulson said. He was wearing a buttoned gray blazer, blue jeans, and boots for an extra inch of height. He placed the laptop on the bar counter, glanced up at the camera, and filled his glass.

"Don't look so surprised, Daniel."

The revelation was pulsing through his veins. Coulson, the mastermind, in control of a ragtag gang of hackers. It seemed obvious and impossible at the same time.

Coulson tested the wine. "Exquisite. A Meerlust Rubicon 2004. I think I should buy a share in this club too."

He looked at Le Fleur.

"I've heard about casual dress for Friday, but this is ridiculous."

Le Fleur took a deep breath. He relaxed. Somewhere in the recess of his consciousness, it was as if he had suspected Coulson all along. But his emotion, honor, loyalty had refused to allow the permutation to develop.

"You know what they say about a good lawyer," Le Fleur said. "He'll take the clothes off your back."

"I'm glad you still have your sense of humor. Good! It's not unusual to be undressed in this room. The Common Room, isn't that ironic? Hardly anything common happens. You're not the first to strip inside here."

"I was talking about the *against your will* variety? Luckily, I'm wearing clean underwear."

"You're not drunk at all, are you?"

Le Fleur lifted his half-filled Black Label. "Where'd Marx go? We were having such an interesting discussion. Why'd he call you?"

"I suppose he doesn't care for some John Wayne hacker making crazy allegations. He knows all recuperating hacker felons do a stint with Cybercrime."

"Ah, and your favorite recidivist," said Le Fleur.

Coulson swallowed a mouthful of wine and held the glass up to the light. A red tear ran down his chin. He wiped it away. He opened his laptop and connected with Gorky Park's CCTV cameras. He swung it around so the display could be seen in the room.

---

"How are those pixels?"

He toggled through a sequence of cameras: street wide, reception, main floor, manager's room. Ynez was sitting sulkily at a chair across the desk from the manager.

"I didn't think you'd take me literally when I told you to go out and fuck cheerleaders, Daniel. Anyway, I'm in the mood to celebrate. We have enough evidence to write Nial Townley's story. I recently took possession of an incredible device. A Stingray. You know what it does, of course, since you had a hand in the design."

Le Fleur did not comment. Coulson's eyes shone.

"Of course *I* already had one working years ago." Coulson laughed. "But this one has a Western Digital connected to the chassis...You know where this is going? I downloaded the data from the drive. Turns out it has been used for all sorts of nefarious deeds. Among others, it recorded Townley's conversations on the day of his disappearance."

"Sounds like a handy device, where'd you get it?"

"I would tell you, and what was said, but that would be reckless of me, don't you think, given my position? It's such an amazing story. Those bastard Austrians contract an elite gang of hackers to mastermind the takeover of Supertech. Townley thinks his son has been kidnapped. NETWORX sets up the scam on cell phones to make it look like Townley was at the airport when he was actually at home. Then SUPERCHARGER deletes the video surveillance. Your friend Sean, a financial genius, designed the super-duper laundry. Then you, Daniel, what *would* we have done without your sleuthing skills."

Le Fleur squared his jaw.

"You put Carla onto me."

"On the contrary, I warned you to stay away from Townley, if you remember? More than once...You made your choice. You should never trust yourself around pussy. Someone should've taught you that."

The irony of those words sent a flash of anger through him. He suddenly imagined Jake Le Fleur in the room, siding with Coulson. *Fussy doesn't fuck.* He took a deep breath. He tried to stay cool with limited success.

"Fuck you, you little piece of shit. You act like this is a computer game. Jeremy is dead. I suspect Richard is too."

Coulson looked at the screen. A number of cars were backed up outside Gorky Park's entrance. He downed the remnants of his glass and pulled out a packet of cigarettes. He lit up.

"Can I pour you a glass of wine?" Coulson asked.

"No, thank you."

"Perhaps you'd like some sushi from the kitchen. They have the best chef."

"No."

Coulson took a seat opposite. "What are you trying to do, Daniel? You come here extorting the GALI reward. Is that your game, surely not? Commercial have all the evidence they need. GALI's activities in Africa are over. Unless they come up with some significant money, that is, which I don't discount."

"GALI will hire the best lawyers, the best cyber forensics. They'll uncover what happened."

"Wrong. There'll be no case. Not in this country anyway. And GALI is fighting multiple lawsuits in South America. It's a massive accomplishment for the State. We have outwitted GALI and the Venezuelan Government. On my recommendation, the State will elect not to prosecute GALI in South Africa. It's too costly. Pittman can be lynched by his own people. It's over."

Le Fleur nodded slowly. "What happened to Townley?"

"You don't know?"

"I didn't know anybody knew."

"It's all on the Stingray's hard drive." Coulson drew on his cigarette. "We're still piecing it together but it seems Townley received a call from a parent of his son's school. The 'catalyst call,' as Carla called it. They told him his son had mistakenly accepted a lift and could be picked up at a Claremont shopping center. Cavendish Square. Anyway, I'm sure this call will prove false. I am sure the GALI agents did this to shift the impact zone from the school. Then Townley's cell phone was switched to the Stingray. When he got to the shopping center, we think he was accosted in the parking lot. We know he received off network instruction that his son had been kidnapped. And later that he received further off network calls regarding the ransom."

There was an air of triumph on Coulson's face.

Movement on Coulson's laptop distracted them. Le Fleur felt a cold wave of anxiety. On a street-facing camera, Coulson's fat black Lexus was parked in a No-Parking zone. A white Saab was being driven away. Coulson laughed.

"Man, they are getting strict about parking these days. The council must be short of cash."

## 70

**Le Fleur walked to the door of the Common Room in his boxers and banged on it.**

"Is everything OK?" The bouncer's voice echoed over the intercom.

"Everything's fine," responded Coulson. He stood up.

"I want to leave," said Le Fleur. "You can't hold me against my will. This is illegal."

"Illegal? Hacking websites, stealing private data, there's quite a penalty for that. I don't need to warn you. Especially with your record...I suggest you sit down before it becomes unpleasant."

Le Fleur hesitated. It was pointless trying to force his way out. He felt naked and vulnerable in his shorts. He returned to the couch and hugged himself. "Can you turn up the heat? It's cold in here."

Coulson's eyes narrowed. He pulled out his cell and pressed some keys. "Zaheer? Did you test the aircon with the sniffer? OK, thanks."

Coulson spent another minute fiddling with his cell then toed the switch. "Has there been any maintenance work in the Common Room?"

The manager's voice came over the intercom.

"No maintenance."

"Good, thank you."

Coulson approached the heating unit and fiddled with the dials. "Twenty-one OK?" He returned to the bar counter, leaned back.

"What was that all about?" asked Le Fleur.

"Your phone had a recording device." Coulson tapped his temple with his forefinger. "Amateur, Daniel, you can do better. Anyway, please do explain why you approached Marx with this...your theory."

"I spoke to Helga Lombardy. She found Karl's diary and confirmed Townley and Marx had lunch with him a year ago. They knew about GALI. They brought Pittman to Cape Town. They set this whole thing up."

"Interesting. So you were you hoping to trap Marx confessing that he'd killed his best friend?"

Le Fleur remained silent.

"I've jammed all the comms now." He held up his phone. "Other than this little baby, nothing comes in and nothing goes out." He smiled smugly. "I like to stay on top of things. I think that's common among hackers. Maybe it's because we don't play competitive sport."

"I've never heard you refer to yourself as a hacker before."

Coulson opened the buttons of his blazer and shifted the flap. Underneath

---

Le Fleur saw the flash of a holstered weapon. Coulson smiled and nodded slowly, his eyes twinkling.

"By the way, Daniel, if someone's tracking your cell phone, they'll be looking in Lentegeur because that's where you are."

Le Fleur breathed in and out to stay calm. His backup plan related to triggers, one was the removal of his cell phone battery. But a Stingray could falsely register his cell in the gang riddled Cape Flats.

Strip searched, possessions removed, and car towed away, realization of the danger swept through his body. Many days he'd woken up on an ordinary day and considered that something may happen, something may end his life. But that was only paranoia. *If it all ends here then that is what it is,* he thought. He had never feared death. He wished he had religion and could believe he would be reuniting with his mother. It would mean bumping into Jake Le Fleur again, but he could live with that.

"You are appreciating my genius?" Coulson closed the gap, leaned forward arrogantly, his face less than a ruler's length away. His eyes were magnified orbs behind the rimless glasses. "I am ZAPPER."

Le Fleur nodded slowly.

Coulson backed away. "For some reason, I feel you are not so surprised."

Le Fleur paused and waited. Eventually he broke the silence.

"You're wrong, Ian, it *is* a surprise. It's hard for me to believe you're involved in this. I am bad with puzzles, real life ones. You had access to the technical skills. You were the Fagan and the hackers your pickpockets. I should've suspected you from the outset. But we confuse loyalty and truth. That's a failure of humanity, isn't it? We sacrifice truth for loyalty and gratitude. But who's the most surprised? Perhaps we will discover."

"Ha ha, you're good value, Daniel. But I must tell you the rest of the story. There's the twist. I need you to know what happens next. The hackers concerned, the lowly pickpockets as you called them, do have a master, a GALI agent. Unfortunately, some changes I have made to the Stingray's data will point fingers at you. And your servers will have more criminal DNA than a defrosted mortuary."

Coulson opened his blazer and fully revealed the silver pistol.

"It's a Ruger."

Le Fleur did not move. Coulson removed the weapon from his waistband holster and pulled back the stainless steel slide.

"You're not clever enough, Ian. Even if you doctor the Stingray's data, my servers are totally secure. If you think I'll allow that to happen, you've got a fat chance."

Coulson pulled a box of bullets from his jacket pocket and placed them on the bar counter.

"You won't be around to defend yourself and your systems. None of the others are. Why should you be any different?"

*None of the others are.* Le Fleur closed his eyes temporarily. In one sentence, Coulson had confirmed the fate of Richard Chinkanda and Sean Coppis.

Coulson removed the magazine and deliberately loaded ammunition, one by one, counting to twenty. He de-cocked the weapon and clipped in the magazine. He holstered it back under his gray jacket.

"You're not going to shoot me in here," he said.

There were too many people involved. Mary, the manager, Marx, the bouncer...

"Oh, you think so."

Coulson filled his glass, lit another cigarette, and fell into a comfortable chair.

Le Fleur had no watch, but he estimated forty-five minutes since Zaheer removed the battery of his cell.

"So how did they meet you, Ian? Townley and Marx. They needed a lowly internet dog to do the dirty work. ZAPPER. They came to you. Was it Marx? You met at the University of Cape Town? Same degree, same year, same University and same framed copies on your walls. Your alma mater would be so proud of your achievements."

Coulson smiled.

"Maybe Gavin was in my class, I couldn't tell you. I didn't know him then." His eyes twinkled. "I never deleted the Dark Video client list. Marx used the Mickey Finn club. Only once, so he says. He tells me it was the most exciting sex he ever had, almost as good as shooting a storm south-easter on his yacht. Now Daniel, if you'd kept the Dark Video client list, you would've been able to piece the puzzle, no?"

Coulson tweaked his mustache between his thumb and index finger.

"What happened to Townley's body?"

Coulson blew out smoke. He looked over at the pictures of the naked beauty queens.

"What happens to a body that can never be found? I'm not saying this happened, but there are roads trailing off the N1 past towns like De Doorns, Touws River, Laingsburg. It's the Karoo. Moordenaar's Karoo. It's space and koppies, dust and sun and low shrub and nothing else, nothing. You can dump a body out there and in a week, it is bones. The fucking sun and sky sucks up all the wet stuff. You drive over those bones with a tractor and put all the pieces in a hessian bag then spread it across veld and dumpsters and dry riverbeds. I'm not saying that's what happened. It isn't that these bodies aren't found. They don't fucking exist."

Le Fleur felt a cold chill of finality. At the back of his mind, he had considered Nial Townley could be alive, perhaps a hostage, or collaborating with Marx in his own disappearance.

"What was Carla's role?" he asked. He wanted to keep the conversation flowing.

"She's Gavin's partner."

"You're lying."

Coulson ground out his cigarette and tossed the butt into Le Fleur's half-filled beer glass. He swallowed the remains of his wine glass then stood and refilled it.

"That reminds me. Look what I saved for you, Daniel." Coulson reached into his pocket and removed a pair of striped panties. He waved them back and forth. "They're a souvenir from your trip down the coast. I was going to auction them off on eBay, but since they're Carla's, I thought you may want them more."

Le Fleur frowned.

"You look confused. I thought since we're airing our dirty laundry, I should give you hers. You surely remember that she left her suitcase in a shuttle bus when you were being chased from Plettenberg Bay."

Le Fleur looked away. He was determined not to give Coulson any satisfaction.

"Ah, shame, Daniel." He tossed the panties at Le Fleur's feet. "You've been hanging for her for so long and now the last thing you'll remember is you never had a chance."

Coulson's cell rang. He took the call.

*Yes. OK. Stay at Mouille Point. She'll come back.*

The Sea View Holiday Flats were in Mouille Point. Le Fleur knew it was a call about Fallon. Coulson ended the call.

"You had a fortunate escape this morning, Daniel. Fallon paid you a visit. She somehow got it in her head that you are JACKER." Coulson held his glass up and winked.

"How many people have to die, Ian?"

"I haven't killed anyone. I brought two forces together. The hackers assist GALI in kidnapping Townley. And Dark Video knocks off the hackers. It's a balanced double-sided equation."

"Dark Video doesn't exist. You know that."

"Well, Fallon doesn't. Not until recently anyway. I can't stop her rampage of vengeance. She and Carlos De Palma were tight."

"That's such crap, Ian. We both know you are paying her."

"Prove it."

Le Fleur's vision focused on a framed portrait of some yesteryear beauty queen, but he was thinking about weapons. A wine bottle, two glasses, and a Ruger. Sounded like the beginning of a bad joke. He breathed in and out. Nowhere to hide. Was there an order, a play that suited him? Aqualung joked about showdowns pitting the wits of computer nerds on opposing keyboards. This encounter might depend on his ability to nullify the weapon of choice.

"I offered you a choice, Daniel. I don't think you realized how serious it was. Leave it alone. You couldn't. GALI's a bunch of crooks. They deserve no better."

Coulson removed a fresh cigarette and lit it.

"That's a lie, Ian. No matter what I did, your plan was always the same. Someone had to take the fall. Fallon would've come for me. Like she killed Jeremy and Richard and Sean."

Coulson drew on his cigarette and his eyes glazed behind the rimmed glasses.

"Fallon discovered an address in Gardens which had clues for an aspirant detective. There were cameras at the entrance. Unfortunately, she screwed up and forgot to take you."

Le Fleur's heart skipped a beat. No.12 Marlborough Court was a set up. The towel, newspaper, the shoe were plants. Coulson had planned for Fallon to lead him there.

"But don't worry. The evidence will turn up and you'll be credited as the famous GALI agent. You see, you and I, we're the last of the great JACKER hackers. ZAPPER and CRACKERJACK. You thought you were the greatest. But you couldn't beat me, Daniel. I am the winner."

"Maybe I won't win, Ian. But you'll never be a winner. You'll never outwit me. And to beat me, you'll have to stoop to the ultimate low. You'll have to kill me, because otherwise you're finished."

Coulson took a mouthful of wine and rolled it around his mouth. When he smiled, his teeth were reddish.

"Ah, that's how these games end. It's your destiny, Daniel. You'll be remembered as a legend, a hacking martyr. You've pulled the online crime of the century. The script kiddies will worship you. You'll be up there with Carlos De Palma in the Darknet lights."

He stared at Coulson. "So I take it the reward's out of the question?"

---

Coulson opened a stick of gum and popped it in his mouth. He checked the screen of his laptop. He toed the switch. "Is Zaheer back?"

"No." Mary's voice.

Coulson looked at his watch.

"He said he'd be five minutes, where's he?"

"He had to drive a car somewhere."

"He only had to take it around the block. He should be back by now."

"I'll let you know as soon as he arrives."

"Where's Ynez?"

"She was in the manager's office."

Coulson frowned. "I hope she's not back on the floor."

"No, she's in the office."

"Will you check?"

After a short interval, Mary's voice came over the intercom. "She's in the manager's office."

Coulson smiled.

A movement on his laptop screen attracted Coulson's eye. He drew nearer, frowned.

## 71

**Coulson stared at the screen.** On the camera covering Gorky Park's entrance, two well-built men in civilian clothes were in a conversation with the bouncers.

Coulson narrowed his eyes then toed the switch.

"Mary, call the manager. Tell him to look at the reception camera."

The manager's voice came on.

"Yes, Mr. Coulson."

"Who are those guys?"

"Yes, I'm looking. They could be the liquor license guys."

Coulson checked his watch. "Friday, five o'clock. They don't look like liquor license guys."

"We've been raided three times this year."

"Pay them and tell them to fuck off. Where's Zaheer?"

On screen, a bouncer reached for his walkie-talkie. Coulson toggled to the street side camera. "Check the street camera."

"What is it?" the manager asked.

"There's an unmarked police car outside," Coulson said.

There was a pause before the manager's voice returned. "How can you tell?"

Coulson toggled back to reception. A scuffle had broken out between the two men and the bouncers. He jumped to his feet, toed the switch, and barked into the intercom. "Shut it down, shut it down."

Le Fleur rubbed the palms of his hands slowly along the top of his bare quads.

"Shut the doors," Coulson shouted. "You've got steel bars and bullet proof sheets, for fuck sake. You can't get in with a pickaxe."

"We have a problem at the door," the manager's voice came over the intercom.

Coulson swapped cameras to the street view. A vagrant was leaning against his black Lexus. Behind the Lexus, a car was reverse parking.

Le Fleur tensed, his attention switching between the screen and Coulson. Timing was crucial. Too slow and he would die; too quick, same result. He knew any minute Coulson would realize what he had to do, regardless of the consequence.

The scene at the entrance of Gorky Park was now a full-on brawl. The lock down order had come too late. The two men were inside the club. He estimated two to three minutes before they could find him.

Coulson's tongue flicked up and over his mustache. He toed the switch again and screamed for the manager. "Jesus, send someone down there. Zaheer! Where's Zaheer?"

"He's not back yet," the manager said.

On screen, one of the bouncers was wrestled to the ground. A second bouncer put his hands behind his back and was cuffed.

"Zaheer must've gone to Lentegeur to look for my clothes and wallet," said Le Fleur, his heart pounding, every muscle alert.

Coulson turned and stared at him. Disbelief was inaction; it used up precious seconds.

"This is you? You fucking—" Coulson teeth were bared. "You have no idea what I can do to you."

Then he saw it in Coulson eyes. The mustache twitched, the nostrils flared.

As realization struck Coulson, Le Fleur sensed the moment. He sprang to his feet and charged. Coulson's hand went for the holster. Le Fleur grabbed the hand and holster, his shoulder slamming Coulson's chest.

Coulson bellowed and kneed him in the face. But Le Fleur had Coulson's right hand and the holster gripped with both hands. He kept his head down, felt Coulson's left fist battering the back of it.

*You can stick a knife in my back, I'm not letting go.*

He could not let Coulson free his weapon. Coulson would shoot him without hesitation. The questions could be asked later.

He used momentum to his advantage by alternatively pulling at the holster or ramming with his shoulder. They reeled around the room, smashing a nude beauty queen off the wall.

Coulson redeployed his left hand as a claw, scratching and tearing at Le Fleur's hand in an effort to open his grip.

A minute is a long time.

The padded room blocked all noise. With the cameras turned off, whatever transpired could be ultimately revealed by the recount of two individuals only. It was his word vs. Coulson. He had to stay alive and have a voice.

He wrestled Coulson backwards, got him off balance. The continual movement denied Coulson room to land a significant blow.

"Arghhh!" An instinctive growl rose from his chest, the sound rallying his resistance, releasing a fresh wave of adrenaline.

They crashed into the bar counter, sent Coulson's laptop flying.

Coulson freed his trapped hand, but Le Fleur maintained his death grip on the holster.

A minute is a long time. Two is forever.

---

He heard banging at the door.

Coulson's nails raked across his face.

Coulson drew back his hand, made a fist, and lunged forward. Le Fleur rotated and flicked his head away. The blow caught him on his forehead.

*Not even if he sticks a knife in my back.*

He bent his neck suddenly and thrust upwards like a ram, the top of his head connecting with Coulson's face and shattering his glasses. He pinned Coulson against the wall. Without releasing his grip on the holster, once, twice, he butted him then slammed his shoulder against Coulson's chest. A bronze statue tottered and toppled over.

Coulson ripped the holster upwards, desperately trying to break the hold.

The banging against the door intensified. Le Fleur held on desperately. Then the banging became violent hammering until a panel broke open and the door splintered into fragments.

## 72

**"Don't move. Nobody move."**

Le Fleur maintained his grip on Coulson's holster. Even now he feared Coulson wouldn't hesitate.

Two plain-clothed men, who had minutes earlier appeared on Gorky Park's entrance camera, kicked away the remnants of the broken door, weapons drawn.

Coulson removed his hands from the holster, stopped struggling, and straightened up, his breathing ragged. "Get him off me!"

"Can you step away, please sir," the first man said. His collared shirt had a lumberjack check pattern and was tucked into jeans.

"He's got a gun," said Le Fleur.

"He's trying to kill me, get him off," said Coulson at the same time.

Le Fleur felt the man's hand on his shoulder.

"Step away, please, sir."

He released the holster and stepped back, ensuring the man was between him and Coulson. He did not take his eye off Coulson.

Coulson fingered his bloody nose. There was a deep cut on the bridge from his spectacles. "Jesus, fuck," he said.

At the door, the second man, older, held stance, weapon readied, pointed down at 45 degrees.

"Put your hands on your head."

Le Fleur raised his hands. He could feel blood running down from above his eye.

"Jesus, you guys got here in the nick of time." Coulson's hands were at his side. "I'm Ian Coulson from Cybercrime. What unit are you?"

"We're with the Tactical Response Unit. Can you place your hands above your head, sir?"

"He tried to grab my gun." Coulson blew his nose into his hand and flicked blood onto the carpet.

"Sir?"

Coulson hesitated then raised his hands. The man instructed Le Fleur to sit then patted Coulson and located his weapon.

"That's my service pistol. I head up Cybercrime. And I'm a reservist."

The man removed Coulson's weapon, unclipped the magazine, and placed both items on the bar counter.

"He was causing trouble with one of the strippers," said Coulson, lowering his hands. "They have it on camera. They brought him in here to try cool him off and he went ape shit."

The man frisked Coulson's coat pockets, placed the contents, his wallet, cell, keys, crushed cigarette box, lighter, and a pair of striped panties on the bar counter.

"Who called you boys in?" asked Coulson.

Neither man answered.

"Do you need medical attention, sir?" the first man asked Coulson.

Coulson fingered his nose gingerly. He shook his head with a scowl.

"And you, sir?" the man asked Le Fleur.

"I'm OK."

"Could you sit down, sir," the first man requested Coulson.

Coulson ignored him. He toed the switch. "Mary, could you send the manager in?"

The first man gripped Coulson's arm. "I've asked you please to sit down."

Coulson shook free. "Do you guys know who I fucking am?"

Boots crunched on the debris at the Common Room's entrance and a uniformed officer ducked under the remains of the broken door. Parks looked around the room without acknowledgement.

"Parks," said Coulson. "Good to see you, my man. What brings you boys to the Russian ballet?"

Coulson wiped his nose on his sleeve, reached out, and offered his hand to Parks. Parks ignored it.

"We got a call about a disturbance."

Coulson walked towards the bar. The second man stepped forward with his weapon raised.

"Sit over there please, sir."

Coulson reached for the crushed packet of cigarettes on the bar counter.

"We've got things under control," said Coulson, walking into the center of the room. He fiddled with the packet then threw it on the floor in disgust and sat.

"Whose weapon is this?" Parks asked.

"It's mine." Coulson looked around the room. "Anyone got a cigarette?"

Parks toed the fallen laptop. He walked to the silver pole, seemed about to grip the metal then retracted his hand.

"Why's he in his underwear?" Parks asked. "Where are his clothes?"

Coulson cleared his throat. "He came here making crazy allegations, Parks. They have footage. He accused one of the ladies of killing Nial Townley. Can you believe it?"

Parks walked slowly around the room. He stepped over the broken picture frames then looked up at the ceiling.

---

"Is there camera footage inside this room?"

Coulson cleared his throat.

"There normally is, but—well, as you can understand —important people come in here."

Parks put up his hand. "I understand."

He continued to circle the room. He stopped at the semi-open bathroom door. "What's in here?"

"It's a bathroom. A shower and a toilet cubicle for clients."

Parks pushed the door with his toe, entered the bathroom, and disappeared from sight. The two men were positioned at the door, weapons drawn.

"I'm not going to fuck around here with this little Captain," Coulson muttered under his breath. He raised his voice. "The thing is, Parks. We must contact the big boys. Le Fleur is in serious trouble. He's the mastermind behind Townley's disappearance."

Parks returned to the room and held up a thin beige object by its zip.

Le Fleur felt a warm wave of adrenaline rush though his body.

"What's this?" said Parks, frowning.

Coulson stared and stood up.

"It looks like a makeup bag," said Parks. "It must've dropped out of someone's handbag."

"That's been planted." The color drained from Coulson's face. He looked on in disbelief. "That wasn't there earlier. I checked the room myself."

Parks walked across the room.

"It must belong to one of the strippers," said Coulson. "You can give it to me. I'll make sure she gets it."

Parks unzipped the bag and emptied the contents onto the bar counter: a powder case, eye pencil, lip gloss and an object the size of a Lion matchbox.

Le Fleur cleared his throat. He raised a hand in the air and looked directly at Coulson.

*"Every win fails eventually,"* he quoted rule #17.

# 73

**"It's done," he said softly to Carla from the phone at Gorky Park's reception.**

The paramedic had stitched the cut above his eye, disinfected scratches on his cheek, and bandaged the hematoma on his forearm. He was still in his underwear, had a towel over his shoulders.

"Oh my God, oh my God," Carla said. "And Ynez?"

"She was star of the show. Thanks to you for helping convince her last night or was it this morning? Time has merged into one long tunnel, I can't think straight."

"I can't believe it, Daniel. Gavin was Nial's best friend. I keep asking myself: how could he kill him?"

Le Fleur did not know the answer. It was bugging him too.

"What's going to happen to him?"

"There's a warrant for his arrest."

"Are you OK?"

"I'm fine."

"I want to come to the club."

"No, don't. It's chaos. Coulson is still here. I'll contact you later."

Behind him, Captain Parks hustled the acting police commissioner out of Gorky Park's turnstile. Girls in lingerie and slinky outfits, the ironic ambassadors from Europe, had flowed into the street. Afternoon punters were headed for their cars and taxis.

Le Fleur left the reception and stood behind Parks. Parks turned and looked at him, could not help a grin. "You've been in a catfight, chief."

A semi-clad stripper tried to push through the turnstile.

"Nobody's allowed in," Parks instructed the policeman guarding the entrance.

There was a buzz from the girls. "What we do, hey, what we do?" one shouted.

"Swing on the telephone poles," Parks muttered. "Come with me, Le Fleur."

He followed Parks up the circular stairs. Coulson was cuffed inside the Common Room.

"His nose is broken," said a paramedic.

Park's eyes glinted. *"That's* a first for the hacker community."

They passed the manager's office. Parks looked in. "Hey, can we get this guy a gown?"

In a vacated office, Parks placed the matchbox sized audio receiver and

---

transmitter in a plastic sleeve.

"What you call this thing, chief?"

"A shotgun," said Le Fleur. "It's an Israeli make."

Le Fleur had modified the storage of the audio device to record a maximum of four hours instead of the specified forty which had reduced the weight to fifty grams. It could record eighty feet away through a brick wall.

Parks shook his head. He had brought in his own IT specialist to make copies of the memory card.

Coulson had jammed the transmission signal in and out of Gorky Park, but the conversation in the Common Room was clear and undistorted.

They played it twice.

*If someone's tracking your cell phone, they'll be looking in Lentegeur.*

*You can throw a body out there and in a week, it is bones.*

*Unfortunately, she screwed up and forgot to take you.*

"Tell me again, chief, what's the story with the evidence. Who's Fallon?"

"Coulson paid Fallon to lure me, by force or otherwise, to a flat in Gardens where there was evidence linked to Townley. The newspaper, the shoe...He'd then have a physical link between me and Townley and I wouldn't be able to defend myself because I wouldn't be around."

*You'll be up there with Carlos De Palma in the Darknet lights.*

"Will it be admissible?" he asked Parks.

"It is for now."

"And in court?"

"That's for the highly paid hot shots to argue about for six months. You know the drill, it usually ends up what's right is wrong and what's wrong is right."

"Yep."

"I have to warn you. Coulson's connected. And this matter is going to be complicated. He has long lines of influence into Government. Probably because he's got the inside track on everyone's browsing history. You see the police commissioner? They're still shitting themselves from the Gupta leaks. He must've asked me a hundred times if I know what I'm doing."

Parks's cell rang. He answered and listened, pulled a face.

"You're keeping the services busy, chief. There was a shooting outside your apartment this afternoon. I haven't got the whole story, but it seems two people were shot."

"Who was it?"

"Apparently two guys, both with records, one out on bail."

"Dead?"

"As a donkey."

"The shooter?"

"Some bystanders have described a woman."

Parks's eyes bored into him. He rubbed his chin. Fallon would either be dead or would disappear into a tunnel and emerge many miles away. She would think he had set a trap for her at Crystal Place. She would think he betrayed her.

"You know anything about this?" asked Parks.

He shook his head.

"No?"

"Maybe it's a coincidence?" Le Fleur said.

Parks's eyes sharpened and he nodded deliberately. "Oh yes, a coincidence maybe, an anonymous act of God."

When Parks went downstairs to address an issue, Le Fleur went to the bathroom and washed his face. He could not stop his hands shaking. Coulson would wriggle out. Millions would be spent on hired lawyers to manipulate the legal system. He knew the taped transcript was not enough.

He needed more.

When Parks returned, he read his statement.

> She gave me a lap dance. It must be authentic
> because I knew they'd watch the footage.

Parks looked up and smiled at him. "Authentic, chief, what's that mean, exactly?"

> I slipped the recording device to her as
> we were being taken to the Common Room.

He looked up as Ynez walked past with one of the original assault squad officers. She stopped outside the Common Room.

"You fucking careverga," she screamed at Coulson. "I hope they fuck your asshole into pieces."

The officer led her away.

"That's the girl?" Parks asked.

"Yes."

In the early hours, Ynez had arrived in a taxi at Crystal Place under the impression he was in the mood for some paid fun. Together with Carla and some monetary persuasion, he had convinced her to cooperate in his scheme to pressure Marx into making an admission.

Shortly after day break, he had met Captain Parks with Carla, handed over the towel, newspaper, and shoe and laid out his plan. He explained to Parks that the items had been dropped in his mailbox by an anonymous source.

The plan was to crack Gavin Marx with the revelation about Geneva and Livigno.

Parks was still reeling from the midnight tip off to secure a crime scene at Marlborough Court.

As he replayed the dizzying sequence of the day's events, everything suddenly seemed unreal.

Carla thought the plan was crazy. She did not believe that Marx could possibly have harmed Townley. Le Fleur doubted Parks would consider it, but Parks was still smarting from Marx's false lead about Carla's abduction. Le Fleur convinced them that if the plan failed, nothing would be lost.

How wrong he was about that.

The assault squad member followed Ynez down the stairs. The guy had dropped a few bouncers, smashed down a door, and now was gentlemanly escorting Ynez to the exit. He looked like he had come to the club to watch the rugby. Except for the shiny assault boots...Sometimes you have to look down to see what's going on.

"We so nearly fucked this up," said Parks.

Someone brought Le Fleur a gown and a cold drink.

"The phone trace had you in Lentegeur. We were about to follow your car."

He felt a chill. If they had not have stormed the club, he would be dead for sure.

"If it wasn't for your security guy insisting you were still in the strip club, we wouldn't have found you," said Parks. "He was watching your car. He said you didn't get in."

He grinned. *Your security guy.* Technology could be a screw up. In the end, his rescue and life relied on words whispered to a hobo.

Parks got a call from downstairs. "Speak of the devil. It's your security guy."

## 74

**Le Fleur pulled the hoodie of his jacket over his head and dug his hands into the pockets.** He walked slowly along the jetty. His body ached. The back of his head was bruised, cuts on his face stinging.

Yachts were lined in neat order, poles swayed, and rigging sighed. The dockside was empty even though it was weekend, neither leisure nor hard core enthusiast interested in braving the wild weather and stormy seas.

"Over here."

He spotted Gavin Marx aboard a yacht. He wore long weather proof pants and his jacket bore the badge of the Cape Royal Yacht club.

"You bring anyone along?" asked Marx. He was standing on the deck of *George's Escape* looking down at Le Fleur.

"The police are in the parking lot."

Le Fleur braced as the wind whipped spray across the surface of the water. Even within the protection of the harbor walls, the sea seemed to be surging back and forth.

"Are you planning on going out in this weather?"

Marx nodded. His hair was wet with sea and weather.

The water in the dock was dark and foreboding. Le Fleur thought if he fell into that he would never emerge.

"Thanks for coming to see me, Daniel. You want to come aboard?"

"No thank you."

Marx nodded slowly. He looked away for a moment as if considering a final change of heart.

"I want you to know that this conversation is recorded," said Le Fleur.

Marx turned over the palm of his left hand and looked back at Le Fleur.

"I understand. I've sent you a collection of documents. Hashtag Townley leaks. I think you'll have everything you need including a record of all the payments made to Ian Coulson and Cybercrime."

Le Fleur fingered his cell. He decided not to record. They stood facing one another. Marx broke the silence.

"We were in trouble in South America," said Marx. "The Venezuelan Government were withholding funds and freezing our investments. We stood to lose the Supertech business, not only in South America. We couldn't have recovered from such losses."

"Then you heard about Karl Lombardy?"

"Yes. Nial did the research. We went to see Lombardy in Geneva and he shared his private research. Of course it was unfinished then, but it was plain what GALI were doing to us, what they had done to others. GALI were deliberately sabotaging us in Venezuela. They had contacts in government and agents everywhere. On the Eurorail returning to London, we had the time to discuss the problem. That's when we formulated the plan. It was called Livigno as you rightly worked out."

Le Fleur wiped the sea mist off his face and pulled his collar tight. Marx continued.

"We thought we had a perfect plan to break back. It was like a business deal, straight. We knew it was us against GALI and the cleverest would win."

"How did you get involved with Coulson?"

Marx looked down. "I've made some poor decisions in my life. I don't want to go into detail, but it involved young women and was highly illegal."

Le Fleur nodded. It tallied with what Coulson had told him: Marx had once belonged to the Mickey Finn club. Young women were drugged in bars and delivered, mail order, to rich clients.

"Coulson was blackmailing you?"

"Yes. Perhaps blackmail is not the right word. But he was on my payroll for among other things protection services at Gorky Park." Marx hesitated. "I—"

Le Fleur raised his hand. "No need to explain."

"Anyway let's just say that Ian and I were acquaintances. I introduced him to Nial who thought he may have the kind of skills we needed to outsmart GALI. We took him into our confidence. Ian had access to vast technical skills and associations in the protection business—some real underworld characters."

"Like Jacky Valens?"

"That's him."

Marx wiped his brow and shook his head slowly.

"We thought Ian was the right guy. He taught us how to communicate secretly. No reference to Livigno was ever spoken about in an open office, or over a cell, or in an email."

The yacht rolled from side to side. Marx bent and lashed a plastic box to the deck.

"But what exactly was Livigno?" asked Le Fleur.

"The plan was that Nial would disappear with the remaining Supertech funds. This would precipitate a crisis. We knew GALI would jump at the chance to play white knight and snap up our assets. For good measure they also resolved our problems in Venezuela. Once we had secured our withheld funds, Nial could return and the blame for Nial's disappearance would be placed at GALI's door."

"He would return. Just like that?" asked Le Fleur.

"There were times in the lead up when I thought we were crazy. But we were caught up in the challenge. Everything was planned to precision. It was agreed only Ian would know when it was coming. We handed it over to him to orchestrate so that our reactions would be as authentic as possible."

"Nial had no chance to say goodbye?"

Marx shook his head and looked towards Lion's Head.

"Excuse me a moment," he said. He walked to the back of his yacht. Le Fleur heard a small engine whirr. Marx returned.

"Who dumped Townley's vehicle?"

"One of Ian's people. Nial was already—" Marx stopped mid sentence. He pursed his lips and continued. "The forecasts had been terrible for that week. We should never have put to sea."

Marx rubbed his wet face.

"I'd created a false charter for *George's Escape*. The skipper was a Brazilian guy called Cardosa who was flown over from São Paulo by supposed GALI agents. The guy couldn't speak English. On the Monday after Nial's supposed disappearance, Cardosa set sail with Nial for a private lodge on a small island off Seychelles."

Marx's voice wavered.

"About five hours into the trip, the boat did an accidental jibe and the mast crashed down and struck Nial."

Marx halted.

"He was killed?"

Marx nodded. He did not continue so Le Fleur prompted him.

"What happened then?"

Marx cleared his throat. "Ian had people—some perlemoen smugglers from Hawston. They put a motor launch to sea and got Nial's body off and Cardosa sailed back into Table Bay."

"They stored his body in a fridge?" said Le Fleur and Marx looked into the distance.

"I don't know exactly. I think so..."

For a moment Le Fleur and Marx stood in silence.

"Sorry, excuse me again," said Marx.

He disappeared below the deck. Le Fleur could hear him talking on the radio. When he came back, he was composed.

"It's the greatest tragedy of my life. I wanted to give up the plan and go to the authorities. To this day, I don't know where I found the strength to continue."

"What did Coulson do?"

"Ian was unwavering. He has this ability to look at a situation without any emotion. I remember he said: 'This has happened. It is fate. Nothing changes.' So I pressed on with this business in Nial's memory. He would have wanted that. He lost his life to save his company. I couldn't pull out of that obligation although it meant nothing to me anymore."

Marx's body expanded as he took in a long breath.

"As hard as it is to say, the plan was successful. We defeated GALI. We restored Supertech. We've done South Africa a favor."

"Unfortunately it's not that simple," said Le Fleur. "Three associates of mine have been killed in the process of validating your successful plan."

"That was never *our* plan," said Marx. "Nial and I would never have agreed to that."

"That may be so. Maybe. I don't know. But when you choose to partner with criminals, you don't also choose their methods."

"This is true. I take responsibility. I take full responsibility."

"What about Carla's attack?"

Marx shook his head. "I was shocked. Ian swore to me it was Pittman. I want you to know, Daniel, that Carla had nothing to do with this. She was never involved in Livigno."

Le Fleur nodded. "You used Carla to get to me. I was to be just another of the fake and dead GALI agents."

"I didn't know this."

"How *did* you think that Coulson would prove that GALI abducted Townley? Surely you must have thought about this, surely you discussed this?"

"The Lombardy reports, the court cases…You were at the press confer-ence, Daniel. Who did not believe that GALI were guilty? Only you…"

Le Fleur swallowed, a sour taste in his mouth.

"I don't know what more to say, Daniel. Can you untie that rope?"

Le Fleur untied a rope and tossed it onto the yacht.

"Where are you going?"

"Not far. Want to come?" Marx smiled thinly.

"Bumpy water." Le Fleur rubbed his stomach.

"*I* gave that Winnie the Pooh tribute to Gregory. He wouldn't take it with him to London. He left it behind at his bedside because he was certain his father would return."

Le Fleur thought about his own mother. He was also certain she would return. Maybe she did. She was inside him somewhere.

Marx reached out his hand and sighed deeply "I know this may sound odd, but I'm glad Carla chose you."

He shook Marx's hand then watched as Marx eased George's Escape off the jetty and out towards the open sea.

## 75

**Two weeks passed like ten years, days filled with intensive interrogation by a specialized Hawks digital forensic team.**

The news avalanche continued: slain gangsters, murdered IT hackers, a missing yachtsman, a hit woman on the run and a prominent cyber law enforcement agent in the dock.

A man found dead with his throat slit on Monwabisi Beach was identified as Jacky Valens, an underworld boss with links to drug supply and protection racketeering. Evidence suggested he was killed at No.12 Marlborough Court Gardens and his body dumped.

Richard Chinkanda's body was found hidden in dense fynbos in a slipway off the West Coast Road.

Le Fleur attended Sean Coppis's funeral held on Muizenberg Beach. It was cold and rainy, and people waded into the shallow water and spread flower petals, which he thought ironic since Coppis hated nature and anything to do with outdoors. He thought they should've held the memorial inside some dark gaming conference hall while attendees played party poker and flamed each other with online messages.

*George's Escape* was found floating off the coast near Gordon's Bay. No one was aboard.

Fallon had not returned to the Sea View Holiday Flats since the day of the Gorky Park bust. The camera in the foyer captured her leaving the flats at 10:45 on that day. His LPR camera captured the shooting in Victoria Road a few minutes after 11:00. Le Fleur had supplied Parks with the LPR footage. Her Chevy was located in the parking lot at Cape Town International Airport. CCTV cameras caught a Patricia Fitzsimmons boarding a flight to Johannesburg. Then the trail went dead.

He had spoken to Carla on a few occasions. She had been offered a top job in Brazil with GALI's competitor, the UK multinational Standard Engineering.

On a sunny Cape winter's day, he pulled on his baggies, sun hat, and slipslops and wandered along Victoria Road to a deserted First Beach. Earlier that morning he rode his new bike to Muizenberg and back.

He was lying on a red and white towel, staring through dark glasses at an empty blue sky, when Parks came to find him, struggling across the sand in a first-class suit, cursing the white light and the crassness of the palm lined frontage.

"Nice office space, chief."

---

"Go away," Le Fleur said.

"What's with you white people and the sun?" Parks emptied sand from his shoes, removed his jacket and two bottles of cold drink from the pockets.

"You don't like it?"

"My mother used to put me outside when I was naughty." Parks laid out his jacket and sat on it. "Your security guard told me where to find you."

"Has he forgiven you for chucking him in jail?"

"I think so. He said you'd gone to the beach for a beer and hard-on."

"He's a funny guy."

Parks twisted the top off a cold drink and offered the other. He took it and pushed himself onto his elbows.

"The life of the rich and famous," said Parks.

Last Saturday, Le Fleur had been received by Willie Schroeder from GALI at the Mount Nelson Hotel. GALI bestowed the R5m reward on him.

But GALI were under siege. Supertech agent Jorge Ramos and local police in Caracas had successfully identified a whistle blower who had fingered three corrupt business officials for taking bribes to illegally block payments to Supertech. Willie Schroeder and his team had canceled a planned trip to Caracas to meet with authorities for fear of being arrested at Simón Bolivar International. GALI's attempt to access the funds repatriated from Venezuela to South Africa, and now held locally at Standard Bank, was blocked by the Reserve Bank.

He sipped the icy cold drink, enjoyed the sting of carbonation.

"Are those pineapples on your pants?" Parks pointed at his baggies.

He nodded.

The blue water was perfectly translucent. There was another couple on the beach with a small child but no one swimming.

"He got bail," said Parks.

"I heard."

Coulson had posted bail of R1 million.

Besides Gavin Marx's admission and a record of payments made to Coulson, the flash drive Fallon dropped into his mailbox would be crucial uncensored evidence in the case against Coulson. Parks had offered Le Fleur police protection against possible intimidation or reprisals from Coulson and his gangster connections, but Le Fleur declined. He made it clear the evidence was in digital form and with or without him, it would stand up.

"Everything's fucked-up," said Parks. "Not only do the likes of Coulson cheat, kill, and steal, but now it's us, society, spending millions prosecuting their asses so they receive a few years inside. Where's the justice in that?"

Le Fleur did not want the conversation, not politics, not crime, not white bones in the Karoo or a boy without a father in London, not a disgraced lawyer floating in the Indian Ocean, not empty justice, simply the empty blue sky and the weak but bright sun on his body.

"How are *you*, Parks?"

Parks slapped his hands to remove the sand. "If I could find that hit woman, I'd be pretty chuffed."

Le Fleur lifted his cold drink.

"You should've seen how she lived, chief," said Parks. "Like an animal. She hadn't thrown anything away."

He had told Parks that Fallon was the anonymous donor of evidence from Marlborough Court as well as the Stingray backup.

"I don't suppose you know anything?" asked Parks.

Le Fleur put his head back and streamed the cold drink down his throat. "I didn't think so."

After Parks left, Le Fleur got up and deposited the empty cold drink bottles in the bin, traced the arc of the water from the rocks to the other end of the beach. His cell beeped with a message, the details of a conference call later.

Then he took lunch at a nearby café.

When he returned to the beach, Carla was standing on his towel, bare feet, fully dressed.

"I suppose Aqualung told you where to find me."

He turned the towel sideways and she settled alongside.

"Freddy's an Oracle," she said. "He's carrying a flipping big stick these days."

Her shoulder pressed against his.

"It's gone to his head, I think. He's impossible. He wants me to buy him a gun."

"He wants to save your life."

She scooped a handful of sand, closed her fist, and allowed it to run slowly out.

"How are *you*, Carla?" He looked ahead, not wanting to make eye contact, to see her eyes flicker, to see the pain.

"I'm numb," she said. "I had no idea how hard this would be. It's like everything I believed in life has been shattered. But my issues are minor. I spoke to Gregory on the phone yesterday. He keeps talking about when he's coming back, when his Dad —"

She stopped. They sat for a long time staring ahead in silence.

---

"So you're going to Brazil?" He spoke eventually.

"Not sure if I'm excited or terrified. But I must get away from Cape Town. I can't live here with the memories of Nial." She closed her eyes. "And I hope I don't bump into Pittman."

Pittman had pitched up at a GALI subsidiary in Chile. He had been reinstated then fired. Who was responsible for the attack on Carla? Gavin Marx had insisted he knew nothing about Carla's attack or the murder of a hacker gang. Coulson was claiming not guilty on all accounts, but it was evident he or Jacky Valens had engineered Pittman's meeting with the gangsters at Gorky Park and the appointment of his gardener.

"You think Pittman was behind the attack on me?" asked Carla.

"It depends who you believe. Pittman says he was set up by Supertech. Coulson is sticking with the GALI blame story and hoping for political assistance. Or a miracle..."

"But what do you think?"

"Perhaps Pittman got carried away with the company he was keeping."

"Seriously? Well, I won't be kicking anyone in the balls again in a hurry." Le Fleur shuffled his feet in the soft sand.

"Coulson spoke to me outside the police station. It was the day we got back from Plettenberg Bay. He said something about imagining your attacker with a steel cord or cable around your neck."

"What?" Carla put her hand in front of her mouth.

"You told me your attacker didn't have a weapon. But Parks sent me Quentin Fortuin's confession. That's the guy who attacked you. Fortuin said..." Le Fleur paused. "He said that the plan was to strangle you with a cable."

Carla moved her hand to her forehead, shook her head in disbelief. "Fuck."

"Coulson could not have known that when he spoke to me about a steel cord. Fortuin's confession only came later."

"But then Gavin was involved! I can't believe it. It's hard enough getting my head around Nial and Gavin and this Livigno plan without Gavin being involved in trying to murder me."

"No, I don't think Gavin knew. It was never part of the Livigno plan."

"But why then?"

"Maybe it was something to do with me."

"You? What do you mean?"

"Coulson wanted to show me that he was in control. That's the way it is in the hacker world. You think professional sport is competitive?"

"Will we ever know?"

---

Le Fleur shrugged. He flashed a memory of Coulson dropping Carla's striped panties at his feet. *You thought you were the greatest. But you couldn't beat me, Daniel. I am the winner.*

"Jesus, Daniel, if you'd known what you know now when I arrived at your place that first day, you would've chucked me over the balcony."

He touched her hand lightly and they sat for a moment staring out at the vista before them.

"So when's your next beach volleyball game?"

She laughed. "Hey, I got my pictures back from my stolen laptop. So weird. Someone loaded them onto Dropbox and sent me the link."

"So weird."

The sun was overhead, still no one swimming in the freezing Atlantic water.

"So what about that hit woman. Fallon Trafford?"

"Did Parks put you up to this?"

She shook her head. "Is it safe for you?"

"I've got my security personnel on full alert. See how hard it was for you to find me?"

A beach vendor approached selling cold stuff. He put his tray on the sand and tried to entice them to buy with his verse: *A water for my daughter, if you don't buy one I can't support her.*

Le Fleur grinned at the vendor.

*A lolly to make you jolly,* the vendor continued.

The vendor turned on Carla.

*A wafer to make him styfer.*

They took the water.

"So what are you going to do, Daniel?"

He closed his eyes and eased onto his back. He imagined walking barefoot down cobbled streets. "I'll be fine." He was going to make a joke about his next missing person case, but he was not in the mood. "I've got work to do. European markets are going to pieces and there are opportunities for trading. And there're always *South Park* reruns and *Game of Thrones* and the latest version of *Call of Duty.*"

She touched his arm. "It sounds lonely."

Lying on his back, the blue sky, warm sun, sea air, Carla's voice, the sugar, if he did not hear it again, maybe once or twice, a strange meeting years from now, awkward, painful.

"You can't want that, Daniel. Surely? Nobody likes being alone."

He opened an eye. She was looking down on him. Her hair had fallen across her face.

Maybe because his mother died when he was young, because his father did everything for women, he had no roots, no soil to hold, no water needed, only air. He could live on air alone.

Carla looked at him. "Will you come and visit?"

He smiled at her.

There was something he wanted to tell her, something about the money from Dark Video. He had donated his share to a home for abused women. The Christina Home for Abused Women. It was a trust fund for eternity. Every week they put fresh flowers on his mother's grave with a special message. But then he would have to explain how he could afford the penthouse. He would have to tell her he was a very successful day trader. A lifetime spent watching terminals and numbers and events and trends was the ultimate preparation for gambling on the markets. And he did not want to have that conversation.

He looked away as she walked across the sand towards the grass embankment. He closed his eyes as tight as he could. He would survive on air.

That evening a light drizzle set in and he started to walk. Earlier, he had taken a ride on his dream bike and, when he returned to Crystal Place, selected a new Van Gogh, *Café de Nuit*. He had ordered new canvases and scraped the dried paint off the handles and ferrules of his brushes.

He set out from Bali Bay and walked along the marine perimeter to Camps Bay. He felt the familiar prickle of unprotected space but did not waiver. He continued past Clifton and Bantry Bay and into the CBD of Cape Town.

He continued to walk, past foreign drug dealers, past excited under-age white kids on Long Street then into Orange Street and away from the lights and the people. There were strangers in the shadows, but he was not afraid, did not care. His mind was clear; he had made peace with what he had to do.

On Kloof Street, he ducked into a small restaurant with pine floors, hanging lights, and drab brown walls. And free WiFi. A couple of youths were playing billiards in the center of the room.

He stood in the doorway, closed his eyes and then opened them and considered the differences between the room and Van Gogh's painting. His first thought was of the patrons—no destitutes or prostitutes, but it was still early.

A waitress came over. She was early twenties, hair tied back in a lace bandana, a plain red buttoned blouse and knee length skirt. She leaned on his chair.

"Hi you," she said.

He smiled and removed his jacket.

"So what'll it be?"

"Have you got some craft beer?"

She rattled off a list and he chose Jack Black.

"Good choice," she said.

"You think so?"

He checked the time on a circular wall clock then looked up an address on his cell.

Van Gogh had written about the "terrible passions of humanity." For him, the painting represented his terrible choice. What was justice anyway? What was right was wrong, what was wrong was right.

The waitress returned with a bottle and a glass. She smiled at him and twirled away. He poured the beer and watched as she took up a position behind a cabinet with a vase of pink flowers. He raised his glass and she returned a friendly wave.

Van Gogh had sold the painting to settle a debt. Isn't that what he had to do?

He typed a code into his cell and linked directly to a conference call at GALI offices in Munich.

A shiny head filled the screen of his cell.

"Good day, Mr. Le Fleur. Right on time. You look like you've been in a storm."

Willie Schroeder, head of GALI's acquisition team, was dressed in suit and tie.

"It's wet here," said Le Fleur.

"Are your dams filling up?"

Le Fleur gazed past the screen to the misted glass windows. His gaze continued to the walls of the restaurant. He imagined transforming their color from drab brown to blood red.

"A little," he said, returning focus to the small screen in front of him.

"So I have someone in front of me," said Schroeder.

Le Fleur breathed in slowly and narrowed his eyes.

"She showed me a European passport." Schroeder paused and looked away from the screen. "She looks quite different."

"OK."

"Can you please confirm this is the correct individual?"

Schroeder rotated his screen to focus on a woman. Her hair was long and auburn; she had a scarf around her neck. Fallon lowered her sunglasses and smiled at the camera with her green eyes.

---

"Is this her, Mr. Le Fleur?"

Le Fleur stared at the woman on screen. She had escaped to Europe then contacted him on Whisper. *We made a deal.* He stared into the void behind her green eyes. There was still time to change his mind.

Schroeder's face appeared on screen.

"Mr. Le Fleur?"

He didn't want to spend the rest of his life looking over his shoulder for her.

"Yes, that's her."

He thought he saw a slight flicker of emotion in Fallon's eyes.

"Thank you," Schroeder said but the image on his phone remained Fallon. "So I want to confirm you wish to assign the reward and it be paid in cash to the beneficiary you designated."

He closed his eyes and an impression of the *Café De Nuit* appeared with the pool table center, pine floors, hanging lights and pink flowers.

"Mr. Le Fleur. She is the beneficiary?"

He opened his eyes. Fallon's eyes flickered and he saw her swallow. She had killed three of his colleagues. She had probably killed many more. What was he doing? This could never be justice. *We made a deal.* Did honor come before justice? Promises kept at any cost.

"Mr. Le Fleur. Do you confirm?"

He stared into Fallon's eyes. He wasn't going to have to look over his shoulder. But he couldn't say the same for her. Paying her the GALI reward would be a digital fingerprint. His mind was clear. He was going to go after her.

"I do," he said.

THE END

# ALSO BY PETER CHURCH

**Available in South Africa in 2019
Forthcoming to North America
in 2020 by Catalyst Press**

## DARK VIDEO

A minibus taxi flipping spectacularly on its head; two teenagers engaged in illicit sex in a shopping mall rest room; a raunchy table dance in a Cape Town strip club... What have these scenes got to do with a beautiful young woman running through Newlands Forest early on a Sunday morning?

Alistair Morgan is the key. A gifted law student with a glittering career in the offing, Alistair seems to have it all: looks, charm and money—and the attention of the hottest girls on campus. But his privileged lifestyle is about to be turned upside down as he is lured deeper and deeper into the sinister online world of Dark Video, where reality blurs and morals unravel.

From the ominous slopes of Table Mountain and the murky depths of False Bay to a dusty Karoo farm and the limestone cliffs of Arniston, Dark Video is an intense thriller that will keep you spellbound from the word go.

*peterchurch.bookslive.co.za/dark-video*

# A NOTE FROM THE AUTHOR

The Crackerjack project was conceived during a car trip from Cape Town to our holiday home at Fynbosstrand on 14 December 2010. I was so engrossed in the story and its possibilities that I missed the turnoff.

Since then there have been any number of write and rewrites. The follow up to Dark Video and Bitter Pill seemed destined to end up as a rusty can of beans on a dusty shelf. Characters were born and died. Plots became twisted then untwisted. Seven years passed.

Then I met Jessica Powers from Catalyst Press.

Raised on Hollywood movies and thrillers by James Patterson, most South Africans have a strong North American cultural influence. Under the guiding hand of Catalyst, some spelling changes, swimming costumes became bathing suits, but the story remains a South African thriller.

I would like to mention some special people who have sparked my imagination and tempered my illusions.

Tanya Jaffee for being the best reader of crime fiction and providing me with valuable feedback and support. My sister-in-law Sue Elliott for her careful review and firm advice. Andre Botha for our discussions on Venezuela. Adrian Gebers for advice on Yachting 101. James Green for his local knowledge of Llundudno. Tim Colman for his innovation in suggesting places where knives can be stored. Jessica Powers for her meticulous edits and for having the courage to support South African fiction. The team at Catalyst Press for all their input.

You can contact me on petergchurch@yahoo.com. I promise to answer every communication.

Kind Regards,
Peter Church

❖

Peter Church has provided some commentary and location photographs, which you can enjoy alongside the chapters at the following url:
https://www.catalystpress.org/crackerjack-interactive/

**Available in South Africa in 2019**
**Forthcoming to North America**
**in 2020 by Catalyst Press**

# BITTER PILL

Inside the heaving party hub that is Cape Town's student playground, someone is preying on the young and unwary. As allegations of drink spiking and illicit sex hit the local papers, university authorities move quickly to limit the damage...

A world away in Seattle, Carlos De Palma, the shadowy operator behind Dark Video, is plotting his survival strategy in the ever-changing Internet landscape. With his precious clients clamoring for heightened thrills, Carlos begins tapping into a new service that blurs the boundaries between the real and virtual worlds...

Enter Robbie Cullen, nice guy and average student, dumped by his girlfriend and struggling with grades. But when it comes to the crunch, Robbie doesn't know the meaning of stepping back. Once he encounters the beautiful and mysterious Fallon, his small-town bravado is set to make him some powerful enemies.

Bitter Pill is a gripping thriller that sweeps through the intoxicating haunts of Cape Town's nightlife and lingers on the sugary sand of Plettenberg Bay—before exploding on the streets of the Mother City's exclusive southern suburbs.

*peterchurch.bookslive.co.za/bitter-pill*

# PETER CHURCH

Peter Church is a Cape Town-based writer.

After a successful career in Information Technology, Church's first novel *Dark Video* (2008) was published by Random-Struik in South Africa and New Holland Publishers in Australia. Reviewed as 'one of the best debuts in a long time' by Lindsay Slogrove of *The Natal Mercury*, *Dark Video* was a Sunday Times "Book of the Week."

In 2011, Church followed up with the "drink spiking" book *Bitter Pill*. *Cosmopolitan* magazine's "Hot Read of the Month," the plot was described by Gillian Hurst of The Drum as "adrenalin-laced, [the] gritty (plot) will keep you furiously turning pages long after your bedtime." *Bitter Pill* was nominated for the 2012 Sunday Times fiction prize.

In 2015 Two Dogs published *Blue Cow Sky*, a novella of sexual proportions.

Peter Church is a member of SA Pen and the Kimberley Club. His acclaimed sporting articles are featured on M&G's *Sports Leader* site.

A short story, *The One*, about compulsive love, appeared in a compilation of South African crime fiction called *Bad Company*. Another shortie, *My Side*, was selected for the annual Short Sharp Story collection *Bloody Satisfied*, edited by Joanne Hichens.

Peter lives in Cape Town with his wife Paula and three children Christopher, Megan, and Ross.